Moving Pictures

a novel of early Hollywood

by K.L.A. Hyatt

ISBN-13: 978-0-615-69753-6

www.movingpicturesbook.net

To Anita Loos, for your wonderful memoirs of
the early entertainment industry. Those works
were a great inspiration to me.

Foreward

I first met silent-film star Maggie Savoy several years ago when I was a Ph.D. candidate at USC's film school. Through some lucky research, I located the home she had purchased at the height of her career in 1917 and was even luckier to find that she still lived there.

At that time there was a great resurgence of interest in early cinema and part of my thesis project was to garner first-hand information from primary sources. In my enthusiasm for the filmmaking art-form in its nascent years, I located many forebearers to what we know as cinema today. Fred J. Balshofer, an early director and producer; Charles Inslee, the actor; Arthur Miller, the Academy-award winning cinematographer; Constance Talmadge and Maggie Savoy, both actresses from the teens. It was an amazing few months when I met with these people who all had a hand in creating the art form that cinema has become today.

The Motion Picture Patents Company had held a monopoly over film cameras and film for most of the early part of the 20th century. When it was finally broken up in 1914 and the use of the cameras with Edison patents became more widespread and accessible, the creativity of film making really began to hit its stride. No longer did a burgeoning filmmaker have to film his scenes on the sly to avoid agents from the Motion Picture Patents Company. Now he could build sets, large and small, on permanent property. With the small fact that film corporations now purchased land and created permanent buildings to film in, the scope of their films was allowed to expand in ways that was limited only by their imaginations.

At the same time, due to the World War in Europe, the pioneering film making that had been taking place in France and Germany were brought to a stand still. World-wide film making became concentrated in the Western United States as the influential directors and performers from Europe sought to live out the war in the United States. This brought an influx of creative people to the warm weather of Los Angeles, as well as those who were drawn to the glamour of the creative lifestyle. Thus was born Hollywood, the entertainment capital of the world. Drawn to it's, back then, muddy avenues were the expats, the displaced, the artists, the dramatists, all of whom were enamored with the newly birthed creative industry of cinema.

This sudden broadening of scope of the way films were created and the lifestyle that surrounded film making in the late 1910s was exactly the time that Maggie Savoy entered the cinema industry.

Maggie Savoy, born Magdalena Santoya, was only in silent pictures for a few years, but her contribution was enormous. Working with some of the top stars and major directors, she was close to many of the movers and shakers of early Hollywood. She acted in the now legendary Solomon and Sheba and was close personal friends with both the star and the director, and was close to the scandal that continues to surround it even today. It is also rumored that she had a hand in 'discovering' the lost director's cut of the film.

Her film career was cut short by her own choice to see the world. She gave up acting to marry and move to Europe just after the end of World War I.

I think I can say this for all of my peers that the day she left Hollywood was a sad day indeed.

Once you have read her account of her years in Los Angeles, you will see why I have been completely charmed. Following is her memoir of the early years of cinema in Los Angeles. I have learned a great deal and hope you will too.

Steven R. Patterson, Ph.D.
Film Critic, Los Angeles Herald
Los Angeles, 1971

Chapter 1

When I was a girl of eighteen, I ran away from home. I knew for certain what I was running from, but as to what I was running to, I had no idea. All I knew was that I needed to find my own way in the world, no matter the consequences. And I found myself, nearly a month after I left, staring out a fourth floor window of a boarding house with nothing to say for myself, watching listlessly as the people below went about their business.

Yet, life has a way of moving on, even when you yourself are so uncertain. And that night, twenty seven days after I left my home, things changed for me. It was the night my cousin was arrested for being an "actress" and it was the night I found a way.

My grandfather, my Papa, when I was a child and upset about the little hurts and bruises that life heaps upon everyone, would say to me, "You can be whoever you want, Mija, you can do whatever you want as long as you are true to yourself. Take heart in who you are and things will work out just fine."

As a child it meant little to me. Yet at that time, as a grown woman, I couldn't get his words out of my head. Who was I? What did I want for my life? I had no answers. I only knew what I didn't want. I didn't want to be married against my wishes. I was certain I didn't want to marry the odious Mr. Henry Johnson.

My mother had accepted, on my behalf, a proposal of marriage from Mr. Johnson. Mr. Johnson was fine as far as boring bachelors went. My mother liked him for he was fairly rich and had excellent prospects. I am certain, even after all these years, that her real object was to get rid of me at last. But I couldn't marry him. The man was too shy to speak to me directly and looked at me as if I were a trophy he had won through some talent of his own. He had no trouble conversing at length about me with my mother. I knew for certain that to marry Mr. Johnson would have been betraying myself.

In the way that I could not refuse my mother, in my heart I refused to settle for a loveless marriage and the rearing of children. I wanted more. What exactly, I did not know.

That is why I found myself staring out the window of the fourth floor window of a boarding house on Main Street in Los Angeles. The boarding house where my cousin Dolores had settled after she left home and also where she worked.

I remember that night in so much detail. I watched the last of the sun disappear into a fiery orange glow behind the bank buildings on Spring Street. I watched out the window long after the light had faded and there was only a small band of light on the far horizon.

My cousin, dressing in the closet behind me for her night's work, admonished me for leaving the curtains open after dark. I said to her, "Dee, no one can see in. We're on the fourth floor and there are no other tall buildings nearby."

"Still, it just doesn't seem right," she returned, running a brush through her hair. I can still see the gloss shining on her stylishly short dark hair as she raked the brush quickly.

"You sound just like my mother." I smiled at her to let her know I was joking. She laughed too.

I then turned back to the window. I could make out very little below me. On the corner was a street lamp that offered some illumination of the automobiles and people passing by. As I wasn't staring out the window for any particular purpose, it didn't bother me one way or the other if I could see anything. Next to me lay my diary. I had always been a very committed diarist, but I had found myself unable to write anything for the past month. There was so much I was confused about, yet I didn't know where to begin.

I heard rustling sounds behind me and knew that Dolores was putting on her dress. When the room again became silent, I turned to look. Dolores was wearing a beaded burgundy evening gown. The hemline was very short, nearly showing her knees. She looked spectacular. The color perfectly accented her dark skin and black eyes. Even though we were first cousins, the only likeness we shared was our dark hair. I was pale with hazel eyes. A dress like that would have made me look as if I were trying to dress up in my mother's clothes. On Dolores the dress made her look even more beautiful.

"You look lovely, as usual," I said to her. In response she smiled broadly and did a little dance for me, turning in the process. Her dress swished around her.

"I have to get downstairs, the car will be leaving any minute now." Dolores checked her make-up in the mirror, smoothing down a stray hair. "Have a good night primita. Don't sit in the window all night."

Since I had run away from home, I hadn't had much energy or motivation to do anything else. Dolores was right. I needed to do something.

Even though I found myself with no prospects more than sixty miles from my family, I did not regret my choice. The idea that frightened me the most in my new, unfamiliar surroundings was my undetermined future. Once I was sure that I would not be found and forced back home, I found that I had no idea what my future would hold. Now what? I constantly asked myself. Now what, now what, now what? I was immobilized by my utter fear of what tomorrow would bring. What would I now do that I'd abandoned all my previous plans for the future?

Not that I had ever had any concrete plans. I had always thought that I would perhaps fall in love one day and then get married. Until then I would help my father run the ranch and family businesses, and ride my horse. Maybe I would give horseback riding lessons to girls who wanted them. Perhaps I would take a correspondence course or two, since my mother wouldn't allow me to attend a university. I knew where I would be living. I knew where my meals would come from. I wouldn't have to worry about money or what to do with my days. There would be no worry other than how to avoid my mother. Such a simple life, a possibility no longer.

The bright spot of hope among my fears at that time was Dolores. She was my best friend and, to be with her at last, made me at least feel safe. She had run away nearly two years before I had, and we had secretly corresponded. My nosy, officious mother had never caught on. When I told Dolores of my intentions to leave my home, she more than graciously offered me her support.

In a moment, I decided that I'd had enough of my self-imposed seclusion and decided to take a walk. I was apprehensive about being out at night alone in the city, having only left our rented room in the company of my cousin. As the boarding house we lived in also housed a genteel gentlemen's club, I was certain that the neighborhood was a relatively nice one.

The boarding house had been an old hotel, the kind in fashion a half century before. It had four floors with two wings that were parallel to each other. In one half of the old hotel lived the girls. The other half was used exclusively by Dolores and her fellow hostesses while they were working the gentlemen's club. The original dining room was now the salon and the basement had been converted into the gaming room. For show, there was a sign in front, on Main Street, that read "Esther's Boarding House, No Vacancy." Esther Barton was the proprietress and the meanest woman I have ever met.

The front and rear entrances were off limits to me so I eased down the service stairs that led to the delivery entrance on the side. It opened onto a small lane and gave me easy access out of the building. When I pulled open the door, I found myself facing a broad back – a man was standing on the steps. There was no way around it, and I worried that I would be in trouble if I were caught talking with a customer on my own at the side exit. I was sure it must be a customer because of the leisurely way he smoked a cigarette. Passersby wouldn't have lolled in the doorway. My fear mounted as I hesitated. I was just turning to go back up the stairs, when the man turned and saw me.

"I'm sorry Miss, am I in your way?" He bowed slightly and stepped away from the door. Still hesitating, undecided, I didn't move. The man looked at me straight in the face. I was surprised to find myself staring back into the man's dark eyes. Stung with nerves and worries, I hurried out the door and down the lane, walking quickly to make the street and the safety of the gold light of the street lamps. As I reached the corner I glanced over my shoulder. The man was watching me.

I walked, in as composed a manner as I could up and down Main Street between 7th and 8th Streets, past many similar buildings to the one I lived in. Many were apartments, there were some businesses and a bakery that I visited as often as I could. I was flustered by the encounter with the man. He was young, he was handsome, and he was dressed very finely. He had also been so chivalrous to me. I was quite struck. I had never encountered a young man that made my heart jump so. I wondered if he were one of the customers that Dolores had described to me.

Relaxing into the exercise, I remembered Papa's tale about how he left home as a young man. He had been born to a family of poor ranch hands and had always worked the ranch himself. Papa had left the ranch in Southern California as a young man because he'd had enough of the poor treatment and even poorer pay. The Americanos had just taken California at that time and he found from them that in their country you were expected to make your own fortune. Papa liked the idea and he left home. "Mija, it was the hardest thing I ever did. I left behind my sisters who had families of their own, but needed the extra money that I earned. I left behind everything I ever knew with no idea about the world I was heading into. Yet, I was so sure that I was doing the right thing, that I never felt regret or sorrow for what I had left behind, even when working the railroads proved to be worse than what I left. For then I left that and tried my hand at gold mining which at least offered more freedom if less food. But whatever job I took, whatever city I lived in, I knew I was going the right way for I was believing in myself. And that, my darling girl, is the one thing you can be sure of."

Tears sprang to my tears and my handkerchief was wet through before I was finished with my walk and my thoughts about Papa. The fresh air and exercise did me a world of good.

I did not venture very far that evening. I was too unsure and wary, but at least the city streets and noises and the strangers I passed, kept me from deliberating over my troubles. It was by far the most pleasant evening I'd had since I had arrived.

Chapter 2

Life always seems to make its most dramatic changes in a flash. After a month of time moving as slow as molasses, that night my future altered drastically. For when I arrived back at the boarding house, there was a flurry of people rushing along the lower floor halls. I went to sneak up the stairs but was stopped short by the words I overheard Esther speaking.

"Mark my words Miss Prentiss, I'll have them out by morning." Her normally haughty voice, now sounding imperious. "The audacity to arrest my girls. They should know better."

Arrest? A worry grew in my chest. Dolores had gone out to a party that night as a rented girl. Arrest? I found that I couldn't go up to my room without finding out what had happened. Once Esther had left the building, the hallways cleared. Usually at this time of night the living quarters of the building were silent, and soon the quiet returned.

I sat on the service stairs, unwilling to go up or down, yet frozen with worry. Had I not been downstairs to hear the commotion, I would never have known that something was wrong. Dolores never came up to the room before three in the morning. Sometimes not until dawn. But I had heard and couldn't rest until I found out more.

I must have dozed off in the stairwell, for I woke to a gentle hand on my shoulder. It was Stephanie, one of Esther's girls. She was the only other girl in the house who had been in any form friendly to me. She was a blonde in her middle twenties. She had a warm, friendly smile, and I liked her a great deal.

"What happened?" I asked.

She gave a nervous glance down the hall and then pulled me to my feet. "Let's have a cup of tea, alright?"

I nodded and followed her to the kitchen. Esther's night time cook had left. I realized that it must be past midnight.

"I'll put the kettle on, why don't you sit down." I did as I was told. Once she got the kettle heating she explained things to me.

"That party that some of the girls went to tonight was raided. Joe got Mary Ellen away in the car, but the other five girls were arrested." Seeing that I didn't quite understand why people had been arrested, she continued to explain. "The cops sometimes raid the parties. Especially the parties of the rich movie folk." Stephanie explained matter-of-factly. "I have heard that they do it to confiscate the booze or illegal drugs, but I don't know for certain. Tonight, though, they arrested some of the people and all of the rented gals."

Raided? I asked myself. What I knew of raids were shipping officials or federal officers raiding warehouses for contraband and pornography. What would they raid a party for?

Stephanie continued, "Esther had a fit. Most of the city officials are in her pocket, so her gals are to be left alone. Now they will all have arrest records. Esther doesn't like those kinds of complications."

I listened silently, trying to understand. "I've heard say that it was some of the city government people who asked Esther to move down here from San Francisco years back. Apparently Esther is quite famous there for a brothel she ran in the Barbary Coast, but after the earthquake she was having trouble making things work. It has been rumored that last mayor, Harper I think his name was, asked her to set up an establishment here."

I didn't know a thing about city politics, but it sounded somewhat impressive. In an illegal sort of way.

"Well, anyway, the cops are supposed to leave her girls alone, but they arrested all of them at the party last night, plus a few other girls working on their own."

"So Dolores is in jail?" I asked weakly, imagining my poor cousin would be stuck there for a long sentence.

"Yeah, but don't you worry, Esther will have them out in no time. She's got connections," Stephanie decided satisfactorily. By then the water was boiling, so Stephanie poured the water into the pot. "Don't you think that its crazy that Esther runs a place for hookers with a gaming room in the basement? Lots of men always coming in and out at all hours and this place hasn't never been raided?"

"Hasn't it?" I asked politely. Frankly, I was very much bewildered at this new turn of events.

"No, of course not. Esther has it all worked out. Heck, half the cops come here regularly."

I nodded in agreement. I started to understand, but was having trouble accepting it. Stephanie came to the table and put her warm hand on mine. "Don't you worry, honey, Dolores will be home in no time. Just you wait."

"Thanks Stephanie. Do you have any idea when Dolores . . . all the girls will be back?"

"Esther has gone to see to them now. I daresay it will be very soon." Stephanie assured me. She poured me a cup of tea and we drank it in silence. She ushered me up to my room. I went to sleep, my head swimming with new ideas and situations.

It was twilight in the room when I woke up, dawn just breaking. I woke up comfortable and comforted. I had dreamed of my Papa holding me in his arms telling me everything would be OK. I heard movement in the room and realized that Dolores must have returned. I bolted up to a sitting position and found her rummaging through her bureau drawer.

"Dolores!" I said quietly but with enthusiasm, "I'm so glad you're back."

She kept digging through the drawer, half bent over it. "Oh, you heard about it? I was hoping you would have missed the news."

I was confused by her answer but relieved to see her back in our room all right. I told her so.

"Aye, it was nothing primita, things like that just happen sometimes." She found whatever she had been searching for in her drawer, it was too dark for me to see, and she began to undress. Her pretty beaded dress was dull now in the morning gloom.

I laid back down meaning to go back to sleep when Dolores continued. "But I got to be an actress for a night Magda."

There was no mistake the sparkle of glee in her voice. Half turning, half sitting up, I asked, "An actress? What were you doing?"

Dolores came and sat on my bed, "We were arrested for being hookers, but when we were booked by the cops, all five of us stated that we were actresses."

"I don't understand."

"Being an actress is legal, primita. And with so many people who come out here just to be in pictures, how can the cops prove that we are not?"

Something clicked in my head when she said that. A distant memory surfaced. "Dee, didn't you want to be an actress too?"

"Ahh, what? What do you know about that?" she answered, a bit alarmed.

"In one of your first letters to me after you ran away, you said that you thought you would like to be an actress."

"Right, I did write that." She sighed and turned towards the brightening window. I could see her profile clearly now. Her eyes shone brightly – too brightly as if tears were coating her eyes. "I did for awhile, but well . . . now you're here and I want other things."

There was something in her manner that made me believe she wasn't telling the whole truth. "Is it hard to be an actress?"

"No, not really. But the work for just an extra is not very consistent and hard to live off of. The real money comes from getting a contract with one of the studios. That's when being an actress can pay off." She sighed again. "I'm so tired, I've got to sleep. Mind if I sleep in today? I may miss lunch."

"No, get your rest. I'm sure your need it."

Dolores was asleep in less than two minutes. She could get to sleep so fast. I tried to go back to sleep and dozed on and off for another hour, but couldn't get back to real sleep. The idea of being actresses struck a chord with me. The movies were filled with girls like us. If so many other girls could do it, why not Dolores and me? We both loved to see movies. We were living in Los Angeles without any real plans. We were both young. I was pretty enough and Dolores was beautiful. Why not try for it?

As I couldn't sleep, I got up and made my way downstairs to the kitchen for a cup of tea.

There was a lot about Dolores that I didn't know. It would be foolish to kid myself that I did. We had only known each other for four years, and until a month before, we had only seen each other once. Dolores's mother, Francis, was my father's sister. When Francis had eloped with one of the ranch hands, my father and mother were outraged (or alternately, pretentious) and barred her and her new husband from their sight. My Papa thought it was a good joke and gave the newlyweds a great deal of money to start a business of their own. They settled up north in Ventura. Papa spent a great deal of time with his family in Ventura. Dolores and I both received reports of one another from our grandfather, and we both longed to know one another.

Dolores was the youngest with four older brothers. I had two much older sisters and a brother whom I never really got along with. To know that there was another girl near to my age who loved Papa as I did made me feel as if I did have a friend out in the world.

We finally got to meet when Papa died four years ago. My father was devastated by Papa's death and invited his sister's family to stay with us while we mourned. My mother did not approve but could say nothing. Dolores and I got along instantly. It was as if we were sisters already. Before the three days were out, we knew all of each other's secrets, and from that time on we had been constant correspondents.

I knew deep down that Dee didn't tell me everything. Her letters were always so enthusiastic, so carefree that she couldn't have been completely honest with me. Even when she was caught with that boy, Jose – the reason she ran away – she was happy. When she left home was the only time that our correspondence was cut off. Yet once she had settled in Los Angeles and we found a way to write to each other secretly, our correspondence had been as open and forthright as it had always been. I loved her too much to doubt her, but now knowing as I did that she didn't always tell the complete truth, I wondered how much I really knew her.

Chapter 3

Those thoughts only lasted a minute before I was again occupied by the idea of acting in pictures. With my tea I went into the common room which was converted from the old smoking room of the hotel. It was a bright, sunny room with lots of old, comfortable furniture. There was no one in the room, as I had expected. On regular nights, no one got up before ten or eleven o'clock. I assumed that today it would be at least noon before I saw anybody.

In the common room there were piles of magazines and newspapers. I took a few newspapers from the top of the stack, most likely the most recent editions, and began to peruse them. The most recent paper was from three days before.

It is strange how when you open your eyes to something, you find that it has always been there before you. As I scanned through the classified ads of the old papers, I saw many advertisements for auditions. I also saw ads for Extras – that was the word that Dolores used. There were whole columns of ads for movie-related positions.

I also read over ads for open positions that were not related to the movie studios. Now that I had broken my self-imposed isolation, I needed to be away from this place before I became a part of it. When I had been walking the night before, I thought that I might look for a job.

It was not at all what I had expected. There were ads for maid service, for factory work. Ads for cooks. I wanted to get a position somewhere that would allow me a modest amount of income, but I didn't want to do the backbreaking work of a servant, nor did I want to burn my hands or ruin my eyes in a chicken factory or laundry.

I mentally cursed my mother for having sent me to a ladies college – really a marriage preparatory school – instead of a proper school where I could have learned stenography or typing. Now that would be a job, I thought, working as a secretary. I just didn't have the skills.

It was not yet 9 o'clock in the morning before I grew bored and frustrated reading through the old newspapers. I went for a walk. It was a lovely, clear morning. The sun shone brightly on the motley array of buildings. It was going to be a beautiful day. Walking through the streets that morning, I took heart in the beauty of Los Angeles. The clear winter air was warm and encouraging. In the North a smattering of snow topped the San Gabriel Mountains making a striking contrast to the deep blue sky. Despite the bleak employment opportunities, I felt cheerful. The weather was so nice, I hardly needed my coat.

I went back up to our room before noon. Dolores was awake, but hadn't moved far from the bed. "Where did you go off to so early?" she asked with a yawn.

"I was reading the newspapers."

"The newspapers? What for," her voice indicated that she didn't think much of the news.

"Well, I was curious about a few things. I think it might be good if I looked for a job."

"A job?" her eyes grew big, "I thought you have enough money." I could hear the worry in her voice.

"Well, for now, but I don't want to sit in this room for the rest of my life."

"Don't even talk to me about that." Dolores's voice was thick with contempt.

I was about to tell her to stop being gloomy, but she continued speaking. "Hey, let's go to Mr. Ross's cafeteria for roast beef sandwiches. Then we can go see if Mr. Stuckey has any new movies."

Her usual enthusiasm was back in spades. I readily agreed to go.

Over lunch, sitting along the zinc counter at Ross's, I tentatively brought up the subject of acting for pictures. "Dee, when I was looking at the ads in the paper this morning, I saw loads of ads for auditions and extras." Dolores only nodded her head. Not much encouraged, I pushed on, "I was thinking that it would be fun to be an actress."

She looked at me from the corner of her eyes, her sandwich poised in midair. "Why are you so interested all of a sudden?"

"I had never really considered it before, but now that the thought is in my mind, I find that it won't go away. If other girls can do it, then why not us?" I said. "You are so pretty it would be a shame if the whole world doesn't get to see you."

Dolores smiled broadly at my compliment. Her skeptical look turning into one of hope, her eyes sparkled brightly. "You really want to Magda?"

"Sure," I responded enthusiastically.

"Well, the best thing to do is to stand near studio entrances or go to auditions." She looked at me sheepishly before continuing. "I got one tiny part by just waiting outside the Ince studios."

"What?" I exclaimed so loudly it was likely I was heard above the din of the noisy restaurant. "You never told me!"

"Hush, I know. I'm sorry. I only had two small parts as an extra. Nothing important." Dolores looked away from me. "When you came I decided I would stop trying. It had been more than a year and I hadn't made a success of it."

The melancholy tone in her voice disturbed me, so I redirected the subject. "What were the pictures Dee? What did you play?"

She enthusiastically described to me the two background roles she played – one in a western and one in a comedy. To me, both roles sounded fabulous.

When there was a lull in our conversation, I brought up the subject of a regular job for me. "I really want to try to be in the movies with you, but I think it is also realistic if I had some sort of steady income. Plus, I don't want to cool my heels at the boarding house. A job would be the perfect thing to keep me occupied."

Dolores mulled it over a bit. "Jobs are hard to come by in this city, Magda. You know, I had to work as a maid in a hotel before I went to Esther's. That's hard work."

"I was thinking I could try for a job in a shop. Maybe in the haberdashery shop in Hamburger's People's Store, or the one in Bullock's." I tried to sound encouraged.

"You would be great at it. Pretty and refined as you are, but I say, those jobs are even harder to come by and they don't pay well. If you apply for one, you shouldn't give your real name. They'd never hire you if they knew you were Mexican." I think Dolores was trying to keep me from getting my hopes up, but she was very much poking a pin in my balloon. It was all right for her to hope for some far off dream of being a famous actress, but not a lowly realistic hope of finding steady employment

"It's okay Dee, I just want a job to supplement the money I have. Maybe I can earn enough so we could move to a real boarding house. Or even get an apartment one day."

Dolores smiled her trademark warm, enthusiastic smile and continued to eat. We spent the afternoon much as we had spent other afternoons since I had arrived – lunch, followed by window shopping and then to a movie house. Dolores generally would talk non-stop, gossiping and conjecturing. But this day she told me a bit about why she began working for Esther.

When she had first arrived in Los Angeles after she ran away, she worked as maid in a hotel. She worked 12 hours a day and made three dollars a week. She was starving, and she wasn't even able to go to auditions – the main reason she had come to this city. She had gotten friendly with a gentleman who often stayed at the hotel, it was he that suggested she go to Esther for work. Her nights then occupied, she had all day to find acting work.

Mr. Stuckey's movie house on 8th Street and Hill – our favorite place to see pictures – was just a few blocks west of our boarding house. That day we found he had two films that we had not yet seen. Mr. Stuckey liked us, so he let us watch the films over and over, only paying once. That day we watched the drama The Cheat. The Japanese actor Sessue Hayakawa starred as the cruel man enslaving the greedy heroine, played by Fannie Ward. It was quite shocking in a very entertaining way. Both Dolores and I were very taken with the handsome Hayakawa. She thought the ending was just fine with the cruel man being arrested and the heroine going free. I thought it was mighty silly that a woman who stole money and then sold herself should get a happy ending. We argued about it the whole walk home.

Much later, after getting to know Mr. Hayakawa, I told him that story. I remember him shaking his head with irritation. Even though that had been his break-out role in pictures and was continually reissued years and years later, he didn't like it. He felt that his character had been unjustly made a villain. Yet, we both agreed, that is just how films were – all shock value, no truth.

That afternoon, Dolores and I had to hurry back to the boarding house. Dolores needed to be in by 5 o'clock – Esther required all her girls to dine and dress before seven – and Dolores had been late too many times before to risk getting into trouble tonight. As we neared 7th Street, I began to feel the fear again. All those hours ahead of me alone. Alone to think on things I couldn't do one thing to change.

It was just minutes after 5 o'clock when we hurried through the side door. Miss Prentiss, Esther's tight-lipped and prim assistant, was waiting for us.

"Late again. After all that Esther has done for you, you ought to be more conscientious about your duties." Miss Prentiss was so awful, she could chill a room just by entering it. Caught in her trap, it was obvious that she was going to lecture Dolores, so I tried to sneak past and go up the stairs. I was just putting my foot on the lowest stair, skirts in hand ready to run up, when Miss Prentiss turned her ire on me.

"Where do you think you are going?" Her haggard, old face turning towards me. Her look, her manner, everything about her reminded me of bitterness. She was bitter to the bone and wanted everyone else to share her fate. "I don't know why Esther, kind woman that she is, lets you stay here. You are not one of her employees. You don't belong here."

She paused for effect, "And now you keep your cousin out all day, making her late. You ought ..." I was starting to grow quite angry with the shrewish woman and nearly lost my temper.

Dolores interrupted her, "Aye, aye, we know. If you keep me any longer I really will be late!" Dolores pushed me up the stairs. It was a struggle for her for I was half turned round glaring maliciously at Miss Prentiss.

The day I left home, Dolores had met me at the train station. We had planned it that way. Once I was safely in her company we discussed my options. Finding that the money I had wouldn't go as far as I had hoped, we had decided that I would apply to her boss, Esther, to live in the boarding house (which was really only a boarding house for the girls who worked for her) sharing a room with Dolores.

Upon first meeting Esther, I felt less like one woman being introduced to another and more like a large succulent deer being laid before a wolf. Esther was a well-kept woman in her fifties who was lavishly draped in expensive clothes and jewelry and wore the coldest smile I had ever seen. When Dolores introduced me, the old wolf eyed me for a full two minutes – a professional appraisal I'm sure – and then treated me with such kindness that it was oddly disconcerting.

Her manner cooled a bit when she found that I didn't want to work for her but only board with her. Miss Prentiss objected from the first mention of it. Esther went into her office to think it over and discuss it with Miss Prentiss. When they returned a few minutes later Esther named her price. It was terribly expensive for me, but I would be in a clean, somewhat safe house with Dolores at my side. We agreed to it.

Miss Prentiss's sour face did not change from the beginning of the interview til the end. I felt I had made an enemy from the first time I ever spoke to her. I'm sure she felt the same way about me. Esther always treated me with obsequious kindness that was obviously false – even incongruous with her true nature – but I returned the favor and was very polite back. She had ulterior motives I knew, but as long as I could live in peace, I did not care.

When I struck my bargain with Esther, I didn't really understand what I had gotten myself into. Dolores had written to me that she was working as a hostess in a fancy salon. I thought it sounded glamorous. I soon found out that Dolores began each evening as a hostess but generally finished the night as a prostitute. Esther's boarding house was actually the city's most notorious and successful brothel and gambling house. While I loved Dolores and admired her unreserved approach to life, it was very difficult for me to accept how she lived. To me it was about as low as one could fall. I tried to hide my reactions from Dolores, for she was my best friend, and I knew she must have had her reasons.

In reality though, it was a piece of information that was hard for me to comprehend. I resolved, soon after arriving, that I had to do what I could to get Dolores out of Esther's grasp.

Once back in our room I had the whole night to go over the events of the day. Actresses, I thought gleefully, hugging my knees to my chest. We could be famous film stars like Lillian Gish.

I had always loved going to see the pictures up on the bright screen. My mother had not approved of moving pictures and thought it was low to go to see them. Shaker's, in downtown Redlands – the town nearest our ranch – had closed up their shop and turned it into a movie house just before Papa died. When my mother was off visiting family, I would sneak down and watch the pictures they showed. I loved the stories and the drama. Comedies were my favorites back then, for I was always in desperate need for a good laugh.

It was amazing to me that I could now go nearly everyday to see the pictures and nearly always see a new one. Dolores and I liked adventures, especially with handsome stars.

I spent my night in a dreamy state thinking how fun it would be to pantomime for the camera. Too see my face dramatically lit up on the screen.

I imagined my Papa laughing with delight at the idea. He had loved the old nickelodeons and would have been so thrilled and proud to see his granddaughters up on the screen.

"Magda," he would have told me, "that dimpled smile of yours will capture the heart of every man from California to New York. You are the darlingist girl to be seen on the screen."

I laughed out loud. Papa would have complimented me like that. Then he would have angled to be an actor himself. He probably would make a terrible actor, being a man that was far too straightforward, but he would have loved to have seen himself projected life size on the screen. How I wished he was there with me, with me and Dolores.

Chapter 4

Over the next few days, which was the weekend, Dolores and I made our plans to go to the Chronicle Studios first thing on Monday morning.

On Saturday afternoon as we were window shopping, the only kind of shopping we could afford then, Dolores said to me, "When you came, I thought maybe it was time to give up on the idea." She looked off in a corner as she told me, "After all, I've been at it for almost two years with only a couple of day jobs to show for it."

"What was it like being at a film studio Dee?"

As she told me about her limited experiences on sets at film company studios, I could see how much it meant to her to be an actress, how terribly she wanted to be a film star.

As was generally the case, Dolores's enthusiasm affected me to such a degree that before the afternoon was over I, too, couldn't wait to be cast in a film, especially after we watched Mary Pickford in The New York Hat at Mr. Stuckey's that night. That short picture was years old, but was so darling we both loved it. Who wouldn't want to be Mary Pickford?

We had originally intended to go the Chronicle Film Company studios on Monday morning, but while we were watching movies at Mr. Stuckey's on Saturday afternoon it had begun to rain. It rained all day on Sunday and didn't show any signs of letting up by Monday.

That was my first lesson in the making of films. Unless the rain stopped, we would not be able to go to the studio the next day.

"When you wait outside the studio gates," Dolores explained to me, "There are sometimes some benches to sit on, but no cover of any sort. Besides, film companies can't really film any scenes when it's as dark as this during the day." She then explained to me how the houses in films have no roofs, or only opaque panels, to let in all the sunlight. Without sunlight, stories that take place inside houses would be too dark to see.

We decided that we would go to a studio lot when the rain let up, or when we found out about an audition, which ever came first.

This was not unwelcome news to me. I couldn't begin pursing my future career the next day, so I would apply for supplementary employment instead. That Sunday morning, it was too wet to think about going out, so I had made a run for it to buy some food and magazines to keep us busy during the day. While I was reading the ads in the newspaper, I came across an employment ad that seemed most promising.

The Hat Box seeking qualified woman to work the counter. Must have experience in hat trimming. Please apply in person. 226 W 5th.

If there was one thing that I knew how to do it was to trim a hat, that as well as hemming skirts and handkerchiefs, embroidery, properly tying a bow, many other useless things, and, above all, curtsying properly. Apparently Ladies College had been good for something after all.

The next morning, I put on my best suit and left Dolores sleeping. As it was still raining, I took a trolley car up to the hat shop. I was very nervous, not having applied for employment before. Getting off at the street corner nearest the shop, I dashed under an awning to straighten my clothing and smooth down my hair. Taking a deep breath, I walked into the shop.

A bell tinkled as I came through the door. A young woman, maybe five years older than myself, was sitting at a table near the back of the room. She put down her needle and unfinished hat and greeted me.

"Good morning Miss, can I help you?" she asked pleasantly.

I was tongue-tied. It hadn't occurred to me that I would be greeted as a customer. My confusion only lasted a second before I blurted out, "I saw the advertisement for employment in the weekend newspaper and would like to apply."

The young woman looked me over and then excused herself to get the manager of the shop. An elderly lady came out from the back. She didn't walk very well, but her expression was cheerful.

"Well, my dear, you have come to apply for our shopgirl," she began kindly. "I am Miss Tanner and this is my niece Miss Jennifer." The younger woman made a slight bow. "And your name?"

"My name is Magda Santoya, it is very nice to meet you both." I made a small curtsy by way of being polite.

"I see that you are a properly mannered young lady. Have you any work experience?" As she spoke she waved me over to an empty chair at the work table. Jennifer took her spot at the table and began to work again on a hat. Miss Tanner sat next to her.

I sat down across from Miss Tanner and Jennifer. "No ma'am, I do not. I have never before applied for a position either."

"Well, you certainly are educated, speaking as formally as you do."

I colored and I felt my face flush. My mother had been so insistent about speaking correctly, I had never really had a chance to learn any slang. If Miss Tanner could understand Spanish, she would be shocked to hear the pigeon slang I use when I speak that language. "Yes, ma'am," I answered, "I attended Worth's Ladies College in San Francisco."

Miss Tanner and Jennifer exchanged a quick glance. "You did now. That is an impressive school, so I've heard," Miss Tanner continued. "I believe, then, that you are likely well-trained in embroidery and such?"

"Yes, ma'am."

"Would you mind showing us a sample of your work?" Miss Tanner rifled through a pile of fabrics and pulled out a piece of yellow cotton. She gave it over to me and put a workbox of thread between us. I took up the piece of cloth and Miss Tanner began working on a hat. It was very cozy to have an interview while sewing. As if we were members of a sewing club.

I began a small flower pattern that I knew wouldn't take very long. Miss Tanner continued her line of questioning. "Miss Santoya dear, why do you seek employment?"

I understood the unspoken part of the question: If you are so educated, well-mannered, and from a wealthy family why do you need to work?

"I am just moved to the city and would like a part-time position to keep me busy and productive." I answered as smoothly as I could. My phrasing was awkward, but I didn't want the Miss Tanners to know I was a runaway. Both women nodded appreciatively.

"Jennifer and myself do all the work here. We don't carry a large amount of stock for most of our work is custom ordered. Our helper would need to be able to take detailed orders, perhaps sketch out ideas and also help us with the work."

I nodded to indicate that I understood.

"What days would you be able to work, my dear?"

"Any days that you please. My time is my own." I hoped that my answers weren't too cryptic.

"That is good. We would need you Saturday, of course. Jennifer and myself were thinking that having some extra help on Tuesdays and Thursdays as well. Maybe with a Friday, now and then, depending on the season. Would that suit you?"

"Of course, that is highly acceptable." Miss Jennifer nodded and smiled at me.

We talked while we worked for a few minutes more. We talked about the weather, good books to read, and pictures that we had seen. Both women were very pleasant to talk with and, in less than a half hour, I had finished my sample.

Miss Tanner and Miss Jennifer each examined my handiwork minutely. While Miss Jennifer further scrutinized the sample, plucking at the threads, Miss Tanner said, "I see that you have an even hand and solid work, even if it is somewhat unimaginative." She turned to her niece. "Jennifer, what do you think?"

Jennifer held the piece up close and rubbed a finger over the design. She frowned a little and then nodded decisively. "It's as you said Aunt, solid but unimaginative. Miss Santoya seems quite capable. As we won't need her to do much designing, she would do."

"Well, then, Miss Santoya, would you like to work for us?"

I couldn't help but smile. "I would very much like to ma'am."

Miss Tanner reached across the table and shook my hand. "Its all done then. Can you start tomorrow?"

"Of course. What time would you like for me to come in?"

We spoke for a few minutes more – hammering out the details of my hours and wages. I left the shop feeling as confident and hopeful as I ever had.

Dolores and I celebrated that afternoon with a fancy lunch in a posh hotel. The rain had cleared by the late afternoon. We agreed that Wednesday we would begin pursuing acting jobs and would do it every day that I didn't go to work.

The next day was a thrilling and anxious day. The confidence I'd felt the day before started to wither as I began to doubt my abilities. There was nothing to be done for it, so I put my chin up and went to work.

The Miss Tanners were both very kind women. They took turns throughout the afternoon showing me around their small shop, how to take orders with customers, and so many things more. It was a fatiguing day, but a good kind of fatigue. The shop closed its doors at 6 o'clock and I was treated to a cup of tea before I headed for home.

As I walked the long way back to the boarding house, I felt much of my confidence had returned. I was glad for it, because I would likely need it the next day.

It had always been my Papa's philosophy that nothing could be accomplished well on an empty stomach. Having grown up on a prosperous ranch, I had never known personally if his philosophy were true or not. However, as my Papa was the wisest man I've ever known, I was more than willing to take his word for it.

When I arrived home after my first day of employment, I made preparations for the next morning – the first morning we would attend the cattle call for extras at the gates at the Mack Sennett studios. Dolores had heard that they were hiring extras for a Western feature. Since we were planning on leaving by 8 o'clock, I knew Dolores would be very tired, so I took out the clothing we would need the next day.

Then I went downstairs to the kitchen. Esther retained a night time cook, an older Mexican woman named Consuela. I had never spoken with her much, but she and Dolores were great friends. I had the idea that I would take some food along with us the next day, maybe sandwiches, so while we waited we would not go hungry. From what Dolores had told me of her experiences, waiting was the one thing to be expected the next day.

During the daytime the kitchen was open to anyone who wanted to use it. However, Esther charged an exorbitant fee for board and paid close attention to those who helped themselves in the kitchen. Always trying to be careful with my limited means, I didn't eat from her kitchen often. That night, for the economy of time, I thought it would be expedient to supply myself with food from the kitchen. Consuela came in at four in the afternoon and made dinner for the girls. She stayed until midnight making hors d'oeuvre and other food for Esther's guests. Her night's work was in full-swing when I went down to the kitchen.

Consuela had her back to me as she whipped something in a mixing bowl. I watched her for a short while as she went about her work in a professional manner. She reminded me of old Marie, our family cook when I was a child. She was a very old woman and very small and had worked for Papa since Grandmother had died. Older even than Papa, she didn't stop cooking for us until the day she died, arriving in the kitchen every morning at seven and leaving everyday twelve hours later. I could see that Consuela was the same type of woman.

"Excuse me, ma'am," I started in Spanish. Startled Consuela turned suddenly to see who had addressed her so.

"Aye, aye, Dolores's little cousin. I thought for a second that one of the house maids was still here. Miss Esther would have a fit if that were the case." She answered me in Spanish and, as she spoke, she turned back to her mixing bowl.

"I'm sorry to bother you, ma'am, but I was wondering if I could possibly have some sandwiches wrapped up for tomorrow?" I inquired politely.

Consuela, never missing a stroke of her mixing, looked me up and down critically. "Aren't you a polite one. No need to call me by that old lady name. Just call me Consuela. Have a seat," she nodded to the chairs along the wall. "I need to finish this batter and then I'll fix you up something."

After another minute of whipping, Consuela filled a pan with the batter and set it aside. "I don't see much of your cousin these days since you arrived. How is she getting along?"

"Very well, I believe."

"She was very excited that you came. Told me all about you, she did. Bragged really. I can't say that she was wrong, you are very pretty." Even though Consuela wasn't looking at me, I still blushed. "And she is not so sad as she used to be."

I was not sure what she meant by "sad" as I had never seen Dolores down at all. I replied, "No, ma'am."

Consuela only responded with a "hmmm." Her hands never stopped working, and it looked as if she concentrated only on her work. Yet she was very aware of me and everything that went on in the kitchen, never having to look behind herself. She brought me a cup of tea. I thought for a moment that she was going to sit with me and rest, but she immediately went back to her work.

"Dolores has a heart of gold," Consuela began after a few minutes in silence. "But she is too passionate and wears her heart on her sleeve. Be sure you look after her."

Surprised by this unasked for definition of Dolores, I was taken aback, automatically responding, "Yes, ma'am."

Consuela brought over a paper sack in which she had packed some food. "I'm glad you are here for her. She never would think to take food with her when she would be gone all day. She always came back half-starved. There are some cakes on top for your breakfast."

Even as I thanked her, she was already busy at the stove. I headed back to our room, up the service stairway. I couldn't help but look through the small window in the door to see if there was anyone there.

Chapter 5

The next morning, I woke Dolores up at half past seven. She couldn't have had more than four or five hours of sleep, but she got up and began to get ready. I laid out clothing for her to wear. Every time I helped her with anything, Consuela's words came back to me. "Be sure you look after her." I hadn't been able to sleep for thinking of my talk with her. She obviously cared for Dolores very much, but she was wrong to think that I was the strong one. Dolores, so brave and carefree, she didn't need me to take care of her.

Dolores was ready in 15 minutes, then we headed out to catch the red car up to Hollywood.

The morning sun cast deep shadows on the city streets. The morning was still chilly, but you could feel that the day would be hot. The streets were becoming alive with cars and carts and people. Several Chinese peddlers with their carts of fresh vegetables padded by. The baker's van rumbled and choked to a start. Even though it was January, the weather was very warm and dry with no sign of the rain that poured down just a few days before. The Santa Ana winds were blowing in fits and bursts.

While waiting for the streetcar to Annendale, I found myself becoming more alert and excited. Dolores was still yawning and very sleepy. The stop at Main and 6th Street was close to the boarding house and we got there in good time. I was eager for the streetcar to come. I felt that I now had a real goal, a purpose to work towards, and I couldn't wait to get started.

I saw the streetcar coming up the hill and pulled the sleepy Dolores away from the street lamp pole that had been supporting her. "Come on. Here it comes." Dolores perked up for a second and we both went to the curb and climbed in. The ride took about twenty minutes, while Dolores slept, I enjoyed the scenery. The streetcar wound through the hills north of the city, where there were ravines green with lush vegetation.

Dolores had been to the studio gates several times before and knew the way from the streetcar stop. Outside the gates there were already a group of five girls, two very old women, and several men of a variety of ages. We took a place along the wall. There were two benches for sitting, but those had already been taken by the earlier arrivals.

A long hot day of waiting began. As the sun rose higher, I soon realized that it would soon be beyond the wall that offered us shade. While leaning against the wall, Dolores and I split the cakes and a bottle of sweetened tea that Consuela had packed. There were many people, mostly men and mostly craftsmen, who came and went through the gates. Trucks and cars came and went as well. Now and then one of the workmen would stop and flirt with the group of girls nearest to the gate who talked and laughed merrily. The old women were flirting with each of the men who were waiting along with us. They were talking like schoolgirls, giving demure looks and playfully bantering with the much younger men. I would have thought each of the women, while still handsome in an aged way, were at least 50.

Before the first hour was out there were two other groups of people waiting along the wall behind us. Mixed groups of boys and girls, they looked young enough that they must have been skipping school to stand among us.

Two remarkable things happened during the course of the morning. The first was when the older of the two ladies stepped away from the wall and presented a song and dance from her vaudeville act of 30 years ago while an entertainer in San Francisco's Barbary Coast.

I'm a timid flow'r of innocence,
Pa says that I have no sense
I'm one eternal big expense;

But men say that I'm just immense!

Ere my verses I conclude,

I'd like it known and understood,

Tho' free as air, I'm never rude

I'm not too bad and not too good!

Ta-ra-ra Boom-de-ay

Ta-ra-ra Boom-de-ay

Ta-ra-ra Boom-de-ay

Ta-ra-ra Boom-de-ay

Ta-ra-ra Boom-de-ay

Ta-ra-ra Boom-de-ay

Her voice warbled more than it should have, but her dancing was excellent for a vaudevillian. Dolores and I both applauded, as did all the men. The group of girls in front looked on with horror at the old woman's display. Those snobby girls had no sense of fun.

The other remarkable thing was when Mabel Normand's large touring car was driven past. The top was down and Mabel was wearing a large hat, but despite the hat, we could see her face clearly. She looked horrible. We had a good laugh over it.

About 1 o'clock the group of increasingly irritating girls left. They were all hungry, apparently, and were tired of waiting. Dolores, the old women, and myself moved to the benches. Under the blazing sun, it was a small relief to be able to rest our legs. Many of the men had just sat on the ground. Had I had to stand up much longer, I would have joined them.

I was very thirsty somewhere around 2 o'clock and I decided to risk missing our big opportunity to run down to the market we had passed near the train stop. During my brief absence, the most incredible event of the day took place. I was sorry to have missed it.

When I arrived back to the line there was one less man and everyone was talking excitedly. Dolores immediately told me that a short man, most likely a director, had stopped and talked to the tall, lanky man who had been squatting silently next to the wall all morning. The short man had asked if he knew how to ride a horse. The silent man nodded and mumbled a quiet 'yes' and then followed the short man through the gates.

The event gave everyone fresh hope, but the waiting continued. Dolores nodded off against my shoulder. Her weight was very uncomfortable, especially given the heat, but I didn't have the heart to wake her. After all, she had to report to work later.

At half past four, we decided it was time to leave. The flow of people was now steadily streaming away from the gates. Dolores was very tired and we still had the ride back into the city.

As long as the day was, as tedious as the waiting had been, it had still been a wonderful day. While we may not have been doing much, it still felt like we were doing something. Something that might lead to a better tomorrow. Something other than gossiping and window shopping.

After that first day, we soon settled into a routine that had us waiting by some studio gates Monday, Wednesday and Friday. I worked every other day, but Sunday. Sundays Dolores would sleep all day, that being her only day off. Often we would go with Allison and Natey, two other girls who worked for Esther, to wait at the studio gates. Sometimes one or two of the other girls from the boarding house would come along.

Our most informative connections came through Esther's gentlemen's club. There was hardly a man in town that didn't visit Esther's at some point. Her gaming rooms were about as legitimate as any gaming house could be. Newly wealthy movie people often wound up at Esther's – it had an excellent reputation and was quite expensive. And very often, it was the place many of the newly rich came to prove their worth by buying rounds of drinks and gambling away all their money. There were many nights when Dolores would wake me up when she came in to tell me where we needed to be the following day.

No matter how discouraging it was to wait all day, we hung on to the hope. The hope did fade after days and days of disappointment, but would immediately resurface when, now and then, people were picked from the line. Our hope levels were topped off the few times that Dolores and I were picked to be extras.

The first time we were picked was about six weeks after we had started our waiting campaign. It was a comedy caper called Times Two. It was a Keystone Cop short, filmed out at the Mack Sennet Studios in Annendale. I can't begin to tell you how excited we were to finally be the ones following the director through the gates of the studio. There were about a dozen of us picked, but I felt as special as if I had been the only one. Dolores, never one to be tongue-tied, was absolutely silent with awe. There was so much going on once through the gates that it would have been enough to just stand to the side and watch.

After explaining to the group what we were meant to do, the assistant director placed us and told us not to move. Another hour of waiting went by, but there was so much to see that it could have been five minutes. We saw, up close, Fatty Arbuckle go by with a tall slim man, both of them joking and laughing. Dolores was about to run out and get his autograph, but thought better of it. Neither of us wanted to risk losing this opportunity by being star struck.

The actual filming only took a few minutes. We played two bystanders, on a sidewalk, who were splashed from head to foot in mud as the Cop's van careened out of control down a street. Unfortunately, we were not dressed in costumes for the scene. I spent the following day cleaning the mud from our clothes. Getting home, covered in filth, was an event in itself. We were paid three dollars each for the work. Neither of us could have been more delighted to be doused in mud.

Once Mr. Stuckey got the reel for the short, he let us watch for free as often as we wanted. It was amazing to see us both up on the flickering screen. And embarrassing too. I made the most unfortunate face upon being covered in mud. The audience always laughed hysterically during the scene, and I was glad for the concealment of the dark room.

The second time we were picked out of the extra line was about 3 months later. It was a drama in which we played old women waiting in a bread line. We were wrapped in rags and our faces smudged with kohl. There happened to be no other women in the extras line-up that morning, so even though very young for the roles, we got to play them. The shooting for that scene was very long, for we had to stand still, hunched over for most of the day. It was worth it at the end of the day when we received five dollars for our work. We treated ourselves to a fancy lunch the following day.

When the movie came out, we went to see it right away. Dolores and I were both dismayed to find that our scene had been taken out. It was a sad lesson to learn that not everything filmed actually made its way into a feature.

Chapter 6

In a way, the months that we were aspiring actresses was the most hopeful time I have ever known. There were small disappointments, but no histories to regret. There was hope and encouragement in spades, but I think just hope would have been enough.

Following this routine of visiting the film company studios three days a week, we pursued our dream of being actresses for many months. I went to sleep very tired every night, but I had never felt more fulfilled.

Even though I didn't see Dolores as much as before I started working, since our working hours conflicted, I felt I knew her better for all the hours we talked while waiting at the gates of studio lots.

My employment was a great source of pride for me. I enjoyed the atmosphere at the shop. Miss Tanner and Miss Jennifer were wonderful friends. Kind and patient, they taught me a lot. Soon after beginning employment there, I had improved enough with my handiwork that I was allowed to put together hats myself. We always sat around the table in the back to work, talking and laughing like old friends.

In the evenings after I left the shop, or sometimes when Dolores had gone downstairs for work, I would take long walks all over the city. As winter started to pass and the days lengthened, so did my walks. I learned to love the city as I had never loved a place before. Even my secret hideaway in the ravine near my childhood home did not hold my heart as the city did.

I would walk the different districts: Spring Street – the banking street – eerily silent after 5 o'clock. Broadway crowded with theater goers to watch the latest vaudeville imports. I would go to the top of Bunker Hill, sometimes taking the Angel's Flight funicular, sometimes walking the steep incline. I would walk amongst the grand houses, stopping now and then at a steep railing to view the city below me. On very clear days, twinkling lights from the beach cities of Santa Monica and Venice were visible.

My lonely night walks were wonderful. The crisp winter air and the clear skies gave me a beautiful view of the mountains to the North. I began to love the city, not only for the anonymity that it offered to me, but for its sheer loveliness, situated as it was between the mountains and the sea.

Those evening walks had become my inspiration. I had always been a solitary person. Walking the city streets at night gave me the sense of aloneness that I relished. From Miss Prentiss I received lectures warning me about how unsafe it was for me to be out at night, but I never listened.

It was a beautiful, mild winter that year and I enjoyed my freedom thoroughly. Dolores was not faring as well as I was. It looked to me as if her spark were diminishing, her enthusiasm ebbing. On mornings we went to the studios she was cheery and hopeful. Though at the end of another long day of being overlooked and unchosen, her mood became dark, and she became uncharacteristically silent.

I worried for her. She never complained about her work, but I could see it was taking a toll on her. I think in many ways she envied me my shop girl job. It was not a position that made one question one's soul. Every time I saw Dee go from happy-go-lucky to very sad, I vowed to find a way to get her away from Esther.

My worry for Dolores's welfare was chief of my anxieties now that my prospects had smoothed out. Consuela's admonition that I take care of her loomed large in my thoughts. How, though, could I take care of her if she would not let me?

A few times, I had caught her wiping at her eyes or choking back a sob only to immediately put on a winning smile. Once, when she didn't know I was there, she threw down her eye pencil, put her head in her hands whispering, "I can't do this anymore." Seeing her like that, my heart caught in my throat. Yet I didn't go to her, I didn't try to comfort her. I didn't want to force her to admit defeat. To comfort her, I would take her mind off it. I would read her articles from the papers about how the latest famous actress was discovered and think of scenarios in which we too would become famous.

It never took much before Dolores would take up the story. We could wile away many hours with the tales we told ourselves. It never seemed tawdry or fantastical as long as we were doing it together. In later years, I would try to distract myself in the same way, but it always seemed futile and ridiculous without my best friend.

I saw how the life was drained from the faces of some of the girls who'd been with Esther the longest – the ones who had accepted that this was all that life had to offer. As prostitutes go, Esther treated her girls well. They had the best of clothes, food and living quarters. After all, none of them were reduced to loitering on the street and, on my walks, I had seen those women. Yet, it was still a hard life. Esther didn't pay any of them enough to ever earn a way out.

I often visited Consuela at night in her kitchens. I thought that we were friends, but I really didn't know. I considered her a friend and confidante, but how she viewed me I could never quite tell. Esther hated that I spent time in the kitchen at night. Consuela had a form of dominion over Esther that I never saw in anyone else. "As long as the food was made right and on time," she told Esther, "I can have visitors."

Consuela always greeted my entrance with a cup of tea and a bit of whatever she had just made. She generally remained silent except to now and then urge me on with a precise sentence or two. We talked about Dolores quite a bit. Consuela was very fond of her. One night I had mentioned that perhaps Dolores should bargain with Esther for more money, that way we could move out more quickly.

Consuela's transformation was sudden and alarming. Her usually menacing silence was replaced with active anger. She had put down her knife and turned to me,, "Don't you ever let her even try that. When you get ready to leave, go. Don't ever try to bargain with that woman."

Stuttering I asked "But why?"

"Esther may look like a lady but she is made of steel without a heart. She'll take no demands, questions, or bartering. And if she gets half a chance she'll make you one of her girls as well."

Consuela continued, for once ignoring her cooking, "Esther would like nothing better than to ruin you both. Just last year she threw out her best girl on her ear, a pretty Mexican girl named Rosalie. Rosalie had demanded a large increase in the money she earned. Esther said nothing and threw her out. Last I heard the girl was working the shanties down by the oil fields." She gave me a grave look then turned back to her work.

It wasn't long before I witnessed first-hand Esther's reaction to demands for money from one of her employees.

One afternoon, just after Dolores had gotten up, we heard a commotion on the floor below ours. We rushed down to find a crowd around the stairwell. Stephanie was carrying a small overnight case and walking before Esther who looked like she would have strangled the insubordinate woman had she the opportunity to get away with the crime. Stephanie walked with her nose in the air as if she could care less about the whole situation, but just as she passed me and Dolores, she gave us a quick wink. Dolores and I exchanged wondering looks, neither of us understanding how she could be so cheeky at such a time.

Rumor had it that Stephanie had been picked as a local commissioner's special girl. As a result, she had demanded more money from Esther. Esther did what she always did when someone tried to bargain – she kicked her out.

I was very upset when Stephanie left, for she was the only woman there besides Dolores who was friendly to me. I was treated with disdain by the other girls there, even more so after I began working at the shop. I didn't pay too much attention to it, for I was too busy saving my money and plotting ways out. Yet I sorely missed Stephanie's companionship after she was gone.

During those months, more than once I ran into the man who smoked outside the servants' entrance. He was always very polite to me and would sometimes try to joke with me or talk to me, but I always became too shy, too embarrassed to speak to him.

Once I saw him while I was working at the hat shop. I was helping a customer near the front of the shop when I happened to see him from the corner of my eye passing on the sidewalk. He caught a glimpse of me as well, for he stopped and looked in through the window. Our eyes locked, then he winked at me, smiled and walked away.

I was so flustered I nearly knocked over a stand full of finished hats. The customer, a wealthy woman shopping for a large boat of a hat, looked at me as if I were ridiculous.

A week later I was straightening up the counter at The Hat Shop when I was interrupted by the bells jingling on the door. When I looked up, I saw him. I tried to remain calm as was required in my position as a salesgirl, however, I think I may have become quite red.

"Hello." He began quite simply.

"May I help you sir?"

"I'm looking for a hat," he stated looking around at our small supply of ready-made hats. "For my sister," he added.

"We have these few here that are ready made. However, we generally take custom orders. Did you have a particular style in mind?"

As I walked over to the display stand, I felt his eyes following me closely.

"No, I have no thing in mind." He fingered the hat on the lowest hook. I hardly dared look him in the face. He was so handsome, and uncomfortably near. He looked at me eagerly, seeming almost as nervous as myself. "My name is Del Wolham. Del."

Flustered, I looked up at him. Yet I still controlled my well-bred manners. "It's nice to meet you Mr. Wolham. You may call me Miss Santoya."

"Santoya . . . that is a Spanish name then? They told me you were Dolores's cousin, but you look so dissimilar." I am afraid my face flushed red then. I turned away, meaning to put space between us by means of the counter top.

Del Wolham lightly took my elbow so that I couldn't escape. "I'm sorry. I don't mean to be so forward, but I've been running in to you for months now and I just had to know who you were."

"I'm s-s-sorry," I stammered for no reason at all.

"I saw that you worked here and thought I might be able to introduce myself this way. If I knew where to find your parents, I would introduce myself properly."

I looked at him then and burst out laughing. He looked so earnest. Bringing my parents into this awkward situation just made it that much more ridiculous. He laughed with me, not quite knowing what to make of my reaction.

"I'm sorry," this time I meant it. "Let me try again. My name is Magda Santoya." I felt more confident after my outburst. I gave him a slight curtsy by way of acknowledging our acquaintance.

He bowed as well, then leaned over, took my hand and kissed it. "I'm glad to meet you Miss Santoya. Which hat would you say is your favorite?" He turned again to the hat display.

He must have heard, what I had heard. Footsteps approaching the door between the rooms.

"Do you need any help Miss Santoya?" Miss Tanner asked kindly. She looked at both myself and Mr. Wolham with more than a little anxiety. I assured her that we were getting along fine. After another thorough look at the two of us, she returned to the back room. I knew that she and Miss Jennifer were working on a large order for the Follies company that was in town.

"Which hat is your favorite?" he asked again.

"I like the maroon with the feather," I answered pointing to a hat Miss Jennifer had made the week before.

"I will take that one."

Disconcerted once again by his manner, I took the hat and returned to the counter. I wrapped the hat in a nice fitted box and then filled out the bill of sale. He stood behind the counter directly opposite me next to the till. Had he meant to embarrass and fluster me, he could not have chosen a better position.

"That will be five dollars and twenty five cents."

He pulled out a billfold from his inner pocket and handed me six dollars. As I was making change, he began, "I see that the store closes soon. I would dearly love to take you to an early dinner."

"I'm sorry?" Again with the apology instead of a proper sentence. My eyes floated up as if to look at him, but I was far too embarrassed and looked down again immediately.

"I know I'm being terribly forward, but I've been trying to find a way to talk to you for weeks." I turned away in embarrassment at the compliment. "I know it's not proper etiquette and all, but I'd really like to get to know you."

"I . . . I . . .," I stammered insensibly.

"Okay, you're right, tonight is too soon. And we wouldn't even have a decent chaperone." He spoke as if he could read my mind. Maybe he read my face, but from the way he looked around, his eyes settling on nothing, I don't think that was the case.

"How about luncheon? Next week? Say Tuesday?" He asked.

"Well," I hesitated, "I believe I can't . . ."

He interrupted me, "Perhaps Dolores would consent to chaperone if you are so hesitant." He looked away, quite embarrassed himself. "Although, I don't know that she would make the most responsible of chaperones."

Here I burst out laughing again. The idea of Dolores being responsible for any girl's safe-keeping was absurd. The awkward nervousness of the situation overcame us and we both laughed heartily. When I got my breath back, I answered him. "It's not a chaperone that I need. I can't go on a Tuesday because that is one of the days I work here."

The surprise in his face made him look at once very genuine and even more handsome. "Is that all? Then why not Wednesday."

I did want to meet him, but the inappropriateness of the situation was not easily overcome. However, I did run away from home to be my own person and in this case it meant stepping out with a gentleman that my parents might never know or approve of. So, after some hesitation, I accepted.

"Luncheon it is then," he beamed. "I'll pick you up at. . .:"

This time I interrupted him. "Why don't we meet on the corner of 7th and Los Angeles?"

His face, flushed with happy smile, made me a bit woozy. Or perhaps it was the strangeness of the situation I had just got myself into. "I will see you next Wednesday at 11:30 at the corner of 7th Street and Los Angeles Street." He bowed to me slightly and walked to the door.

"Mr. Wolham, your package." I called out after him.

His hand on the door, he turned to look at me. "Call me Del. That package is for you." With that he left. He left me holding a nicely wrapped hat and a mouth hanging open in a most uncharming fashion.

I felt as if I were flying when I left The Hat Shop an hour later. I half feared and half hoped that Mr. Wolham would be waiting for me as I left the store. I didn't see him, but I wasn't completely convinced that he wasn't somewhere nearby. I carried the hat box clutched to my chest. To the Miss Tanners I had fibbed. I told them that the hat was a delivery that I could take care of on my way home.

Once I was back at the boarding house I flew up the stairway. It took me a long while to settle down. From my window, I stared at the stars and devised what I should wear and how I should act. Del's handsome face never more than a few thoughts from the front of my mind. The giddy feeling, the elation and excitement, I had never before felt. Poor Mr. Johnson never elicited more than a feeling of obligation from me. With every step I took in this new life, I felt more sure of the decision I had made. I felt more secure in the feeling that my life held more for me than boring domesticity.

When I told Dolores the next morning she was elated.

"Mr. Del Wolham," I said quietly to myself. "I had seen him a few times before, when I went out at night. I thought he was so handsome."

"Handsome you say? More than that, perfect! Except he is not very tall. Besides his gorgeous looks, he's educated and very very rich." Dolores rocked herself on the bed. "Just think cousin, you are stepping out with the most sought after bachelor in town."

Dolores looked as if she'd swallowed a canary. I wondered that she was even pausing for a moment before telling me the news she obviously wanted to tell me, and which she knew I was dying to know.

"Well, it is common knowledge that his family owns half the oil wells in Southern California." Dolores told me with glee.

"So his family is rich, I want to know about him."

Dolores rolled her eyes at me. "I see now, you are in love with him already," she said to tease me. I put on a haughty look, with my nose in the air, and looked away.

"I think he's very handsome and has very nice manners, is that a bad thing?"

Dolores laughed, pulling her knees to her chest. She looked at me with such joy in her face that her eyes shone brilliantly. "Yes, primita, you are right. It is not such a bad thing."

"Then will you please tell me what you know?"

"I will. I can tell you that he is the favorite of every one of the girls in this house."

I threw a pillow at her. It knocked her off balance and she nearly fell off the bed, still laughing at me. "Okay, okay," she said, "I'll tell you what I know."

Del Wolham had been raised back East, Philadelphia or New York or someplace. He was 24 and had barely graduated from Yale a year earlier. His family was old money. Del was supposed to be learning the family business while in Los Angeles. His family had a lot of oil interests in the area and Del was meant to do something about them. No one was sure what he was supposed to be doing, but everyone was quite sure that he was mostly just enjoying himself while in town.

When Dolores was finished with his history, as she knew it, I awkwardly asked, "Does he often ... well, does he often come here?" My face burned with embarassment. I looked away.

Dolores found too much hilarity in this situation and laughed at me some more, "You mean, does he often come for the girls? Of course that's what you meant. Your face is turning scarlet. That red face of yours gives everything away! But he doesn't. He only comes here to gamble. Which, I think, he does a lot of. But he is supposed to be very very rich. Did I mention that already? Anyway, a man that handsome and rich wouldn't have to pay for it. I mean, he shouldn't have to. Who knows? He is a man after all."

I couldn't stop blushing. I knew I lived in a brothel. I knew what went on here, but I still was sometimes embarrassed by the open way Dolores spoke.

I was also blushing to find that my interest only increased. To be sure, gambling was not a particularly welcome vice, but if that was his only one I could overlook it. Had he frequented the ladies of the establishment, I think I would have found his looks and manners far less appealing. I say this in hindsight of course. At the time I was completely smitten.

Dolores and I had several days to plan and to speculate about what the date would be like. It was the only thing on my mind and the only thing we talked about. We spent our Monday shopping instead of auditioning. By Tuesday night I had worked myself into such a degree of expectation that I was practically terrified. The Miss Tanners kept asking me if I were all right, but I didn't want to confess to the two spinsters about my romantic affairs. I considered cancelling our appointment, no matter how much I had spent on a new dress. Fortunately, I had no way of contacting him. I was committed.

Chapter 7

When you are young, you think love is the end, when really it is only the means to an end – happiness. When I began seeing Del Wolham, I thought that I was well on my way to happiness. To be so young and so naive! That almost painful feeling of heart-stopping attraction is pleasant to remember, even if it is with a rueful smile.

Years later, when I watched my own daughter go through the elation and disappointment of first love, it was like I was reliving my own. As I watched her suffer, my only consolation for not being able to console her was that time would wear down the sharp edges of memory for her as it had for me.

The day I fell in love, Wednesday, I woke up very early and spent hours sitting at the window staring out. I was terribly nervous about what the day would bring, but I was also very much resolved on making it wonderful. Even Dolores got up early that morning. I had purposely stayed in the night before, but Dolores had been out as late as ever. I had a suspicion that she would likely be back in bed as soon as I left.

I think Dolores was as nervous as I was. She was abnormally quiet, even for so early in the day, but by 11 o'clock my hair was arranged, my dress complete, I was ready to go. I went down the stairs quietly and quickly, as if I were sneaking out. In a way I was. I really didn't want anyone in the house, especially Miss Prentiss, to see me leaving alone in a fancy new dress. I didn't want anyone to suspect I had a rendevous, innocent or not.

I stood on the corner just a few buildings up from the boarding house. The baker's son, Jed, nodded a hello to me as he passed, heavily laden with deliveries. I started to worry about who else might see me before Del Wolham came to meet me. I was very near to working myself into a panic, when it occurred to me that there was really no one I need hide from. In the past months I had gotten too used to worrying about being caught, being found out. If Miss Prentiss or Esther found out, so what? They would threaten to throw me out, but something could be arranged, I was sure. As I relaxed, I felt much more confident.

Then Del Wolham drove up in a large, shiny car. I had not expected to be taken out in an automobile. Putting the car in neutral, he got out of the car and gave me a small bow. "I'm glad you could make it," he said and then ushered me to the passenger chair. Now I was smiling for a completely different reason. To be treated with chivalry and elegance! As if his charming appearance weren't enough, there was a small bouquet on the passenger seat. As I went to climb in, he picked it up and handed it to me. My heart was thumping so hard, I feared I wouldn't be able to hear myself speak.

"Ready to go?" he asked. "I can put on the top if you don't like the wind."

I indicated that I didn't mind, so Del Wolham ran around the car and climbed into the driver's chair.

As he worked the gears he said, "I just got this beauty a few days ago. I'm still working out her quirks."

"Is this a racing car?" I asked, more out of politeness than curiosity.

"Yes! Its a Stutz Bearcat, specially made. The engine is finely tuned for long distance speed races, so she doesn't idle very well. No matter, I'll get her going in a heartbeat." After a few seconds more, the car lurched, then shot forward smoothly, speeding down the street. I turned to look back at the boarding house and, I couldn't be very sure, I believe I caught a quick glimpse of Miss Prentiss looking out the second floor window. I would have gotten a better look but for the car swerving widely to avoid a street vendor's cart.

"Sorry Magda." Del said sheepishly. "As I said, she's a racing car and not meant to slow down."

"Is it safe for you to drive it on the city streets?"

"Of course!" he beamed, "It all comes down to the skill of the driver, and I'm an excellent driver." I couldn't help but smile back at him, but I made very sure for the rest of the trip to hold on.

He drove us down Los Angeles Street. We were both silent, now and then taking shy glances at one another. I felt that I was in danger of having a very bad date if I didn't do something about it.

"Mr. Wolham, I understand that you are not from California and that you are from the East?"

The car audibly slowed, jerking us both forward. He quickly caught his mistake and shifted the car into the proper gear. He turned left.

"Please don't call me that. Del is my name and what I answer to."

I mumbled my apologies at the mistake, looking down too embarrassed. As cumbersome as it was to have a chaperone, at least I would have been saved from an embarrassment such as this.

"I'm from Philadelphia originally but have lived all over since my father got into the oil business."

"What place have you liked best?" I inquired, politely trying to keep the conversation going.

"Why, I'm not sure. I really like Los Angeles. It's not so stuffy as the East. It's more casual and relaxed. I like it." As he spoke he concentrated on the road. It was the first time I got to really look at him without having him return my look. His profile was very handsome with a foppish lock of hair falling into his eyes. He had very dark hair, not quite black, that seemed to take in the sunlight, not reflecting it, but making the color richer. His dark eyes sparkled in obvious enjoyment.

He turned right onto Wilshire Boulevard. As he turned the wheel, he looked over and caught me scrutinizing him and smiled more broadly. I could feel a blush tingle my skin. I felt destined to spend the afternoon with red cheeks.

"What kind of name is Magda?" Del asked.

"Its a nickname really. My full name is Magdalena." I answered shyly, somewhat embarrassed by my ethnic name.

"Like the saint?"

"Well, in a way. Its actually a quite common name in Spanish. I was named for my great-grandmother who lived in California when it still belonged to Spain." I was trying to make it seem as if I were not just some farm girl from the sticks.

"Then your family has lived here for a long time," he said more to himself than to me. "I didn't think people had really lived here that long."

I was about to get indignant about my family, spurred on by both pride and shame, when he turned to me, "Mind if I call you Maggie?"

I couldn't deny his charming smile a thing. Blushing so wildly my ears burned, I answered "Not at all."

That was the substance of our conversation as we drove along. After a half a mile he pulled to a stop at Westlake Park. Del parked the car at the curb and jumped out just as he had set the hand brake. He ran around the car and opened the door for me. Once out of the car, he took my arm and placed it on his, retrieved a basket out of the back and then guided me to a picnic spot along the lake.

I waited patiently while he threw out a large blanket and set down the basket. The park was recently built and many of the trees, palms and maples, were not yet grown in. Del had picked a spot right down on the lakeshore next to a small tree. Still holding the small bouquet of flowers, I felt that this was the most picturesque scene imaginable.

Adjusting my skirts for sitting on the ground, I awkwardly sat down. As Del set out the picnic items he picked up our conversation, "You and Dolores are cousins?" he continued, "You don't seem much alike."

I was slightly confused by his words. I didn't know if he meant it as a compliment or not. "I wish I were like Dolores, she is so bubbly and enthusiastic, I don't think there are many like her."

Del laughed, "I meant that you were not alike in looks. Although both of you are very pretty. Now that you mention it, you are quite different."

Again, I was embarrassed, but I refused to be unequal to the situation. I took a deep breath and gave Del a brilliant smile, even if I wasn't quite able to look him in the face.

"Yes, we were raised very differently. Dolores is the most vivacious and sincere person I know."

"Vivacious she is, I will not argue with you on that point. It doesn't mean that your manners are any less interesting, even though more refined."

It was all I could do not to cover my face with my hands. I couldn't take many more compliments without running the risk of having a heart seizure. I resolved to change the subject, but what topic would be safe? Occupation, it was always safe to ask a man about his occupation.

"Mr . . . I mean, Del, what is your business?"

It was his turn to look confused for a moment and then he answered evasively, "This and that for my father's company. Nothing of consequence really." That question seemed to have killed the conversation.

"I'm sorry, I didn't mean to be too inquisitive." I looked out at the lake. It was very pretty reflecting the clear blue sky. As it was still early spring, the grass was not very green and it was a bit chilly out.

Del seemed to recover himself. He reached into the basket and brought out an insulated bottle. "Its nothing, really. I'm sorry for being such an idiot." He laughed a little and poured tea from the bottle into fine china cups. He handed me one. "I know it is the proper etiquette to ask about business, but I always hope that I won't be. I'm always disappointed." I looked away, uncomfortable. "No, not you!" he cried at the sight of my downcast face. He sighed and looked away. I tried my tea.

"It must be you, you know," Del said to me, glancing at me from the side. I was just about ready to be quite offended when he said, "I've never bungled a conversation so badly. I'm usually the 'sweep a girl off her feet' kind. Yet for some reason I can't say anything right. I think it's you." Here he looked at me directly. I smiled in spite of myself.

"Perhaps I should start over then. How about this for a question: What are your hobbies, Del? What do you do to enjoy yourself?"

He grinned wickedly. "That's a much better question! I even think I will answer it. I like racing - whether it is cars, horses or people."

"Are you an athlete, then?" I inquired.

"I ran track in school, but was never very good at it."

"I've never seen a car race, but I love horse races and horses."

"You know horses?" he asked me.

I finally had a real reason to smile largely and graciously, "I know something of horses. My grandfather was a great afficionado and breeder." Del's smile reflected my own.

"Then I would imagine you are a great horsewoman?"

"Not a great one, no, but an enthusiastic one. Riding my horse is the one thing I miss most about home, I think." As I said it, I realized I had said too much. The inevitable question to follow would be why I had left home. I cringed waiting for it. It never came. I didn't even have a chance to wonder that it didn't, the conversation was so pleasant.

"You haven't had a chance for a ride in some time, I would imagine, why don't you come to my club another day and we'll go for a ride."

I glanced up at him, eyes shining with embarrassment. "I would like that."

From there the conversation ran smoothly, so smoothly, in fact, that I felt I had never talked to someone so thoroughly before. It felt as if everything each of us said was of so much interest to the other that the conversation could have branched out and gone on forever.

We lunched by the lake. When the sun became too hot, Del took me for a drive. It was one of those rare days in Southern California where there wasn't even a hint of cloud or haze. We drove North to view the ocean, and all the settlements in between, from the hills above Hollywood. Then we drove through Annendale and on to Pasadena. Del said he hadn't really planned what to do with me besides lunch, but now he wanted to take the incline railway up to Mt. Lowe. We found that the train wasn't in operation from all the rain we had the week before, but Del and I had a lovely walk among the lower parts of the canyon along a rushing stream.

It was along this path at the far end, where it stopped at a wall of rock, next to a waterfall and bright green glade, that Del kissed me. Had I been one for romantic visions, this would have surpassed anything I had dared dream. The sun was shining bright in the Western sky, birds were flittering in and out among the green bushes, the water gurgled merrily. Early wildflowers colored the hills. I took it all in and realized none of it except for the face of my lover in front of me. It was the perfect day.

We made our way back along the path slowly, walking very close to one another and talking little. We stopped at a nice hotel in Pasadena for dinner, the Raymond according to my diary, though I hardly knew where I was or what I ate. Then Del drove me back. We had agreed that he should drop me off a few blocks away. He had wanted to drive me up to the front door, but I insisted, and he relented.

He parked on 9th Street and came around to open the door for me. He took my hand to help me out. We said our goodbyes, he kissed the palm of my hand, then we parted ways.

I was too full of love for him to try and analyze the day. All I knew was that it was perfect. I didn't go back to Esther's immediately, for I knew I would have to be sneaky about going in. It was just about time for the girls to be going down to the salon and I wanted to give everyone enough time to be fully at work before I tried to enter. Besides, going back would dampen my spirits and I wanted the feeling to last my lifetime. Cupping my palm to my chest, I wandered the streets.

Finally, I went back. Thankfully, I saw no one when I sneaked in the back way. I stopped off in the kitchen to get some food for the morning. I was scheduled to work on Friday that week, instead of Thursday, so Dolores and I decided to go to the film company lots the next day to make up for our missed days.

Consuela, as usual, had her back to me. As soon as I entered she said, "I wondered if you would come in tonight. I packed some food for you. It's on the table."

"Thank you Consuela. How did you know, I . . ."

"Everybody knows Magdalena. Miss Prentiss saw you drive off in an expensive car."

"So she did see me." I sighed. I had been sneaky for nothing. "How is it that Esther hasn't barred me from this house?"

"Miss Prentiss saw you leaving in a big car. You know how nearsighted she is." Consuela was silent for a few moments while she took a pan out of the oven. "Today hasn't been any easy one for your cousin. She told them that you were meeting with your father and that he is trying to get you to go home."

"She said what?" It was a brilliant excuse, yet I was alarmed. I felt that the time I could stay here unmolested was ticking away quickly. Esther would either charge me more money or kick me out entirely if she could get away with it. She would charge me more money, of course, and that was a pressure equal with time.

"Be careful, Magdalena," was all that Consuela said in reply.

Sitting in my favorite spot on the window sill that night, I listened to the peaceful rustling of the wind, staring at the dark sky, not quite believing the day I had experienced.

I wanted to tell Papa about it. I wanted to know what he would think of Del. He would say, "He is quite a charmer that boy." I think Papa would really like him. Even my mother would like him, as he was from a rich, connected family. Better than any Mr. Johnson she could come up with.

I laughed. I had reminded myself of a conversation I had overheard when I was a girl. I must have been about 12 years old. My whole life I had worked with my grandfather on the ranch. I had four or five different uncles amongst the ranch hands and cattlemen. My Papa inspired loyalty, so many of our employees had been with us since my father was small. The argument I overheard was between my Papa and my mother. My father was in the room, but I don't believe he made a comment.

"My dear Ingrid," Papa said to my mother, "She's been riding among the ranch workers her whole life."

"And it is far time that she starts behaving more like a lady than as a cowman," mother replied indignantly. She and Papa disagreed on nearly every subject and in all the years they lived together, she never once willingly compromised.

"Be reasonable, please," Papa said soothingly. Of course that made Mother even more indignant. I remember having to bite my finger in order not to laugh at her.

"I mean it, she is not to spend time amongst the employees any longer. She is of an age where she certainly could be taken advantage of. She is also silly enough, that girl, to become smitten with some common boy and ruin her chances at a good marriage."

"Now, now Ingrid." Papa could calm wild cats, but my mother he always had trouble with. "Think about it a moment. If you deny the girl, she will want to spend time with the ranch hands. That is a far more dangerous risk, I think. Then we won't even know she may be in trouble."

"I'll make sure she has plenty to do to stay out of trouble."

"Please listen for a moment. You know Tomas and Jimmy. They've both been with the family since Edward was a boy. Do you think they would stand by if something were to happen to the girl? I happen to know for a fact that young Enrico took to task that boy we hired last year for looking too long at the girl. If she is known to the hands, they'll take care of her like their own. Take her away from them, she'll be on her own."

At the time I didn't quite grasp what it was that Papa meant. He had gained mother's silence, which generally effected a win in their arguments. "Edward, what do you have to say." My father didn't answer verbally, but he must have made a movement for the tension was broken at that point. I hurried up to the top of the stairs, out of sight, before my grandfather came out of the room.

At the bottom of the stairs he stopped and looked up as if he knew I were there. "Did you hear that little Magda?" he asked me. I softly answered 'yes.' "Please behave yourself then and prove your mama wrong." He chuckled to himself and walked on down the hall.

The next morning I got Dolores out of bed at 7:30. She mumbled something about my date, but as she was not even remotely awake, I held off descriptions until later. After we arrived outside of the Nestor Studios, at Gower Gulch, and took our places in line, Dolores took a great yawn and demanded all the details.

I told her while having our breakfast rolls. Mostly I described the things Del and I did, not having the words to tell her how it felt.

"That's amazing, Magda!" Dolores declared more than once. She also said more than once "Really, he did that?" Telling Dolores, in a way, made it feel more real to me. It was as if I were watching the movie reel over as I was talking about the day.

"What did you talk about all day? I can't believe you weren't back before 7:30." Dolores demanded.

"Well, horses and things we like. We talked about books and movies and afternoon drives. I don't know really, but we never suffered from a lack of conversation."

"Cousin you are holding out on me! What is his job? Is he really all that rich?"

"He didn't want to talk about his job. I didn't see any reason to press him on it. After all there are quite a few subjects I didn't want to talk about." I replied sanguinely.

"He didn't ask anything about you?" Dolores looked suspicious.

"Well, not about my personal history, if that's what you mean." I didn't understand why Dolores looked suspicious and it made me nervous. "It's not that he didn't tell me anything about his family or growing up, just nothing specific. I conversed likewise."

"I know why he didn't ask you any particulars." Dolores answered smugly.

I gave her a sardonic look, "Why is that?"

"He asked Stephanie all about you months ago."

"What? How long have you known this?" I cried.

"I think she must have mentioned it to me sometime soon after."

"And you never told me?" I was practically indignant.

"I didn't want to bring it up without knowing what his motives were." Had she not said this with such a straight face, I would never have believed it of her.

I searched her face for clues as to her true meaning, but couldn't fathom what it was. "Then why didn't you tell me before my date?"

"I wanted to see how well he treated you. What if he were just a jerk who tried to use you? If you knew he had been interested in you beforehand, you would have been ready to let him. With his handsome face, I know I would have." I couldn't quite grasp where she was going with her reasoning, but I knew it was something important to her. At that moment, I didn't give it much consideration for I was too impatient to learn what Stephanie had said about me.

"I trust your reasons cousin. But tell me more about what Stephanie said."

"Your Del and Stephanie were quite good friends it seems. I mean, I had seen them talking a lot, but I didn't know that they were actually friends. It seems that Del did Stephanie a good turn soon after he moved here. They were friendly ever since."

"Yes, but what did she say about me?" I demanded.

"She said he asked her about the girl who lived at Esther's but didn't seem to work there." Dolores was practically floating off her bench seat as she lived in the fantasy of my melodrama. "She said he had wondered who the pretty girl was."

My face was burning, but it was very gratifying news. He had been as much struck by me as I had been by him. "And you, sitting there with your shy smile so quiet. You've snagged the best catch in the city." Dolores laughed loudly as if to make up for my silence. "Now, tell me more details."

"I've told you everything really." Except for the things I have no words for, I thought to myself. Except for how my heart is near to bursting from the love for him.

"You are blushing again. You are holding out." Dolores looked me over from head to foot. "I can see that you are going to be too shy to tell me the good stuff."

We both sat silent for a few minutes, watching the cars go by.

"I know. You just answer yes or no when I ask you a question." I wasn't sure that I liked the idea of being held to the truth by just a word, but I agreed to it. "Okay, let's start with an easy one.... Did he order for you at the restaurant?"

"Yes." Much easier than I would have thought.

"Did he help you in and out of the car."

"Yes."

"Such a gentleman," Dolores said clucking her tongue. "Did he hold your hand?"

"Yes." I could tell where her questions were leading and I was growing embarrassed in anticipation.

"Did he kiss you?"

I was quiet for a moment, not really wanting to answer, knowing that Dolores would demand the whole story. I flinched as I answered, "Yes."

"Cousin!" Dolores shrieked. I shushed her, but she was not about to be quieted. "Did he do anything more?"

"No!" I shouted back. Our conversation had turned hysterical and was starting to garner attention. In an effort to quiet us both down, I scooted closer to Dolores and whispered to her the details of our kiss by the waterfall.

"Ah Magda, how romantic. You are so lucky to have landed him." Dolores sighed, satisfied at last with the details.

"I don't know that I have landed him, or caught him. I do know that I am quite interested in him. I hope he feels the same way."

"Ah cousin, he would be a stupid guy to let a girl as beautiful and smart as you get away." She smiled at me. "When do you see him next?"

"Tomorrow." I smiled back.

The day passed quickly enough as we had so much to talk about, although we weren't called in for work nor did we see any cinema stars.

Del met me as I left work the following night. He was waiting for me at the front door as I said goodbye to the Miss Tanners. We had agreed to meet for dinner.

After greeting me charmingly, he said "Do you mind walking?"

"That would be a pleasure," was my reply. He offered his arm and I took it. His closeness, his warmth thrilled me. I became quite embarrassed just from the intensity of emotions I felt. It was dark already and I hoped that Del couldn't see my face. If he noticed my hesitation he never said anything.

We walked along the sidewalk making small talk. We didn't move very fast, not that I really took any notice. I was full to bursting with emotion. Just being able to touch him was enough then. I can't say for certain how he felt, but from the way he held my arm close to him and covered my hand with his own, he probably felt very similarly.

I know it sounds so silly and trite. Part of me wishes to gloss over the puppy love I had for Del, but it happened and that is how I felt. Having known him for only a few days, I don't know how I could have possibly felt as strongly as I did. The flush of first love was upon me and I would never have thought about trying to shake it off.

We walked for sometime taking a circuitous route. The spring evening was mild and the breeze reminded me of the ocean. Del took me to a small restaurant set in the basement of an office building on upper Spring Street called Rosemary's. It was very quiet as it was still early in the evening. As I found out later, even when filled with patrons, it remained very quiet, very private.

"Did you have a nice day at work?" Del asked me when we had taken our seats.

"It was much the same as usual," I replied. "The women I work for are both very kind and pleasant to be around. I would ask you how your work day went, but I fear you won't like the question." I teased him with a smile.

"I will tell you how my day went, for no work at all was involved. At least not the paying sort."

He had been racing his auto all day, practicing for an amateur race he wanted to enter. "Have you raced before?"

"Never," he laughed. "I hope I don't crash and break my neck."

I frowned. "That isn't something to laugh about."

"It'll be okay, I swear it," his enthusiasm was as catching as Dolores's. "Will you come to the race with me? It will be the first Sunday in May."

"I'll come, if you promise that you won't crash. I don't think I could stand to watch." I was truly pleased that he was offering to make a date with me a month in advance.

When that line of conversation closed, I decided to ask him about himself, "Del, I find that you know quite a lot about me, yet I know nothing of you."

"What do I know about you," he asked with impish innocence.

"Dolores tells me that you consulted with our former housemate Stephanie, many months ago."

Del was rarely embarrassed, but I could have sworn his color grew just a little redder. "Well," he began by way of explaining himself, "I didn't think it would get back to you."

I looked at him questioningly, inviting him to explain more. "Look, it just won't do to have the girl you'd like to woo knowing you've been asking about her."

We both laughed. He held my hand over the table. Heart pounding, I was determined to conceal my delight. "I understand you were good friends with Stephanie? She was always very friendly with me."

"Was? No, no. I'm still good friends with her."

"Then you know where she went after she left last month?"

"Of course, she's taken up with Harry Stewart. Did you ever meet him?"

"No, I . . ." I didn't have an explanation. It didn't seem to matter to Del.

"He's a lawyer she met at the . . . um . . . where you live. She told me that she got Esther to throw her out. Harry got her an apartment and everything." Del explained.

I could finally put a reason to her wink to me and Dolores. "That's wonderful news." I was truly excited. "I was very worried about her."

"If you come to the races with me I'm sure you will see her. Harry, like me, loves races of any sort."

"I already said I would." I squeezed his hand.

The night was wonderful. We spent hours in the restaurant talking and laughing. Looking at each other. Del walked me back to the boarding house, giving me a lingering good night kiss before we said goodbye.

I found, when I got to our room, that it was after 11 o'clock. I couldn't believe how late it was. It seemed like only a few minutes had passed since I had left the hat shop. I also began to get a niggling worry. Being out so late would definitely come to the notice of Esther.

My worry didn't have too much time to fester. The next morning, as I was leaving for work, Esther waited for me at the side entry. "Miss Santoya, a moment of your time please," she beckoned to me and I followed her into her office.

Once we were both seated, she began "I have noticed of late that you have not been respecting the rules of this establishment. I allowed you to stay with us on the premise that you would be no trouble and would not disturb my business."

No, I thought to myself, you allowed me to stay because I pay you a great deal of money.

"However, it has come to my attention that you have a job outside this establishment." She gave me a steely look. I returned it. "I also believe that you are involved with some man."

Ah, now she's getting to what she's mad about, I thought. I didn't say a word in response.

"This may appear to be a regular boarding house, but as I'm sure you are aware, this is my business and I cannot have my business interrupted for your whims. Perhaps it is time that you seek shelter at a more appropriate house."

My mind began to whirl as I did sums in my head. I knew she was angling for more money. I just wasn't sure how much would be too much. She must have known that I wouldn't leave Dolores. Now I had to figure out how much I could afford.

"How much would you like for me to be able to stay," I asked finally.

"Seven dollars a week should cover my expenses." That was robbery, plain and simple.

"Esther, I believe that your business could not be too harmed by my comings and goings, especially as I'm always very careful about staying out of sight." I took a deep breath. "However, if you truly think that I am harming your business, I'd be more than happy to help compensate your losses. I will give you six dollars a week. Two extra from what I am now paying, as payment for inconvenience."

Esther held her chin up high, scrutinizing me closely. We were then playing a game of bluff. If I left she would be losing six dollars extra a week. If she held to her original price she could make more, but I wasn't as likely to pay it. Her reasoning won, but I'm certain her avarice was not satisfied.

"Very well then. Six dollars a week." I nodded and left for work.

I had to walk quickly to make up for the time I had spent talking to Esther. Six dollars a week! That was my whole salary at the hat shop. I had to find a way to get Dolores away from that place soon. The exercise of walking quickly went a long way to soothe my nerves that morning.

Chapter 8

I know I am supposed to tell you about how I became a famous actress of silent films, but for a short while I must take a detour, as life often does. After my confrontation with Esther, it became apparent that my most immediate purpose was to get Dolores and me away from the boarding house. But it was still some months before I could make it happen.

The next few weeks went by in a whirl. I spent as much time with Del as possible, but I spent any free time of my own perusing ads for jobs that might be appropriate for Dolores and looking for cheap rooms for rent. I was nagged by my worries over money. My reserves would not last through June, but I didn't want to have to pawn more of my belongings than I had too, for who knew what Esther would try to charge me next time. I had decided that Dolores should have a job. If we could get a real job for her then we could move away with no other worry than avoiding Esther.

Dolores and I had only one friend outside of Esther's place, so I asked Mr. Stuckey if he knew of any jobs that might be available for Dolores. I would have asked the Miss Tanners as well, but they knew nothing of my private life and I wanted to keep it that way. I didn't want them to get the slightest idea about where I really lived.

The time I spent with Del was as much a relief as it was unreal. Getting to know him proved to be as exciting and interesting as our first few meetings. My puppy love for him grew and deepened into a feeling I didn't even know existed. I was living in a dream. Dolores teased me endlessly.

I finally met Stephanie again when Del took me to the amateur auto races at the Ascot Park course south of the city. I cried out when I saw her and threw my arms around her.

"Harry said that Del would be here today, I hoped he'd bring you along." Stephanie said convivially, as if the last time I had seen her she hadn't been walking the plank in front of Esther. "Del told me he'd finally had enough courage to step out with you."

Del and Harry greeted one another and I said hello to Harry. "But what happened to you? Dolores and I were so worried."

"I planned it that way," replied Stephanie. "Didn't you see my wink? I wanted you to know I'd be all right."

"You planned it? How?" I had to know the particulars.

We had all started walking toward the railing as the first race was about to start. Del had walked off ahead, no doubt to make his bets. "You know how Esther is. You try to leave and she slaps you with tons of unpaid bills. Ask her for more money and she kicks you out, granted, she withholds your pay, but you're out free and clear." I was listening intently. This might be just what I needed to know for Dolores's sake. "Harry here had offered to take care of me, set me up in my own place." She looked up at him with a look of love in her eyes that I certainly recognized. The man was very quiet, just looking straight ahead and walking in pace with us. "So I got Esther to let me go with no strings attached, I told her I wanted more money and that was that."

Stephanie looked very happy. I thought the plan was brilliant in its simplicity. "That was a wonderful idea Stephanie." I stopped to give her another hug. "Do you like your new place?"

"Oh you wouldn't believe it. It's so wonderful. I'm going to school to be a stenographer and maybe one day I can work for old Harry here at his firm. Hey look here." By this time we had arrived at the railing and taken our places. Stephanie pulled a pen and a card out of her purse. "Here, I'll give you my address. You and Dolores should come see me some afternoon."

I gladly took the card. Del came up then and the first race began. Del didn't take part in the amateur race that afternoon as he'd badly damaged his car the week before in a crash. The day was a very pleasant one, as if all my afternoons with Del weren't. It was like we were on a double date. After the races we went out for cocktails and dinner. Harry, while a quiet man, was extremely good natured. I found that he could converse with ease on many subjects. He was not given to outbursts and never laughed aloud. He obviously loved Stephanie. It was wonderful to get to know Stephanie as a person, away from the awful place we'd met. She was much more relaxed and easy going among her friends than I had seen her before. I felt as if she could truly be a great friend.

Before we parted company that night, I let Stephanie know, as discreetly as I could in front of the gentlemen, that Dolores needed to follow in her footsteps. I inquired if she knew of any jobs that might be available for Dolores.

She was very understanding, of course, but knew of nothing. "I'll keep my ears open for you," she told me. "Maybe old Harry here might know of something." It was all I could hope for then.

As May wore on the weather became warmer. Nearly every Sunday now, Del would take me to the beach in Santa Monica. He had rented a bungalow tent there. Back in those days a whole tent city was built along the beach every summer. With the pier just down the beach, it made for a wonderful weekend get-away from the city.

The first time we went, it was for a party among some of his racing pals, and not a few of them were part of the movie business. I spent the day at Del's shoulder listening to him speak easily to anyone and everyone. I knew nobody there and was relegated to watching the activities more than participating in them. It didn't matter to me. I loved to watch Del laugh among his friends. His easy manners and playful antics were an entertainment in their own right. Even as he charmed and fawned over the professional auto racer Norman Foy, I was fawning over him. It was enough for me that I could just be there with him, standing attentively at his shoulder, enjoying his presence.

The following Sundays we would arrive early in the day long before the fog had lifted, before any one else arrived. The whole beach was quiet with only a few seagulls squawking over their finds in the sand. We spent the morning alone among the fog. I learned a lot about him during those quiet times.

We would take long walks along the shore and talk quietly. I learned about his sad, lonely childhood with no mother, but a father and grandfather who pulled at him and used him, his older sisters who still treated him as a child.

I told him all about my Papa. I told him the stories Papa always told me and how he was both teacher and comforter to me. I said little about the rest of my family. All the fights with my mother, the distance of my father and brothers and sisters, the left out feeling of being different from your family – those things I kept to myself. I had left those behind when I had left home.

By the afternoon, the fog would clear and the beaches would fill up, the atmosphere like a carnival. But it was those mornings alone that I treasured most.

It was after one of those wonderful Sundays, when I arrived back at the boarding house late one Sunday night to find Esther waiting for me. "I thought we discussed this Miss Santoya. You are not to be disturbing our customers." Every nerve in my body tightened readying for a fight.

She was lying, we both knew it. No one had seen me go in. I was standing in the small side door entry way, Esther was in the adjacent room that served as a laundry. No customer would be here and if they were, it would not be me that was disturbing them.

I remained silent, unwilling to add fuel to her fire. "I think it is high time that you start looking for a new place to live. Until then you will pay me ten dollars a week for my inconvenience."

I was shocked and livid, but Esther held the cards. I couldn't argue with her, it was her place. She could kick me out right then and we both knew it. It didn't help that I very much agreed with her about finding a new place to live.

I started up the stairs when she continued, "I'm not finished with you yet." I looked down at her steely eyes and rigid face. "Don't be giving Dolores ideas that she can leave as well. She owes me too much money to think of leaving here."

Liar! I wanted to scream in her face, but I remained silent. To take her on verbally would mean to lose ground in our little war. I had precious enough ground as it was. I sealed my lips tight and waited for her next round of lies.

"If you can't come up with the money to pay me this week, perhaps you should ask your Del Wolham, he's rich enough to keep ten sluts like you." With that bit of name calling she turned and walked away. I went up the stairs.

So she had found out about Del. No wonder she was so bitter towards me. I think I really had been "disturbing" a customer. I had been keeping Del from losing his money gambling in her crooked parlor.

Rather than waking Dolores the next morning for another round of waiting at studio gates, I let her sleep and went to find a job for her. I was determined. I couldn't stay for another two weeks, my money would run out. I was not going to leave Dolores in Esther's employ.

I bought a newspaper. Looking at the employment ads for Dolores was a very different thing from what I had done for myself. Any position I saw that I would find promising, I could see Dolores wrinkling her nose at. There were many I thought she might be terrific at, but she would probably be overlooked for her sparse work history and unproven talents. After an hour of searching and frustration by what I found, I went to Stephanie's apartment.

Answering the door in a simple house dress, she explained it was her cleaning day. She looked so domestic and happy that I wished the same fate for Dolores. Well, maybe not the domestic part, I couldn't see Dolores settling into that, but some equally happy future.

Stephanie knew of no jobs that would be suitable for Dolores. I didn't stay with her long, for I was on a hunt and she had other things to do.

My next stop was to see Mr. Stuckey. He was washing the floor in his little converted theater when I knocked on the window. Smiling at me, he opened the door. "Goodness gracious Magda, you know I don't start showing the flickers until noon."

He was teasing me, I knew. He loved to tease me and Dolores about our love for the cinema. "Mr. Stuckey, I've come to find out if you know of any job openings for my cousin."

Mr. Stuckey leaned against the mop handle in a thoughtful pose. "Well, Miss Magda, I've been thinking on that. Seems to me I could use a pretty girl to sell tickets from my ticket window. Especially in the evening."

With every word, my eyes grew wider and wider. "Oh, Mr. Stuckey! Would you really give her a job?" I cried with delight.

Mr. Stuckey laughed at my eagerness. "Sure thing. As for the terms, I can't pay very much. I would need her Friday and Saturday for certain. Plus a couple of nights during the week. I can pay $5 a week. I know that isn't very much."

"But it's enough, Mr. Stuckey. It's more than enough."

I discussed things with Mr. Stuckey for another half hour. I found that his sister had a room to let and that she lived nearby on San Pedro Street. He wrote a note to her for me and I went to visit her.

Mrs. Haelstrom looked nothing like her brother, but she had an equally warm, generous nature. She had a small attic room to let and was willing to let both me and Dolores share it. There was a separate stairway on the outside, so we wouldn't disturb the family. Rent was $6 a week, with two meals a day if we cared to join the family meals. The whole time I talked with Mrs. Haelstrom we were bombarded by her children. I never did get an accurate count that morning of how many she had. All of them were moon-faced, toe-headed, and full of energy. They all looked so similar that I was never sure if I were double counting.

Mrs. Haelstrom and I agreed that I get Dolores's approval before we made a final agreement, but if everything went smoothly, we would move in by the end of the week.

After my interview with Mrs. Haelstrom, I hurried back to Dolores. I found her dressed and combing her hair. She was terse with me when I came in, mad, I supposed, that I hadn't woken her that morning.

"Dee, are you hungry! Let's get some lunch." I was so excited, I'm sure she could sense it, for she dropped her sullenness and immediately took up with high spirits.

Over lunch, I told her all about my morning. Dolores took the news differently than I expected. At first she was thrilled, then she became disheartened, and finally she became resolute.

"I don't know what kind of luck you have on your side primita. Whatever it is, I think you must have some magic to make all this happen. I hope it holds out when we try to move out from under Esther's nose."

"I don't think it's luck Dee. I think its determination." She rolled her eyes at me.

The next step in my plan was to sell to a pawn dealer some of my expensive things in order to have a money reserve. Del had offered me any money I might need, but I would never have been comfortable taking it from him. I had to do it on my own, with my own resources, or not at all. Dolores and I decided to go to the pawn dealer on Wednesday. We also decided that we should start moving our things out piecemeal that day, so that when we actually left, neither of us would have too much to carry. Stephanie happily agreed to store our things for the week.

That night, Monday night, it seemed like a year since I had so peaceably been with Del walking along the beach. Sitting in the window seat, for what I hoped would be the last time, I enjoyed the warm spring breeze. I could just hear my Papa saying, "Well done, my girl, when you put your mind to it you can make things happen." I dozed off thinking of his stories and knowing I was living one of my own.

THE COUNTRY COUSIN

Directed by Edward Dillon
Produced by Joe Schenck

CHRONICLE FILM COMPANY

List of Players
Mae — Maggie Savoy
Violet — Virginia Lee
William — Kentley Crain
Dexter — Wallace McCutcheon Jr.
Violet's Beau — Lane Meyer
Mae's mother — Frances Raymond
Violet's mother — Mathilde Brundage
Mayor's Son — Bert Sprotte

SCENARIO

On a porch in a rural area are sitting two young men, one on either side of the doorway. One young man is very handsome, although dressed rather shabbily. The other young man is a dandy, but rat-like in appearance. He wears a look of confidence and takes out his gold pocket watch to show off rather than to tell the time.

Inside the house a mother is berating her daughter who sits weeping. The mother stands above her daughter, wagging her finger.

THAT YOUNG STUDENT MAY BE HANDSOME, BUT HE'LL NEVER MAKE ANY MONEY. THE MAYOR'S SON WILL DO FOR YOU FINE.

The mother continues to wag her finger, but the daughter stands up and confronts her mother. She refuses to marry the rich man's son, flinging out her hand in a universal symbol meaning no. It is the student that she loves and she'll marry no other. The mother crosses her arms in contempt.

She takes a letter off the desk, points to it and explains.

SOME TIME IN THE BIG CITY WILL COOL YOUR HEAD. YOUR COUSIN EXPECTS YOU TOMORROW.

The daughter weeps in despair and refuses to go. The mother threatens to force her, shaking a finger at her head.

YOU WILL GO AND YOU'LL ENJOY IT! AND WHEN YOU GET BACK YOU'LL MARRY THE MAYOR'S SON.

The daughter tries to deny her mother, but cannot. Instead she runs from the room. The mother looks after her daughter with pity, sighs heavily and exits to the front porch. The gentlemen rise to greet her. She looks coldly at the handsome young student and wishes him goodbye, waving her hand that he should go. She then turns to the young dandy and applies him with her old lady charm, flattering him, which he accepts as his due.

The handsome young student walks away sullenly. At the end of the walkway, he looks back over his shoulder and sees his young lady waving to him out of the window. She indicates that he should come around the side of the house. Glancing back to make sure he isn't seen by the mother or the dandy, he walks the edge of the fence and goes back along side of the house. The young lady leans out an upper floor window and indicates her love for the young man.

MY DARLING MY MOTHER IS MAKING ME GO TO SEE MY COUSIN IN THE CITY, BUT I ONLY WANT YOU.

The young man heartily returns her love.

BUT MY DARLING VIOLET, WHAT SHALL WE DO?

The girl thinks for a moment. Looks around her to make sure no one is nearby.

> MEET ME AT THE TRAIN STATION TOMORROW. IF MY MOTHER IS WITH ME DO NOT LET HER SEE YOU.

The handsome young student and the young lady bid their fond farewells and the scene fades.

The next scene opens on a farm house with no other buildings in sight. There sits a pretty young woman knitting on a rocking chair. She drops her needles and looks far away. She stiffles a sigh, but continues to look far away.

A moment later an automobile appears on the horizon, its going terribly fast, but making its way towards the farm house. She stands up to look, trying to discern who it is. When the occupants become visible, she smiles as she sees it's her friend, Violet. She runs out the meet the car.

Violet jumps out of the car and embraces her friend. She starts explaining what is going on as the young student gets out and comes around the side of the car. The young man shakes the farm girl's hand.

> DEAR MAE, MY MOTHER INSISTS I MARRY THE MAYOR'S SON BUT WE HAVE DECIDED TO ELOPE INSTEAD.

Mae is at first affronted by the news, but when she sees how much it means to her friend and the young man, her sensibilities are overcome. She congratulates the pair. Violet turns serious and asks Mae for a favor.

> I AM SUPPOSED TO VISIT MY COUSIN IN THE CITY. WILL YOU TAKE MY PLACE SO THAT NO ONE KNOWS WHERE WE HAVE GONE?

Mae is abashed. She waves her hands in front of her to indicate that she doesn't think she could. Violet and the young man plead with her. Mae objects saying that Violet's cousin would not be fooled so easily. Violet has a simple retort.

> I HAVE NOT SEEN MY COUSIN SINCE I WAS A GIRL OF 5. HE WILL BE LOOKING FOR A GIRL IN A BLUE DRESS WITH A YELLOW BAG.

Violet holds up her yellow suitcase, pointing to it. Mae begins to waver. She wants to be a good friend and help, but can't decide if it is right or wrong. Then Violet finally persuades her.

> MY COUSIN LIVES IN THE BIG CITY AND I KNOW YOU HAVE ALWAYS WANTED TO VISIT. NOW IS YOUR CHANCE.

Mae agrees. Violet says to tell her mother, but not the truth.

> TELL YOUR MOTHER THAT YOU ARE STAYING AT MY HOUSE FOR A FEW DAYS.

Mae runs in to the house to the kitchen. She cries out "mother?" Her mother, washing up from breakfast, turns and smiles at her saying "What is it Mae?" Mae explains.

> VIOLET HAS COME TO ASK IF I CAN STAY WITH HER A FEW DAYS. YOU WOULDN'T MIND, WOULD YOU?

Mae's mother indicates that she should go. She happily waves goodbye as the girl runs off. Mae meets Violet in her bedroom where they quickly repack Violet's bag. Violet pulls out the blue dress that Mae needs to wear. Mae goes off to change.

Violet and her young beau drop Mae off at the train station. Mae wishes them luck then takes the ticket that Violet has given her and gets on the train. It is the first time she's ridden on one and she is in awe. As the train takes off, she stares out the window.

On a train platform a young man looks at a letter. William is a well-dressed young man, although rather conservative and serious, but with an honest good-natured face.

DEAR COUSIN WILLIAM,

THANK YOU FOR ALLOWING MY DAUGHTER VIOLET A CHANCE TO SEE THE BIG CITY. SHE WILL ARRIVE ON THE 4:30 TRAIN. SHE WILL WEAR A BLUE DRESS. HER SUITCASE IS YELLOW. PLEASE TAKE CARE OF HER LIKE SHE WERE YOUR SISTER.

YOUR AUNTIE

The young man looks up from his letter and nods in affirmation. He will treat Violet as his own sister. As the train rolls into the station, he stands at attention. His hands grasped in front, his back straight. Just to make sure, he takes a second to square his hat.

Eagerly he watches the passengers exit the train. Finally, as the passengers clear the platform, he sees a lone girl in a blue dress holding a yellow suitcase looking around shyly. He smiles to see that he has found the person he is waiting for at last.

Then he gets a really good look at the girl – from shoes to her very lovely head, her hair in a very comely old-fashioned style. He gulps, and then grows very nervous.

MY, THIS COUSIN OF MINE IS VERY PRETTY INDEED.

The young man waves to the girl he thinks is Violet and walks over to her. Mae asks him if he is her cousin William. The young man nods. He makes a gallant bow and indicates that he'll carry the suitcase. Mae is a bit flustered. She hadn't imagined that the cousin would be so young and so nice. She accepts his offer and he turns to lead her away from the station.

William keeps checking over his shoulder to make sure she is following. Although it seems that he looks back at the pretty girl too often. As they near the platform stairs, a large crowd of people push past William and Mae. Mae is nearly knocked back by the crowd and reaches out and grabs William's hand to steady herself. William stops suddenly. He looks a bit frightened with his eyes growing wide. He half turns to see that Mae is scared and is holding his hand. He looks straight again and visibly gulps.

Meaning to continue on, William takes a large step, not realizing he is at the very top of the stairs. In the instant before he hurtles down the stairs, he drops the suitcase and Mae's hand, flails his arms a bit and flips over instead of tumbling. He lands, somewhat painfully, on his rear end at the bottom of the stairs. Then falls backwards, hitting his head on the bottom stair.

Mae screams. She picks up her case and runs down the stairs to aid the poor man. William is dazed and Mae kneeling beside him, places his head in her lap. From the viewpoint of William, his vision is unfocused, blurry. As his eyesight comes back to normal, he sees Mae above him, but upside down. She's speaking to him, asking him if he is all right?

Enjoying the view and the female ministrations, William suddenly realizes what a compromising situation he is in and he springs up like a jack knife. He gets up so quickly, in fact, that he nearly tumbles backwards again. Mae still very much concerned, picks up his hat, which had fallen nearby, and gets up to give it to him.

> YOU ARE CERTAINLY ACROBATIC COUSIN WILLIAM.
> YOU COULD HAVE BEEN SERIOUSLY HURT.

She reaches to touch his head, but he backs away, hands stretched out before him to stop her.

> NO, NO COUSIN VIOLET, I AM ALL RIGHT. JUST
> FINE, REALLY.

To prove that he is fine he walks back to the suitcase, but two steps towards it and his legs become very droopy, making him walk funny. He makes it to the suitcase and he picks it up. He speaks to Mae.

> PERHAPS WE SHOULD TAKE A TAXICAB. MY LEGS
> SEEM TO BE OPERATING FUNNY.

Mae consents and they head out to the street. Mae is googly eyed while taking in the enormity of the big city. There are tall buildings and people everywhere. William hails a taxicab from amongst all the automobiles and street cars. He opens the door to the cab and ushers Mae in, she barely notices as she looks around wide-eyed. Once inside the car, she gaps out the window. William notices Mae's wide-eyed behavior and leans over to look out the window to see what she's looking at.

Mae jumps a little when she turns and finds William so close. They look at each other for a long second, then William jumps back. Mae looks at him and then something on his side of the vehicle catches her eye and she leans over him to look out. William shrinks back against the seat as far as he can go. His hands up in the air, palms out-facing, as if he were scared to touch the girl. His eyes go from looking at her form to looking at the roof as he thinks of his aunt's request.

. . . LIKE SHE WAS YOUR SISTER

William finally gets his bearings. He pulls against Mae's shoulder and makes her lean back into her own seat. He tells her firmly:

ENOUGH OF THAT COUSIN VIOLET. WE WILL GO SIGHT SEEING TOMORROW.

Mae is delighted with the news, clasping her hands in front of her. She is so excited, she nearly throws her arms around her pretend cousin, until she realizes that he is not her cousin, but a stranger. Each of them sits back in their respective seats awkwardly, looking away from one another.

William opens the door to his apartment carrying Mae's suitcase. He ushers her inside. William's apartment is small, but neatly furnished. He takes her suitcase to the bedroom and sets it down inside while explaining things to her.

YOU CAN USE MY ROOM VIOLET. I WILL STAY NEXT DOOR WITH MY FRIEND.

Both William and Mae turn to the door as if someone has knocked. Outside the door is waiting a well-turned out man. William explains that he knows who is at the door.

William opens the door and ushers in the well-dressed man.

WILLIAM'S FRIEND DEXTER, A REAL LADIES' MAN

William introduces Dexter to Mae. Dexter immediately comes on to Mae. She becomes quite shy and looks away while offering her hand to Dexter. Dexter takes her hand a little too lovingly for William's taste and he pulls the ladies man away from his cousin.

Dexter looks at William meaningfully, as if he is asking why. William puts his fists on his hips and looks sternly at his friend. He heads into the small kitchen, saying he will get refreshments. Dexter helps Mae to the couch and sits beside her.

In the kitchen, William loads a tray with drink fixings. In the living room Dexter is flirting madly with Mae who is very embarrassed by the attention. William rounds the corner to the living room carrying his large tray. He sees Dexter close to his cousin on the couch and his eyes grow wide. The tray tips a little and the ice in the ice dish falls to the floor.

William sets the tray on a nearby table, then squares himself to confront his friend. He puts on a menacing posture and begins to move forward. Unfortunately, he does not look where he stepped and placed his foot on a square of ice. He slides forward, arms flailing, trying to make his way to the couch. But every time he puts his foot down he steps on another piece and he slides along the room, behind the couch, his eyes never leaving his cousin and his friend. He slides off scene and a second later comes sliding back into the room. He crisscrosses the room several times before flying through the door of the kitchen and landing heavily.

As he lays sprawled on the floor, he says:

I GIVE UP!

William ties a block of ice to his aching head and leans against the cabinets. He sighs heavily. He can't forget his Aunt's request.

LIKE SHE WAS YOUR SISTER

In the living room Dexter wonders where William went. He stands up and heads into the kitchen.

I WILL JUST BE A MOMENT DEAR VIOLET. I SHOULD JUST CHECK ON GOOD OL' WILLY.

Dexter finds William on the floor of the kitchen looking ridiculous with the ice on his head. He immediately becomes concerned. What's the matter?, he says.

William brushes him off. Dexter comes over and takes the dripping ice off of his head.

I HAVE NEVER SEEN YOU LIKE THIS WILLIAM. YOU ALWAYS HAVE EVERYTHING TOGETHER. WHATEVER COULD BE THE MATTER?

William attempts to brush off his friend, but instead sighs deeply and forlornly. Dexter begins to grow very worried for his friend, but doesn't know what to do to help. He asks William if there is anything he could do. William again sighs. Then finally speaks.

I HAVE NEVER SEEN SUCH A PRETTY GIRL AND SHE IS MY COUSIN!

William looks so sad, but Dexter, after recovering from the shock of such an announcement, laughs merrily. He points down at William and laughs with his whole body. William frowns, then gets angry. Finally he stands up. He points at Dexter.

LOOK, YOU JUST DON'T UNDERSTAND!

Dexter says in return, what do you mean I don't understand. He puffs out his chest and points to himself. The two men are just about to get really angry with one another when Mae pokes her head in the door. Is everything all right, she asks with such a sweet look on her face that both men immediately melt. Dexter straightens his tie. William smooths back his hair.

> **EVERYTHING IS FINE, COUSIN VIOLET. WHY DON'T YOU HELP YOURSELF TO SOME REFRESHMENTS. THE TRAY IS ON THE TABLE.**

Mae leaves the kitchen. The two men look at each other as if they are going to get angry again, but instead they just laugh. Dexter places a consoling hand on William's shoulder. William is toweling off his face.

> **SHE MAY BE YOUR COUSIN, BUT IT DOESN'T MEAN YOU CAN'T ENJOY HER COMPANY FOR A FEW DAYS. THERE IS NOTHING WRONG WITH BEING FRIENDLY TO A PRETTY GIRL, EVEN IF SHE DOES HAPPEN TO BE RELATED.**

William nods in agreement at this good advice. He finishes putting his suit back to right, then follows Dexter out of the kitchen.

WILLIAM SHOWS MAE ALL OVER THE CITY.

A montage of scenes shows William and Mae visiting museums and parks and famous buildings and nice restaurants.

In one museum, Mae is scrutinizing a work of modern art. She screws up her nose at it and cocks her head to one side and the other. She turns to William saying "I really don't understand this." William is only looking at her. He sighs and begins to lean against a large crate just when the movers began to pull it away. He falls, sprawled on the floor. Mae doesn't notice as she's moved on to the next picture.

In the park, William rents a row boat and takes Mae out on the lake. It is a beautiful sunny day and Mae is enjoying the view of the shore. William is enjoying the view of Mae with the sunlight on her hair. He sighs and locks the oars so he can rest his chin on his hand. He did not properly lock one oar and it floats quietly away. Mae turns to say something to William and sees the oar behind the boat. She points to it and shouts, waking William up from his reverie. He awkwardly tries to maneuver the boat around with just one oar. Finally, he makes it back and fishes it from the water.

Mae laughs at him and then coos.

YOU MUST BE TIRED, LET ME HELP

Mae sits next to William on the rower's bench and laboriously pulls the oar. William watches her in half amusement, half agony. He turns away from Mae, inches away on the seat and gulps.

William and Mae walk all over the city. Sometimes stopping to look at buildings, sometimes pointing out sites. They have a marvelous time together.

In a restaurant, William and Mae are seated across from one another and laughing together. There is a third place setting at the table and soon enough Dexter joins the pair. William rises to greet him.

Mae watches all the fancy dressed women and men enjoying their dinner. Her eyes grow especially wide as one lovely woman passes their table.

**LOOK AT ALL THOSE PRETTY DRESSES! I WONDER
WHERE EVERYONE IS GOING SO DRESSED UP.**

William and Dexter explain that the people dressed up are likely on their way to the theater. There is a scene cut in showing a busy theater district with signs bearing the names of plays all lit up. Mae says that she would like to see a play. William immediately agrees to take her. But Mae refuses, shaking her hands in front of her to object.

I HAVEN'T A PROPER DRESS TO WEAR.

Mae looks away sadly. William also looks disappointed. Dexter's face lights up and he puts his hand in the air, snapping his fingers. I have an idea, he says. Both William and Mae look at him hopefully. Dexter looks over at Mae while pointing to William.

HE CAN BUY YOU A DRESS.

William looks at Dexter with a look that says: what a wise guy. Mae abashedly says no, that it wouldn't be necessary. William thinks about it for a minute, itches his chin as if in deep thought, then speaks to the others.

> **ALL RIGHT, I WILL. TOMORROW WE'LL GET YOU
> A DRESS AND GO TO THE THEATER. AFTER ALL
> IT WILL BE YOUR LAST NIGHT IN THE CITY. WE
> SHOULD MAKE A NIGHT OF IT.**

Mae is profoundly thankful. William is overjoyed that he can do so much for his dear cousin. Dexter looks on the two others as if the cat got the canary. The scene fades out.

> **WILLIAM AND HIS "COUSIN" GO SHOPPING THE
> NEXT DAY. IF ONLY WILLIAM COULD THINK OF
> THIS GIRL AS ONLY HIS COUSIN.**

The next day William and Mae are in a posh dress shop and Mae is going crazy over all the beautiful clothes to choose from. They are shown at least 15 dresses. Mae can't take her eyes off the clothes. William, as usual, can't take his eyes off of Mae. He begins one of his usual sighs, when he is disturbed by an attendant standing near to his side and bowing over him. The small elderly woman is offering him coffee. William looks up quickly, then jumps, nearly falling off his ottoman chair. He flings out his arm to get his balance, hitting the attendant and knocking her over. Both struggle right themselves. The attendant walks off in a huff, straightening her hair as she goes. William, as usual, is completely embarrassed by his behavior.

Just then Mae turns to him and tells him that she has whittled her choice down to three. The three she has chosen are quickly shown. All are tasteful and elegant. William gets soppy-eyed again thinking of how Mae would look wearing the dresses. She gets up and follows the saleswoman. William gets up too and follows Mae. Just before she walks behind the curtains, she turns and see that William is following her. She stops and he nearly runs into her. She puts a hand on his chest and waggles a finger at him, telling him he can't come along.

William says to her, before he has figured out the situation:

**HOW AM I TO SEE YOU IN THOSE DRESSES IF I
DON'T COME ALONG?**

Mae's mouth opens in shock. William realizing his error immediately begs for forgiveness. He shows her he is a little crazy today by making a circle with his finger at the side of his head. She laughs at him, but pushes him back towards the seating area. She then turns and goes behind the curtains.

In the dressing area, with the seamstress helping, Mae tries on all three dresses. She looks smashing in each of them. After the third, the seamstress steps back and admires Mae. She is an older woman, but still strapping and strong.

**YOUR YOUNG MAN IS GOING TO BE KNOCKED
OUT WHEN HE SEES YOU.**

Mae looks at the seamstress with wide eyes and hesitation. She looks as if she is going to explain to the seamstress, who has already begun her work of fitting the dress. After a few seconds, Mae only nods her head and then looks at herself in the mirror.

Mae is in the waiting room of the store with William. The saleswoman comes through the curtains with Mae's dress all packaged up and ready to take home.

William looks at the package and then at Mae. Mae takes the package and then puts her arm through William's. He looks down at her intimate gesture, clearly pleased by it.

DON'T I GET TO SEE THE DRESS?

Mae smiles like a darling and shakes her head no.

IT IS A SURPRISE FOR YOU.

William gets sentimental and looks at Mae lovingly.

In William's apartment, he is adjusting the cuffs on his tuxedo. In the bedroom, Mae is finishing her dressing. William calls out to her.

I AM GOING OUT FOR A FEW MINUTES. BE READY
IN A HALF HOUR TO LEAVE FOR DINNER.

Mae smiles as she arranges her hair. When she hears the door shut she goes into the living area. She looks gorgeous in her new dress and shoes. Her hair is made-up in a very modern fashion. She looks stunning.

Mae looks around the room and then chooses the couch. She sits down and folds her hands in her lap. That doesn't suit her. She shakes out her hands and shoulders, loosening up. She then reclines in a sophisticated way. She stays like that for a few seconds, then sits up and shakes her head 'no.' She looks around the room again. She then gets up and goes to the mantle. Facing the camera, she puts her left hand on the mantle then looks over her shoulder towards the door. She smiles. She decides this is how she wants to look when William comes back.

A hand is knocking on the door outside. Inside the apartment, Mae jumps to get the door. Then, remembering her pose, she strikes it. Looking over her shoulder she calls brightly, Come in. The door begins to open. A full-length shot of Mae starting at the floor and moving upwards shows her as a stunning beauty.

Mae is smiling waiting for William to notice how great she looks. Then suddenly, her smile becomes shock because its not William at the door.

At the door is the real Violet and her new husband, the young student. The real Violet's mouth opens in surprise to see her country friend so city-fied. Mae leaves her post and rushes over to hug Violet.

Violet returns the embrace. The young husband looks on with satisfaction.

Mae pulls away from Violet and asks what she is doing there.

WE THOUGHT WE WOULD TAKE YOU BACK WITH
US. WE ARE ON OUR WAY HOME NOW.

BUT MAE, YOU LOOK SO BEAUTIFUL, I WOULDN'T

HAVE KNOWN YOU. BUT WHY ARE YOU ALL DRESSED UP?

Mae, looking downcast that her friend has arrived and her good time will be over, explains things.

WILLIAM IS TAKING ME TO THE THEATER TONIGHT.

Violet looks at Mae in wonder and surprise. The young husband looks on the pair with a look of satisfied bemusement.

Mae turns away from Violet's scrutiny. Just then, the door still being open, Dexter lets himself in. He sees Mae and greets her, then asks:

VIOLET, ARE THESE FRIENDS OF YOURS?

Dexter looks expectantly at Mae. Violet reacts to Mae being called her name. Mae continues with her back to everyone else.

MAE, DIDN'T YOU TELL THEM THE TRUTH?

Dexter looks on in confusion. Mae answers Violet's question, grabbing her breast with emotion.

WILLIAM TREATED ME SO KINDLY, I DIDN'T WANT IT TO STOP BY TELLING HIM I AM NOT HIS COUSIN.

Violet's heart melts at Mae's confession. She walks over to console her friend. Mae is overwrought, on the verge of tears. Her final night, the night that was going to be perfect, is spoiled.

Dexter mouths the words, 'not his cousin.' He thinks about it for a moment, then his face begins to brighten. He says "Violet" and both Violet and Mae turn to him. He points to Mae, saying "this Violet." Dexter is just about to tell Mae that William likes her, when William himself comes to the door.

His sight immediately goes to Mae who is a vision of loveliness. Her heightened emotion has only made her look more beautiful, more passionate. William is frozen. He doesn't notice any one else in the room. His eyes meet Mae's and they lock. Violet heads towards

William, as does Dexter, but William doesn't notice either of them. Finally, he tries to talk but the words don't come out. His eyes waver from Mae's eyes and the spell is broken.

Before anyone can say another word, Mae rushes from the apartment. She takes everyone by surprise, so no one tries to stop her. William turns and reaches after her, longingly. Then he turns back and asks.

WHAT IS GOING ON? WHO ARE YOU?

Violet runs to William and throws her arms around him, embracing him. William's face becomes even more confused. Violet explains, introducing herself and her new husband.

SO YOU SEE, MY FRIEND MAE TOOK MY PLACE HERE SO THAT MY BEAU AND I COULD ELOPE.

Violet smiles up at William. William smiles back at her. His face looking dopey as he realizes what is going on. William's face brightens and his index finger points up as if he has just had a bright idea.

THAT MEANS I AM NOT IN LOVE WITH MY COUSIN, BUT WITH A PERFECT STRANGER.

Violet repeats his words, shocked and amazed. Dexter stands behind them both laughing heartily. The young husband laughs along with Dexter, although not quite so enthusiastically. Dexter stops laughing long enough to say to William:

WILL YOU GO GET YOUR GIRL ALREADY?

William realizes he's just let the love of his life run off. A split second later he runs out the door after her.

He runs out the front of the building, but doesn't know which way to go. He looks down the street, both ways, searching for a glimpse of Mae. His search is in vain. He puts one hand on his side and the other up to his chin, thinking of where she could have gone. He snaps his fingers and says, 'I know.' Then takes off down the street.

Mae is draped, elegantly, across a bench in the park sobbing, her shoulders shaking. Her face is in her arms. William runs into the park, sees Mae and approaches her. She doesn't hear him coming, so she is quite shocked when he puts his hand on her shoulder.

She looks up at him, her eyes sparkling with tears. He sits next to her and takes her in his arms.

WHY DIDN'T YOU TELL ME?

Mae pushes him away, then turns away from him. She puts her handkerchief to her eyes.

YOU WERE SO KIND TO ME AND I VERY MUCH ENJOYED BEING WITH YOU. I THOUGHT IF YOU KNEW I WEREN'T YOUR COUSIN, YOU WOULD SEND ME AWAY.

Mae puts her head down, shoulders bent, handkerchief covering most of her face. William puts both hands on her shoulders and turns her to face him. He lifts her chin up and kisses her. Mae's eyes are wide with surprise. She pulls away, looking at William straight in the face. William laughs a little, wipes a tear from her cheek with his handkerchief. They smile at each other with an understanding. Now that they know each other's meaning, they kiss again. Then William pulls back and asks:

BUT WHAT IS YOUR REAL NAME?

Mae throws her head back with laughter. She says her name then leans forward to kiss William again.

THE END.

Chapter 9

When I had first arrived in Los Angeles, Dolores and I had sought out several different pawn shops. I didn't want to become known in any of them in case my family thought to look for me through the missing silver and jewelry. Unfortunately, when I had left home, I did not have an abundance of ready cash and had brought with me items of value, not all of them belonging to me.

Wednesday, I went back to one of the first shops I had visited. I had been to that shop more than once, for the first time I had visited it the owner there had given me a top rate price for the necklace that I sold to him. Since I needed to replenish my money reserve for our big move, I wanted to be sure that I was not taken advantage of and got the best price possible. As soon as Dolores was up and dressed, I packed my silver and tortoise shell brush and comb, and we set off.

Martini's Fine Wares was on Fourth Street near Spring Street. It was near the heart of the financial district.

The shop was situated in the middle of a block and for all purposes looked like a fine jewelry shop. Dolores had found out, through one of Esther's customers, that it bought and sold under the table.

The store windows of the little shop were spread with Martini's wares. Some very beautiful pieces and, I noticed just as I entered the door, my necklace. It put my nerves on end to see something of mine so prominently displayed in the window. I wanted to make this quick.

Fortunately there were no other customers in the store, so I could get right to business. Mr. Martini was on his telephone that was hung next to the entrance to the storeroom. He was taking his time, apparently waiting to be connected through by the operator.

He winked at me as I stood in front of the counter. Another minute passed before he spoke.

"That's right sir, your item has just arrived. Very good. We'll see you then." Mr. Martini hung up the phone and turned to me.

"Ah, it's the young Miss come back to visit" said Mr. Martini in his booming baritone voice. He was a short, portly man, finely dressed with a large, greased mustache and always wore a very friendly smile. That he recognized me so easily made me nervous and a glance at Dolores showed me that she felt the same. She had entered before me, but had now moved back closer to the door. For all our customary habits in our new lives, we were still just fugitives from our families.

"Good morning sir," I greeted him, but before I could say anything further Mr. Martini put up his hand to stop me.

"I know, you have come back for your necklace. Am I right? Hmmm?" Mr. Martini headed for the shop window. He reached over and pulled the necklace from the display. I watched him do it and noticed him take a long look up the street before he leaned back.

"No, sir. I've come to trade another item," I said in a rush, feeling eager to get the transaction completed.

"Why, you mean to say that you don't have the money to take it back?" Mr. Martini made a clucking noise with his tongue. He put the necklace back in the window. "I am sorry to hear it."

Mr. Martini moved behind his counter. It seemed to me he moved very slowly. And maybe he was. Settling himself on his stool, he said to me, "Now, let's see what you have for me." I laid my bundle on the counter and began to take out my items.

I heard the bell on the door jingle and turned to see who had entered.

"Magda."

With the second ringing of the bell on the door, I knew that Dolores had been much quicker than myself and had escaped. I stood frozen to the spot by the sound of my father's voice.

"Magda!" He came forward quickly and embraced me. Holding me so tightly I could hardly breathe, not that I had dared take a breath since he had first called my name.

I was stunned. I didn't even raise my arms in attempt to hold him in return. Fear was creeping into my heart. Fear that I would be going back to the dull, quiet life my family had decided upon for me. Fear that I would lose everything I had gained on my own.

I hardly heard my father's words as he told me how glad he was to see me, how scared he had been for my safety. His embrace and reverie were broken, however, by the large voice of the shop owner.

"Ah, how glad it makes my heart to see a family united." The fat man was beaming, his happy face a direct contrast to how my own must look. Father finally let go of me and turned to the owner.

"Thank you sir, for all your trouble. I will take that necklace now and in the envelope you will find something for your troubles." Father laid a fat envelope on the counter then moved to the window and removed the necklace, placing it in his inner pocket. I had remained motionless in the same spot during the whole interlude. I felt I should run, but how could I run, again, from my father? The first time had been much easier since I had left in the dark of night. Now here I was, facing my father with the sun shining brightly outside. I couldn't try to escape, not when he looked at me so earnestly.

"Come, let's go," he said as he took me by the arm. I didn't have it in me to resist. We left the shop and turned up the street. I vaguely looked around for Dolores, but she was smartly nowhere in sight.

Neither of us spoke as we walked. I didn't even wonder where we were going, I was far too sad believing that I would soon be home. Past Spring Street, just a few buildings down from the pawn shop, Father entered the Stowell Hotel and ushered me to the adjoining restaurant. In a daze, I saw him indicate to the host that he would like a table for lunch.

Lunch? I thought, lunch now that I wouldn't see Dolores again? Would I be able to send word to Del?

We sat at a small table near to the window. I gazed out at the passing people, unable to look my father in the face. An uncomfortable silence ensued, but I had no heart to break it. I was deeply unhappy. I was very scared. And enveloping it all, I felt guilty. I had abandoned my family. They had worried about me and I was so selfish that I had left them with no word of my welfare.

The months of putting my childhood behind me came crashing in on me. The weight of the sudden guilt was heavy on my heart. I felt I would be smothered there in the middle of a fancy hotel restaurant for all the diners to see.

"You are not happy to see me." Father said. His voice was dejected and sullen. "Perhaps you fear that I will take you back home. You have no need to fear that. I won't make you if you don't want to go."

I looked at him finally and began to cry. The tears overflowed, but I did not sob. "I'm sorry Father. I am truly sorry. I knew you would worry and I knew the harm I would be causing, but I did it anyway."

Father, always so gentlemanly, took his handkerchief from his pocket. He leaned across the table and wiped my face as if I were a child. I took it from him as he stroked my cheek, finishing the job for him.

"If only you had told me that you were so unhappy. We wouldn't have forced you to marry Johnson. You're mother and I . . ." his voice trailed off and he stared at my sullen, puffy face. "No, we would not have understood."

We were both silent for a few minutes until the waiter came to our table. I looked away from him, staring again at the people going past the large plate glass windows. How often I had stared this way in the past few months. It was an irony that a girl, like myself, who had always been so busy and purposeful could take solace in the quiet pasttime of watching people go about their business in the streets of a big city.

Father placed an order with the waiter and again we were left in silence.

"I think I understand better now why my father took such an interest in you. I can see now how alike you are." I looked at my father, much braver now, and let a small smile brighten my face. His words were just what I needed, what I had always needed from him.

"I just wish I had seen that sooner."

"Thank you, father." The tears streamed down my face. I couldn't help it. All the emotion I had been bottling up seemed to burst forth from my eyes. I did my best to wipe them away, but couldn't do anything about the source.

"Now, if you will, please stay and have lunch with me."

I nodded, looking down at the table. The silence felt heavy. I wanted so much to ask about my home and family, but felt as if I shouldn't bring it up. Father probably felt the same. It was too awkward. There were too many subjects that would be painful, if not to me then to him. The silence continued. My tears continued to flow, although not as fiercely. The waiter brought our drinks and then our first course, yet still nothing was said.

Father finally broke it. "It makes me glad to see you, Magda, it really does."

"How is home and mother and my sisters and brother?" I blurted out. Once the silence was broken I could contain it no longer.

Father smiled his most gentle smile. "Ah, I see that you are a little homesick." He laughed a quiet, rueful laugh. "Your mother is as busy as ever. Your sister-in-law is to have a baby and your mother is making arrangements to be in Chicago for some months to help."

"She must be pleased that Edith is finally having a child. They have been married, what, six or seven years now?"

"Something like that. I think she really just wants to spend time in the East. You know she prefers it to Southern California."

"Yes." I answered, relieved that the conversation was going so easily. "And the ranch? How are things? I imagine you've been to the cattle sale already."

"Yes, last month in fact. The price of beef keeps rising since the war began. I'm thinking of opening the North pasture and adding another 200 head."

The conversation continued along these mundane lines through the first course and into the second. While eating our roast chicken, the conversation trailed off having covered all the available topics in that line.

Staring down at his plate Father said, "Magda, can I ask you a few questions?"

My heart leaped and I started to feel trapped again, but Father had been so gracious, I couldn't deny him. "Yes," I stammered.

"I saw that you are with your cousin. Her mother will be very relieved to know. Is she okay? Are you okay?"

"We are both well Father. Neither of us want for anything. We live here, but ..." my voice dropped off to a whisper, both of us knowing that I meant not to tell him more.

"I would ask how Dolores has taken care of herself all this time, but I know that if you kept her secret before, you will not divulge it now." I nodded assent.

"To tell you the truth. I had planned on taking you home. I had convinced myself that you were starving in the streets. But after I first saw you I knew that you could take care of yourself." He sighed. "I have been stifling in the hotel lobby here for ten days, since I first saw your necklace in the window, waiting for you. I was sure that you couldn't be happy."

He paused to look out the window. "We knew that you were probably with Dolores. Annie told us everything after you left, except for the most important piece of information, Dolores's address. But I imagine that is why you chose to go through Annie." I remained silent.

After Dolores had run away we had corresponded through the housemaid Annie. Annie was a sweet girl, but illiterate. I had told her I was corresponding with a secret lover. She was happy to help me with my intrigue.

We were both quiet again. We had finished with our meal and father was drinking his coffee.

"Can you tell me what your plans for the future are?"

"I don't really know. I've thought about it a great deal, but I haven't made any decisions." I paused, thinking over how much information I wanted to give him. "Dolores wants to be an actress."

Father smiled broadly. "Yes, of course. Dolores has always been very dramatic. Do you?"

"I don't know really. I love to go to the cinema, but I don't know that I would be any good at it."

"I think you would be a wonderful actress. I think you will be wonderful in whatever you choose."

I felt the color rise to my face. "Thank you Father."

"I imagine you've been wanting to leave for some time now."

"No Father! I've enjoyed seeing you. Really."

He raised a hand to silence me. "Now, now. You have a new life to lead and here I am interrupting it. But please, is there a way to contact you so that I don't have to worry?"

"I don't know. What about Mother? Does she know that you have located me?" I felt the tears rising again, but was determined to stifle them.

"No. I haven't told her anything. She thinks I am in Arizona now on business."

Again we fell silent. Our meeting had been made up more of heavy silences than actual conversation. What a strange pair we must seem to anyone paying us attention.

"Magda, how about this? Meet me here for lunch in two months time. 1 o'clock?"

I readily agreed.

Father reached into his pocket and pulled out his billfold. He took out some cash and then reached in and retrieved my necklace from his inner pocket. It was a platinum chain with a pearl pendent. It had been a gift for my sixteenth birthday. He now offered it to me again along with the folded bills. "Take it. I don't want you to sell your things." It took all my nerve not to break down and agree to go home with him. "I don't want you to have to want for anything. Please, please take care of yourself for me."

I couldn't stand it any longer. I rose from the table, hesitantly kissed my father on his cheek and then exited the hotel as quickly as possible, shoving the gifts into my bag without looking.

Once outside I stopped to take several deep breaths. I didn't think that he would follow me – not after our talk, but I wanted to be sure. I went to the nearest streetcar stop, about a block away. He couldn't follow me on the streetcar without being seen.

I had been waiting at the streetcar stop for about five minutes when I was joined by Dolores. She had followed us from the jewelry store to the hotel and then had waited for a few minutes after I left to make sure I wasn't followed. Once we were safely on the streetcar, I told her everything.

Exiting the streetcar a few stops down, we went into a small cafe. Dolores was starving and I needed a chance to think it all through. Upon pulling out the money and my necklace, I found that he had given me over $100 dollars. To me that was a small fortune. It made for a cash reserve that far exceeded my expectations.

"Aye!" Dolores started, "I always knew your father was a good one. Maybe not so good as Papa, but still a good man."

I sat staring down at the cash in my hands. I was stunned. In a way, I felt like I had never known my father before.

"Dee, with this amount of money neither of us would have to work for several months. Maybe we should just concentrate on finding work as actresses?" I said, clearly not thinking things through in my excitement.

"Ah, primita, that is your money your father gave to you. It wouldn't be right for me to live off of it too."

"But Dee, he'd want you to be safe too. I'm sure your father would do the same."

Dolores answered in a steely voice, "My dad wouldn't. He'd whip me with a cord and lock me in my bedroom." The gravity of her voice startled me. "Your father isn't going to tell my mother is he?" Her eyes were hard with fear.

Trying to soothe her fierce reaction, I soothingly explained, "He said that he was going to tell her that you and I were safe. Nothing else."

She turned back to her luncheon. "I hope that's all he says."

Dolores went down to work late that night. Now that our freedom was certain, she was not behaving so well. Our plan now was to leave Friday morning and not come back. Later that night I went down to visit Consuela. There were few things that I would miss about the boarding house. My conversation with Consuela would be one of them.

I'm sure she knew that Dolores and I were plotting something. She didn't ask. After settling in a chair and accepting the cup of tea that she offered. I told her of meeting my father.

"And he let you go? That's a good man, I tell you." That was what Consuela decided once I'd finished my story.

"I'm ashamed to say that I never fully realized it. Although, when he went against my wishes and agreed that I should marry Mr. Johnson, he wasn't so good."

"Maybe not. I'm sure he thought he was doing the right thing." Consuela rejoined, pouring sauce into a serving dish. I lapsed into silence.

"I think Dolores's father may not be so nice as mine. I always thought that they must be similar, but maybe not."

"You may be right," answered Consuela.

"Papa always seemed to like Mr. Esparza. But Dolores said something today that makes me feel as if he weren't very nice to her."

"Dolores always puts on a good front, remember. I would bet she always has."

We were silent. Consuela pulled a tray of cakes out of the oven. They smelled delicious. In as nonchalant a manner as ever, Consuela finally broke the silence. "You two are planning on leaving now, I take it?"

"Um, yes," I replied. "Very soon, I hope."

"Good. The sooner the better. Miss Prentiss gave Dolores hell tonight for coming down late. And if I didn't know better, Esther is planning on punishing her in her own way."

Despite the tea, my mouth dried out and I found it hard to swallow. I was thanking my lucky stars, or whatever magic Dolores thought I had, to know that we had a safe place to go to in just a few days more.

Dolores got up very early the next day, at least early for her. I didn't even have to wake her. I had to go to work in the afternoon and sometimes she would have lunch with me beforehand. I was arranging my hair in front of the bureau mirror when she came up behind me. When our eyes met in the mirror, when I saw the haunted expression in her face. I knew something had gone wrong.

I turned to face her and embraced her. "What's the matter?"

"Esther knows that we are plotting something. Before I came in last night, she stopped me. She threatened me." Dolores held out her arm for me to see. Above the elbow there were deep black bruises in the shape of fingers. I couldn't help but reach out and caress her skin, doing what I could to soothe the damage. "She threatened me, Magda. She said she would hurt me if I tried to leave."

"Its okay, she can't hurt you if we aren't here."

"But Magda, I was terrified. I've never seen anyone as scary as she was last night."

That was the last straw. We were leaving that day. We would leave for good that day.

"Dolores, get dressed. We are leaving now."

In thirty minutes time, Dolores was ready. We couldn't sneak out the four remaining bags. We each took a suitcase and crept as silently as we could down the hallway and stairs. I know more than one girl saw us, for it was about the time of the morning when the girls started to wake up. No one said a word. Once outside, we splurged on a taxicab to take us to Stephanie's apartment.

From Stephanie's apartment, I called the Miss Tanners and told them I couldn't come into work that day. "My cousin and I are moving house today and I have gotten caught up with moving our bags. I can come in tomorrow to make up for today." Jennifer did not protest and wished me luck on the move.

After having a late luncheon with Stephanie, I decided to go back for the last bags. Dolores made an attempt to accompany me, but she could not go back there. What if Esther saw her? She would never let her go.

As I entered the side door for the last time I took a large breath, letting it out as I rushed in and up the stairs. I was lucky and saw nobody else. I entered our room and grabbed the bags. It didn't look to me as if anyone had been in there during the day, but it was hard to say. I checked around the room to make sure we hadn't left anything. There were still several dresses hanging in the closet, but they were cheap, flashy things that Esther made the girls wear. Dolores was happy to leave them behind.

The final bags in hand, I peeked out the doorway and didn't see or hear anybody, so I walked out quietly. It was just after 4 o'clock and I knew Consuela would be below in the kitchen. I couldn't help but go in to say goodbye.

I passed several of the girls now and hoped they didn't take notice of me carrying two bags, one small and one large and heavy.

Consuela was in her habitual spot, stirring a large bowl of something. When I entered the room she said, "I see your cousin is not coming back." I set the heavy bag down, meaning to give her a hug goodbye, but she was not the affectionate type of woman. The hug, like the farewell, would be for me only.

"No," I returned.

"Well, you better hurry out of here, before Esther figures it out." She looked up at me, something she hardly ever did.

"I wanted to say good bye to you and to thank you for being my friend."

"No need for you do that." was her quiet response.

"We'll come back and visit. I'm sure Dolores .. ." She interrupted me, abruptly.

"Don't you dare. Don't either of you dare come back here. Go on and live your own lives."

Feeling that I had said as much as I could, I reached down for the bag. Before I could pick it up, Consuela rushed over and kicked it under the table then stood still beating her batter.

I stood up, confused by her sudden reaction, when the door slammed open and Esther stepped in. I know she meant to confront me and likely to stop me from leaving, but she stood so close to me I couldn't cross my arms without touching her.

"What do you think you are doing? Trying to sneak out from under me? Do you really think you could leave taking my things." She leaned into me, her breath little spikes of air in my face.

I couldn't look in her face, she was far too near, but in looking over her shoulder I could Miss Prentiss looking as if she were dying to say "I told you so." Anger boiled under my skin, but this was not the place to become demonstrative. All the advantage was on the side of Esther.

"I have taken nothing of yours."

"I've been to your room and its been cleaned out."

"Not entirely, there are several dresses of yours that remain."

Esther reached to grab my arm, but I shrugged away. Trying to menace me with her bulk and demeanor, she said, "The room is cleaned out, I say, are you trying to tell me you had nothing to do with cleaning it out?"

"I packed my own things and have taken them to my new home. You did tell me this past Sunday that I was no longer welcome here."

Practically breathing fire, "Where are Dolores's things? Where is Dolores?"

Holding up the small bag I still held, "I should hardly think I could fit Dolores's things in just this little carpet bag. Dolores must have taken them herself. I am sure I haven't done anything with them." I did my best to sound and appear mildly perplexed that she should be speaking to me in such a manner. I took a step to the side, out from under her intimidating stance and smoothed out my sleeve.

"Don't you believe her Esther," cried Miss Prentiss. "I haven't seen Dolores all afternoon. This one must have done something with her things."

For a moment there was silence. All that was heard was the steady beat of Consuela's mixing. Esther appeared to be calculating how to persuade me. Ignoring Miss Prentiss entirely, I turned back to Esther.

"Ma'am, I have lived here on the condition that I could leave whenever it suited either of us. It now suits me to leave this place." I put on my most important air, copied directly from my mother's supervision of her maid. "My accounts are paid up, there is nothing left binding us. If you will kindly let me pass, we will not need have anything else to do with one another."

Esther had no objections. Her momentary fit of rage subsiding, she knew she couldn't do anything to me but take the small bag and that wouldn't be the property she was after. The large bag had still escaped her notice. The scrape of the spoon against bowl was the sound that accompanied my exit. Miss Prentiss said as I passed, "This won't be the end of it."

I answered without turning, "Oh, I think it will be." I heard Consuela chuckle behind me and say, not above a normal conversational tone, "Tell her she can say goodbye to me where I live."

Then I was out the door with the future bright ahead of me.

Twenty minutes later I was at Stephanie's. Dolores and Stephanie were sitting at the dining table celebrating our escape over a bottle of gin. I joined them.

"You got out easy, Darling. I wonder she didn't search your bag however small." Stephanie concluded. I had wondered that myself at the time.

"I know I did. She must either think it was a better business decision to let me go peaceably or she felt that she could get more out of us later. Either way she is sure to benefit."

"That she is. I never met a woman better at making a profit of any person or anything." We all laughed.

The next morning Stephanie accompanied us to our new home with the Haelstrom's. I don't think I was ever happier to arrive home.

Chapter 10

Our lives changed dramatically over that summer. Dolores regained a carefree, girlish air, much like she had when we had first met at my Papa's funeral.

Living with the Haelstrom's was very pleasant. Mrs. Haelstrom had seven children altogether. Mr. Haelstrom worked on the train lines on a very erratic schedule and I very rarely saw him. Dolores and I kept erratic schedules as well. Dolores quite often worked late for Mr. Stuckey and within weeks had several boyfriends to keep her busy afterwards. An unfettered Dolores was a force to behold. I loved to see her with all her energy, free to be who she wanted.

She loved working for Mr. Stuckey. He was so sweet to us both. I no longer had to pay the entrance fee and would often visit in the evenings after my own work was finished. One evening he told me how his profits were increasing due to Dolores sitting up front in his ticket window.

"I swear Magda, I should have hired Dolores months ago. If I had only realized how a pretty girl can increase sales!" He raved. "I see men walking by who had no intention of going to see a picture, stop just to talk to her and that Dolores, she is the best sales gal I ever saw."

And I knew how Dolores loved to flirt. "The best part about flirting with all the strangers at the ticket counter," she told me, "is that there are three feet between me and them and that is as close as they will ever get!"

Dolores and I kept to our same schedule for attending auditions and waiting at the studio gates. For me, in many ways, it was less about becoming famous screen stars and more about enjoying time with Dolores. We always had so much fun. I always had so much fun, despite the waiting and all the disappointments. We laughed and talked and made up stories.

I spent as much time in my new window seat as I had when we lived at Esther's boarding house. My new seat faced North, so I didn't have the sunsets or the foot traffic to watch, but it was a very pleasant aspect. When the moon was out, I had a commanding view of the San Gabriel Mountains, framed by two old maple trees in the neighboring yard. I found it tremendously peaceful. It was with a light heart that I stared from the window in those days, Papa never far from my mind.

I met with my father twice that summer. Each time was a little easier. He never told mother about my whereabouts and he always insisted I take some money from him. I began to genuinely enjoy my father's company in a way that I never expected I could.

Since I no longer had to worry about running afoul of Esther, I spent as much time with Del as I could. Mrs. Haelstrom just adored Del and welcomed him in every time he came calling. If Mrs. Haelstrom ever took notice of the late nights I spent out with him, she never said anything to me. I know that it was not proper for me to spend so much time, unchaperoned, with him, but in many ways I already felt as if we were married. I knew that I would spend my whole life with him, so nothing else mattered to me.

We went to the beach on Sundays, and Dolores sometimes accompanied us. She talked up and flirted with the movie people we met. Dolores discovered all sorts of inside information about who was hiring and even got one audition out of it. I had never thought about our goal of being actresses when I had met some of those people before. When I was with Del, I had never considered that part of my life with Dolores. My heart was all for him.

Weeknights, Del and I went to dinner and sometimes to the movies, although that was a treat I still preferred to share with Dolores.

Dolores was never shy with her boyfriends as I was with Del—perhaps she had lost all of her womanly virtue when she worked for

Esther. Although, there were times when I, perhaps unfairly, wondered if she had ever had any.

She teased me constantly that I hadn't given myself to Del. We had been courting for nearly six months and Dolores thought I was the funniest prude around. I thought it very unfair of her to tease me so and it embarrassed me greatly. We had a huge argument over it one afternoon while at home, upstairs in our attic apartment. I thought her teasing had become rather spiteful, and I told her so.

"Dee, it is not that funny. It seems to me as if you are being intentionally malicious by this constant teasing. Del and I don't have to operate on your time table."

Her eyes took on a dark gleam. "Well, why shouldn't you sleep with him? He is your man. You should please him." The way she spat out the words made me think she had been wanting to say them for a long while. She folded her arms across her chest and looked smug.

It was too much for me, I confess. My response was full of venom and I regretted the words as they came out of my mouth. "You must have an awful lot of men the way you get around."

I might as well have slapped her in the face. It would have done less damage. We both stood stock still for a minute, Dolores staring at me. I was frantically trying to think of a way to smooth out the acidity of my words, but I could think of no way to take them back or make it better. When Dolores finally moved, she took her bag and left.

We didn't talk for several days. It was horrible trying to share our small room without speaking to one another. Dolores avoided all the meals with Mrs. Haelstrom's family and I sat through them sullenly. So many times I opened my mouth to apologize, but the words just weren't there. I know I had hurt her far too deeply.

Finally, on the third afternoon, after work, I stopped by the sundries counter at the Broadway Department store, her favorite shop, and bought a hair comb that would look perfect on her. I took the small package to Mr. Stuckey's where I knew she would be at the ticket window. When she saw me walk up, she put up her magazine as if she didn't know I was there. Trying not to roll my eyes at her stubbornness, I placed the package on the counter in front of her. "Dee, I'm sorry. Please take this as a peace offering."

She looked at the package and then at me. Her face was a conflict of emotion, like clouds passing over the sun. I thought to leave her alone to think about it, when she finally said, "Magda, I'm sorry too. Friends again?" She stuck her hand over the counter. I gladly shook it.

It was a strange few days for me. Perhaps for Dolores as well. We had never argued like that before. Until then we had always been the best of friends. As I walked away from Mr. Stuckey's that night, I felt like something had changed between us. Something imperceptibly small, but a part of the foundation of our relationship. It did not please me at all.

One particular night, in late summer, Del met me after work as usual. It was a hot night in the city with barely a breeze. We walked to Rosemary's, our favorite restaurant, and Del seemed to be a bit sad. He wasn't nearly his usual talkative self.

Trying to cheer him up I told him a silly joke that I had read in a magazine. I wish I could remember now what it was. I thought it very funny, but I barely got a smile from Del. He kept walking, pulling my arm close to his body despite the elevated temperature on the sidewalk. As we neared the restaurant, he reached across and kissed me. I was embarrassed for the sun was still out and there were other people on the walkway. He took no notice and ushered me down the stairs. It was much cooler in the dark of the little basement eatery and I basked in the cooler air.

Del stared at me intently while I unbuttoned my collar a small bit and rolled up my sleeves. The heat didn't seem to be bothering him. When I had settled, he took my hand in his, not letting it go even as he ordered from the waiter.

"What's wrong?" I asked him. Convinced now that his quiet mood was more than just a temporary thing.

"I found out today that I have to leave for awhile." He pulled my hand to his lips. "I would do anything to not have to go."

"Go where?"

"Go home, to Philadelphia. I need to be there in three weeks. My father says that I should plan on being there for a full month before I will be able to return." He held my hand to his cheek. "I am so sorry to leave you. Even for a few days would be too much."

His tenderness snagged at my throat. "I don't want you to go either," I somehow choked out.

Dinner was mostly silent, neither of us knowing how to breach the sadness of our impending parting. Generally we would sit and talk for hours over dinner and drinks, but that night, nearly as soon as we were finished eating he wanted to leave. "Let's go for drive," he told me, leading me out by the hand. "I just want to be alone with you."

After a short walk we came to his car and were soon buzzing through the streets away from the main city. Del drove faster than I would have liked, but I had no heart to scold him. The air felt good on my skin. After driving for a half an hour, Del made his way up to a housing development off of Franklin Street. We had been there before. It was high up and since it had been leveled off, commanded a good view of the basin below.

From that vantage point we watched the last of the sunset fade away. The moon, a week past full, hung low in the sky. Del and I sat close holding hands.

"I can't wait for seven weeks from now," I told him.

"Me neither. At least you will be here, among your friends. I will be henpecked by my sisters and my father." He sighed. "Believe me, if I had a choice, I wouldn't leave you."

I squeezed his hand and nuzzled into his shoulder. "We have two weeks until you have to leave, right?"

"We do." Again we sat in silence for some time enjoying the night air, being close to one another.

Del pulled me onto his lap to kiss me. Gently kissing me, his hands around my waist, I felt a longing for him as if he were already gone. When he unbuttoned my collar to kiss my neck, I did not object. And before my head knew it, my hands were unbuttoning the rest of my blouse and my camisole. He looked into my face questioning my actions while he wound his hand between my shirt and my bare skin. In answer to his unspoken question, I kissed him.

"Oh Maggie," was all that he said.

The next few weeks were a dream. We made love every chance we could and the rest of the time my mind was in the clouds. I thought only of what it was like to be in his arms, not letting myself for a second think about the month he would be gone.

While Dolores was working, we would spend the whole time loving each other. I tried to be careful, so that she wouldn't know, but one night she came home a few minutes early. Del was just finishing dressing and I was in my nightdress. When she saw the state of things, a wicked smile lit her face. Del gave me a peck on the cheek and was out the door in a flash. Dolores watched him go, all the way down the stairs.

"Ooh la la, primita. I see that you are pleasing your man," she clucked.

My face burned hot with embarrassment. Having been caught in so immodest a situation was embarrassing enough, but for Dolores to tease me was just unfair. "Please, Dolores. Don't tease me. If you can't see, I am already embarrassed enough."

"If you won't let me tease you, then at least give me the dirt?" she responded good-naturedly. "When did this all begin?" She sounded like we were gossiping about the latest film stars, not my love life. I gave her the rough details and she seemed to be satisfied. Either that or she noticed my extreme discomfort.

"Just be careful. You wouldn't want to be getting with a baby." She said as she started to change her clothes.

"Um, how does one be careful?" I asked with mortification. She looked over at me and laughed, not meanly but as if I were trying to be funny.

"I guess no one would have ever told you, huh?" And she kindly explained.

The thirteen days we had together went so fast. The day before he was to leave, we decided to spend the whole day at the beach, in his rented tent bungalow. It was a Monday so there were hardly any people on the beach. I wanted to enjoy my time with him to the fullest, but I'm afraid that my sadness at having to let him go got in the way more often than not. We ate dinner in Santa Monica, but instead of driving back to the city we went back to the tent. Those bungalow tents were furbished like homes with carpets and couches, tables and closets. We spent the whole night together on the couch, very close. Sleeping in his arms was the most perfect way that I could ever sleep, I decided. I woke up sometime in the early hours of the morning to Del's urgent kisses.

Whispering softly to me, "When we are married we'll have a house on a private beach so that we can hear the waves and I can love you on the sand and in the water. We'll never have to part. I'll never have to go away. Never."

We didn't sleep another wink, neither of us. We were already missing each other, even while our arms and legs tangled on the couch.

In the morning, Del drove me home and then left to catch his train. I openly wept as I watched him go, hoping that he wouldn't be gone one day past four weeks.

Chapter 11

You are wondering when we became actresses, as this is supposed to be my memoir about my years as an actress. For me this is the story about my early years in Los Angeles. However, that time before I became an actress came to an end shortly after Del left me for the first time.

Shortly after Del went back East there was a huge casting call for the Chronicle Film Company. Dolores had found out about it through some friends. That pioneering film company was casting for a picture with only women characters and extras. It was excellent news, for that meant there was a great chance that we could be picked.

The casting was to start at 11, so Dolores and I left for the line-up at 7 o'clock, an hour earlier than we usually left. Dolores' eyes were heavy with sleep, but she was as determined as I was. She had the great ability to be able to fall asleep anywhere, so I was sure she could catch up on her sleep the hours we were to wait in the line-up.

We wanted to be at the Chronicle studio lot early because we both knew that with a casting call such as this, the number of girls would be overwhelming. As we got off the streetcar and headed the remaining blocks to the studio, I felt that it was going to be a big day for us. Even though, when we turned the last corner, we saw that there were already at least 60 girls in line. It was not even 8 o'clock yet. The line was going to be huge.

Dolores hesitated at the sight of all the competition and held back for a second. I stopped too and looked at her. She set her jaw and said "Let's get in line."

Walking to the end of the line afforded me a good look at the competition. Many of the women were young, some were very, very old. There were more than a dozen that we passed who were dressed up so finely they could have sat down to dinner with the governor. I felt very small under the heavy stares of the bored, waiting women. Dolores appeared to take no notice.

It was a clear, sunny day and many of the girls, especially the heavily made-up ones, had resorted to sitting on the ground, shading themselves as best they could. Dolores had been one of the first to wilt. I fanned myself, leaning against the wall of a building. After waiting for what seemed much longer than three hours, I noticed a perceptible ripple of energy coming from the front of the line and like a wave gaining energy, the women in front of me began to stand up and straighten themselves up. I shook Dolores awake and pointed to the movement.

"It's starting." Dolores stated as she stood and brushed herself off. "It won't be long now." I took a few steps away from the wall and looked towards the end of the line. There were probably another 100 women that I could see behind us, and it seemed more were lined up around the corner. Indeed, we had arrived early enough.

Dolores was digging through her handbag, "Did you bring the lipstick? I don't think I have it in here." I handed over my bag.

In a few minutes I could see three men moving quickly down the line, stopping every three or four girls, pointing and talking, and then moving on. After they moved on, the girl they had spoken to went towards the entrance. When Dolores finished up powdering her face, she took a quick glance down the line and then turned to give me the make-up treatment.

By the time the three men were twenty girls away, Dolores was finished with her fussing. She gave me a quick hug, held her chin up, put on a big smile and turned towards the approaching judges.

I followed Dolores's example, although I feared I was blushing more than smiling. The leader of the trio was a stocky middle-aged man dressed in a coat that was more fashionable than tasteful and wore a lot of pomade in his receding hair. Whenever he stopped, he looked a girl from toe to head and back again. As he got nearer, I heard him giving rough instructions to the girls he looked over. "You, go in the gates and go straight to the big stage."

As he drew near, Dolores's smile did not fade, but I could tell that she was tense. I felt like a bag of nerves – embarrassed by my awkwardness and scared of making a bad impression.

The man stopped two girls in front of Dolores and thumbed her towards the entrance. I held my breath then, hoping that I was still smiling. The little man only gave Dolores a cursory look and nearly walked by me. He stopped just on the other side of me and gave me the same head-to-toe inspection. The woman behind me did everything possible, except actually stepping in front of me, to gain the attention of the little man.

The man's look made me feel like I was naked, he was so thorough. He paused at my face and looked me in the eye before his gaze again descended to my shoes. He barked the usual instructions to me and turned to go down the line.

Without even thinking I blurted out "But can't she go too?" grabbing Dolores's hand. The little man grumpily turned back, gave a quick look at Dolores. I was deflated when he turned to walk away. As he moved away he said "Take her." Not hesitating for a second we hurried towards the entrance, not looking once at the disappointed girls already passed over and still waiting to get in. Never before had we made it past the first cut at an open audition.

Inside the gates, we went down a short walkway and came to a door with a sign that read: Auditions. Through the door, there was a huge stage set up on one end of a clearing, the other girls were arranging themselves in the front. The stage consisted of a platform raised about two feet off of the ground, three walls, and what looked like curtains for a roof. The fabric over the stage kept the direct sun off the platform, but lit up every corner so there were very few shadows.

Once on the platform we waited for the actual audition to begin. Waiting, always waiting. Once we entered the dim stage area we had to wait for another two hours. Mrs. Haelstrom had taken over Consuela's place and I was always sure to ask her for a box lunch when I knew we were going to be gone all day. I was especially thankful for the bottle of cold tea she had packed that day. Dolores and I ate our lunch amongst the envious looks and snide comments about being too fat.

Somewhere around 1 o'clock, the small man came onto the stage clapping his hands for attention. Many of the women jostled to be in front. Many, like Dolores, took the high road and composed themselves by smiling brightly and lifting their heads. All and all, there were about eighty girls on the platform.

"I am Mr. Griply, the audition will be starting in just a few minutes. I need you girls to line up in rows of 10 facing me. No elbows ladies, this is a high-toned affair." He read something off his assistant's clipboard. "Now, everybody in a line? Great. What I need you to do is stay in your line and turn to the right so that you're facing the front of the stage."

There were some cries of outrage from a few of the girls who now would be in the back. There were eight rows altogether. Dolores and myself were in the third row at the far left. Turning towards the open area in front of the stage, we saw a small group of people assembling in front of us.

"Now, girls in the front row, show your gams. When I tell you to, you will turn to your left and walk off the stage. There my assistants will further direct you. The next row of girls will then take a step up and show your legs, et cetera et cetera. Got it? Great." Mr. Griply finished with a shout.

I couldn't see the people below us very clearly from the two rows of girls ahead of me. The ones in the first row kept moving from pose to pose, showing off their "gams" I suspect, so I just had to be patient until I got to the front.

A man's voice called out, "Fourth from the left, step forward and turn in a full-circle." I could just see the head of the girl who was called. She did as she was told and then returned to her place in line. After some whispering from amongst the people assembled below, Mr. Griply called for the first row to exit. The second row moved forward as if one body. The third row, mostly because I wasn't paying proper attention, did not step forward so smoothly. The procedure was repeated the same as before, with two girls being called out to circle around.

"Row two exit, Row three up." shouted Mr. Griply. Fumbling slightly as I moved up with the other girls. Now that I was at the front of the stage, I got a big dose of stage fright. I felt as if my muscles were loosening and that I would fall over any second in front of important people I didn't know. I took a breath and smiled while lifting my skirts a bit. How awkward, I thought, showing one's legs so obviously. I dared not look around to see how the other girls were bearing it. I knew that Dolores was looking bold and beautiful.

"Second from right, more leg and do the turn." Unfortunately, I did not realize at first that the voice was barking at me. A discreet nudge from Dolores brought me to my senses. Without thinking another thought, mostly because I was too embarrassed to try, I hiked up my skirt nearly past my knees and stepped forward to showcase my whole body. The most ominous aspect of my ungraceful turn was the silence. I knew I had goofed by not understanding that I had been called, I knew that I had taken too many steps to swivel gracefully, but the stage was silent.

More whispering ensued from the people sitting below. The fifth girl from the right got called out. Finally, and mercifully, Mr. Griply called row three off the stage. As soon as I had turned to exit the stage, I saw that the first two rows had been lined up behind the last row. Once all of the third row was off the stage, one of the young silent assistants pointed us in the direction of the stage.

The relief I had felt upon being released from the stage crumpled as I returned. Being in the far back, Dolores risked a smile in my direction. I smiled back and then felt guilty. I hadn't even thought about the fact that Dolores hadn't been called out. Although it wasn't a bad thing. Heaven knows, I would have said something inappropriate. Poor Dolores, what if she didn't get called? I resolved right there that if Dolores were not cast then I would decline. It would happen for both of us or for neither of us.

The stage once again became an arena of boredom while the last rows were made to step up. When finally the first row was again the front row, the girls waited. I could see movement among the half dozen people below. There was low talking and after twenty minutes the man who did all the talking boomed out again.

"If I call you, move to the front," one of the man below said and then proceeded to call out about twenty five girls. All of them pushed their way to the front, not taking the easy route by going around. It was much harder for them to make their way through the lines of girls, for the girls who were not called were as immovable as statues. Once they were all in front, smiling smug smiles and looking down their noses, Mr. Griply ushered them all off stage.

I was deflated and didn't worry about looking around now. I had felt so certain that today would be different. There were many other girls who must have shared my feelings because I caught the eye of many of them, but Dolores held firm. Her eyes still sparkling, she stared ahead. I, as I so often did in awkward situations, imitated her. After a brief silence and wait, those of us remaining were rewarded with some good news.

"The rest of you waiting will all be background actors. There are four of you who are up for additional roles. Those of you who are not called now, please follow Mr. Griply. The four called please stay on stage." The voice from the anonymous man below paused before calling out the places of the four chosen girls. I barely listened, I was too ecstatic about being a background actress in a feature film! When the other girls started to leave I started to follow but was waylaid by a fierce hug from Dolores.

"I just knew that they couldn't help but notice how pretty you are." I stared blankly back. Had I been called? Dolores knew the expression on my face, "Didn't you hear them? You are one of the four! Stay here and Wow them, okay? I'm off with the herd." Laughing, she ran off the stage after the other newly cast actresses.

I turned to face the shadows off the stage, feeling the panic well in my chest.

It was nearly 4 o'clock when I finally caught up with Dolores in the costuming room. I had been looking for her for some time and when I saw her I was not surprised to see her talking intimately with one of the young men who had been holding a clipboard for Mr. Griply. She was smiling brilliantly at him and inching closer by the second. As discreetly as I could, I got Dolores's attention.

"You're back! I'm so glad to see you. Charlie, this is my cousin Maggie. I just know they are going to cast her in one of the roles." Dolores said enthusiastically. Charlie shyly said hello to me. "Charlie is so sweet, he's offered to give us a lift into town if we wait until five." Dolores beamed at him. Charlie was obviously on the shy side and looked awkward in the face of Dolores's charm.

"Thank you very much Charlie." I said politely.

"No trouble really, there are three of us going that way anyway. A couple more won't hurt." He smiled shyly. "I have got to get some things finished before we can leave. I'll meet you out front, okay?" He said this to Dolores.

"We'll be there Charlie." she said sweetly. As soon as he was out of earshot she turned back to me. "Spill it, tell me everything. I can't wait to hear."

"There isn't much to tell." I let Dolores steer me into the dressing room. Most of the other girls had already been fitted and were on their way out.

Dolores exaggeratedly rolled her eyes at me. "Well, did you get picked for the close-up roles?"

"Is that what it was for? I wasn't sure."

"Well, didn't they tell you? They had to have said something. What did you do in there for over an hour?" Dolores was getting impatient with my usual lack of details.

"They made us walk around with our skirts hiked up," I pantomimed the operation. "Then, each in turn, they asked us to make a sweet face, a scared face, and relieved face. Then . . ."

"Let me see! I want to see what kind of acting you can do." Dolores interrupted with a teasing smile.

"Okay, sweet face," I opened my eyes wide with a dreamy look and pursed my lips. Dolores giggled. "Now, a scared face" I opened my eyes wide, tilted my head to the side and back and covered my open mouth with my hand.

"Good, good, now the relieved face." Dolores demanded giggling. I half shut my eyes and put my hand to my cheek and then burst out in laughter. Dolores was laughing too merrily for me to try and remain serious.

"That was the hardest one. I went third, so I had time to think about it." I said as the laughing died down.

"Your sweet face and relieved face aren't that much different," we both giggled. "What else did you have to do?"

"The man asked if any of us played instruments or could sing."

"I wonder what that was about."

"Well, I told him that I played guitar and sang. You know I used to play the love ballads for Papa? They seemed pleased with that."

"Hmmm, did any of the other girls play?"

"Yes, the very tall blonde woman plays piano."

"When do you find out?" Dolores continued. I was interrupted from answering by the costume lady shouting,

"All girls fitted up? Anybody left?"

"I haven't been fitted yet. They said Monday when they start the filming." I hurried off to the costume seamstress.

The very capable wardrobe woman took my measurements in a flash. She pulled a white garment off a full rack and handed it to me to try on. There weren't any private changing areas so I began to undress right there in the room. The wardrobe woman must have felt I was taking too long for she began to undress me. It was very awkward. I struggled against her at first, but she was not one to be dissuaded.

After a bit, I got the costume on. It was a short dress that was all gathered together like a roman toga. I had never shown so much of my legs to anyone on purpose, but Dolores and the draft on my legs was very unpleasant. The seamstress made some adjustments to the costume, poking me with pins in the process several times, and then bade me take it off. She didn't have time to dress me as well, for she was labeling the outfit with my name and moving on with her business.

Freshly dressed, I met Dolores and we went outside to wait for Charlie. We were both in high spirits, understandably. The next week we were to start shooting a film for which we had been chosen especially, not just picked up off the street at random. I felt as if all the hours we had put in trying to be noticed were paying off. We were finally getting somewhere.

On the ride back home into the city, with the three of us scrunched into a cab of a truck, Dolores pumped young Charlie for information about the studio and producers. She disguised it as flirting, but I could tell she was trying to get something from him. Charlie, gawky and lanky, despite working at a studio where aspiring actresses were always trying to get something, completely fell for Dolores's charms. I nearly felt sorry for him.

Dolores was never short of admirers and never thought twice about using them for her own gain, but the fellows always went along willingly right to the end. This one was no different. Some men are just attracted to exotic beauties. Dolores, with her large black, almond-shaped eyes, high cheek bones, and wide mouth certainly fit the bill.

"Ah so that is why they need so many girls for the picture. An island of women, how fun," Dolores said with a well-placed giggle. "But who is directing it? Who are the stars?"

"Well, it hasn't been announced yet, but seeing as you girls are both going to be in it, I guess it wouldn't hurt to tell you." Charlie looked at the road enjoying being the center of Dolores's attention.

"Tell me, please." Dolores cooed back.

"The director is none other than H. Phillips Monroe himself." Charlie allowed himself a self-satisfied look at Dolores's face, show-ing obvious excitement by the news, before turning back to look at the road.

I perked up at his announcement and clutched at Dolores's arm. H. Phillips Monroe! The most famous director in Hollywood next to D.W. Griffith – maybe even more famous. His Gentleman's Agree-ment and Hounds for Harry were my favorite movies at that time.

"Aye! He is amazing. We just saw Pearls for Irene and loved it." Dolores responded with enthusiasm, placing her hand on Charlie's upper arm.

"I worked on that one with Monroe – he goes by Monroe to all his friends. That man is a genius." Charlie was loving this. "I'm his number one assistant you know."

"Well, Mr. Monroe is a genius, of course he'd pick someone as talented as you to be his assistant. Who will be the players for this one?" Dolores may have been reading my mind. Sarah Esseter was often the star of Monroe's films and was one of my favorite cinema stars.

"Wyndham Standing is the hero. I think the heroine is going to be played by Norma Talmadge, but I don't know for sure." Charlie gave a smug shrug, "After all the picture is being funded by Joe Schenck."

Dolores was still making eyes at Charlie but took my hand and squeezed it with excitement. I didn't know where to look or what to think. I couldn't believe our amazing good fortune. Not only to be cast in a feature, but one that had so many important people working on it. I had forgotten how to breathe. I became even more nervous when I realized that we were now actresses and were supposed to know how to act.

Dolores had Charlie drop us off on a corner near the Haelstroms. I didn't pay much attention to our goodbyes to Charlie and his friends in the back, although I'm sure that I must have said it. As we started walking back home, Dolores happily chattered away. I wasn't meaning to ignore her, but I was still dazed by all that had happened.

"Magda! Are you even listening?" Dolores shouted in my ear.

I was about to defensively say 'of course I am' when I realized that I hadn't been. "I'm sorry Dee, What were you saying?"

She put her arm around my shoulder and repeated herself "Didn't you hear Charlie say that they often put the pretty girls on contract?" I shook my head no and Dolores sighed. "You're lucky you have me here cousin otherwise you'd lose track of your head."

The weekend was busy for both of us. On Saturday at work, I asked the Miss Tanners for week days off for the next few weeks. Both of them were very excited for me and told me it would be perfectly fine. Dolores made similar arrangements with Mr. Stuckey. Everything in place, we were ready to give a chance to a new life.

Chapter 12

The night before we were due on the set for the very first time, I had reason to be very glad that Del was not in town, even as much as I missed him. Dolores and I were both nervous wrecks. Even though we would be in costume while on the set, we both fussed about the clothes we were going to wear on the way to the lot.

Monday morning came quickly enough, despite all our fears. We were waiting on the corner of 8th Street and Spring by 7:45. Dolores had talked Charlie into giving us a ride and we were due on the set by 8:30. I wasn't the only quiet one that morning as we drove along the busy streets. Charlie kept cracking jokes trying to perk Dolores up, but she was so nervous she could barely keep up her side of the conversation.

Once we got to the lot, we had to check in at a booth just past the gate. Dolores was told to go to the dressing rooms we used before. I was sent along the opposite path to a room on the other side of the small bungalow. Apparently I had been given a role. As I walked around the corner of the building, my stomach turned with knots. We had arrived a bit early, so there wasn't any one else along the way.

Once through the outside door I came into another dressing room. This one was much better lit and seemed more comfortable than the one from the week before. There were two women already in there. One applying make-up to the other. Mr. Griply was in the room as well, leaning over a counter and pouring over a large folder. He looked up when I entered and gave me a curt nod.

"Finally, some actresses that can be on time." In his nasally voice he emphasized actresses. It sounded to me as if he didn't hold the denizens of the profession in much esteem.

I waited by the doorway for someone to tell me what to do. Mr. Griply noticed and said, "Don't dawdle, come in and start getting costumed. Your dress should have been transferred to this room. Look for it over there." He pointed with his pen to a rack with lots of dresses hanging on hangers.

"Did I get a role then?" I asked, trying to sound casual. Each of the hangers had a tag with a name on it and I looked for my name.

Mr. Griply gave me an annoyed look. "Didn't they tell you? Must I do everything around here?" he said with a huff. "You are the minstrel to the Queen. You are to play the mandolin or ukelele or something to entertain the Queen and her guest."

I looked at him passively. I understood the part about play-ing instruments, but nothing else. "I suppose you haven't read the scenario either." Mr. Griply shuffled through his paperwork. "Ah ha. Here it is. Found your costume? Excellent. Please change into it. Don't you worry, I'll be leaving shortly." Mr. Griply gathered up his folder and held out some paper in his free hand, "Here is the scenario, please familiarize yourself with it. Take this pen and fill out this paper. This will be your temporary contract for the duration of the filming." He handed them to me awkwardly, and I had to throw my costume over my arm to take the papers and pen. "I have got to check on the carpenters' work. They had barely begun to paint the pavilion yesterday and we wanted to start shooting that scene today."

He was off, puffing with each step as if every breath he took was an annoyance. I watched him go, then turned to set my bag and the paperwork on the counter next to the two women. "Hello." I said meekly.

"Don't worry about him darling. He's all steam." said the one woman who was fixing the other woman's hair.

The woman being made-up said "He frightens everybody at first, but he is all cream puff on the inside. You'll get used to him." She smiled at me. She was very pretty and somewhat older than I was. I was feeling very inadequate again. I smiled back at her, at a loss as what to say. I set the contract down and began to read it over. It wasn't long and seemed straight-forward. I was no attorney, but it seemed fair, so I signed it. Below my signature it asked for my name to be printed as it was to appear in the 'players' title.

Dolores and I had long ago decided to use aliases when we became actresses. Dolores had already been using one while working for Esther. Once we had gotten our first roles as extras, we had decided that it was time for new names. Dolores had thought we should use less Spanish sounding names. We had great fun coming up with lavish stage names, but in the end settled for more run-of-the-mill names. Dolores was Dottie Sparks, since she already used the nickname Dottie. At first I was going to be Mary Savoy, but after I met Del and he began calling me Maggie, I changed it to Maggie Savoy.

That is how I wrote my name on the contract. Maggie Savoy.

The pretty woman getting her hair done said to me, "You don't look like a Maggie." She must have been reading the contract upside down. Next she spoke to me in Spanish, "You and that girl you came in with are not white girls. I can tell a Mexicana when I see one." She laughed and I joined her.

"Professionally, I go by Virginia Lee, but my real name is Maria Constanza Vega." She held out her hand to me.

"Magdalena Santoya. Pleased to make your acquaintance." We shook hands.

"Now if one of you girls would like to explain what you've been talking about," the beautician said testily.

Virginia, in a very good-natured way, explained. Turning to me, she said, "You better hurry and get changed if you want a chance to have Minnie make you up." Virginia hiked a thumb in the direction of the woman behind her.

"Once Norma gets here, I won't have a chance to work on anybody but her," explained the beautician.

I went behind the curtain and changed quickly. I hung my dress on the same hanger and brought it out with me. Virginia had just stood up from the chair. I could see she had a similar costume as mine, but a little longer along the hemline.

"What role will you be playing?" I asked.

"I'm the general of the female army," she answered me with a laughing smile. "Here, put your dress back on the rack. Take a seat with Minnie and I'll see what they did with your shoes."

I sat down on the chair and felt like a queen myself. Minnie started right in on my hair. I had put it in a loose bun that morning, not knowing how I should arrange it. I'm glad I hadn't spent too much time on it because I never would have done what Minnie was doing. While she worked I took up Mr. Griply's paper work and looked over the scenario.

THE SIREN'S SONG, *Photoplay by H. Phillips Monroe*

The director wrote it too! I was very impressed. Although, after a few paragraphs, I began to grow alarmed. I didn't have a tiny background role, as I had supposed, I had quite a large role and was likely in as many scenes as the star. The fear gripped my stomach again and I leaned forward a little.

"Relax, darling. You'll be fine. Everybody gets nerves, some of them even after they've been doing this awhile." Minnie had a soothing voice. A plump woman in her forties, she wasn't very pretty, not by the standards set by the actresses, but she was pleasant and comforting. She was the perfect antidote to my fear. She started asking me questions to get me talking and not thinking. Just then two more women came into the dressing room.

They were veterans and went right to work fixing themselves up. I found that they were to be the waiting women for the heroine and therefore in front of the camera as often as myself. I felt better finding I wasn't going to be alone.

Virginia came back then with a box of shoes. Well, not shoes really, but the footwear that we were to wear as part of our costumes. The footwear was leather booties with thin ropes sewn on that were meant to wrap around our legs. The five of us had a good laugh trying to figure out their application.

Mr. Griply came puffing into the dressing room. "Girls out to the set immediately. Minnie, Norma's just arrived so do with her what you can and get her out there as soon as you can. Monroe wants to start presently." He turned and was off in a second.

I followed Virginia out the doorway. Instead of going across the yard to the area where we auditioned, she turned right and took us towards a high wall across an empty lot. There were trees and buildings visible over the top of it. Soon we made it to a large gap in the wall and on going through I found that we had entered the set. The scenario had said that the story takes place on a mythical island and I found myself in a place very mythical indeed; except for the smell of paint and turpentine and the sight of carpenters in dirty dungarees finishing up. The colors of the fake plants weren't quite right, nor that of the gazebo-type buildings, but I soon learned it was due to the black-and-white nature of film.

Virginia marched us up to the center of the set where a large building with no walls stood at the top of a number of steps. It was very grand looking. Inside, I could see rolled up carpets, an ornate chaise lounge and low stools, and potted ferns on pedestals. The only thing that marred this lovely place was a large crane with a camera on the end that was positioned next to the building.

Several men and girls in costume were milling about. We waited at the bottom of the steps. I was wide-eyed and staring, taking it all in.

Only a few minutes later H. Phillips Monroe came strutting through the foliage. I knew who he was immediately from the way he barked orders and everyone jumped when he looked at them. He had been at the audition, but I don't recall that he said anything that day. He was a normal looking man, neither tall nor short, well-built but not fat or thin. He had a receding hairline, his dark blonde hair combed straight back. He moved quickly, in sharp quick motions that put me in mind of a military unit marching in procession. For a man that wasn't much to look at, he was very impressive to watch.

There were a number of extra girls following behind him. Ahead of all of the others was Dolores. She smiled and winked at me when she came to the open ground before the raised building. I thought she would come over and join me, but she stayed in her group. I was still grouped with Virginia and the two other girls, Maryanne and Dorothy, who were sitting on the steps. I didn't dare sit, or move even, for fear of being caught out, of doing something wrong. I wanted to blend in and not be noticed. I think I was the only one who did.

Mr. Monroe spent the following hour reviewing the sets and checking the camera positions. Finally, it must have been past 11 o'clock, he started placing the extras and then those of us with roles. Norma Talmadge still hadn't arrived on the set, so Mr. Monroe sent young Charlie to summon her.

I was placed in the interior of the wall-less building on one of the pedestals, a small guitar was put into my hands as a prop. I think I was sitting very stupidly, for Mr. Monroe made me get up off the seat so he could show me how he wanted me situated. I was in too much awe to verbalize my acceptance, just shaking my head 'yes.' Mr. Monroe only spent two or three minutes with me before he was off instructing someone else. The man was full of energy. He seemed to always be moving.

I saw Dolores milling about on the steps of the building with a group of other girls. She waved at me when she saw me looking, but that was about all the interaction we had that day.

Norma Talmadge finally made her appearance. She was so beautiful my mouth opened involuntarily. Mr. Monroe yelled at her for being so late and told her to move up to her place on the set. She only laughed at him and hurried to her place. She reclined in the chaise lounge dramatically, covering her eyes lightly with her hand.

Maryanne must have been acquainted with Miss Talmadge because she said, none too quietly, "Some of us get our sleep at night, not while we're working." Ms. Talmadge shot her a sarcastic look and went back to relaxing under her hand.

Mr. Monroe finally came up the stairs to the platform and described to Ms. Talmadge – and to us – what is was we were supposed to do when the film started rolling. Mr. Monroe made Miss Talmadge go through the whole scene, some parts several times, before he actually began shooting the film.

I was supposed to be entertaining "the queen" with a ballad and actually did play the small guitar I had been given, but the strings were so loose as to not make a correct note and my singing was therefore out of tune as well.

During the first break Miss Talmadge shouted to Mr. Monroe, "I don't mean to knock this kid, but could you get an instrument that works? That song is killing me."

My face burned as everyone laughed. I tried to laugh to, but it was an empty effort. Mr. Monroe shouted to me, "Tune that thing, if you can." So I did. It was an awful, cheap little thing, but I got it into tolerable tune and was rewarded later in the day when Miss Talmadge said to me, "You ain't half bad."

The day went by quickly, even though not much of it was actually spent acting. At a little after 3 o'clock, Mr. Monroe dismissed the supporting actresses for the day so that he could do some close-up work with Miss Talmadge. He gave us a stern warning about being late the next day then sent us off to change out of our costumes.

By the time I met up with Dolores at the entrance to the studio it was 4 o'clock. We were both exhausted from the little that we had done during the day.

"I can't believe how hard it is to stand around all day," yawned Dolores when we took our seats on the streetcar back to town. We had a twenty minute ride back to our neighborhood and Dolores slept the whole time. My eyes were heavy, but I couldn't relax on a streetcar, not like Dolores. We spent a quiet night, resting up and preparing for the next day.

The next day was boring. Much of the day was spent waiting for the sky to clear. Heavy rain clouds obscured the sky and ruined the lighting for filming. It never rained but the oppressive clouds made the waiting even harder. The allure of the cinema lost much of its magic when you saw the painstaking process of filming.

I was standing with the girls who I had started to consider my own group, Virginia in particular. I saw Dolores now and then with a number of different people, including Charlie who seemed to work as near to her as possible. I noticed later in the afternoon Dolores having a tete-a-tete with Mr. Monroe and marveled at her audacity.

The hours rolled by slowly, and at last, when there was no hope of getting decent sunshine out of the day, we were dismissed.

As soon as we were out of the gates of the lot I questioned Dolores about Mr. Monroe. "Oh, it was nothing, really." She said off-handedly.

"It seemed to me that you were talking with him for quite a while for nothing to have been said," I eyed her suspiciously.

She laughed me off, "I guess so." That was all I could get out of her.

After the bout of bad weather, filming went quickly for the following two weeks. It seemed unreal. The costumes, all the people, the way the story was filmed in small pieces and would later be fit together.

I worked hard at my part in the picture but never felt really sure about it. While I got many compliments for my work, even from Mr. Monroe and Miss Talmadge, I never felt comfortable. Everybody said I had done a wonderful job in the scene where the hero saves me, I hoped it was true.

Dolores was getting attention as well. Charlie told us that many of the other directors for Chronicle loved the way she looked on film. Her broad cheekbones and bright eyes were particularly suited to the starkness of the black-and-white film. When Charlie told us, as he was giving us a ride back into town, Dolores played off the compliment, but I know it was deeply satisfying to her.

In those few weeks of filming, Dolores took on an air of gravity that I had never before seen in her. It was a determination that edged out much of her usual mirth. Maybe a sense of direction and maturity was replacing her girlish spontaneity. I didn't know what it was, but I could see the change in her.

More than once while waiting for Dolores in front of the studio, she came out with Mr. Monroe. They were talking in a most friendly way. I knew what Dolores wanted – a contract. Although there was a look in her face that seemed to make more of the situation than just flirtation on her side. Mr. Monroe was not a boy, like Charlie, and I couldn't see him being swayed half so easily by Dolores's charms. Yet I saw them together quite often.

It was two days before filming was due to end when we got the good news. It was a Tuesday. Sid Hawthorne, the manager for Chronicle Film Company took me and Dolores aside that morning as we arrived at the lot. Nearly everyday we had been given a ride from Charlie and had always arrived early.

"Dottie and Maggie, just the girls I wanted to see," Mr. Hawthorne said with a condescending smile, "Early as usual. Just wonderful."

We both greeted Mr. Hawthorne and followed him into his office bungalow near the front gates to the studio. "Girls, we'd like to offer you each a contract here with the studio," he began.

My heart leapt with his words. Dolores actually did leap to her feet.

"Oh, Mr. Hawthorne that is terrific. You don't know how much this means to me." She reached across the desk and shook his hand. "Thank you so much."

"Now, now. I haven't even discussed with you the terms." Mr. Hawthorne, a conservative man in his late 50s, was off put by Dolores's exuberance. "Don't you want to know what we intend to offer you."

"Whatever it is, Mr. Hawthorne, I'm sure it will be generous." Dolores beamed back. She took her seat again and waited, this time, to hear what Mr. Hawthorne was offering.

"Ahem, now. Chronicle Film Company would like to contract with you for a term of 6 months at $30 a week, with the option to renew for another six months to two years at the end of that term. Is this amenable to you both."

"Oh yes," declared Dolores.

"And you young lady?" Mr. Hawthorne looked at me for an answer.

"Well, I . . ." I wasn't sure how to respond. I was glad of the offer, but a six month contract seemed like a long time. Del came first to my thoughts. What if we should be married before then, would he object to me having to work? I was conflicted.

Dolores was staring at me, her dark eyes boring holes into my head. "This is a good offer, Maggie, I don't think you'll get a better one in the next six months." She must have been reading my mind. I had always suspected that she could.

"Young lady, is there another offer you are seeking? I will have you know that Kingston Sam has especially requested you for a primary role in the short feature he begins shooting next week."

Dolores turned to him, her mouth wide with surprise. Kingston Sam was perhaps the most famous vaudevillian in the country and had just begun a successful film career. I was surprised as well and was beginning to soften.

"Um, no," I stuttered at Mr. Hawthorne, "I'm not entertaining any other offers, Mr. Hawthorne. I am just unsure about the length of the contract."

"Well, you don't need to give me an answer right away, but I do hope you'll consider our offer seriously." Mr. Hawthorne said this with an air of a man not used to being turned down. "Young Dottie, I'll have your contract ready tomorrow morning. Please stop by my office when you come in."

We got up to leave, Dolores furiously thanking Mr. Hawthorne. Once out the door her obsequious smile turned into a frown of rage, directed towards me. She yanked me by the arm to a quiet corner.

"What do you mean you need to think about the offer. They've already lined up your next feature and you are hesitating. For what? For Del to take you away from all this?" I should have been angry with Dolores for such treatment, but I was completely surprised by her anger. I was starting to work up to a healthy dose of defensive ire, when she stepped back leaning against a door frame and said "I should have realized sooner that you didn't like it with me, that it's beneath you."

She looked away from me, arms folded across her chest. She may have been playing on my sense of duty and guilt, or she may have been seriously wounded by my foreseeable abandonment. Whatever her intent, I was moved by the latter. I loved Dolores too well to take her at anything other than face value.

"I'm sorry Dee, I don't know what I was thinking," I reached out and gently took her arm. "I think I was just overwhelmed, you know. Let's go now and tell Mr. Hawthorne I'll take the contract. Okay?"

She made a sniff and tossed her head and wordlessly went with me back to Mr. Hawthorne's office. She waited outside as I told him I'd accept the contract. When we finally were headed towards the dressing rooms, now rather later than usual, Dolores said to me as we walked arm in arm, "I think this the beginning of my real life primita. I think now I'm really going to start to live."

THE SIREN'S SONG

Directed, Written & Produced by
H. Phillips Monroe
Produced by Joe Schenck

CHRONICLE FILM COMPANY

List of Players
Antonia, Queen of the Amazons — Norma Talmadge
Shipwrecked Sailor — Wyndham Standing
Amazon Army Commander — Virginia Lee
Amazon minstrel — Maggie Savoy
Pirate Captian — Barry Resnor
Pirate #1 — John Feilder
Pirate #2 — Samuel Anderson
          ...and hundreds of beautiful women

SCENARIO

Fading from black, a hazy view of a landscape appears blurred with a deep fog. A figure struggling forward. It is a man, bedraggled and wet and struggling to walk. He clutches a life preserver with the name "Old Queen" inscribed on it. The fog begins to lift and it becomes clear that the man was on a beach having swum ashore from a shipwreck.

A BRAVE SAILOR LOST AT SEA, FINDS HIMSELF ON A STRANGE SHORE

As the sky becomes clear, he gazes long and hard at the horizon looking in vain for his fallen comrades.

COULD IT BE? COULD I BE THE ONLY SURVIVOR?

The man is wretched and after some further searching he turns to behold the place where he has landed. He sees that it is a lush land, filled with slowly crumbling Grecian-style buildings. Every where he looks he sees beautiful tropical flowers on lush vines. He takes a few steps off the beach only to be surrounded by the most lovely of gardens.

WHAT COULD THIS ISLAND BE?

The man explores the garden he has stepped into. There is a gazebo with marble floors and ionic columns. The man climbs the four stairs to get a better view of his whereabouts from the view. All he can see is paradisical foliage. He climbs down the stairs and sits on them.

I HAVE NEVER HEARD OF A PLACE OF SUCH WONDROUS BEAUTY. PERHAPS IT IS AN UNDISCOVERED ISLE?

The man puts his chin on his fist and thinks of his situation. From a close-up view of the sailor, the scene widens and now the man issitting on the steps of the gazebo on the right hand side, and on the left side there is a path. Two ladies appear on the path. They are dressed as the ancient Greeks dressed in flowing robes and with swept back hair.

The two women see the man before he sees them. They are partially concealed by the foliage and they point to the man and whisper to each other. Then both women laugh. The man, hearing the laughter, looks about him for the source. The two women reveal themselves and smile. The man is immediately taken with their beauty and elegance and walks towards them.

The women each take an arm and guide him along the path. The man looks stunned and goes along willingly.

WHAT BEAUTY! ARE THEY ANGELS? HAVE I ARRIVED IN HEAVEN?

The women guide the sailor to a small city all built in the same style as the gazebo. White marble is everywhere, all the plants are in bloom. There are hundreds of beautiful women – some doing chores, some lying in hammocks, some playing musical instruments. The man is overawed by the grandeur of the place, but most of all by all of the women.

WHAT SORT OF PLACE CAN THIS BE?

The man allows the women to guide him through this paradise. He offers no resistance. They arrive at a grand temple and walk up the twenty steps to the platform. There the man sees the most beautiful woman in the world draped across a lounge chair being entertained by a charming girl strumming the guitar and singing.

Upon his arrival, the beautiful woman looks up and the player halts. The beautiful woman sits up and looks the man over closely. She whispers something to her playing girl and the girl giggles in an embarrassed way. Then she speaks to the man.

**ANOTHER SAILOR HAS FOUND OUR SWEET ISLE.
WHAT, SIR, HAS BROUGHT YOU HERE?**

The sailor, sensing royalty, bows deeply and explains that he washed ashore. He demonstrates how his ship sank and he swam to shore with the lifesaver. He still holds it in his hand.

The woman smiles graciously at him and stands to speak to him.

**SAILORS OFTEN ARRIVE ON OUR SHORES. YOU
ARE WELCOME HERE UNTIL YOU ARE READY TO
RETURN. I AM THE QUEEN OF MY PEOPLE. MY
NAME IS ANTONIA.**

The sailor goes down on one knee and the queen laughs. The sailor looks up and smiles at the queen.

**YOUR HIGHNESS, THANK YOU FOR YOUR
GRACIOUS HOSPITALITY. I AM CALLED LAWRENCE.
I AM HUMBLY GRATEFUL TO YOU.**

Lawrence offers his hand to the Queen and she takes it for a moment. She calls to her serving women. Half a dozen women appear on the platform and the Queen gives them instructions. The women usher the man down the stairs. As he goes, he takes a long backward glance at the Queen. She stands at the edge of the platform, lit up by the early morning sun, and watches him go.

Lawrence is taken to a bath made out of hot springs and allowed to bathe. When he exits the baths in just a large towel he is given fresh clothing. He goes back behind the screening foliage to change.

WHAT'S THIS? I CANNOT BE EXPECTED TO WEAR …

Lawrence comes out wearing the garb of the native women, flowing togas and skirts. He is obviously embarrassed and tries to pull the skirts lower. The attending women giggle and admire him, but the brave sailor will not be appeased. He frowns with embarrassment and displeasure.

IS THERE NO OTHER CLOTHING FOR ME TO WEAR?

Just then two women run up carrying a pair of pants and a shirt. Lawrence is surprised and pleased that there are regular clothes for him to wear. Yet he wonders where they have come from. One of the girls who brought him the clothes explains that they washed up on shore.

ANOTHER BRAVE SAILOR LOST TO THE SEA.

After a short pause for reflection, Lawrence goes back into the cove and changes. When he reemerges, he is wearing a very well-fitting uniform of a swashbuckler including a sash around his waist.

The attending women lead Lawrence to a large table heavily laden with a variety of delicious looking food. After a short hesitation while he admires the food, Lawrence sits down and applies himself to the meal. The attending ladies, about 10 of them, watch with delight as he takes in his meal. The novelty of a man is something they do not get used to. Once Lawrence is satisfied, the ladies lead him away to a hammock set in a splendid glen. Offered the chance to rest, Lawrence at once accepts and goes to sleep.

LATER THAT DAY …

Lawrence awakes from his peaceful sleep in the splendid glen. He rises and stretches, yawning. Not sure of where he should go, he glances around. Then he catches a snippet of sound and puts his hand to his hear to hear better. He follows the sound to the source and finds three women just outside his natural bedchamber making wreaths and crowns with the lovely tropical flowers.

Once the ladies see him they get up and arrange the flower jewelry on him. Lawrence gently tries to dissuade the ladies from decorating him in this manner.

FLOWERS ARE BETTER SUITED TO ENHANCE A LADIES' BEAUTY AND ARE ENTIRELY UNFIT FOR A GENTLEMAN.

The ladies look at him in confusion, but continue their work. Lawrence give in and allows himself to be decorated. His look shows his exasperation. Once completed they take him by his hand and arms to see their queen. He passes beautiful vistas with ocean views in the distance and white marble structures dotting the landscape. He is very impressed with the beauty of the place. Even more so now since he has had a chance to rest. Along the way, he sees many women employed in a variety of occupations. Each woman stops as he approaches and looks at him in wonder.

As he draws near to the Queen's pavilion he begins to notice something. His eyes grow large and round as his head cranes round on his neck. He is astonished.

WHY, WHAT KIND OF PLACE CAN THIS BE?

He stops the women who are ushering him and takes a hard look around him.

THERE ARE ONLY WOMEN HERE. YOUNG

BEAUTIFUL WOMEN! HAVE I REACHED HEAVEN?

The women only laugh at his declaration and pull him along to see their mistress. Once again Lawrence climbs the stairway to the pavilion, but this time in wonderment at where he must be. At the top of the stairs he bows low to the ground in respect for the Queen. She motions for him to rise and he does so. Walking forward a few steps he entreats the Queen, hands grasped in front of him.

YOUR HIGHNESS, WHAT IS THIS MOST GLORIOUS OF PLACES? WHERE IS IT THAT I HAVE LANDED?

The lovely queen laughs gaily at the awe-struck Lawrence. She stands up from her low couch and takes him by the arm. She turns him to gaze at the beautiful view. There are white marble villas and large trees in flower all down the valley from the Queen's pavilion. In the distance is the sea with the sun setting. The Queen raises her hand telling Lawrence where he is.

THIS IS AMAZONIA. THIS IS OUR HOME AND OUR PARADISE.

The Queen laughs brightly and Lawrence smiles at her. He looks around in amazement at the women and the scenery.

THEN YOU MUST BE THE QUEEN OF THE AMAZONS AND I HAVE REACHED PARADISE!

The Queen wags her finger at Lawrence.

NO, THIS IS NOT THE TRUE PARADISE. FOR THOSE OF US WHO LIVE HERE IT IS OUR HOME. WHICH IS LIKE A PARADISE TO US. MY PEOPLE HAVE BEEN CALLED MANY NAMES, BUT HERE WE HAVE NO NAME. WE LIVE IN PEACE AND HARMONY.

Lawrence, overcome by the beauty and strangeness of his surroundings, kneels before the Queen. She reaches down and lifts his face to see her.

YOU ARE WELCOME HERE, DEAR LAWRENCE,

UNTIL THE TIME FOR YOU TO LEAVE COMES. FOR NOW, ENJOY YOUR TIME HERE. SEE THE MANY BEAUTIES OF OUR LAND.

Lawrence turns his gaze from the Queen's face and looks at the faces of the maidens surrounding him. Each girl is viewed close-up showing just how pretty each one is. After looking at all of the pretty girls, Lawrence looks out at the vista and then the sea. He gazes at the sea for a long time. His face shows that he longs to be out at sea again, despite all the pretty women. He bows before the Queen again.

THANK YOU, YOUR HIGHNESS. I ACCEPT YOUR OFFER. PLEASE TELL ME WHAT I CAN DO FOR YOU IN RETURN.

Lawrence, with his hand over his heart, offers himself to the Queen. She leans towards him and after a long gaze into his face, she pats him on the shoulder and turns away. He is led away by his many attendants.

The Queen lays across her couch and motions for music to be played by the young guitarist. The girl starts to play a melancholy song. The Queen dramatically puts her arm across her eyes and sighs.

THERE IS SOMETHING ABOUT THAT MAN THAT ATTRACTS ME SO. IN ALL THE AGES AND ALL THE MEN WHY DOES HE TOUCH MY HEART?

The Queen lays silent while the girl plays and sings.

DAYS GO BY …

Lawrence spends happy days with the women of the island, he helps them in their chores, and they lavish attention on him. He is very merry among the women and helps them with the washing and cooking and even with the carpentry and carving of new structures they are building. He is amazed when he first learns that all the buildings were made by the women themselves.

LAWRENCE IS HAPPY DURING HIS TIME ON THE
ISLAND OF WOMEN. THEIR COMPANIONSHIP IS
MOST REWARDING. BUT ALAS, IN HIS HEART HE
LONGS FOR HIS HOME.

He always spends several hours a day on the shore looking at the
sea for signs of a ship, for he has not forgotten where he comes from
and must return. He stands at the edge of the beach, looking forlorn,
scanning the horizon for that one ship that can return him.

HIS HEART GROWS LESS HOMESICK WHEN HE
SPENDS TIME WITH THE QUEEN.

At a dinner feast, the Queen's pavilion is lit up by glass lanterns.
Lawrence and Her Highness are enjoying an intimate repast. They
laugh gaily with one another as Lawrence tells the Queen of some of
his adventures on the sea. Lawrence stands up suddenly thrusting his
arm in the air then staggering back a few steps, his hand to his heart.
The Queen looks surprised and then she laughs again as Lawrence
sits back down by her side to continue his anecdote.

After their laughter has quieted down, the Queen looks at Lawrence shyly and begins to speak earnestly.

DEAR LAWRENCE, YOU LIKE IT HERE VERY MUCH
DO YOU NOT?

Lawrence explains that in his heart it is truly the most beautiful
of places. The Queen continues her line of questioning.

YET YOU LONG FOR THE SEA AND YOUR HOME. I
SEE IT IN YOUR FACE WHEN YOU WATCH THE SEA.

The Queen looks down, very melancholy. Lawrence admits that
his heart does lie elsewhere and that he longs to go back to it. The
Queen turns away from him and speaks to herself so only she can
hear.

THEN I SHALL NOT KEEP YOU FROM YOUR HOME

When she turns back to him she is once again gay and merry and asks him questions of his home life.

DEAR LAWRENCE, TELL ME OF YOUR HOME. TELL ME OF YOUR FAMILY.

Lawrence tells the Queen all about his home and family with great fervor and love.

Lawrence is once again walking along the beach, looking forlornly out to sea. Very far ahead, around a bend in the shore, he thinks he sees a ship off of the shore. He begins to run.

CAN MY DREAMS AT LAST BE REALIZED?

He continues running until he has to climb some rocks that are in front of him. As he carefully reaches the other side, he sees that a ship is anchored in a small harbor there. His face shows his rapture, but all of a sudden it falls into a look of anger. For on shore there are two men badgering the young minstrel. She is very frightened and tries to run, but the men grab her wrists and hold her back. Her guitar getting smashed in the process.

Lawrence is very angered by the scene he is witnessing.

PIRATES!

He runs to the aid of the girl, taking her captors unaware. He beats them off, leaving them unconscious. Then he shoves their boat away from the shore. The ship's crew spies him do this. All the hands on deck shake their fists in fury at him.

Lawrence knows that it is just a matter of time before the whole ship lays siege to the island. He takes the girl by the arm and runs off with her into the forest. They run through the city and up the stairs of the pavilion.

Lawrence appears in front of the Queen with the young minstrel in tow. As soon as the girl makes it to the platform, she throws herself across the Queen's knees, weeping. The Queen tries to soothe her.

The Queen looks to Lawrence for explanation.

PIRATES CAME ASHORE AND ATTACKED HER. IT
WILL NOT BE LONG BEFORE THEY COME TO LAY
SIEGE ON YOUR FAIR CITY!

The Queen puts her wrist to her mouth in shock and shakes her head. The young minstrel looks up imploringly at the Queen.

MADAME THEY WERE AWFUL TERRIBLE MEN! WE
MUST DO SOMETHING.

The Queen pats the distraught girl's head. She raises her chin and composes her features. She looks noble and brave.

WE WERE ONCE WARRIORS, BUT HAVE BEEN A
PEACEFUL RACE FOR THOUSANDS OF YEARS. YET,
WE MUST REPEL THIS ATTACK ON OUR SHORES.

When the Queen finishes her inspiring speech, she turns to the gazetteers and motions for them to sound the alarm. The ladies raise their trumpets and sound the call.

The laundresses working with large tubs look up on hearing the call. Immediately and in unison they empty their large tubs, pick them up and cart them off to fill with nearby rocks. The master carvers, working on marble pillars, drop their tools at the sound of the call and begin to gather up the marble pieces and fragments scattered around the ground. The women roofers stir their cauldrons of pitch. A group of women open ancient cabinets that are filled with bows and arrows and swords. Rows of women walking single file towards Her Majesty's pavilion. The Queen stands at the top of the stairs surveying her people. Her nobility radiates. Her stoic expression determined.

The pirates are all on shore now and beginning to set up the base of their operations. A rude fort for their imminent attack. Brandishing their muskets and knives at one another, all of a sudden they cower in fear.

AS THE CALL OF THE TRUMPETS REACHES THE
EARS OF THE PIRATES, THOSE SCOUNDRELS
QUAKE AT THE PURE AND RIGHTEOUS SOUND
THAT THEY HEAR.

Lawrence and Her Majesty are standing halfway down the steps
to the pavilion addressing the ladies of the isle. Her Majesty tells
them of the threat on their shores and benevolently asks them to
fight the scourge on their shores.

Lawrence takes over the battle planning and animatedly directs
the different groups of women. As he gives a direction, groups peel
away to fortify themselves. The last group of women are the swordswomen. The tallest woman, their leader, ceremoniously hands Lawrence an elegant, mighty sword. He leads them away.

The Queen watches him leave with love-sick eyes. She is comforted by a pat on the arm by the little minstrel. The Queen turns to
the girl with a sigh.

IT IS SUCH A COMFORT TO HAVE SUCH A BRAVE
MAN WITH US NOW IN THIS TIME OF TROUBLE

The beautiful face of Her Majesty fills the view, her look sick with
love and worry.

MEANWHILE ...

AT THE PIRATE CAMP, THE THIEVES READY
THEMSELVES FOR AN ATTACK!

The Captain of the pirates lands ashore. He is a large brute of
a man, with a large dirty mustache and fancy, but dirty clothes. He
holds himself up high as he steps on the beach, laughing a maniacal
laugh. As he climbs the beautiful beach he rallies his troopes with a
roaring speech about plunder and women. When he has shouted
them into a fever pitch, he raises his sword and his gun and leads the
men on the path to the center of the island.

Once they are moving along the path they make their way slowly.
The tropical foliage is thick. In a short time, they run into the washer

women along the stream. The pirates get ready to attack them. The ladies scream and run away, the pirates chasing after them.

The pirates chase the ladies into a clearing, but once they are in the clearing the ladies are nowhere to be seen. Out of nowhere, it seems, comes a volley of rocks and shards. Taken completely by surprise, the pirates run ahead as the volley is coming from where they just were. They start out along the path, but don't want to get too far from their base of operations, so the Captain leads them into the bush to double back.

Unbeknownst to his men, he soon becomes lost and when he comes across a path he tells his men that he knows exactly where they are going.

HA HA! THIS IS THE PATH WE STARTED FROM. WE SHALL MAKE IT BACK TO CAMP SHORTLY.

The pirates gamely take the path, but it leads them right into the heart of the city. As soon as they enter it, they are attacked on all sides by the ladies. No matter which way they turn they get hit with rocks and arrows. The pirates are taking great injury and some of the men go down. In no time at all, the women warriors have embargoed the pirates into the main forum of the city. Her Majesty stands above them on the stairway to her pavilion. She is grandly surrounded by her archers who all have a deadly aim on the hearts of the remaining pirates.

Lead by Lawrence, the swordswomen surround the pirates.

The Pirate Captain, fearful after being so easily penned in, lashes out at Lawrence. The other pirates cower under the aim of the archers and swordswomen.

Lawrence meets the Captain in a fierce sword fight, both men capable with their weapons. Her Majesty looks on in terror as the men fight it out.

They cover a lot of ground, the ladies always keeping the way out barred with their bodies. At last Lawrence steps aside from a great thrust by the Captain. In doing so he takes a small cut on his arm, but has enough space to run the Pirate Captain through, leaving him dead.

The island women all cheer. The remaining pirates sink to their knees begging for mercy from the Queen. She looks at them fiercely. Then she waves her hand at them and turns her face away.

> TAKE THEM FROM MY SIGHT. PUT THEM ABOARD
> THEIR SHIP AND LET THEM FOUNDER IN THE SEAS.

The pirates are ushered away by the swordswomen. Lawrence leaps up the stairs to the embrace of the waiting Queen. She laments his injury and calls for it to be dressed. Before Lawrence will allow it he begs a favor of Her Majesty. He goes down on one knee in supplication.

> YOUR MAJESTY, I ASK YOU THIS FAVOR. PLEASE
> ALLOW ME TO TAKE THE LANDING BOAT OF THE
> PIRATES THAT I MAY FIX IT UP TO SAIL ME BACK
> TO MY HOMELAND.

Overcome with emotion the Queen grants his wish and then turns dramatically away running up the stairs to her pavilion.

With his arm well bandaged, Lawrence appears on the shore where the pirates are being forced back onto their ship. Lawrence takes the last man out himself and brings the landing boat back to shore.

The pirate ship sets sail. As it leaves the small bay, a shroud of fog closes in behind it. The pirates will never find their way back.

> AFTER SUCH A TERRIBLE BATTLE, LAWRENCE
> HAPPILY BEGINS TO MAKE THE LITTLE BOAT
> SEAWORTHY.

Lawrence is mounting a mast on the little boat while groups of women sew his sails. In a short time, they are done and they begin to load supplies onto the boat. When it is all done, Lawrence goes to visit Her Majesty in her pavilion.

He bows deeply to Her Majesty and she gets up from her lounge to greet him.

> **WE SHALL HAVE A FEAST IN YOUR HONOR ON THIS YOUR LAST NIGHT ON OUR FAIR ISLE.**

The women begin to bring out large platters of food and the feast commences. There are lots of festivities. Some women are playing on instruments, some are dancing. There are groups laughing and everyone is having fun. In the center of it all are the Queen and Lawrence quietly sitting close together on a low couch.

After enjoying the festivites and laughing along with the others, the Queen turns maudlin. Lawrence inquires why she is sad. She takes his hand and puts it to her face, overcome with her love for him.

> **DEAR LAWRENCE, I KNOW THAT YOU WANT TO GO BACK TO YOUR OWN PEOPLE, BUT I AM TERRIBLY IN LOVE WITH YOU.**

Her Majesty's declaration moves Lawrence. He takes his hand back, still holding hers, and kisses hers tenderly. He speaks to her, pouring his heart out. No one else seems to notice the two in the center.

> **MADAME, YOU ARE TOO BEAUTIFUL AND TOO KIND. I WOULD BE A LUCKY MAN TO LIVE OUT MY DAYS HERE ON THIS PARADISE ISLAND . . .**

The Queen's face becomes hopeful as she listens to Lawrence speak. Her free hand rises to her breast in anticipation.

> **BUT I CANNOT STAY HERE. I HAVE A HOME AND A FAMILY TO RETURN TO. IT WOULD BE WRONG OF ME TO STAY**

Her Majesty's hand now flies to her forehead as she is close to tears. Lawrence continues to prostrate himself before her, but she won't look at him. Lawrence finally entreats her to look at him. When she finally does, he takes her in his arms and kisses her. Then they both stand and the Queen leads Lawrence away from the party.

On the beach is Lawrence's little boat, a group of women are pushing it into the water.

Lawrence emerges from the foliage with the Queen on his arm. They walk to the boat. He turns to all the women who have gathered on the shore to see him off. He wishes them a hearty farewell and they all wave back to him.

He turns to the Queen, looking deeply into her eyes. He brushes her tears away with his fingertips. They embrace. Lawrence gets into the boat and it is shoved off. He begins to row away, smiling broadly. In just a few strokes the wind picks up his sails and he is carried out of the small bay. The Queen watches in the direction he has gone, long after he has gone out of sight, her eyes bright with tears.

THE END.

Chapter 13

The next morning we arrived early, as usual, and went straight to Mr. Hawthorne's office to sign our contracts. Half an hour later, Dolores and I emerged as professional actresses.

I was the last one to the dressing room that morning, Virginia and the others were already finished and about ready to head out to the set. The last scene to shoot required as many costumed women as possible. The studio was bringing in every woman on the lot today out for this scene.

Norma – Miss Talmadge – was having her make-up done as I came in. After the first few days of filming, she had grown quite warm to those of us who shared the dressing room with her. She had a quick sense of humor and a wonderful smile. Something she rarely did in her pictures since she always played the romantic parts. I was just getting my costume off the rack when she escaped the hands of Minnie and turned to me.

"Maggie dear, I hope you are coming to the party on Saturday." Mr. Schenck, the producer of the picture and Norma's boyfriend, was throwing a huge party down at the Vernon Country Club. Over the course of the last week I'd heard of the party, but I hadn't been invited. I was quite honored to be asked by the hostess herself.

"I'm not sure if I can make it, but I'd like to go," I answered simply, if not plainly.

"Do come if you can. I have a feeling you'll be the belle of the ball." Norma said mysteriously turning back to the mirror. "I've heard already that there a number of men who have their eye on you." She laughed slightly and I blushed profusely. I didn't want to tell her, in case my invitation was revoked, that I would likely be attending with my boyfriend.

Filming went quickly. When we wrapped for the day, Mr. Monroe said we didn't have to come back. The only scenes that remained were some of the pirates and the hero. All the girls ran back to the dressing rooms. I was taken by surprise by the rush, after all we had been let out early. Virginia told me while we changed that the last day of shooting is when the money is paid out. There was going to be a long line for the day girls. Virginia, who was already on contract, didn't realize that my own pay would be coming from there until next week.

Knowing that I would already be at the back of the line, I took my time changing.

Dolores hadn't known what the rush was about either. Or she didn't care, which was a good possibility. She was only the third from the end of the line and when she saw me she let the other two in front of her.

We were both quiet at first, never really having made up from our argument the day before. Then Dolores suggested, "Since we both will be making so much more money now, maybe we should move to a bigger place where we can both have our own rooms."

"Certainly," I answered. This time I felt it was she trying to get rid of me.

"Don't give me that turned up nose of yours," Dolores chided. "Why should we stay crammed up in that attic when we can afford proper rooms?"

I knew what she said made sense, but things were changing so fast, I was beginning to feel overwrought. "Where should we move then?"

"I know a lot of the movie people live at the Hollywood Hotel. We could get rooms there." She suggested. The line inched forward.

"We would be a lot closer to the Chronicle lot if we moved there." I was trying to be reasonable. "But what about Mrs. Haelstrom? We can't just move out on her like this."

"Why don't we pay up for the month. It will give her plenty of time to find someone else." I nodded in agreement. Dolores continued, "What are you going to tell your boss ladies?"

"I don't know." I replied and meant it. I was certain the Miss Tanners would be happy for me, but I was really going to miss them. On the Saturdays I had worked, they had loved hearing the tales I had of the studio lot and shooting the picture. I had been working for them for the better part of a year and they had always been so kind to me. Like aunts, really, both of them. It was foolish of me to be so sad about it. I had a much larger opportunity in front of me, but there was part of me that knew I would never be so proud of a job as I was at the hat shop. That, I found, is the way of the world.

"What will you tell Mr. Stuckey?" I inquired after a reshuffling of the line.

"Oh, you know him, he'll be so happy and supportive." She sighed, "Still, I'll miss the old guy, you know?"

"I know exactly, Dee."

Retrieving our pay for the three weeks work was thrilling. I received $45 for my work and Dolores got $30. We felt rich. In many ways we were.

Later that afternoon, after buying some new clothes, Dolores and I went our separate ways. We agreed that we would move out the next day. Del was due back in town the next afternoon and I wanted to surprise him with all the news that had happened in his absence.

Dolores, I suspected, had a rendevous planned with one of her beaux. I intended to resign from my job at the hat shop, but needed a bit of time to steel my nerves. I knew it shouldn't have been such a big deal, but the gratitude I felt for the Miss Tanners made me really regret having to leave them. My worries, as usual, turned out to be unwarranted. Both women were delighted with my prospects.

"Just to think, our little Magda will be in the flickers," Miss Tanner beamed.

"Well, she's beautiful enough, Auntie," Miss Jennifer returned. I grew shy from their praise. "And don't you dare worry about us."

"She better not," Miss Tanner continued, turning to me, "Especially if you keep sending your movie friends in for hats." I smiled at them both.

All the hats I wore came from the shop and were all custom made – not for me, but I bought cheaply the hats that had mistakes. The girls on the lot had all loved the hats I wore and I, of course, had sent them to the hat shop.

"Of course I will. Now I can be a customer too," we all laughed.

Dolores didn't come home that night. The next morning she came in while I was packing. I didn't even bother asking her where she had been. I knew she would tell me only if she wanted. My asking would make no difference. She didn't tell me.

At dinner the night before, I had told Mrs. Haelstrom about our decision to move. As befitted her kindly nature, she was both very happy for us and sad to see us go. I paid her for the remaining part of the month, just a week or so. We were free to go.

I finished packing long before Dolores. While she worked on her own luggage I asked her if she had told Mr. Stuckey.

"Aye, I did yesterday," she answered with a tiny bit of regret in her voice. "He was so happy for us. You know what he said?"

I shook my head no.

"He said he would only play movies from Chronicle Films now that we were going to be big stars. He wants to show off that he knew us first." She made a slight choking sound, a hiccup or a stifled sob. I would have sworn it was the latter, but her eyes were dry. Mr. Stuckey had been good to her, good to us both, my chest ached that we wouldn't be seeing him so often any longer, if we saw him at all. He was the first to befriend me when I had first come to Los Angeles so many months before. It seemed like I had known him for much longer.

Mrs. Haelstrom telephoned for a taxicab. She gave us both bear hugs and cheek kisses and admonished us to "be good." The cab loaded, we climbed in and watched as our safe, comfortable house was left behind.

Arriving at the Hollywood Hotel we took two rooms that were joined by an interior door. With the connecting door it was like we had one large room. We began unpacking immediately, enjoying our spacious and fancy new environment. We laughed and joked as we went about our business, not touching any topics that would cause an argument.

By five o'clock we were finally settled in. Dolores picked up a large bag, straightened her dress and headed for the door. I tried to act like I didn't notice. I concentrated on folding my underclothes, pursing my lips in silence. With her hand on the doorknob, Dolores looked back at me. "I don't mean to keep anything from you. I'm just scared and I don't want to jinx things by telling you my plans." She opened the door, but didn't go out. "I'm sorry. I'll see you at the party tomorrow night, right?"

I didn't look at her, though I could see her from my side vision. I nodded as she left. Her behavior towards me was shocking. As close as we were, it came as a blow to me and I didn't know how to handle it.

But my attention was soon diverted. Del was to have arrived in town that afternoon and I meant to surprise him.

I went down to the lobby and asked Miss Hershey, the spinster who managed the hotel, about the use of the public phone. She looked at me severely through her thick spectacles before pointing down the hallway to the kitchen.

"That phone is for public use. Please don't be long as there may be others who want to use it." I looked around the empty lobby waiting for one of those others to appear. Miss Hershey went back to her account books.

I called the operator and asked for the Alexandria Hotel. Once I got put through, I asked the hotel operator for Del's room. We had made plans before he left to meet that night.

"Hello?" said his familiar voice on the other end of the line.

"Hello Del, it's me."

"Maggie? It's so good to hear your voice. We're still on for tonight, aren't we?"

"Of course!" I replied hastily. "There is a change in plans though. Could you pick me up at the Hollywood Hotel? Ask for Maggie Savoy." I suppressed a giggle.

"What? What happened, are you ..." I cut him off.

"I'll tell you all about in a few hours. See you then." I hung up the phone. I thought a little suspense never hurt anyone. Plus, I was delighted to be able to surprise him with such good news.

I went back up to my room and got ready. At just before seven, I went down to the lobby. Del was usually very punctual, so I wanted to make sure I was earlier than he was. I sat in the sitting room just off the main entrance. In not too many minutes, I heard his familiar step at the door and then heard him get Miss Hershey's attention and ask for Maggie Savoy.

Before Miss Hershey had a chance to respond, I walked into the entrance lobby. Del turned immediately and saw me.

"Maggie!" he came to me and leaned in to kiss me, but Miss Hershey's stare of indignation weighed heavily on us, so instead he kissed my cheek and offered me his arm.

"Thank you," I said accepting the offer. We walked out nobly as if we were King and Queen of the place. Just outside and to the left of the entrance windows, Del stopped and kissed me deeply. An old woman and her husband were just passing as he did it and I saw the woman's face shocked with scandal.

We didn't speak much as we got in the car and drove off. I was too happy to see him. My good news seemed insignificant by then. He took me to Levy's for dinner and we got a quiet table in the back. After ordering drinks, he took my hand in his. For a little while we just looked at each other. As corny as it sounds, it was deeply satisfying and comforting. Finally, he broke the silence.

"Tell me everything, Maggie Savoy," he said with a wide grin.

He was excited by my news about being cast in *The Siren's Song*. It was gratifying to me, above and beyond what I already felt, because now he was excited too.

"Enough about me," I declared, "Tell me how you've been. What have you been doing? You won't have to leave again soon right?" and then with mock anger I added "You've better not been flirting with any pretty girls."

A number of emotions flickered across Del's face. He leaned back in his chair and said "What if I have? What would you do?"

I sat up straight, putting my hands on my hips and screwing up my face, as if in anger. "I'd lock you in a basement so you couldn't do it again!" Then I laughed. I couldn't keep up the charade for more than a few seconds. At the time, I could never have been angry with Del.

He laughed along too. "If only you could," he said half under his breath as the waiter arrived with our dinner.

"Really Del, you won't have to leave again soon?" I asked again, timidly, as if I were scared of the answer.

"No, not for several months at least." He gave smiled at me, but it was not very reassuring. For awhile at least, I had him and that is all I wanted.

Del dropped me off early that night. He'd been traveling for several days and was exhausted. He agreed to go with me to Mr. Schenck's party. I found myself looking forward to it.

The next morning, feeling lonely after waking up in a new place all alone, I decided to treat myself to a new dress for the party. It felt good to be an independent woman of some means.

I headed for the best shopping in town, down at the brand new Ville de Paris department store on Olive and 7th Streets. I had seen a dress there some months before when the store had just opened that would be perfect. I just hoped that it was still there.

The streetcar ride from Hollywood took a long time. It gave me a solid half hour to do nothing but stare out the window and think – something I'd had little time to do in the last few months.

The tension between myself and Dolores still stung, especially having woken up without her – something that hadn't happened often since I'd come to Los Angeles. I was probably worrying for nothing, making more of our argument than was warranted. And while I was extremely excited about my new prospects, I was apprehensive. What would happen when my mother found out? When both of our mothers found out? With our faces looming large on screens across the country, I wouldn't imagine that my mother would not find out.

Del and I would get married in a year, maybe less. Then things would be all right. My mother wouldn't be able to resist a young man who was rich, of a good family and handsome. She would have to accept me for myself then, I hoped.

My thinking was circular that morning and I always came back to thinking about Papa. He would be overjoyed at our new prospects. I think he would buy a projector and set up his own screening room. Then he would invite everyone he knew, friend and foe alike, to show off his granddaughters. I hoped he would be proud of me.

That half-hour streetcar ride may have been the longest I had experienced, as heavy as my thoughts were that morning. Finally I arrived in the main part of the city and spent as much money as I chose.

By the time Del picked me up that night, I was feeling much better. I felt pretty in my new dress – it was a gauzy mauve with sequins sewn along the hems – and was really looking forward to the party. While waiting for me in the lobby, Del had so charmed Miss Hershey that her attitude was completely changed. When Del leaned in to kiss me on the cheek, Miss Hershey now looked on with approval. I marveled at his ability to charm even a fussy old woman like her.

The party was being held in the main ballroom of the stylish club. As soon as we walked in the door of the party, I saw Virginia. She was standing near the dance floor talking with two other girls, but as soon as she saw me, she came right over.

"Maggie, you made it. And who is this handsome man?" Virginia openly and obviously looked Del over. Had I not known her before-hand, I would have been completely affronted. Virginia was as bold as she was thoughtful.

I introduced Del as my fiancé. Saying that he was just a boy-friend made him seem too inconsequential, or maybe it made me seem that way. It very much impressed Virginia, for her eyes widened in amazement for a second before she again started flirting with him – although in a much more subdued manner.

Del took my announcement in stride and didn't even blink. My heart swelled so much that I felt it would burst. He really did want to marry me, enough that I could announce it to my friends.

The ballroom was decorated extravagantly with red velvet draper-ies and crystal chandeliers. Not very many people were there as of yet, but it was pleasant enough talking with Virginia and her friends. Del almost immediately found some friends of his own and left me to be social with my new coworkers. I spoke with Norma and was introduced to Joseph Schenck, the producer of our film and Norma's fiancé. He was a very kind and gentle man, although not so handsome as Norma. I also met Norma's mother, Peg, and younger sister, Natalie. As the evening wore on, I did my very best not to become star struck. David Griffith came to talk with Mr. Schenck while I was being introduced. I saw Mack Sennett with Mabel Normand on his arm. Norma, who was so friendly and sweet, made me feel right at home. Although I think that if I had seen Mary Pickford or Lillian Gish I would have fainted right in the middle of the room. Fortunately for me, neither of them appeared.

I was on the lookout, from the moment that I arrived, for Dolores. Upset with her as I was, I couldn't help but worry. An hour or more after I had arrived, she finally made her entrance. And a grand entrance at that. She came through the doors on the arm of Mr. Monroe, as I half expected she would, in a gorgeous satin and fur get-up that I couldn't believe. Mr. Monroe looked as if it were commonplace for him to appear with a stunningly beautiful woman on his arm – and that very likely may well have been. However Dolores beamed a smile so bright as if to show every other woman there that she had trumped them all.

Virginia, who I was standing next to at the time, nearly choked on her drink and I heard one of her friends gasp in shock. Charlie, who was chatting up one of Virginia's girlfriends, gave a start, his eyes wide. I gave Virginia a questioning look.

"You knew about this?" Virginia asked me. I shook my head no. "That man screws any woman who'll lay down long enough, but has never, ever been seen with one on his arm."

I had my suspicions about Mr. Monroe, but it didn't seem all that shocking that he should bring Dolores as his date. Virginia, seeing that I didn't quite grasp the nuance of their appearance, continued.

"Either your cousin has some dirt on Monroe, or he actually likes her." I nodded my head understanding a little better, trying to look concerned, but all the time bursting my heart with pride in my beautiful cousin. If anyone could tame a womanizer, it would be she.

Dolores sought me out after she had made the rounds of the party on the arm of the most distinguished director in Hollywood. She drew me away from the group I was talking with. Embracing me, she apologized for her recent behavior.

"I'm so sorry primita, but I was too worried that if I didn't play my cards right I wouldn't get him."

"You could have told me," I spoke in Spanish, since it was a very private conversation we were having. Dolores held her hand up for me to stop and looked around us worriedly.

"Not in front of other people Magda. Do you want them to think we are Mexican or something?" My mouth dropped open out of sheer shock. "Don't stand there gaping" Dolores said and pulled me out into the hallway.

"Dolores! We are Mexican." I stammered at her.

"I know. I know, but everyone out there doesn't need to." She gestured towards the ballroom. I glared at her. "Come on Magdalena, don't look at me like that!"

I was so angry with Dolores right at that moment, that it was all I could do to only glare at her. Dolores took my arm by the elbow and gave it a little squeeze.

"Don't be mad at me. I just want to make this a fresh start . . . for both of us. If we go out there speaking Spanish it will just make us different. This is my chance to fit in. Our chance."

"You practically abandoned me this week to get into Mr. Monroe's good graces and now you don't want to be Papa's granddaughter?"

Dolores frowned. Her eyes became bright with tears. "Don't say that to me. I'm doing what I can."

I knew it was true and I also knew that this was a fresh start for her, but I was too cross to just let it go. I told her so.

"I don't blame you. It's just the way it turned out. I won't do it again. I'll never leave you out like that. I promise." She looked at me hopefully.

"You were forgiven before you started, but I'm still mad." I remember my tone of voice sounded shockingly like my mother's. That just made me angrier. "Let's get back to the party. We can talk tomorrow." I turned to go back in the double doors and said, with my back to her, half-scared of her answer, "You will be around tomorrow . . ."

"Probably not until the afternoon, but I will be there tomorrow."

The rest of the party passed uneventfully enough. It was great fun and towards the end of the night a couple of the guests got quite inebriated and were making speeches from the table tops. Del and I were some of the first to leave as we still hadn't been alone together since he had returned. He was a comfort to me. I was still upset about Dolores, but Del made me feel as if everything would be all right.

Dolores did return late the next morning and we made amends – as much as we could.

The rest of Sunday flew by and before I knew it, Monday morning had arrived. Our first official day of work. Dolores and I held hands in excitement as we pushed open the gate to the lot. We arrived at 8 o'clock sharp and went to the casting office for our assignments. Mrs. Mercer, the office secretary, was surprised to see us so early.

I was to begin work on the next Kingston Sam comedy, as Mr. Hawthorne had told me. What he had neglected to tell me was that no Kingston Sam picture ever started filming before noon. The great comedian was too used to his old schedule of playing vaudeville and couldn't be moved out of bed before 11:30 and a pot of tea.

"Do you think you could come back after luncheon? Maybe about 1 o'clock?" Mr. Hawthorne asked me nicely.

"Of course," I replied, but what else could I have said. I waited to see what assignment Mr. Hawthorne had for Dolores, but it wasn't any more interesting. Mr. Hawthorne assigned Dolores to the costume department for the day. He didn't have any roles for her and the seamstresses were working on the costumes for a historical picture and needed as many models as they could get.

Dolores and I each parted with a sigh. So much for the glamourous world of movie making. I headed out the studio gates. I hadn't taken any breakfast. I walked down Hollywood Boulevard avoiding the ankle-deep puddles that lined the misnamed street. It was no wide grand boulevard as it is today. At a nearby newsstand, I bought a daily paper and a lady's magazine. I found a small diner to have breakfast.

On time, I returned to the studio. This time I found a ruckus taking place in the foyer just outside Mr. Hawthorne's office door. The scene I came upon could have been a movie, except for all the yelling and shrieking, issuing mostly from a woman. I had seen her in Kingston Sam movies before, but I didn't know her name. She was beautiful in a full-bodied feminine way. She was pacing up the floor shouting at Mr. Hawthorne and Kingston Sam who sat in a chair elegantly sipping a cup of tea. He was quite ignoring the angry woman.

I didn't know if I should intrude upon the scene or come back later. Before I decided, the woman saw me and began to take her fury out on me.

"That is the one, isn't it?" she said hysterically. "How could you possibly think that something as slight and insignificant as that could take my place? Its absolutely ridiculous. More funny than your last three pictures!"

Mr. Hawthorne was trying to calm her with soft shushing sounds. Kingston Sam continued to ignore her. Ignore everyone, actually. He took no notice of Mr. Hawthorne nor me. After a few more vile remarks about Kingston Sam's talent and my looks, the woman stormed off, slamming the door on a set as a final exclamation mark.

Mr. Hawthorne, already a nervous man, wiped his forehead with a shaky hand. I was still standing twenty feet away, not having moved since the woman began yelling at me. Mr. Hawthorne turned and said a few quiet words to Kingston Sam, then turned to me.

"My dear Miss Maggie, I apologize that you had to witness that scene. Unfortunately, Miss Beard didn't approve of our choice for Kingston Sam's new picture, but we are both confident that you are the best choice for the part." As he was speaking to me and walking towards me, Kingston Sam stood and walked away – never taking a glance at me.

"No need to apologize, Mr. Hawthorne. I can see that Miss Beard was just upset." Mr. Hawthorne smiled with relief, then explained that the players were gathering on Set 1 and gave me directions.

I was very nervous as I stepped into the large, open room. A group of players were assembled, some sitting on chairs and tables, a few sitting on the floor. All of them were watching the two men in the center of the room performing a funny dance. The performers had their back to me and were between me and the assembled group. I went in as quietly as possible, but everyone turned their attention on me. I must have looked very timid and troubled for Kingston Sam turned from his dance to welcome me. He walked over to me with his arms outstretched and said, "There's our new girl."

I began to smile when Kingston Sam stepped up to me and kissed me deeply on the mouth. Our audience roared in laughter. I felt my face turn red. It must have been very dark for I heard someone say quietly that I'd need a lot of face powder to be seen on film.

Without another word Kingston Sam ushered me over to the group and pulled out a chair for me. He took a sheaf of papers off a table and handed them me. In his Scots-Irish brogue, he announced, "Everyone, this is Maggie. She'll be the shop girl. Maggie, this is everyone. Why don't you read over that scenario. Me and Jonny are practicing our pratfalls."

I looked at "everyone" and tried to smile with more confidence than I felt. Kingston Sam and Jonny started in on a comedy routine.

The way they moved seemed like a complicated dance that entailed some flips and lots of falls. The two men moved effortlessly, but what they were doing seemed very physically demanding. I'd never noticed it in the comedies reels they starred in, but Kingston Sam and his sidekick Jonny were very athletic.

As they were practicing their moves, now and then someone from the group would call out an idea or an instruction or even an improvement on what they were doing. Immediately, many times without even acknowledging that anything had been said, the two men would incorporate the suggestion into what they were doing. I became very impressed at their abilities. No wonder Kingston Sam was such a popular vaudeville performer.

I read over the scenario – the narrative of the picture we were to shoot. It was to take place in a department store. Kingston Sam and Jonny were janitors for the store and I was the counter girl with whom they were both in love. The scenario was very short, I assumed because they didn't write out all the comedy gags that were to take place to keep the story moving. At the end, Kingston Sam saves the girl from a robber using a broomstick and wins her heart. My heart.

I didn't think much of my acting skills as it was, but I was certain I was no comedienne. I hoped that Kingston Sam was so much of a comedian that he could bring out a funny side to me.

Filming didn't get started until several hours later. After Kingston Sam and Jonny finished their practice, the set had to be put up and the cameras placed. The familiar face of Charlie appeared through the doorway in the middle of the setting up, and I was very happy to see it. He told me he had been assigned to be assistant director to Kingston Sam. I didn't understand what the job entailed, so Charlie told me.

"Ol' Sam can't direct himself if he's in a scene, so I will call out directions to him and you other actors as needed." It made perfect sense once he explained it to me.

I was sent to wardrobe to get suited up in an costume more appropriate to a lower-class working girl. I laughed to myself as I went through the courtyard to the dressing area. Not a week ago, I had been a poor working girl. I ran into Dolores in the dressing room. She was made up to look like an angel. She looked beautiful in the flowing robes and her dark hair loose around her face. She was being fitted and the seamstress had pinned her all over, so she couldn't move without being pricked. We waved at each other and I explained, to both her and the seamstress, why I'd been sent over.

"What's he like, Cousin?" Dolores asked of Kingston Sam while the seamstress draped some dark fabric over her shoulder.

"He's dramatic," was all I could think to say about him without explaining how he greeted me. I would have gladly told Dolores, but I was too embarrassed to tell the story in front of a stranger.

Once I was fitted up, she walked back with me to the set. I told her about my introduction to the company and she nearly collapsed in laughter. It was much funnier explaining it than experiencing it.

The filming went well and was loads of fun. I found that to be the straight-faced person in a comedy was not so different than being in a drama, except that I had to keep a straight face. Every time I was having a romantic scene with one of my "suitors" the other one was sure to be off camera making faces at me. The first day was the worst. I was very much surprised that I wasn't thrown off the set. I think King and Jonny loved that I laughed so easily, after all, they were comedians and this was their milieu.

We finished filming on Thursday and I found that Mr. Hawthorne had already filled out a schedule for me to last a month. By the end of the week, Dolores had been assigned to another drama. This time she was the jealous, naughty sister of the leading lady. I watched her film many of the scenes and she was spectacular as the villainess. Her wicked grin, the one she wore when she was being mischievous, was perfect for the part.

Chapter 14

The weeks sped by. During the day, my work schedule was always full. I spent nearly every night with Del, going to parties and meeting with friends. The quiet life I had led until then vanished in a blink. All of a sudden, I wasthrown into a busy, social lifestyle that sometimes was too much for me. Del was a darling. He was so proud of his "cinema star," proud of me.

Within a month of the release of The Siren's Song, I was being recognized on the street, in restaurants, everywhere. It didn't happen too often, thank heavens. Del would beam when I would be recognized in public, loving the attention. I was very nervous when a stranger would greet me and tell me how much they liked me. It was disconcerting, really.

Most of the people who came up to me were girls, not so dissimilar from myself. Each of them would be excited to meet me, some more timid and others more bold. I tried my best to be open and friendly, although my primary instinct was to run away. Every time I felt like turning and running, I could imagine Papa standing behind me giving my shoulder a nudge forward. He would be saying "Go along Magda, you're a brave girl." He would have been like Del – proud of me and the attention I was receiving.

Dolores became a big hit too. After the release of Eleanor Straight and True, the drama where she played the villainess, she began to be recognized as well. Unlike me, she took the attention in stride. She lapped it up, encouraged it. A few times when we were out together and either of us was recognized, Dolores would encourage conversation with the person. If it was a man, she'd flirt cleverly. When it was a woman, she would charm them in a more subdued way.

Of all the actors and actresses I met, very few of them had the same personality off screen as they had on. Dolores was one of the few. Many of the best dramatic players, were lively and funny off-screen like Norma. The same with action stars and others. Only Douglas Fairbanks was the same person all the time. But Doug never claimed he could act, either. Dolores was as vivacious on camera or off and I think it delighted her fans. She never disappointed them.

As we became well-known we both hid our fear of being caught-out by our families. She and I only spoke of it once in passing, both of us trying to play it off. Yet, I believe that it was Dolores's main source of anxiety, for she had so much more to lose than I, having had no contact with her family in at least three years.

I rarely saw Dolores outside the studio. She spent, perhaps, one or two nights a week in her room at the Hollywood Hotel. I was constantly having to make excuses to Miss Hershey for Dolores's absences. I told her Dolores had a sick mother that she often attended. Miss Hershey, I'm sure, had other suspicions. She was always cold and prim with me, but Del made her laugh like a school girl. I think if it weren't for his continual presence, she would have kicked me out soon after my arrival.

Dolores was, for all intents and purposes, living with Monroe. It was the talk of all the film companies that Monroe had settled for one girl. I also heard that there was a rather large gambling pool being organized as to how long it would last. I hoped Dolores didn't know about that as well.

She never said much to me about her relationship with Monroe. She never told me if she really did like him, or if she was in it for the status it gave her. Not that it would be anything she would admit, even if she were. I knew that Monroe was completely smitten with her from a conversation I had with him several weeks after their grand appearance at Joe Schenck's big party.

One weekend Del and I went to see the fights out at the Vernon Country Club. I wasn't much of an afficionado of the sport, but that was where the social scene was taking place that weekend. Del, of course, loved boxing and was glad it had turned into a social spectacle.

Marcus Loew, the movie theater mogul, had reserved a private room where his personal friends could relax. About 500 people were crammed into a small ballroom to enjoy the party. Early on I had stationed myself on a couch and I planned to stay there the whole night. Del would always be able to find me that way and I wouldn't have to elbow my way around the room.

As the night wore on there was a constant parade of friends and acquaintances who dropped by the couch to rest and chat. I felt like the queen bee perched on my thrown and was having a marvelous time. At some point I was sitting next to a very quiet man named Mr. Clayton who I understood to be a financier of several studios. We were talking politely when Monroe joined us on the couch, sitting between us both. He had a few words with the financier before we were joined by some more friends. We were all having a pleasant, yet loud, conversation about Monroe's latest film project.

About then the main event was announced and the room cleared considerably. Abandoned by our small group, Monroe turned his attention to me. The room was nearly empty, so we could speak in lower voices. A point which I appreciated as Monroe began to speak of Dolores. It consisted mostly of his praise for her.

"That cousin of yours is a grand girl. You know she made me wait weeks before she slept with me? No girl has ever done that." At this turn in the conversation, I tried to mask my horror with a straight face. Monroe was taking no notice of me, I believe, so I could have been openly offended instead of trying to cover it up. "Smart and sassy is how I like them, and that Dottie has it all plus an unbelievable ass."

I really was offended. He was talking to me as an intimate male acquaintance. I think I was nodding while he talked, the whole time I was wishing myself far, far away. He kept on in the same manner for a few sentences longer. Fortunately, the fight was over quickly for people began streaming back into the ballroom. Del sought me out right away.

At least, from our too intimate conversation, I knew that Monroe really did have a sincere interest in Dolores. I hoped that they could make their affair work. Dolores seemed to be very interested in him, and I wanted her to find a man who would do right by her.

After a month on contract, Dolores and I were cast in the same film as sisters. We were cast as the daughters of a rancher in a Western called *The True-Hearted Cowboy*, roles that were not so far from the truth.

We were filming on location at the site of an old adobe farmhouse in the San Fernando Valley. Dolores was originally cast as the lead sister, but when the director, Ferdinand Kranz, found out that I was an experienced rider, he switched our parts. Dolores wasn't too upset. She got to play the bad sister and had some excellent scenes in which to have fun "doing wrong."

The picture was meant to be a western and was being directed by the upcoming director Ferdy Kranz. He had worked as Monroe's cameraman before branching out into Westerns. The story goes that Monroe was asked to make a series of Westerns – a genre that he detested – and he gave his best cameraman the job. In the year since Ferdy started directing, he hadn't had a flop.

The hero of the picture was Floyd Howard, the famous horseman. He had gotten his start in the very early days of motion pictures when they still filmed the "wild west" in the untamed forests of New Jersey. He was a great deal older than I was, not very tall, but handsome in a toughened way. I had loved his films growing up – the few that I saw. Even on the screen, I could tell how much he knew about riding and horses. To me, his Westerns were always the most accurate.

In person he didn't make much of an impression. At least not like Kingston Sam. I'd met him socially once or twice during the month that I had been working at the studio and I hadn't taken too much notice of him. When I met him again on the first day of filming, I was very daunted. He had a gravity about him that was easy to overlook in a large crowd. He had pale blue eyes that were both laughing and sad. I soon found in him a kindred spirit.

The filming was only meant to take a week, but due to some stormy weather, none of the interior scenes could be shot. By that time, I was very much used to all the waiting involved in shooting pictures. Dolores spent her extra time joking with the filming crew or taking naps. I got to know my co-star Floyd.

I made good use of the extra time we had on that picture. In the year since I'd left home, I had hardly had a chance to be around horses, only a couple of visits to Del's sporting club. While growing up, my horse Bailey, a handsome roan, had always been a huge part of my daily activities. I had found that I missed my horse more than my family. On that first picture I made with Floyd and Ferdy, I spent hours riding around the location. And when the weather was too inclimate, I would work with the horses in the stable. I got to be close friends with the horse trainers as well as Floyd.

Floyd was famous for the love he had for his horse and was constantly working with her, training her for tricks and stunts. He worked with some of the other horses as well, but his heart belonged to Black Baby, his personal horse.

One rainy afternoon I was helping to brush down the horses when he came up to the stable fence. "I see you sit a good mount on your horse."

I hadn't noticed him behind me and jumped a little when he broke my concentration. "I have been riding all my life," was my reply.

"I see," he drawled slowly. "Ever do any rodeo riding, trick riding?"

I continued to work on the horse, a large Appaloosa mare. "No one would ever teach me. I grew up on a ranch so I learned to ride cattle and trails. My mother thought it was unbecoming and made me learn what she called proper equestrian with an English saddle and proper clothing." I stood up and looked at him. "I was never any good at that."

Floyd grinned back at me. "How'd you like to learn now?" We spent the next day and a half working on the moving mount and some other very fun tricks. It was Floyd's idea that for the rescue scene in the film instead of having the hero bring his horse to a full stop, he could catch up the girl as the horse ran. He was teaching me that trick.

First he had to teach me the trick of swinging off the horse at a full run, hitting the ground, and rebounding into the saddle. I must say, that it was exhausting work. By the end of the first day I was sore from head to toe, sore in the head from taking a fall off Black Baby. By the middle of the next day I had fairly managed the trick. Floyd told me it was one of the hardest maneuvers to master for it involved strength, balance and lots of concentration. If you weren't completely focused on making it work, you could easily miss your footing and be flung from the horse. Unfortunately, that happened to me several times before I finally got the hang of it. I never did it very prettily, but I could do it.

The trick we were going to use on the film was similar, but instead of coming off the side of the horse to rebound up, I had to jump up into the saddle, being pulled by Floyd. After a few practice sessions, Floyd and I got the hang of it. Ferdy couldn't have been more pleased by the new choreography. After all it was an action film and this new maneuver would add a lot to the excitement of the picture.

The filming, I think, went particularly well. Of the films I worked on, it was one of my favorite to watch. After that first Western, I made several more pictures with Floyd as my costar and Ferdy as our director. Floyd once even played my father! Maybe it was the horses, with the addition of a gifted co-star and excellent director, but those were the films I most loved to make.

Floyd and I became close friends. He didn't like the shallow atmosphere that surrounded much of the picture industry in Los Angeles and spent his free time on a small ranch he had bought just over the hill from Hollywood. Knowing my love for horse riding, he would invite me over now and then for a long ride through the hills where he lived. It was the one thing I did without Del or Dolores. Floyd's steadiness and the Southern California scenery did a lot to make me feel grounded. I missed my childhood home, sometimes very dearly, but riding out with Floyd returned some of it to me.

A few months after I signed my contract with Chronicle Film Company, I received an offer from a rival company. It wasn't a proper offer, more of a hint that I could make more money if I broke contract with Chronicle. I paid no attention to it, but a few days later Mr. Griply, with a face that looked like he had smelled something rotten, told me that Mr. Hawthorne wanted to see me in his office.

"Miss Maggie, I understand the California Film Cooperative has offered to make you a better contract," he began.

I was surprised that he knew. I stammered out, "Well, not an official offer."

"But they have intimated that they would like to hire you away?" I nodded in agreement. Mr. Hawthorne bounced his fist off of the desk. "I knew it. Have you considered it?"

"Well, there has been nothing as yet to consider."

"But you would consider it?" Silence fell heavy as I weighed my answer carefully. I had never thought to consider accepting an offer from another film company, but Mr. Hawthorne clearly thought I would. He answered himself before I could frame a proper answer. "Of course you would. You'd be a simpleton to pass by more money."

Mr. Hawthorne's answer was certainly reasonable. I remained quiet while Mr. Hawthorne leaned back in his chair in thought. After a few minutes consideration he leaned forward again with a new proposal for me. "My dear Miss Maggie. I don't generally make offers like this, but I would hate for you to think you are not well treated here at Chronicle Film Company. How about we increase your contract to one hundred twenty five dollars a week? How would that be?"

I readily accepted. I would hate for Mr. Hawthorne to think me a simpleton for denying his generous offer. I could not help myself from inquiring if Dolores would be receiving a similar offer. Mr. Hawthorne's replied was full of implied meaning, "Miss Dottie? I don't think she will be having a financial difficulties any time soon."

I was astounded to find, when our interview was over, that without saying much of anything I had come away nearly one hundred dollars a week wealthier. To me that was about as much money as I would ever need.

It wasn't long after my new contract that Del brought up the idea of moving to a place for myself. Miss Hershey's watchful eye was becoming bothersome to both of us. I loved the idea of an apartment for myself. Living on my own would give Del and me more opportunities to be alone.

I thought I would begin by seeking a flat in Stephanie's building, at least then I would have a friendly neighbor. There was nothing suitable in her building. Del and I toured several apartments before getting frustrated. They were all either too small or awkwardly constructed. One that I really liked was too far from Chronicle studios to be sensible. Others were monitored by women very much like Miss Hershey. I just wanted a nice living environment where Del could come and go as he pleased.

It was a nearing the holidays when Del picked me up for dinner with some interesting news. "You know that man I do business with, Dan Forther? He told me he's selling his house. His wife wants to move back East." Del was driving down Sunset Boulevard behind a slow moving streetcar. He looked over at me quickly. I was all ears wondering what it had to do with me. "It's a fairly new house near Echo Park. I have been thinking that it would be a wonderful house for you to buy."

"Buy? I couldn't possibly buy a house!" I was astounded that he would even think it a prospect.

"Listen for a second before you decide anything." We were now past the streetcar and flying down the boulevard. He risked another look at me. "You are making enough money now to buy whatever you want. I could help out too." I smiled at him, despite my misgivings. "It would be good for you to have a place of your own. You know what I mean? A home for you and me."

"You make it sound so easy." I told him.

"It is easy. A house could give us time alone that we can't get elsewhere." He reached across and squeezed my hand. "If you want, we can go see it now."

The house was in a development, barely a year old, just south of Sunset Boulevard on one of the winding streets leading away from Echo Park Lake. We parked at the top of Kelam Street. The house was one story and tucked up against a hillside. It had a lovely view of the basin below, although houses were starting to be built below it which would one day obscure much of the view. It was a nice looking house without being too fancy. Once inside I saw that the Forther's had decorated the inside more elaborately than what was appropriate for the style of the place. I could see that the house had potential to be quite lovely.

After we left, Del spent the evening encouraging me to accept the offer from the Forther's. It was a good price, I was told, but I hesitated at making such a large step on my own. Later that night, on my own in my room at the Hollywood Hotel, I decided that Dolores should go in with me. Even if she and Monroe lived together at his home, it would give her a home of her own as well.

It turned out that my plan was perfect for Dolores as well. Monroe objected to openly living with one another and marriage was not in the plan for the time being. Miss Hershey threatened to throw Dolores out of the Hotel anytime she saw her. We both worried that one day she would carry it through. A house of our own would give us both the full-range of freedoms we craved.

Dolores didn't have the ready funds to pay her half, but Monroe graciously supplied her part. I was suspicious that he was so ready to get her a place of her own. Even though I could see that he was still very much enamored of Dolores, I didn't trust his plans concerning her. Dolores was oblivious to any worries of mine.

We made the deal for the house and were able to move in just after the new year. Along with the house, the Forther's had sold to us many of the larger items of furniture so I didn't have to buy all new things. I didn't realize how many things went into making a house liveable. Del was a sweetheart, as usual, and bought half the wares at the Grand Central Market. Before I had been there a week, my kitchen and living room were fitted up and ready to live in.

I found that I really enjoyed having my own home to go home to at night. It was a safe and comforting feeling. As things turned out, it was a blessing that I moved into the house when I did. Dolores had only been in there two or three times to get her bedroom arranged, but hadn't stayed the night, when she was injured on the set of a picture.

Dolores was working on a comedy for director Henry Fitzpatrick. It was a slapstick comedy. The heroine, Dolores, was being chased by several men who had mistakenly drunk a love potion. The scene in which she was injured called for her to jump out of second floor window and land on a moving cart. The way it was to be filmed had Dolores jumping out of the window and being caught below. That film was to be spliced with another bit of Dolores landing in the cart. Unfortunately, the three men below the second floor window were not too steady on their feet and didn't fully catch her. From what I heard, she landed hard on the ground, as one of the men had let slip his side of the mat that was to catch her. I had thought it rather brave of her to do her own stunts. You would never have caught me jumping from a window.

At first it was thought that she had broken her ankle, but it turned out to be a really bad sprain. From the hospital she was moved home, to my home, where she ordered a dozen gorgeous dressing gowns and set-up in her bedroom to entertain visitors.

The three weeks that she had to remain off her feet were both fun and trying. My house became filled with people. It seemed that all parties had been moved to my house to accommodate Dolores's injury. Monroe was often attending on Dolores. Del and Dolores both loved all the people and parties. I couldn't wait to be alone. I found myself taking long solitary walks as I used to do when I first moved to the city. Those long walks kept my nerves from fizzling.

One Sunday, Mr. Stuckey, having read about the accident in the newspaper, brought his projector and spent the afternoon showing us pictures. I hadn't seen the final cut of The True-Hearted Cowboy, so he showed us that one too.

Dolores healed up just in time for one of the big social events of the year. Although, I'm sure she would have faked being healed in order to make the party. The Million Dollar Theater on Broadway and 2nd Street, Mr. Loew's latest grand theater and the biggest and fanciest of its kind anywhere, opened up its doors that February and everybody who was anybody was there. Taking center stage was Mack Sennett, since he'd talked Mr. Loew into premiering his latest picture on opening night. Dolores told me that Monroe was fuming over being upstaged.

As movie premieres were getting larger and the theaters to show them in kept growing too, more and more photographers and journalists showed up for what used to be very low-key parties for the people who made the pictures. Both Dolores and I made the society pages in the papers the next day. A photographer had taken a wonderfully candid picture of us as we made our entrance to the theater.

Once Dolores was back on her feet she was back at Monroe's house. I was never quite sure why she hadn't set up there to recuperate from her injury in the first place. It seemed silly to me that she didn't. Everyone knew that she and Monroe lived together. However, I was not privy to such intimate details of their relationship and just had to accept it as it was.

Both of us were really busy at the studio. I may have been the first to become well-known, but Dolores was rapidly becoming a huge star. Dolores was cast in lots of dramatic roles. Her wide eyes and composed face were perfect for those drawn out close-ups of the heroine in trouble. She did a lot of costume dramas, which I happened to know she loved. She adored dressing up, being someone completely different.

I preferred to do westerns and comedies, especially if I got to be the straight character. We each made about two films a month. Many times I was in six or eight pictures a month, but only starring in two. Whenever we were needed, we both played bit parts and background characters. It was incredible, back then, how easily pictures were made. Someone would have an idea, someone would hack out a scenario, and soon after we would start filming. Easy as pie.

THE TRUE-HEARTED COWBOY

Directed by Ferdinand Kranz
Scenario by William B. Hartfirth

CHRONICLE FILM COMPANY

List of Players
Bill — Floyd Howard
Ellie — Maggie Savoy
Millie — Dottie Sparks
Rancher Sam — Pat Chrisman
Mr. Henry — Bob Fleming
Mr. Henry's son, Jack — Donald Curtiss
Mother — Enid Markey
Stable boy — Lewis Sargent

SCENARIO

The sun shines brightly down on three men penning cattle up in a large pen. The oldest of the three wipes his face with a handkerchief and examines the cattle. The youngest of the three, who is really just a boy, secures the pen so the cows can't wander off. The third, a handsome man with soft, light-colored eyes, leans against the rail chewing a long piece of grass.

The oldest man wipes his face again and shakes his head sadly.

I HOPE WHEN WE SELL THE CATTLE IT WILL BE ENOUGH TO COVER MY DEBTS AND PAY FOR MY WIFE'S MEDICINES.

Looking forlorn the old man shakes his head and looks across his cattle herd. The boy shouts something positive and gives his fist a swing in a gesture of support to the old man which makes him smile. He turns to leave and pats the boy's head.

In a darkened bedroom an old woman lies on her sickbed. Next to her bed are her daughters. The younger one is busy embroidering while the older one puts a cool, wet cloth on her mother's feverish forehead. The old woman is sleeping a fitful sleep. Her older daughter has a look of sincere concern on her face. The other daughter seems bored and looks longingly out of the window. The older, without looking back at her sister, speaks to her. When her sister speaks the younger girl looks up as if caught in the act of doing something wrong.

SISTER MILLIE, DO YOU REALLY THINK MOTHER
WILL GET BETTER WHEN WE CAN FINALLY BUY
HER MEDICINE?

Millie earnestly shakes her head positively. Although, as soon as she is sure her sister isn't looking, she turns to gaze out of the window again.

Their father, the old cowman, comes into the room. Saddened by his wife's illness, he leans over her bed and holds her hands. He looks in her face and sees that she is sleeping. He turns to his girls and asks them a question.

HAS THERE BEEN ANY CHANGE IN HER CONDITION?
SHE DOESN'T SEEM ANY WORSE OFF DOES SHE?

His older daughter shakes her head indicating that there hasn't been any change. The briefest look of crosses the old man's face. He looks from one daughter to the other. His second daughter, Millie, is staring out the window. He looks out the window too.

DRATS! IT'S THAT THIEF OF A BUSINESS MAN,
ERNIE HENRY.

The old man storms out of the room angrily. Ellie, worried that her mother may have been disturbed, hurries to the bedside. Millie stands as well, in order to leave the room.

ELLIE DEAREST, I'M GOING TO CHECK ON FATHER.

Millie hurries out of the room before Ellie has a chance to reply.

The old man is standing on his porch as three riders come up to the front of the house. A man just about his own age is in the lead. This is Mr. Henry. Mr. Henry is followed by his son Jack. Jack is dressed in finery and looks foppish. The third man is Mexican. He huddles down to his horse under his sombrero, behind the other two men.

The old man stands firmly on his own wooden porch. His chest puffed up he looks like he's ready to take on the world. You can just see his daughter Millie peeking through the window behind him.

Mr. Henry pulls his horse to a stop in front of the old man and looks at him square in the face.

OL' SAM IT'S ABOUT TIME YOU BE MAKING YOUR DECISION. I GOT GOOD CATTLE TO GRAZE HERE AND I'D RATHER NOT WAIT UNTIL FORECLOSURE. BE SENSIBLE, NOW WOULD YA, TAKE MY OFFER.

Ol'Sam stoutly refuses Mr. Henry's offer (whatever it is). He points at himself, he points at the doorway, and he points to the porch, all the while telling Mr. Henry that the property is his.

Mr. Henry and his son laugh heartily at Ol'Sam. Their laughter infuriates Ol'Sam and he yells at the pair some more. However, their laughter does not cease. Just as Ol'Sam is working himself up to some violence his handsome ranch hand walks lazily around the corner. Seeming as if not to care, the lanky man leans against the house and calls to his boss.

BOSS, AIN'T IT ABOUT TIME WE GET THEM CATTLE IN FROM THE WEST PASTURE?

Both of the Henrys jump when they realize someone else is there. The ranch-hand's timely interruption is enough to cool off the head of Ol'Sam.

Mr. Henry shakes his bull-whip at Ol'Sam speaking to him with a mean look on his face.

LOOK HERE OL'SAM, YOU WON'T GET A BETTER OFFER. TAKE IT NOW AND THAT SICK WIFE OF YERS WON'T HAVE TO SUFFER!

With a wild arm swing, Mr. Henry turns his horse and gallops off, followed by the two others. Ol'Sam swings off the porch and hurries away. Its only the lanky ranch-hand who watches the dust of the riders. He watches the three horsemen long enough to see one of them split off and circle back. Only then does he turn and follow his boss.

In the interior of a barn, Millie waits anxiously behind a horse stall. Every few seconds she looks over the top and then ducks back down. The third time she does this she is rewarded for she smiles broadly. She leaves her hiding place and rushes into the arms of Mr. Henry's son Jack. Jack is leading his horse and has come in from the back of the barn. Dropping his lead he takes her in his arms and swings her around. When he puts her back on the floor, she beams up at him.

I WASN'T SURE IF YOU WOULD COME. I'M SO GLAD YOU ARE HERE.

The dashing young man makes love to her, promising her the moon and stars if just she give him a little kiss. He points to his cheek expectantly. Millie gives him the tiniest of kisses. Jack whoops for joy and swings her around again. Laughing they fall back into a pile of hay.

MILLIE, IF YOUR FATHER TAKES OUR OFFER WE'LL BE ABLE TO GET MARRIED. BUT YOU MUST GET HIM TO TAKE THE OFFER SOON.

Jack explains to Millie how she must get her father to see reason and sell the property. With love in her eyes Millie agrees to everything Jack says.

Ellie is working in the kitchen. She leans over to look out a window and checks the front porch.

> **WHERE HAS THAT SISTER OF MINE GOTTEN OFF TO? JUST WHEN IT'S TIME FOR CHORES AND COOKING.**

Ellie goes back to making dinner. Outside at the door, the handsome ranch hand, Bill, knocks at the door. Ellie calls out "who is it?" Then opens the door.

Bill stands there with his hat in his hands looking very shy. Ellie ushers him into the room.

> **IT'S NOT DINNER TIME QUITE YET BILL, BUT YOU ARE WELCOME TO HAVE A REST AT THE TABLE UNTIL IT'S READY.**

Bill slightly bows to Ellie. His movements are awkward and gawky, and he nearly falls on her. She takes a step back but smiles charmingly at him. Unsure what to do with himself, Bill looks around. Ellie points to a chair and indicates he should sit down. He does so and sits shyly at the table. Ellie continues making dinner, but now and then she sneaks a look at the tall lanky cowboy. He is too embarrassed to look anywhere but the table. He is behaving far differently than the cool cowboy he was earlier while amongst his equals.

Ellie turns to him and opens her mouth to speak, but she is also too shy, so she turns back to her cooking. Finally, she works up enough gumption and turns to Bill. She asks Bill.

> **DOES IT SEEM LIKE THE CATTLE WILL BRING IN ENOUGH TO HELP US?**

He starts at the sound of her voice. He stammers a bit and finally answers her with an affirmative. Ellie smiles at him. Just then Millie enters the kitchen from the front door. She sees her sister and the ranch hand staring at each other and makes a face as if to say "These two are so silly. If they are in love, get over it already." Millie slams the door shut. Both Ellie and Bill look up at her, extremely startled.

Ellie collects herself first and goes back to cooking. Without missing a stroke she looks at her sister and points to the pot on the stove. She gives her a grim, angry look.

Millie attends to her duty, although in a lax and lazy manner. Bill tries to make small talk with Ellie and they smile nicely at one another. Millie doesn't even try to stifle a yawn, she is so bored with her too-good older sister and the beau she will not claim.

Ellie finishes making dinner and sets the table. Ol'Sam, her father, comes into the kitchen followed by the stable boy. Everyone but Ellie sits at the table for dinner. After Ol'Sam says the prayer everyone digs into their dinner. Ellie takes dinner into her mother's sick room. Bill, his fork poised halfway to his mouth, watches her go. Ol'Sam sees this and slaps Bill heartily on the back, laughing hysterically at him. With the slap, Bill loses his fork and looks away sheepishly. The stable boy chuckles to himself as he wolfs down his food. Millie has taken no notice of the shenanigans. She looks off into the distance.

In the morning the sisters are in the barn milking the cows. Ol'Sam passes by carrying a calf. Millie sees him and runs after him, glancing back once over her shoulder to see that her sister hasn't noticed.

Ol'Sam lowers the calf into a pen heaped with straw. Millie helps him settle the baby into its new pen and helps make up a bottle with which to feed the calf. As she works alongside her father she speaks to him, looking up at him from half lowered lids.

> DADDY, WHY DON'T YOU TAKE MR. HENRY'S OFFER? MOTHER IS AWFULLY SICK. I JUST DON'T UNDERSTAND.

She looks at her father imploringly. The old man is visibly shaken. He sadly puts his head down into his hands. Millie, not thoroughly heartless, throws her arms around her father to comfort him. Ol'Sam weeps some more and then he speaks to his daughter with heartfelt emotion.

> I COULD TAKE MR. HENRY'S OFFER AND BUY MEDICINES FOR MY WIFE BUT HOW WILL I MAKE MONEY AFTERWARDS TO FEED MY DAUGHTERS?
>
> I MUST MAKE A GOOD PROFIT FROM THE CATTLE SALE TO PAY THE MORTGAGE AND FOR THE MEDICINES. I KNOW THAT IF I CAN MAKE THAT HAPPEN WE WILL ALL BE HAPPY.

Millie is genuinely moved by her father's declaration. As father and daughter are embracing, Ellie turns the corner and witnesses the event. She pulls her apron to her eyes, moved to tears by the emotional scene she has witnessed.

Again underneath the blazing sun, Ol'Sam is leaning against the fence talking with Bill. He points to several heads of cattle and the two men discuss the upcoming sale, on which so much depends.

Peeking around from behind the barn is Jack Henry. He has a wicked look on his face and is listening to their conversation. The two cowboys don't notice the intruder but continue to talk about the cattle.

> WE HAVE JUST GOT TO GET A GOOD PRICE ON EACH HEAD, BILL, OR ALL WILL BE LOST. I WILL HAVE NO WAY TO PAY THE BANKER WITHOUT THESE CATTLE.

A close-up of Jack shows that he just had a great idea. He slinks away without being seen.

A while later, Jack is in the lush office of Mr. Henry. Jack is explaining his plan.

SO IF WE JUST STEAL HIS CATTLE, HE'LL BE
FORCED TO SELL.

Mr. Henry rubs his hands together greedily and both men are
delighted with the idea. Mr. Henry claps his son on the back.

GOOD JOB SON, I WILL LEAVE IT TO YOU TO
BRING IT OFF. DON'T DISAPPOINT ME.

Mr. Henry wags a finger at Jack in a mocking, good-humored
way. The father and son laugh together heartily.

THE NIGHT BEFORE THE CATTLE SALE OL'SAM
PREPARES FOR THE BIG DAY THAT WILL DECIDE
EVERYTHING.

Ol'Sam is working away in the barn. Ellie comes in carrying a
basket with a cloth over it. She interrupts her father and offers him
the basket.

I WAS WORRIED FATHER, SINCE YOU DID NOT
COME IN FOR DINNER. I PACKED YOU A BASKET
SO YOU WOULDN'T GO HUNGRY.

Ol'Sam stops his work and looks at his daughter kindly. He takes
the basket and sits. He eats his dinner with obvious happiness.

I AM BLESSED TO HAVE DAUGHTERS AS
WONDERFUL AS YOU. YOU GO OFF TO BED NOW.
I WON'T BE MUCH LONGER.

Ellie puts her arm around her father's shoulder and then leaves.
Ol'Sam puts away some tackle and makes sure the pens are secured.
He blows out the oil lamp and leaves the barn.

As soon as he is gone, Millie sneaks into the barn to await her
lover. Jack Henry appears soon after. The lovers embrace. Almost at
once Jack asks Millie to help him with his scheme.

I JUST NEED FOR YOU TO ACT AS A LOOKOUT AND
MAKE SURE THAT NO ONE COMES OUT OF YOUR
HOUSE.

Millie's eyes grow wide with terror. She mouths the word no and shakes her head vehemently. Jack presses her. He grabs her arm and shakes her, bullying her into being his accomplice. Still Millie denies him.

WHAT WILL BECOME OF MY FAMILY WITHOUT THE CATTLE?

Millie desperately asks Jack what will become of her family if she helps him. He tries to soothe her with talk of their wedding, but Millie doesn't believe him.

Finally Jack realizes that she won't help him so he threatens her in a very underhanded way. Menacing her by leaning over her with his fist in the air.

YOU ARE NOTHING BUT A LOOSE WOMAN, I WOULDN'T MARRY YOU IF YOU WERE THE LAST WOMAN ON EARTH. YOUR FAMILY IS NOTHING AND DESERVES WHAT IT GETS.

Jack laughs maniacally as Millie, hair flying wildly, pounds his chest with her fists. She is calling him a rat and a liar. Tears stream from her face.

Jack succumbs to even worse villainy for he must dispose of Millie since she knows of his plan. He raises his fist in the air and this time he lets fly, striking the poor ill-used girl to the ground. Millie is knocked unconscious and Jack turns to run the cattle from their pens.

Ellie stays up late sitting in the kitchen. She looks tired and sad, but sits quietly. All of a sudden the door bursts open and Millie staggers into the kitchen. Ellie is shocked to see her sister stumbling with blood dripping down her face. Ellie runs to her and takes her in her arms as she becomes insensible once again.

Ellie tries to revive her sister, slapping her hands, wiping her face with her apron. Finally Millie comes around. Ellie demands to know who did this to her. Millie weakly tells her that Jack Henry has stolen the cattle.

> DEAR SISTER, JACK HENRY HAS RUN OFF WITH OUR CATTLE SO THAT WE WILL BE FORCED OUT OF OUR HOME.

Millie's head lolls as she finishes her sentence. Ellie makes her comfortable on the floor and then stands. A determined look on her face.

> MILLIE, I'VE GOT TO STOP HIM. I'LL GO GET THE SHERIFF.

At once she takes her hat and rushes from the room. Ellie saddles a horse in the barn and climbs up, the horse starting as soon as she is seated. The horse runs out of the barn into the dark of night.

Back in the kitchen, Millie has sat up and is leaning against the wall. She holds her head miserably.

Without knocking, Bill dashes into the room, wildly asking what is going on. He points to the stable and says "Ellie?"

> IS EVERYTHING ALL RIGHT? I JUST SAW MISS ELLIE TAKE OFF FOR TOWN ON HER HORSE.

Millie shakes her head and explains to him what has happened. Bill is at first shocked by the news, but his features take on a grim determination when he hears the whole story.

> WAKE YOUR FATHER AND TELL HIM TO GO AFTER ELLIE.

> I WILL HEAD OFF THOSE CATTLE THIEVES.

Bill stands tall, determined, and heroic as he turns to take on the cattle thieves himself.

Meanwhile, Ellie is racing her horse determinedly into town. All of a sudden, from behind a small hill, ride Jack Henry and his hench-men. The three men cut off Ellie's means of escape and surround her, yanking the reins from her hands. Ellie tries to defy the men. She gets off her horse and tries to run, but it is no use. The outlaws overwhelm her.

Jack Henry puts her across his saddle and heads off with her.

> WE CAN'T HAVE YOU TELLING THE SHERIFF ON US UNTIL WE CAN UNLOAD THAT CATTLE.

> TIME TO JOIN UP WITH MY MEN.

He laughs evilly and urges his horse into a run.

In the barn, Bill saddles two horses and leaves one for Ol'Sam to take. Just as he mounts and is riding from the barn, Ol'Sam comes in, his miserable eyes pleading with his cow hand to retrieve the stolen cattle.

Bill assures him that he will.

> GO TO THE SHERIFF'S AFTER MISS ELLIE . WITH ENOUGH MEN, I AM SURE WE CAN HEAD THEM OFF.

Bill takes off from the barn. Ol'Sam jumps into the saddle and follows.

Ol'Sam rides hard into the town and stumbles into the Sheriff's office, waking up the deputy in charge. The deputy is none too happy about being woken up. Ol'Sam demands the sheriff. The deputy indicates that the sheriff is sleeping and he would like to be doing the same.

Ol'Sam grows worried. He looks all around the small office and jailhouse and there is no trace of his daughter. He pleads with the deputy to find his cattle and his missing daughter. He grabs the deputy's shirt desperately pleading with the young man.

> MY CATTLE HAS BEEN STOLEN! ALL THE COWS I WAS TO SELL AT TOMORROW'S AUCTION. AND NOW MY DAUGHTER IS MISSING TOO. PLEASE HELP ME! PLEASE!

When the deputy understands the gravity of the situation, he jumps into action. He frees Ol'Sam's hands from his shirt and runs to the telephone. Ol'Sam falls into a heap on a chair. The young deputy animatedly talks into the telephone's speaker. When he is not speaking he is nodding emphatically. Finally he hangs up the ear piece and drags Ol'Sam out of the door.

Bill has picked up the trail of the thieves and rushes after them through the dark of night, riding fast and hard.

Ellie is sitting awkwardly by a fire. Her hands and feet tied. The thieves, led by Jack Henry, have herded the cattle to a remote and secret ravine where they can hide the cattle easily. As the five thieves congratulate themselves around the campfire, Ellie tries to work free of her bindings.

Jack Henry is talking to the grimy hired men, each of them in tattered clothes with unkempt beards, Jack's fine clothing stands out. He holds up a bottle of liquor for them all to share, the henchmen cheering and hooting. Ellie cocks her head towards the men to be able to listen better, even as she works at her bindings. Jack takes a swig of the beverage and then hands it around telling the others about their payoff.

> **WHEN WE GET A HOLD OF THAT LAND MY FATHER
> WILL GIVE YOU EACH A SHARE IN THE OIL WELLS.
> YOU WILL ALL BE RICH.**

Ellie's eyes grow very wide when she overhears this information and works all the harder to be free.

Back in town, the Sheriff, two deputies and Ol'Sam have gathered on their horses. They are looking at a map. The Sheriff points at the map and then in the direction of his left. All the men nod grimly and turn their horses to ride out of town.

Bill has come upon the thieves' hideaway. He sneaks along the back of one of the hills that hides the camp. Hidden from view he sees the thieves around a campfire with Ellie tied nearby.

NOT MY ELLIE!

Bill's face grows angry and fierce. He heads back to his horse, torn between trying to rescue his darling by taking on five men alone, or doing the sensible thing and going for help.

I WILL DO HER NO GOOD IF I ONLY GET MYSELF
KILLED. I'LL GO FOR HELP!

Bill chokes down a sigh and pounds the air with his fist. He heads off to get his horse and go to the sheriff.

At the campfire, all the men turn the opposite way from Bill towards where the cattle are penned.

SOMETHING HAS SPOOKED THE COWS, BETTER
GO CHECK IT OUT.

The thieves abandon their campfire and head toward the cattle pen. Ellie has worked herself free of the rope and runs away from the campfire. She works her way over the hill, moving as fast as she can. Once on the other side, on flatter ground, she heads in the direction of town. She nervously checks all around her. She doesn't run, but walks very fast. She tries to conceal herself from one low bush to another.

Then she sees them, coming over the hill are three of Jack Henry's henchmen looking for her. When she sees them, they see her and point at her, beginning to run. Ellie screams, her hand flying to her mouth as she turns and runs away across the low hills.

Ellie runs with all her might, but the men gain on her. The one that is closest, stops to take aim at her with his gun. He shoots and misses, but the sound of the shot nearly does poor Ellie in. She falters, mistepping, nearly falling. She keeps from falling and continues to run, but the men are now dangerously close.

From out of nowhere comes Bill galloping on his horse. He shouts "Ellie," and she looks over her shoulder and sees him coming her way. She gives him a fearful, yet relieved, look. Bill shouts directions to her. He ties his reins about his saddlehorn and reaches both arms down towards the running Ellie. She lifts her arms to him and in an instant she is pulled up into his saddle in front of him and they are on their way.

The henchmen stop running when they see the man pick up their prey and take off at a run. They have foul looks on their faces and swear profusely.

Just then, the other henchmen and Jack Henry come towards them astride horses. They pull up and ask where the girl has gone.

Jack Henry gnashes his teeth in frustrated rage when he hears that she's been rescued.

THE GIRL HAS HEARD TOO MUCH, SHE MUST BE TAKEN CARE OF!

He beckons with his arm for the other mounted thieves to join him and they take off across the plains in a flat run. Soon they are within sight of Bill and Ellie. Bill has slowed his horse to a slow canter (so as not to wear her out). Ellie is draped dreamily in front of him, her arms wrapped around him for support.

Bill turns his head as if he has heard something.

DO YOU HEAR THAT ELLIE?

Ellie who has a better view behind them, looks up in time to see Jack Henry bearing down on them with a gun in his hand. Ellie cries out for Bill to go and Bill wastes no time in looking behind him before setting his heels to the horse and breaking out in a run.

The chase is on. The two thieves chasing the hero, taking shots with their guns but never getting close. Bill handles his horse expertly, weaving through trees, up and down ravines. Never staying on a straight path. But Jack Henry and his henchman don't have a second person on their horse slowing them down, so even with all Bill's skill, they still gain.

Trying to outsmart them, Bill rounds a hill and nearly runs into the Sheriff and the others. Now the tables are turned as the Sheriff and deputies go after Jack Henry. Ol'Sam gets off his horse and runs to his daughter. Ellie likewise slips from Bill's saddle and runs to her father's open arms.

Ol'Sam, remembering that Bill is the one who rescued his daughter, goes up to him and shakes his hand.

> **YOUNG MAN YOU HAVE SHOWN ME TRUE LOYALTY. I OWE YOU EVERYTHING. WHAT CAN I DO TO REPAY YOU?**

Bill grows shy and quiet, he stutters that there isn't anything that he wants. Ellie takes this opportunity to go up to Bill and to take his hand. Standing at his side, she turns to her father.

> **I THINK BILL WANTS TO MARRY ME FATHER.**

Bill probably blushes as he looks away, but at the same time he nods his head in agreement. Ol'Sam is tickled pink and laughs heartily.

> **WELL YOUNG MAN, I THINK YOU'VE EARNED MY BLESSINGS.**

Ellie smiles the delighted smile of the newly engaged. Bill, still shy, turns and looks at her. They grasp hands.

In town the next day, Ol'Sam, Bill, Ellie and another man are standing under an awning. The stranger is paying Ol'Sam handsomely for his cattle. The deputy walks down the street leading Jack Henry, the four henchmen, and Mr. Henry – all of them handcuffed. The sheriff follows holding a shotgun. He nods at Ol'Sam as he goes by.

Ol'Sam holds up the money in his hand, smiling broadly. He looks at his daughter and future son-in-law with pride.

> **NOW WE'LL BE ABLE TO AFFORD MEDICINE AND SO MUCH MORE!**

They all congratulate each other. Ellie puts on a shy smile and asks her father a question.

EVEN ENOUGH FOR AN EXTRA ROOM IN THE HOUSE?

Bill and Ol'Sam look at her with quizzical expressions and then they both laugh.

THE END.

Chapter 15

At the end of that winter, Del had to leave again on business. We had been having so much fun spending all our free time together, it was hard on both of us that he had to go. His family business required him to leave and there was no escaping it. He was to leave on a Wednesday. Although we had said our goodbyes the night before, I thought I would surprise him at his hotel and accompany him to the train station.

My shooting schedule was very open that week and when I asked Monroe, the director of my current film, if I could duck out early, he waved me off with barely a glance. Del had always been checked in at the Alexandria Hotel on Spring Street and 5th, even though he hadn't stayed there very often since I bought the house. His train was to leave from Central Station at 2 o'clock, so I planned on getting to the hotel by noon.

I went to the reception desk and asked if Mr. Wolham had checked out yet and, if not, which room he was in. The clerk, a man as young as myself, began shuffling through his guest book. He didn't get very far before he looked up and said "There is Mr. Wolham now."

I turned with great eagerness to see a distinguished looking older man walking towards the desk from the elevator. I was about to say, "that's not Del," but my instinct got the better of me and I instead turned to the clerk saying "I must have got the name wrong, that is not the gentleman I was sent to meet."

The clerk eyed me curiously, said nothing and turned his attention to the approaching man. As I passed the older gentleman, we looked straight into each other's faces. I knew at once that he was

Del's father. I walked to the telephone counter and pretended to make a phone call, all the while an alarm was sounding in my head.

After just a few minutes Del stepped off the elevator with the porter and a cart of luggage. He saw me at once and looked startled by my presence. He glanced over at the older man who was paying the clerk, then he looked at me and winked.

I was panic-stricken, my throat tight with fear. If that was Del's father, the father who had treated him severely and was unfairly forcing him to work for his company, then why was he here? Staying in the same hotel as Del and leaving at the same time? My mind raced as I held the telephone up to my ear. I didn't even bother pretending to speak into the mouthpiece behind me on the wall.

Del had followed the luggage cart to the street and the older man had finished with the clerk. As he left the counter he looked directly at me. He knew who I was as well, I could tell. His eye color was similar to that of Del's, but his eyes had no warmth. They were shrewd and piercing. I blinked but did not turn. Then he had left the building.

In less than half a minute, Del dashed back through the double doors and moved towards me. Still holding the telephone, I finally let it drop, not bothering to hang it back on its hook. I rushed forward to jump into his arms, but he instead took me by the elbow and ushered me to an out-of-the-way corner. He kissed me. Tenderly.

"Why is your father here? Why didn't you tell me?" I urgently whispered. "What is going on Del?"

Smoothing my hair from my forehead he said, "I didn't want to upset you anymore about my leaving. Father got here last week to check up on my work here. It's nothing really."

He kissed my forehead and then held me to him tightly. When he spoke again, I could hear the emotion in his voice, choking on his whisper, "I've got to go now. I'll miss my train otherwise. I don't think I can bear to look at you again," he held me even more tightly, "I'll never leave if I do."

He pulled one arm away from me and reached inside his coat. He squeezed me tightly again, kissed my hair, then pulled away. He left in my hand an envelope. He was out of the door before I knew it. For some reason, with some bit of intuition, I knew then that he was not leaving for just a few weeks. He was leaving for good. I watched the doors until long after he had gone through them.

Recollecting myself and feeling the burn of the stares from the hotel staff, I walked out through the doors myself. I must have been in shock for I felt almost happy, carefree. I took a streetcar back to my neighborhood and walked the steep hill home. I was thinking of Del's tender goodbye and of the comedy reel we had shot last week in which I played a harlot. I wondered when I would next see Dolores, if she planned on ever staying in our home again.

I thought of anything but my painful realization and the envelope in my hand. I went into the kitchen and put the kettle on the stove. I thought of nothing and everything, my mind jumping from one topic to another. When I had made my cup of tea, I sat down at the table. The tea I had thought would soothe my nerves had the opposite effect. It galvanized my fears into a leaden ball that weighed heavily in my stomach.

I reached for the envelope, stared at it, felt its weight in my hand, then with one smooth movement, I tore it open. In shaking out the letter, out fell Del's class ring. The one he always wore. I was surprised that I hadn't noticed it missing from his finger that morning. I palmed the ring and unfolded the letter. I read it.

Dearest Maggie,

I couldn't tell you in person. I couldn't stand to see your face any sadder than it already was. I am not coming back. My family has arranged for me to be married and by the end of the week, I will be. I know it is horrible that I didn't tell you that I was engaged, but I love you so much and was happier with you than I've ever been before. I was a coward. I am a coward.

I could have left my family and been on my own as you did. I'm not so brave as you. I cannot go without my allowance. I cannot live that way. I am ashamed of myself. I hate myself, but I cannot change who I am. I decided it was best that you know what I am now, that you don't have a chance to talk me out of marrying for money. I know you could. Yours is the only advice I ever want, but you would end up hating me as I hate myself. That is something I could not bear to witness. Even as I break my own heart.

I want you to have my class ring. It is the only thing I own outright that is of any value to me. It will do me good to know that you keep it safe.

I will love you always and forever.

The ring still clutched in my left hand, the letter crumpled in my right. I left the table to go to bed but only made it to the living room before I had to lie down.

It was dark when I felt a pressure on my bladder so strong that I could no longer ignore it. I finally made it to my bedroom. I don't know if I slept or not. I was in shock I am sure. Heartbreak combined with shock is a deadly combination.

When it was light again, I heard Dolores come into the house and call for me. I didn't answer. In a few minutes I heard her from the hallway cursing Del loudly and thoroughly. Feeling my right hand, I found that the letter was not there. I must have dropped it when I moved.

Then she was sitting on my bed next to me, smoothing my hair and talking quietly. "You haven't been here like this since yesterday have you primita?"

I didn't answer. I couldn't find breath enough to spare. "We should get you cleaned up and get some food in you. Things will look better then."

Still I did not answer. Dolores sat by my side for some minutes in silence. Her whole presence was a comfort to me. "I think you haven't even cried over him. Tears would do you good, you know."

I hadn't thought about that, nor anything really. My mind was trying so hard to deny the letter, the ring, his goodbye, that I had dammed up all the heartbreak. Dolores leaned over and kissed my head then took my hand in hers. The tears began to flow, followed by the racking sobs. I cried myself out on her lap as I had so often done with Papa. She was so patient and so tender with me, she might have been my nursemaid and me her very young charge. She never told me to stop crying or to move on. She just sat with me and let me cry out the pain.

When my sobs were at last diminishing, she got me out of bed and into the bathroom. She drew a bath for me. The hot water and pleasant smells helped to quell the last of the hiccups and sobs. I heard her on the phone speaking to someone about how I was too sick to come in for a few days. She was probably telling Monroe. A little glimmer of light sparked in my heart when she said she was going to stay with me.

After my bath, she fed me and put me back to bed, this time under the covers. I felt like a child to be ushered with such care, but it was a good feeling. I couldn't bear the responsibility of taking care of myself that day. To be able to give up all duty and care was a blessing.

I stayed in that semi-conscious, childish state for the rest of the day and all of the next. It really was similar to an illness and I did need the time to recover. By the third day, Saturday, I was up in the morning and dressed before Dolores was up. I had made tea, but once it was made I couldn't drink it and was feeling more and more like I should go back to bed. Dolores found me then.

Sitting down across from me and taking my tea cup to drink from, she said, "Today is a special day. Wait here for just a minute." She left the table. When she came back she had my coat, hat, and bag. "We're going shopping."

I made to protest that I didn't feel up to it, but she had already dragged me out of the chair. Of course, getting out of the house and back in the world was the best prescription possible. We went to our favorite dressmaker to see what she had new in her shop. Dolores took me to the Broadway Department Store. Dolores made me try on about 50 different hats and shoes in the department store. I bought a pair of earrings that were quite lovely. We lunched at Mr. Ross's cafeteria where we had eaten so many times during our months living downtown. It was fun to revisit the place, say hello to our old acquaintances.

And because we were having so much fun behaving in the girlish way we used to, just the summer before, we went to visit Mr. Stuckey. He was very happy to see us. He had a copy of The Siren's Song and showed it in our honor. We howled with laughter at our own parts in the film, much to the annoyance of the other patrons, but it was too much. The wide-eyed girl on the screen was me just six months earlier. I looked so young. I probably still looked that way, but the weight on my heart told me something different.

Dolores decided we should go out for an extravagant dinner. We went home and changed then went to the Brown Derby for a grand dinner.

After the first course, Monroe arrived with several of his lackeys. They all joined us. The merry mood that our day out had produced diminished quickly for me. I wasn't ready for company. I wasn't ready to talk to other people.

"I see you're feeling better Maggie. You'll be back on the set Monday." Monroe said to me. It wasn't a question and I resented his manner.

"Definitely, Monroe," I replied. I was never much of a talker in a crowd, but I was even more silent that night. I was confused and scared, every bit as much as I had been when I first set out on my own.

I drank a lot that night. I didn't mean to or really know that I did. It lifted, just slightly, the weight on my chest and gave me a wonderful excuse not to speak to anyone. Dolores, again taking care of me like a nursemaid, practically carried me out of the restaurant and put me to bed when we got home.

The hangover I had the next day was nasty. Although, just like the shock, it didn't allow me to think. I loved and loathed that feeling.

Chapter 16

The next several months passed in a haze. I remember very little of it and what I do remember, I wish I didn't. I worked some, I drank a lot, I took many lovers, and I hated myself. I couldn't stand to be alone, not for a second.

Dolores stayed with me for the first few days after Del left. It was wonderful having her so near, but by the end of a week she was ready to be back at her real home with Monroe. I've never felt so lonely in my life the night I came home and she was gone again. All I saw were hours and hours of emptiness ahead of me.

The strange thing was, I had often spent many an evening alone in that house. Del and I rarely saw each other two nights in a row. Many nights I had made dinner and sat comfortably in the living room until late at night, reading books or listening to the phonograph. I had never felt the house to be quiet or lonely until that first night that Dolores didn't come home with me.

I didn't stay at home, I couldn't stay there. Before I had even taken off my jacket, I grabbed my purse and left. Where I went didn't matter as long as I didn't have to face the empty house alone. Or sober.

I walked down the street to a taxi stand and caught a cab into downtown. I knew there would be people I knew at the nightclub near the Hotel Del Coronado. Many people who worked in pictures had drinks there when the studios closed shop for the day. Walking in the door I saw two people I knew. Before an hour was out, I was on my way to a private party in the hills. I don't remember the rest really. Even the man I woke up next to. I just remember, the next day, climbing the hill to our house, weeping as I walked.

During one of the early weeks after Del left, I was filming a comedy/western with Floyd. I had become Floyd's favorite costar when trick riding was involved. He and Ferdy loved that they could film me doing riding stunts. I had already made three films with them. That was my fourth.

Filming was not going so well. Mainly due to me. I had gotten to the point where I could put a happy face over my sorrow, but I had a complete lack of interest in anything. I had arrived several hours late the first day of filming and then the second day I just couldn't get the hang of the stunt I was supposed to do. Floyd must have gone over it ten times. I always nodded as if I understood, but when we tried it out at a standstill, I just couldn't get it. I hadn't really been listening, nor could I summon enough enthusiasm to care. I was there because there were people there and I was supposed to be.

Floyd was in the middle of explaining things again and I was looking where he was pointing. I realized that I was looking where his hand indicated on the saddle in front of me, but that he had ceased speaking. I looked up at him with surprise and found that he was scrutinizing me. I was instantly embarrassed and ashamed. I looked to the ground.

"Maggie, I was gonna give you your space and let you be upset if you need to be, but this isn't like you." Floyd said with genuine concern. "Usually you get the stunt in one or two tries and can't wait to do it. Since I saw you yesterday, I could see you are really troubled by something. Is it really so bad?"

I broke down in tears and sobbed on his chest. Yes, I wanted to scream at him, yes it was really that bad. We were screened from the rest of the set by shade trees that were planted to the side of the stables. No one witnessed my scene but him and me.

Floyd patted my back in a 'there-there' sort of way. It gave me great comfort. During those black days any human touch made me feel marginally better. He asked me if I wanted to tell him. I didn't really, but before I could help myself, I sobbed out my tale of woe.

"Ah yes," he said and he put his arm across my shoulders, "A broken heart will do it every time."

We stood side by side for a few minutes as my breathing started to calm. I realized that he had given me his handkerchief and that it was now a sorry mess, crumpled in my hands. "I'm sorry," I mumbled, "I shouldn't have broken down this way. I just get so sad sometimes. I can't do anything else."

He gave me a squeeze and we were silent again. Some of the carpenters walked past us wheeling a cart of lumber. They looked over to say hello and in seeing us, thought better of it and walked on by. I was feeling silly all over again. I was just waiting for the afternoon to be over so I could find a drink and a party and forget how stupid and worthless I had become. Then Floyd began to speak.

"This first girl who broke my heart was a real beauty named Coreene. I think I couldn't have been more than 16 when I knew her. I was working the Triple-A rodeo and we were wintering in Oklahoma. Coreene was the daughter of a shop keeper and had her pick of beaus, but when I saw her, I wanted nothing else than to spend my whole life with her. It seemed like she wanted the same thing from me. We would go for long walks and sit together in church. Her smiles were like nothing I've seen since. Except maybe for yours."

He lifted my chin to look at my face and I couldn't help but give him a smile. "We spent all of the fall and most of the winter courting like we were on the way to the altar. I was saving up my earnings to buy us some wedding rings." Floyd paused for a minute and gave a soft sigh. He looked straight ahead, but his sight was far away. "Then one day, I overheard a couple of old lady's talking rumors about my Coreene. They said it was a shame the way she toyed with that poor cowboy when everyone knew she was to be married in the spring to her father's assistant. I knew it had to be nothing but idle rumors, but I couldn't help myself from finding out the truth."

"Truth was, them old gossipy ladies were right. I was being played with. When I confronted Coreene, she laughed it off as if my heart weren't being torn to pieces. I never saw her again even though the rodeo didn't head out for another five weeks. I didn't leave our compound once after that. I thought I shouldn't be able to hold my head up again."

He stopped to chuckle. I knew what he said made sense, but it was not what I wanted to hear. It would not bring Del back to me again. "You know in the thirty or so years since that happened, I've had my heart broken more times than I can count on my fingers. Yet the first one hurt the most. Once you get over the first one, the rest are all a piece of cake."

His arm was suddenly feeling very heavy to me. I didn't want another heartbreak, I wanted Del. I couldn't very well say that to Floyd who was always so kind to me. He was only trying to make me feel better, I knew that. Having my heart broken by the love of my life ruined me, I was certain. Now, I might as well be a prostitute at Esther's boarding house for I was becoming a wanton woman and my only regret was losing Del.

Floyd gave me another squeeze then removed his arm. He was obviously feeling better, so I did my best to put on an interested face. "Now, this is what I want you to do. When you grab hold of the saddle and jump up, I want you to think of that no-good Del and imagine his face as the springboard that you have to jump off of to get into the saddle."

He ushered me into position and I couldn't help but laugh, a real, genuine guffaw, at what Floyd said. The best part was that it worked. I had more enthusiasm for jumping on Del's face than anything else in a long while and we shot the scene in the first take.

The cheering up didn't last long and before the night was through I was drunk. I wish I had been able to take in Floyd's well-intentioned advice, but I felt so miserable and empty on the inside.

I had a string of lovers then, some names I remember, some I don't. It seemed that as soon as word got around that Del had dumped me, I became a popular item. Dolores said it was because I was suddenly free, single. I didn't quite believe it. Or, more precisely, I didn't care. I didn't care who I ended up with at night. The drinking, the lovers, everything I did was in order that I didn't have to think or feel. There was a terrible pain in my heart if only I stopped long enough to feel it. I didn't want to. I didn't want to feel alone.

Looking back, it was such a foolish way to behave. My heart would have healed far more quickly had I looked my heartbreak in the face and gone on anyway. I had always dealt with pain in that manner - locking it away inside. When my grandfather had died, when I was sent off to boarding school, even when I left home - I would shut my pain away and become someone silent and watchful. This pain was different, it was too much to just shut out.

My biggest regret, second only to my overall behavior, was poor Charlie. Sometime during those months of debauchery, he invited me to dinner and I accepted. We went out together quite often for a short while. For a few weeks, I think he even thought he was my boyfriend. His sweet, earnest face was so hurt when he finally realized that I had no interest in him personally. His hurt face sincerely mirrored my poor heart. If I were a more cruel person, I could have gained some satisfaction by his pain, but it only compounded my own.

Some three months after Del left me, I was at rock bottom. I never made it to the lot on time, sometimes not at all. I was worried that my contract would be cancelled, but not enough to face up to it. The wonderful thing about those early movie days, was there was always a party. I never had to stay alone or sober for long. I think my contract would have been cancelled if Dolores hadn't prevailed upon Monroe to vouch for me and if I weren't so popular a player.

It had been nine months or more since The Siren's Song had been released and I had been in demand as a actress since then. The studios were always very careful about keeping information about our popularity from us actors, but we had ways of finding out. The kids in the mail room were always too eager to tell you who had received the most letters of any given week. We also had an excellent popularity meter in Mr. Stuckey. Dolores and I would go down to see him now and then and he would tell us how we were doing with the public.

As erratic as my behavior became, the films I made, somehow or other, were hits. The bottom line was what really counted at the studio. Mr. Hawthorne saw to that. The moment my pictures started losing money, I'm sure I would have been kicked out with or without Monroe's backing.

I was slinking into the studio, early one afternoon, terribly late for the beginning of a shoot, when I was stopped by Mr. Hawthorne's secretary. The stern, large, elderly woman blocked my path and said my name, "Miss Savoy."

I had been looking at the floor, trying to get through the hallway without looking anyone in the eye, but when I saw the solid shoes and long skirts of Mrs. Mercer on the floor in front of me, I had no choice but to look up.

"I have a telephone message for you. I know you are not in the habit of receiving personal calls at the offices, so I will refrain from reminding you that it is forbidden." She paused to stare at me. "Your father called to say he is in town and would like you to have lunch with him at 1 o'clock at the Stowell Hotel."

I opened my mouth to say I had to be on the set, but Mrs. Mercer continued. "I think you should meet your father for lunch Miss Savoy. The filming for your new picture was cancelled today as the lead actress didn't show up for filming."

I felt my face start to burn. I was so ashamed. Mrs. Mercer turned and stalked back to her desk. I turned on my heels and left the building. I was torn. There was a certain level of comfort I would get by meeting with my father, but my guilt and shame were overbearing. I hesitated for some minutes outside the lot gates. One way would take me home, to my empty shell of a house. The other to my father who would see me at my lowest. My fear of being alone won out. I went to face my father.

I took a streetcar into town, knowing that it would take longer than a cab. I had half a hope that I would arrive too late and would miss him. I guess I was meant to face him that day, for I found him at his usual table.

His face brightened as I approached the table. He stood to greet me, taking my hands and kissing my cheek.

"Magda, it does me a world of good to see you in person."

I managed a half-smile, wondering at his use of words.

"Or should I call you Maggie?" Then I realized it. He had seen the films, he had called me at the studio. How could I have over-looked that in the beginning? Because I am hungover and stretched to my limits, I thought to myself and blushed deeply. Father must have mistaken my blush for humility, for he continued.

"I think it is a very becoming name for you. Your mother thinks so too." I looked up in surprise.

"She knows?" I asked, afraid of the response. I left off the rest of what I was thinking . . . 'and she hasn't come for me?'

"You know she dislikes the cinema, but she was told about it by some of the ladies in her church club."

I gulped, my mouth suddenly dry. "And she saw it?"

"Yes, and she thought you were beautiful." I looked up into my father's warm eyes. Eyes so much like my Papa.

"What did you think Father?" I looked back down at the table.

"I thought that we were very wrong to hold you back as we did." Tears began to flow then. "I see I've made you cry again. Come now, cheer up. Can't a father be proud of his headstrong, independent daughter?"

He offered his handkerchief and I took it, wiping my eyes. The tears stung my dried out eyes, but in my heart they felt like such a relief. My one solid belief was that my parents would disown me once it was known to them how I was living, if they hadn't disowned me after running away.

"Does mother know that you and I meet?"

"I confessed to her a month ago that I had known where you were for a year." He paused to sigh softly. "I can tell you she was very angry with me. But I took up your defense."

I think he wanted me to respond, but I had nothing to say. I just wanted to hear what happened. "Naturally, she wanted to come here and take you home, but I convinced her that we wouldn't be able to keep you for long."

I smiled at the table. A year ago. Del and I were together a year ago. Del.

" . . . playing the guitar. You looked so sweet." Father was talking, but I had missed it. Not getting the reaction he expected from me, he scrutinized me closely. "You look very tired, my dear. Is it hard work being an actress?"

I gave him a shy smile while thinking, not so hard as it is being a failure. I explained to him how the pictures were made and used it as an excuse for my haggard appearance.

"No, I think you look wonderful. More mature, really. As if you had grown up since I saw you last."

I was very tempted to tell him about Del, about my heart being broken, about how I fell into a pit of despair and had no idea how to claw my way out again. But I didn't. We had a lovely lunch. Father was talkative and caught me up on everyone's life.

As we were finishing our coffee, he brought up Dolores, whom I'd completely forgotten until then. "You haven't told me how Dolores is doing." When her name came up, I realized I had totally overlooked another important point.

If my mother knew where I was and what I was doing, then Dolores's mother would know too.

I gasped and asked in a rush, "Does Aunt Frances know?"

Father chuckled at me. "Of course. Although, I don't think she will tell your uncle. Frances is happy that you girls have found your own way and that you are safe. I believe she is under the impression that Dolores's father would come for her immediately and not treat her very nicely if he knew."

"Father, you make it sound as if Aunt Frances knew where to find Dolores and me all this time."

"I confess. She did. I could not keep the secret from her. She is like Papa and is happy to let people live how they choose." My father beamed at me. His love and admiration were disquieting. At once it both bolstered my confidence and made me uncomfortable.

"I know I've said it before, Magda, but I'll say it again. Your Papa would be so proud of you." He leaned over and patted my hand warmly. And I knew what he said was true. It had been so long since I thought of Papa. It had been too long since I'd used his memory to gauge my behavior and actions. Far too long.

"That is the best thing you can say to me, Father. Thank you." Tears were welling up again. I wanted to stay with my father for ever, but I needed to get away to think. To think about the things he said, to think about changing what I'd become.

"I'm taking a 3:30 train back to Redlands, so I need to leave. Why don't you tell your cousin to write to her mother? I'm sure Frances would be thrilled to hear from her directly." I said I would.

As we left the restaurant, Father put his arm around my shoulders and gave me a small, quick hug. "Please write or telephone now and then, now that you don't have to hide. Can you do that for me?"

I nodded. "But what about Mother?"

"If you write to me, I'll fill her in. I don't think she's quite ready for any reconciliation yet, but give her time." I was the one who needed time. Father gave me another squeeze, kissed my cheek again, and left.

I stood alone in the lobby for a split second before deciding what to do. I walked over to the clerk's desk and took a room. Before going up, I phoned Dolores at the studio and left her a message telling her where to find me and that she needed to come.

When I got to the room, I stripped down to my underclothing. I washed my face and neck and laid down on the bed. All the feelings I had held at bay during luncheon, I let wash over me. I cried, I sobbed, I laughed.

It all came down to the fact that my mother and father approved of me as an actress. They weren't going to take me home. A sense of real relief came to me. I was no longer a runaway in hiding.

A nagging worry that I didn't even know was there had been relieved. I laid on the bed for hours staring at the ceiling. For the first time in months, I didn't obsessively think about Del. I couldn't help but think about him. It was a habit now, as much as brushing my hair before I went to bed, or making the bed in the morning. Yet now it didn't bother me so much. The hurt was much less substantial than when I had last taken stock. I hadn't so much as bothered to look at what was going on inside me, I was so concerned with blocking any feeling. I was scared to look inside and see what I would find.

At first, right after Del left, I thought I would find nothing. I thought I would be empty on the inside, that Del would have taken all of me with him. Later, after I started behaving so abominably, I didn't want to look for fear of realizing that I was no longer the person I had been and that what I had become was awful. Lying there on the hotel bed, staring at the white scalloped ceiling, I thought about myself. I gained a clarity that I hadn't known since I was a girl, and it was heartening.

I did weep bitterly over the months I had lost and the dreadful things I had done to myself. Once I had gone through all that, I finally felt like I could face my Papa again. I had been so ashamed of myself, so devastated by my heartbreak, that I couldn't face his memory or what he would think of me. I did that night and found, in my imagined conversation with him, that he was as forgiving as ever.

I was resigned to keep to my room. Waiting for Dolores, I remembered Papa's story of when he first fell in love. It seemed so ridiculous of me to take all these months to remember Papa's inspiring life. He made a lot of mistakes, he always said, but he never let them get him down. Of course, when Papa told me the tale of his first love, I was too young to really understand. Yet it gave me so much hope when I remembered it that day.

"When I first met my true love I had been a sailor for several years," was how Papa started the story. "At that time I was working the merchant line from Valparaiso to San Francisco. Every few weeks we would make the round trip back to Valparaiso to pick up a new shipment of fresh food for the miners in Ol' Frisco. It was a good line of work, no hassles or fears of a shipload not paying off. After visiting that beautiful old port city several times I took to going to a little cantina just to the south of the docks. It was run by a family. Their youngest daughter waited on the tables.

"For me it was love at first sight. Maria was the most beautiful girl I ever saw. She had black eyes that gave off their own light, so much did they sparkle. She had shiny black hair that hung to her waist and she always had it modestly tied back in a braid. Her dimpled smile was enough to make my stomach do flip-flops. She was very shy, but efficient in her work. Every time we dropped anchor I made for the little cantina first thing.

"Maria would always smile at me and after I was seated would wait for my order. In those few minutes we made a little talk, about nothing really, but my heart would always swell from the small bit of attention I received from her.

"One visit, I found that a festival was taking place. It was a festival honoring the founding of the city. When I visited her cantina I was determined to ask her to go with me. Even long after I had finished my meal, I sat at my table trying to work up enough nerve to ask her.

Finally when the shop had only a few other customers and she was getting ready to close, I approached her.

"Miss Maria," I said to her, "I don't know if you are going to the festival or not, but if you are, I would be delighted if you would allow me to accompany you."

"Her eyes grew wide as she considered my offer. She checked into the kitchen to see if anyone was there, but we were alone. She accepted my offer and we arranged to meet at a later hour to go to the festivities.

"I don't think I have ever been as happy as I was that night. Maria met me and we enjoyed all of the entertainments the festival had to offer. She talked to me more than I ever heard her talk to another. We laughed and joked, we were solemn and serious. We stood as close to each other as we could without causing alarm in any would-be chaperone. I bought her candies as we left. We shared them while we walked along the shore as I escorted her home. So overjoyed was I when she held up a piece of toffee for me to taste. We saw into each others' eyes and I knew that I loved her with all my soul.

"I had to leave the next day as my ship was sailing out. We made plans to see each other again as soon as I came back. I promised her that I would visit the cantina as soon as I was free to leave the ship. With that promise, I kissed her hand and said goodbye. Her dark eyes shining in the half-moon light as I walked away.

"When I got back to Valparaiso three weeks later, I made good on my promise and went first thing to the cantina. But Maria was nowhere to be found. In her place an old man waited on the tables. He was gruff and rude and I hadn't the nerve to ask him what had become of Maria. I waited outside the place all of the day and part of the next until I had to go back to the ship. I never caught sight of her.

"The next time my ship returned it was five weeks later. Again I went first thing to the cantina, but there was no Maria. Waiting the tables was a girl a few years younger than Maria, and not nearly so pretty. She was not as intimidating as the gruff old man. Before my meal was through I worked up enough courage to ask her about Maria.

"The girl hastily looked around to see if she would be overheard, then she bent low over my table and told me "Senora married Maria off to that wealthy old Don Hidalgo, the one with all the estates outside of town. Word has it that he fell in love with her at first sight and demanded her hand in marriage." Again, the girl looked around briefly. "And who could blame Senora for accepting the offer of such a wealthy man, even if he is old and ugly. But I have heard that Senora had another good reason for marrying Maria off so quickly. Maria was said to have a secret boyfriend that was just a sailor."

"The girl, satisfied that she'd spread her gossip, went about her business. I could eat nothing more and left some pesos on the table. It took me a long time to get over my failed love affair. Sometimes I think I am still not over it, for those dark black eyes still haunt me. True love is a great thing, but it does not conquer all as they say. There are too many other things that so easily get in the way.

"It wasn't long after that affair when I decided that I had had enough of the ocean and decided to go back home to Los Angeles. I was ready for tall grass and horses. Maybe there was part of me that just couldn't face going back to Valparaiso again and again knowing that it would never be the same."

Papa had sighed a lot during his retelling of the story. As he finished he laughed as he always did. I think he was laughing at the memory of his childish love and how much it had hurt. It was only then, lying prone on the hotel bed, that I really understood how much it really had hurt Papa. How much it hurts anybody who truly loves.

Dolores came late that night. I had decided that I needed a few days to cleanse myself. I was feeling comfortable in the hotel room and wanted to be rid of my need for drink before I left it. She thought it was a great idea and said she would handle Mr. Hawthorne for me.

"Dee, there is something else you should know."

"What is that?"

"My father got a hold of me today by calling the studio. He's seen *The Siren's Song*." Dolores face turned to stone. "He confessed to me that he had told your mother last year that he knew where we were. But she, like him, decided it was better for us to live as we chose."

"My father ..." Dolores said flatly.

"... he doesn't know about where we are or that we are working as actresses. Father said that Aunt Frances thinks it is better that he doesn't know."

Dolores received the news with gravity. She sat still for some time then let out a long breath as she slumped over in her chair. With her face in her lap she said, "So we are safe for a little while." She let out a mirthless laugh.

I went over to her and put my hand on her back. "Dee, we're our own women now. We make our own living. He couldn't make you go back. Not even lawfully." I was trying to be encouraging.

Dolores lifted her head to me. "If my father comes looking for me, he won't be trying to make me go home."

"Come on now. You said it right. You are safe for now. Let's order some room service."

I spent four days in that hotel room. The first two were the hardest, knowing as I did that there was a lovely bar just at the bottom of the stairs. Yet I held out. I wanted to be again that girl who I was before I met Del. Open and optimistic. Maybe not quite so innocent, but a good, kind-hearted woman.

I vowed to myself that I would throw myself into my work. I vowed that I wouldn't go out, but to the most necessary parties. I vowed that I would read two books a week and learn to crochet. I was filled with more purpose than I had been in years and I felt good. I felt as if I were going to be happy.

Once I went back to the lot, I showed up early every day and did as much extra work as they needed. About a week after I came back, Mr. Hawthorne stopped me outside his office.

"Miss Savoy, I am so delighted to see you back in good form. I was growing quite worried for you there for a while. But here you are back to your former good health. I am glad of it."

I thanked him and walked on, only daring to roll my eyes once I was well past him. He was a good sort, I knew, but I also knew he was not so much worried for my well-being as he was for his budget.

Extricating myself from the party lifestyle was easy, it was staying away from all the people who had become used to my presence that was hard. There wasn't a day gone by in my first month of wholesome living when I wouldn't receive an invitation from one of my former lovers or a wild girlfriend.

Those first few months of trying to get my life back on track were nearly as painful as the months I spent wrecking it. Yet I was determined to live my own way. I was determined to be happy.

Chapter 17

It was autumn again. A year since Dolores and I had landed our roles in *The Siren's Song*, now a nearly forgotten film. We'd both had our contracts renewed a number of times and both were making a tremendous amount of money.

Monroe was beginning production on, what was to be, his biggest epic yet. He left early in October for New York to try and secure funding for his new film. He wanted to have a whole ancient city built for the background sets. Dolores stayed at home with me while he was gone and it was a enormous boon to me to have her so close for awhile. We were always close friends and confidantes, but while she lived with Monroe, it sometimes made me miss the days we shared a room in a brothel boarding house. Not actually living under Esther's roof, of course, but how close we had been then.

I had been doing so well on my own, that I had become quite boring. Dolores balked at staying in every night after only a few days and the first Saturday she made me go to a party.

"It's all well and good that you are getting yourself right, but you shouldn't become a shut-in."

I must admit it was fun to put on a fancy dress and do my hair for myself and not a character I was playing. As we were getting ready, Dolores turned on the phonograph and played some catchy popular songs. We practiced dancing in the living room, laughing hysterically the whole time.

It was in high spirits that we headed down to a party at the Darrow estate, in the West Adams district. It was my understanding that Stephen Darrow, the director, was away on a trip and his wife was throwing a gala party to keep herself company. Dolores had driven us to the party in the little roadster that Monroe had bought for her. She wasn't a very practiced driver, so it was a thrill just driving the few miles to the Adams district with her.

We were some of the earliest guests to arrive, so we got a tour of the place from Mrs. Darrow herself. She was a pretty, lively woman in her thirties. I don't believe she was very educated, but she was friendly and meant well. That, to me, was what made a good hostess.

Dolores and I settled in their living room, a huge room full of lovely white couches and gold accents. I accepted a glass of wine in order to look sociable. Dolores, I think, had a gin. Fausto de los Santos, rumored to be a Spanish count joined us on the couches. I had heard gossip that the count was pursuing Mrs. Darrow. Dolores flirted with him tirelessly as only she could. Mrs. Darrow seemed to take no notice. I enjoyed watching the makings of an intrigue I could have no part in.

As the house filled with party-goers, I got quite a warm reception from my former party mates. It was nice to know that despite my formerly drunken ways, I was generally liked.

Virginia arrived with her latest beau on her arm. I hadn't seen her in months, since her contract had been bought by the Ince Company. Her boyfriend was a cowboy actor for Ince's westerns, so we immediately fell into talking about stunt riding. Tom was his name, and he had seen my work with Floyd. He was impressed that I did my own stunt riding, since most of the time when women were riding horses, it was an actor dressed as a woman.

Sometime later, I was still talking with Tom, Virginia and some others, when Dolores came over to pull me away.

"Primita," she started once we were out of ear shot of the others. "I think I'm ready to go. I really think it's time we left."

I must have given her an incredulous look for she immediately continued, "No, really. I'm awfully tired." She had taken my arm and we were making our way towards the front door.

"Are you sure? I mean, isn't this a bit early for you?" I asked. People we knew were waving at us to stop and calling our names, but Dolores determinedly ignored them. I gave half waves and kept on walking.

"O yes, I really need to go. I ..." I stopped short, making Dolores pause. I saw now why she had found the sudden urge to leave. My heart stopped. Across the room was Del. My Del. Del.

I stood motionless. I knew Dolores was speaking, but I couldn't really hear her. Then I ran.

Like a fool, I didn't run from the house. I ran to one of the back bedrooms and dropped into a chair. I couldn't catch my breath, then I could only breathe too much. In a few minutes, I started to calm down.

I heard Dolores calling my name in the hallway, but I was hidden in the dark room I had found. In a minute or two I heard her walk on past. Without another thought, without another feeling, I went down to the back parlour, nearest the swimming pool, and got a whiskey. Then I got another. I got a third that I just sipped. I slipped out the back door to the patio by the swimming pool. It was a very cold October night. No one else was outside. I sat in a lounge chair, enjoying the flush of heat on my skin from the effect of the alcohol.

I hadn't really thought out what I was doing. I knew Del was there for me and I would have to face him at some time. I wanted it over with, I wanted to be over the pain I knew was coming. The cold, aching pain that had no beginning or end. I would have rather faced having my hand cut off. At least that was a visceral pain that would eventually go away, that could be healed. It had been a hard half-a-year – filled with pain and shame and sorrow – I wasn't prepared to do it again.

As I sat in the chill air, gulping at the air and trying to keep calm, for the first time I felt anger well up inside of me. It occurred to me, as the alcoholic buzz took over and the anger began to hold sway, that it was odd that I had never been angry with him before.

I made up for it that night. I was so angry at Del for leaving. I was enraged at him for making me feel so low about myself that I became a person I loathed. I was angry that he was a coward. I was angry at the pain he had left me with that seemed to never go away. I was even angry with myself for allowing someone so much control over me that they could possibly hurt me that much.

With a high-pitched harumph, I downed my drink and went inside for another. That was my fatal error. Just as I was going back outside, I heard my name as only he could say it. I paused, but didn't turn. Without looking back, I went out the door. He would follow me of course, but at least the scene that was coming wouldn't be witnessed by the whole party.

"Maggie, I'm so glad to see you." His voice was soft with emotion. "Won't you even look at me?"

I remained silent. I was so conflicted, I wouldn't have known what to say had I tried to speak. For winning out over the anger was the deep love I felt for him. I knew the wrong thing to do would be to throw myself into his arms, but every moment with him standing just beside me made me want to do it. Take the easy path.

"Maggie, I am so sorry. I am so very sorry. I know I hurt you terribly." He put his hand on my shoulder. The shock of his touch was too much, tears began to stream down my face.

"Listen to me. Please?" He sat down on the lounge facing me, but I turned my face to the side. If I looked at him directly, it would be all over. I would be his again.

"I was so stupid to leave you. I haven't had a moment's rest since I last saw your face so shocked and surprised. Marrying that woman was meaningless to me. We've hated each other since our wedding day."

I looked at him then, anger once again welling up inside. How dare he? How dare he act like he weren't a mercenary? How dare he act as if it wasn't his choice?

He tried to take my hand, but I shook him off. "Maggie, I want you back. Please take me back. I'll never leave again."

I stayed silent, formulating my attack. I longed to throw myself in his arms, but the hurt was still too fresh for me. My pride would not allow him to win.

"Please, say something. Anything, just talk to me," he pleaded.

"And your wife?" I finally spoke, but it was not likely something he wanted to hear.

Del slumped. Then he spoke very softly, "She's nothing to me. She never was. You are the only one who matters to me."

"You are married," was my only reply.

"Yes, I am," he said with a sneer, "I am, but that never mattered before. We can go back to the way we used to be."

"We can never go back."

"But why can't we?" His face was getting intense. I suppose mine was as well, although I felt like I was keeping considerably more calm.

"I had always planned on marrying you. Now it's an impossibility."

He reached for me, his face softening. He made to pull me into his arms, but I escaped and stood up. It was my turn to speak.

"How dare you come back here and expect me to jump into your arms? After what you did to me, can you possibly think I am the same naive girl you left behind?" I paused to choke back a sob. "I want nothing more than to pretend the last six months never took place and to feel your arms around me." Del started to stand and move towards me, but I held up my hand for him to stop. "I won't do it. I won't. I would never be able to rest easy knowing that the next time a hard choice has to be made that you will turn yellow and leave me."

"But Maggie. . ."

"No! You say it won't happen, but my only guarantee is that you will do what you have to that will cause you the least inconvenience."

It was his turn to be silent. I stood over him, face wet with tears.

"Because of you, I have done horrible things. Things so contrary to who I am, that I don't think I'll ever forgive myself for them. Because of the hurt you left me with, I wanted to die, to not feel anything ever again. Do you think I can go back to that? Do you think I can risk being hurt by you again?"

I leaned against the wall, my hands over my face. Del stood and came to me. He slipped his hand around my waist. I was so close to giving in, the smell of him squeezing my heart in half.

"Maggie, it will be all right, you'll see." I pushed him away.

"You don't get it. You don't get me. I . . ."

"Just stop it." Del flared with rage, "We are meant to be together. Stop this."

I had never seen him angry before. It made me shrink away from him. "No Del, we aren't meant to be together." I said quietly inching my way along the wall. "Go back to your wife."

He grabbed the front of my dress and pulled me towards him with a violence I didn't know was in him. "Maggie, you are mine." I was shaking my head 'no.' "Damn it Maggie." He shook me hard.

I don't know what I felt at that moment. I loved him and hated him, feared his violence and felt I deserved it. I stood there, pulled close to him by his hand clutching my clothing, waiting for what would happen next.

"I think the lady has made it quite clear what her intentions are," said a voice from behind me. In an instant the angry moment had passed. Del stared at the man behind me and then released me. With a scowl he walked past me and into the house.

I sat down heavily on the chaise lounge. I could no longer control the sobs.

"You know, it is not his fault that you did things you are ashamed of." I whipped around in surprise, already having forgotten that someone else was there.

"Who are you to say that to me? You don't know anything." I saw that it was Elliot Clayton. I did not know him well enough for him to make condescending pronouncements about my life and behavior.

"I know enough," he said casually, although he looked at me with intensity. "You made your own choices just as he did."

"It's nothing to you, leave me alone." I screamed at him still sobbing on the chair. "Just go away." I was feeling the effects of the drink and my head was swimming. Dolores found me then and took me home. She tried to get me through the length of the house with as few people as possible seeing me, but those we did come across gawked at me as if I were the side show.

Dolores's horrible driving on the curving roads in the hills made me so sick, we had to pull over twice. I was asleep by the time we got home. Somehow she got me inside into bed.

I felt horrible the next day. Not just from the drinking, but from the crying too. All the sobbing had left me with a headache. I spent most of the morning and early afternoon drinking tea and staring off into space. When I could face it, I went to my desk and wrote a letter to Del reiterating my displeasure at seeing him and asking him to leave me alone in a manner much more rational than the night before.

Dolores kindly assented to take it to his hotel. I was certain he was in the Alexandria as usual. When she got back, I was feeling better. I had bathed and eaten a good lunch. I was wearing my favorite dress, the one that made me feel pretty.

I was sitting in the window seat when she came in. She sat on the couch.

"I didn't see him, but he was staying there." She paused for a long while. "I'm glad I didn't see him, you know. I would have scratched his eyes out."

I smiled at her wearily. "So he wanted you back and you told him no." She said it as a statement.

I nodded. "I told him in a lot more words than just no. I think I said some very awful things, but mostly it is just a blur now. It happened so fast. I'm still trying to piece it all together."

"I hope you did say horrible things to him. Whatever you said it wasn't mean enough, I'm sure of it. What he did to you was the worst."

I didn't answer her, I just looked out the window. It was a clear day. I could see the houses at the top of Bunker Hill. He did do something horrible to me, I thought to myself, but I did horrible things to me as well.

Sometime between my headache of the morning and the relative calm I was feeling at that moment, I had realized that what Elliot had said was true. I think it may not have been the best time to bring it up, but he was right. I had behaved horribly, but it had been my choice and I needed to own up to it.

I had known Elliot since we had first started working for Chronicle Films, meeting him at parties and dinners. He didn't work directly with the film studios, but was involved somehow financially. I had never paid him much attention. He was polite and kind and had even driven me home more than once when I was behaving so appallingly and was too drunk to get home on my own.

After realizing the wisdom of his words, I felt bad for yelling at him as I did. After all, he had intervened when things had gotten out of hand. I should have been grateful to him. Of the many things to regret from the night before, that is what I regretted most.

"I am proud of you primita for turning him down," Dolores said after a while. "I don't know if I could have done it in your place."

"To tell you the truth, I'm surprised I did." I pulled my knees up, wrapping my arms around my legs. "I just became so angry with him once I saw him again. I think that is what sustained me."

"Well, whatever it was, I'm glad of it. I don't think I could have ever been nice to him again if you took him back. He didn't see you, he didn't know what you went through. And then he comes back, easy as you please, as if nothing had happened. Humph."

"I love him still, if you can imagine that." I laughed mirthlessly to myself. "I wish so much that he could be a better person than he is. I wish he hadn't acted the coward and left me, that we could be happy together."

"What was it that Papa used to say about wishes?"

"'If wishes were cakes we would all be fat and merry,'" we both laughed. Always with the memory of my grandfather, I knew things would be all right.

All I could think about for the next week was Del. I heard nothing from him. In fact, I heard nothing about him either. This led me to believe that he had again left Los Angeles. I can't say I was sorry for it. There were many times that I would feel a sharp pain in my breast and think I had made a terrible mistake by letting him go. At these times I was mortally tempted to rescind my rejection. It was better to believe that he wasn't within 'running to' range.

Talking to Virginia the following week, I found out much of what happened at the party that I did not witness. When Del had arrived he had asked all over for me. Virginia said that after I had run off, Dolores had marched right up to him and told him what a low-down, miserable dog he was to show his face there. Del had tried to hush her up by saying that he was there to make amends, but Dolores would have nothing of it and continued to berate him until he stepped away. Anyone who hadn't known about our history before, certainly found out then. Virginia then told me how as Del hurriedly left the house, certainly after our argument, he looked as if he had been wounded – his face pale, his arms folded close to his chest. He didn't speak a word to anyone as he left, although many people tried to get him to stay. He just made his way through the crowded house and left.

I don't know that I got any satisfaction knowing that he was hurting. I did, however, get much satisfaction to know that Dolores confronted him. That was my cousin, for you, not one to back down. Dolores never mentioned a word of it to me. All the same, I thanked her in ways just as silent.

Things went back to normal. I did my best to get on with my life. I had my career, my best friend and a home of my own. For now that was enough.

Chapter 18

They say the only constant in life is change. I think there are two constants – change and sudden, flip flop change. Sometimes life can be a whirlwind and sometimes it can be still, but the difference between the two happens with such rapidity, there is little time for warning.

Some weeks after Del's abrupt return and hasty departure, I came across Elliot while at the studio. I saw him come through the gate, heading for Mr. Hawthorne's office.

"Elliot?"

He stopped and turned towards me. "Maggie, how good it is to see you." He came over to me with all his usual politeness. He made a slight bow and opened his mouth to speak.

Not giving him a chance, I said, "I wanted to apologize for being so wrathful the ... the last time I saw you. I also wanted to thank you for standing up for me."

He looked at me with a queer, but sincere expression. He bowed slightly again. "It was nothing, I assure you. Any one would have done the same in my place."

"I'm not so sure," was my reply. "So thank you again. I wanted you to know that, even if it didn't seem so at the time, I appreciated your help." I did my best to convey my deep gratitude, but it sounded so slight to my own ears. "I won't keep you any longer. I'm sure you are here on business."

He waved his hand as if brushing away a fly. "As I said, it was nothing. I am glad to see you here and safe. Are you working now?"

"No, not today. We were doing some rehearsals, but I'm finished now. I was just on my way home."

"In that case, you would do me the greatest honor if you would accept my invitation for a late luncheon." Elliot's words were so formal, but his expression was one of open friendliness. The corners of his mouth were relaxed in a slight smile and his eyes crinkled at the edges in a comforting sort of way.

He wasn't a handsome man, not like Del at least, but he was very distinguished looking. He was most likely in his late 30s. He was always neatly dressed – but not in a flashy way – in well-made suits. He kept a short beard that was beginning to show some streaks of gray. The gray showed starkly in his dark hair. I had known him for awhile, but I don't think I'd really ever looked at him. He was distinguished looking without any distinguishing characteristics as only older gentlemen can be.

"I hadn't even thought about lunch, but I . . ." I started to reply by declining his offer. Before I could get the sentence out I changed my mind. Why not have luncheon with a friend, even a male friend? "I would love to." I answered after only a slight hesitation.

"Wonderful. Can you go now?" He seemed genuinely pleased.

"I need to get my things. I'll just be a minute." I turned and then stopped. "If you have business with Mr. Hawthorne, I can wait."

"No, that won't be necessary," he replied, "I believe my business to be done here for the day."

"In that case, I'll hurry." It only took me a minute to find my bag and coat. In only a few minutes more, I found myself in Elliot's large silver-gray touring car. From the lot he turned onto Hollywood Boulevard, heading East.

"You don't mind Levy's do you? The squab there is delicious."

"No not at all, the food they serve is always wonderful." Even though that had been one of Del's favorite restaurants, I was determined that he wouldn't ruin it for me. As we drove along, speaking awkward small talk to one another, I wondered at what I was doing to be accepting lunch with this man I really didn't know.

Since it was after 2 o'clock, the dining area was nearly empty. We had a quiet table near the windows. It was a perfect afternoon to be sitting inside – for the cloudy weather had finally burst and we were treated to a heavy rain shower. The restaurant was cozy and dry and the company, it turned out, was just to my taste.

Our small talk gradually turned into real talk and we covered many subjects. I found Elliot to be as interesting as he was interested. He sometimes asked more pointed questions than would have been normally polite, but I didn't mind. It was refreshing to talk to someone who wouldn't sidestep large issues, even if it were about my own recent history.

I nearly fell out of my chair when he asked, "Do you despise Mr. Wolham because he left you or because he married someone else."

I was so much at ease with our conversation leading up to that point that I answered naturally, as if it were a natural direction the conversation should take. Leading up to that point we had progressed from the state of marriage in society today, with so many divorces and remarriages, to those we knew personally, to those we knew were unhappy in marriage, and then his question.

"I don't despise him at all, I don't think. I guess if I were to make a choice, I would have to say that it is because he left me."

"I thought that might be your answer," Elliot replied with a disarming smile. "I myself was married off to a girl of good family when I was 21. Unlike Mr. Wolham, I didn't leave behind a girl as charming as you."

I'm sure I blushed. "I must not have been charming enough."

"Family strings are the hardest to cut. I'm sure you know." I did, intimately. "My wife and I hated each other within six months. We were dissimilar in every way imaginable. Fortunately, we got twin sons out of it and didn't bother each other much after that."

"Does you wife mind your boys then?" I asked, not quite sure where to head the discussion.

"Ah, no, my wife divorced me several years ago. My boys are at school now."

"I see, so you are a divorcee as well." I was glad to get some more personal information out of him. So far, I had only learned that he was educated in England, which did a lot to explain his slight accent and formal manners.

"I confess, I am. I've been happier in the last two years than in the last twenty. You can put me down as an advocate. Or perhaps I should declare myself an advocate of better chosen spouses."

I laughed. I was finding that I was laughing more than I thought possible that afternoon. It was a very welcome surprise.

"Do you regret your relationship with Mr. Wolham?" Again he asked me a question that was very pointed.

I stammered a bit as I formed an answer to his question, "I don't think so."

"It is best not to regret, I think. After all, each hurt or failure adds to one's character." He paused and I had no response. He tilted his head a bit while he looked at me, "Even though you lost some of your charming girlishness, you seem to me a better person for it." I blushed thoroughly, I'm certain.

By the time we had finished our leisurely luncheon, the rain had let up. Elliot offered me a ride home and I accepted. As I was attempting to give him directions, he reminded me that he had driven me home before. I was so embarrassed by the recollection that I was silent much of the ride.

As the gentleman he was, he ushered me to my door, bowed over my hand, and said goodbye.

When I entered, I found Dolores waiting for me. Monroe wasn't due back for two more days.

"I thought you were coming home this afternoon," Dolores started by way of greeting. "I thought maybe you had gone shopping without me, but then I see you delivered home by that Elliot Clayton." She reclined on the couch, checking her nails, as if she wasn't all that concerned.

"Elliot offered me lunch" I admitted. I wasn't feeling disposed to indulging her petulant manner, but I wasn't going to lie either.

"Look at you with the eye for the very rich men." I rolled my eyes at her and walked into the kitchen.

She followed me. "I don't mean anything bad by that, cousin. I just wonder at your taste in men." She leaned against the doorway, as I put on the kettle.

"My taste in men has nothing to do with it," I answered sharply, "Elliot has been very kind to me. He is very chivalrous and polite. Does there have to be something more?"

"Don't be a simpleton. I know how he looks at you, how he has always looked at you."

I frowned at her, "What would you know about it? I'm sure you haven't taken you eyes off of Monroe long enough to notice."

"Don't be sharp with me, cousin. I just want to show you what you are apparently too blind to see. Elliot Clayton likes you. Whether it is good or bad is up to you."

"Okay, you've told me what you think." I made a scrunched up face at her, and the kettle began to steam. "Would you like a cup of coffee?"

Over coffee Dolores told me about the comedy she was working on that week. It was meant to take place in a circus and a group of trapeze artists had been brought in to work on it. As she told me how her heart leaped and jumped every time they did their stunts, I couldn't help thinking about what she had said.

It wasn't until some days later that I saw Elliot again. Like the time before, he was in the walkway outside Mr. Hawthorne's office bungalow. It seemed as if he were waiting for me. Again he asked me to luncheon, and again I accepted, but for dinner. I was due on the set that day and knew we'd be filming as long as it was light out. We made arrangements to meet at 7:30 at Sexton's on 3rd Street.

I was quite casual with myself all day. Hamming it up on camera, off-camera joking with the crew and other actors. But it was almost as if I had stepped outside myself, outside the part of me that feels or thinks deeply. It's not that I wasn't looking forward to my date, for that really is what it was, with Elliot. I just didn't know how much I wanted to look forward to it.

Elliot was waiting by the entrance to Sexton's when I came up. I had taken the streetcar and was delayed by an accident. Elliot had dressed for dinner, as had I. He ushered me in and we were immediately seated. He had called ahead for reservations.

After pleasant small talk, just after our salad course was served, Elliot began, "I must confess that it wasn't an accident that I ran into you at the studio last week."

I smiled encouragingly.

"In fact, I went there expressly to seek you out. I had been loitering around the lot since noon hoping that I would see you."

"Lucky for you I wasn't working all afternoon." I think my response may have been flippant, but I wasn't quite sure how to answer such a declaration.

"I know. I was even luckier that you agreed to accompany me. I've long taken an interest in you and have hoped that one day you might do the same for me."

I know I blushed then and was too shy to look up to meet his eye. I believe he was looking directly at me, although I couldn't look up to be sure. I opened my mouth and stammered a bit, but no real reply came out. Couldn't in fact, because there was no real answer in my mind.

"Now, I see I've embarrassed you. Please forgive me, it was not my intention to cause you anxiety on my behalf. I wanted to be straightforward with you."

"No, no … I understand. I just was not expecting such a declaration. It is not unwelcome, but …" I had no further explanation for him. I half glanced up at his face, and I believe he was more flustered than I was. His voice didn't betray him, but he didn't have as much control over his features.

"I do enjoy your company, Elliot."

"Thank you, that gives me a little reassurance that I haven't made a complete fool of myself tonight."

"Of course you haven't." Silence fell upon us, it really felt like the air had gotten heavier. Then I sucked in my breath and said in a rush, "Perhaps if we can just think about enjoying our dinner tonight, we can see what happens tomorrow."

I looked up with a shy smile. Elliot looked away from the windows and smiled back. Being a man of extremely good breeding, he immediately began a very innocuous conversation about the features that Ferdinand Kranz had been planning – several of which I was to star in – and the rest of our dinner went off without a hitch.

We talked a lot. He told me about his twin boys, Wendall and Barnard, who were then 16. Apparently, the pair were quite mischievous. Elliot told me several stories of their misdealings that made me laugh so hard I nearly fell out of my chair. My favorite story, still to this day, was about their sixth birthday party. (Grandfather's themselves now, they will never forgive me for making this story public.) Elliot's youngest brother Simon, who was only about twenty at the time, had given the boys a bag of firecrackers as a present. Barnard and Wen had replaced the candles on their cake with the firecrackers. The maid had lit them, unknowingly, and brought the cake in. Everyone marveled at how sparkling the candles were, not knowing what they really were. Before they were finished singing the birthday song, anyone within ten feet was covered in cake and icing. Elliot told me he was laughing too hard to punish the boys, for they had been closest to the cake and were sticky messes. He told me it was probably punishment enough to miss the rest of the party and have to endure a second bath in one day. He must have told that story to Ferdy for it showed up in one of his 'Little Sweetheart' pictures a few years later.

After dinner that night we walked down 3rd Street enjoying the unusually balmy night air. I was still giggling from the funny stories he had told me. Elliot drove me home and again walked me to the front door, kissing my hand chivalrously as way of goodbye.

I was glad that Dolores had decamped back to Monroe's home. I was glad that she wasn't there to gloat or question or joke. I felt a new door had opened for me. But I wasn't quite sure, yet, if I wanted to go through it.

Chapter 19

Elliot and I began to see a lot of each other. I found that Elliot was really a very shy man and didn't like to be given very much attention. He did like society and was quite satisfied with observing the goings on rather than participating.

In a very short while, I found that Elliot, far from being dull as I had originally imagined – with his impeccable clothing and formal manners – was funny, energetic, well-informed and clever. As I had with Floyd, my first impressions of him had been completely mistaken. He was not a flashy, showy person so was often overshadowed by the many in Los Angeles that were. But for me, I liked his quiet ways. I liked that he had clever things to say and knowledgeable opinions, and he didn't care if anyone else heard them.

His family owned a large financial investment company, for which he worked. As the oldest son he was meant to be running it from the home offices in Boston. Elliot's younger brother Stephen was dynamic, outgoing, and ambitious, so Elliot abdicated his position as head of the family in favor of his brother who was much more suited to the job. Elliot managed several outpost offices.

For years he had been in London and Paris, before the war broke out. Since then he had worked at several of the offices in the United States, but was most happy in the Los Angeles office. The company, founded by his grandfather, had been one of the earliest companies to see that motion pictures were not a fad and could be a solid investment. They invested heavily in studios and directors. Elliot, by residing in Los Angeles, could better manage the company's investments. Also, he had confessed, he loved the people that show business attracted, so for the time it was a wonderful place for him to be – especially since he was surrounded with plenty of British actors he had known since his time in London.

Armistice was declared only a few weeks after I began to see Elliot. For at least a week there were celebrations held all over the city. The war hadn't really affected those of us living in California, but all the same, we were happy to celebrate along with our brethren in the rest of the world.

We went to the big celebration the Friday afterward, held at the newly named Pershing Square on 6th Street in the city center. It was amazingly crowded – half the city must have turned out for the event. We didn't stay too long since it was so crowded and went to Kingston Sam's estate for a large party he was giving.

Kingston hadn't been back to England since he left it when he was seven, but for all his years in America, his heart still belonged in Liverpool. Once we arrived at his house the party was going strong. Champagne, beer, and gin flowed equally. When we finally found Kingston, to say our hellos, he was sitting at a piano drunkenly singing patriotic songs. It looked like he hadn't been sober since the Armistice was announced. Elliot and I said hello, and Kingston and Elliot immediately fell into a conversation about the fine points of England. I wandered off to see who else was there that I knew.

The night was enjoyable although I didn't spend much of it with Elliot. We were both eagerly chatting with friends. Moving about the room, Elliot would stop to make sure I was comfortable, often bringing me a drink. He was so thoughtful where I was concerned, I couldn't help but be flattered to a degree I hardly knew was possible. I believe my face must have been flush for much of the night.

I was to find that Elliot was like that wherever we went. If we were separated in a crowd, I could be sure to always find at least part of his attention reserved for me. I warmed to it and found myself wanting to never be without it.

The holiday season that year was one of the most pleasant I've ever known. There was a very festive feeling about since the Armistice in the middle of November. The holidays the year before had been hectic. I think Del and I had gone to a party every night, he was so fond of crowds. That year, I spent it quietly – enjoying the weather, long dinners with my close friends, shopping with Dolores, quiet time with Elliot. It felt right.

Elliot and I grew very close. I knew that he liked me a lot and that he had for a long while. Not being an outspoken or boisterous person, he showed me in myriad tiny ways. His patience and kindness so often reminded me of Papa, I really wished that Papa could have met him. I thought he would have found a kindred spirit in Elliot.

Elliot confessed to me early on that he had fallen for me as soon as he saw me in The Siren's Song. He hadn't even met me in person, but thought he had already fallen in love. Even after he had met me and saw that I had been attached to Del, he continued his interest in me. All that time I had known him and I never had an idea of his interest. No wonder Dolores made fun of me.

I laughed at him for his secret love of me even as I was tremendously flattered. Elliot was not the love-at-first-sight sort of man and I teased him for having the courtesy to change just for me. He laughed right along with me. From what he told me of his history, it seemed that he did not fall in love often and it had been some time since he last had. More and more I began to hope that he wouldn't fall in love with anybody else again for a long time to come.

We spent a quiet Christmas together. I cooked dinner. Elliot carved the turkey. It was as if we were making up our own little family that day. Although we barely made it through dinner before falling into each others arms. The more I knew Elliot, every facet about him, the more I grew to like him. In many ways, the quiet holiday that we spent together cemented our bond with one another, and I was more glad for it than I ever would have thought.

After the New Year, it was back to the old grindstone. In January I filmed two short comedies and started on a western. Monroe had begun construction on the elaborate sets that were needed for his epic which was due to begin filming the following month. Dolores was cast to play the lead character. I was cast as a side character. It looked like it was going to be a very grand picture. Monroe hadn't let anyone read his scenario yet, but the film was to be called *Solomon and Sheba*. It was easy to guess then why the sets needed to be elaborate.

It was fun to watch the construction go up. The buildings had facades like you've never seen. Every known architecture was mixed to create something entirely new and nearly all of it topped with Persian minarets. The colors it was painted were garish and uncoordinated, but the sets were painted that way to show up well in black and white.

Things seemed to be going well for Dolores and Monroe. Dolores, for the world, made it look as if she and Monroe were the most solid couple one could ever meet. However, I began to notice that perhaps Monroe was reverting to his former womanizing ways. On one occasion in early November, Elliot and I saw Monroe sharing an intimate meal at a quiet, out-of-the-way restaurant with a very pretty woman I had never seen before. I didn't tell Dolores.

Just as filming was set to begin Monroe and Dolores had a terrible fight in front of a large crowd at the auto races. They were at the finish line with a large group of friends. Norman Foy, the former race car drive and actor, was participating in the race. Everybody waiting for him at the end was there for the party, whether to celebrate his win or commiserate his loss. Apparently Dolores was at the front of the crowd at the finish line and had lost track of Monroe. After the racers crossed the line, she went to look for him and found him at the restaurant bar being very cozy with a waitress. Monroe and Dolores were having a very loud argument as the crowd filled the place for the post-race party. She yelled something about his promise and then left the place in tears.

I had been gone for a few days, taking a short trip to San Francisco with Elliot, so I heard all this second-hand from Stephanie, who had attended the races with Harry, the following Tuesday when I got home. Stephanie was worried about Dolores. I was too.

I found her that afternoon on the set at the studio lot that afternoon. She was as chipper and energetic as ever and never once mentioned to me what had happened.

I could do nothing else but respect her silence. As we were both working on *Solomon and Sheba*, I had the opportunity of watching her carefully for the next seven weeks. That was the longest any of us had ever spent working on the same picture. Monroe, the genius director, always got his way. He had a clear vision for his epic and made everyone else work around it. Even if it meant halting the production of a dozen other pictures.

While filming any picture, there was always a lot of waiting, but I have never had to do as much waiting as I did during those long weeks. I was playing one of Solomon's wives and was also an extra in Sheba's entourage. I volunteered for as many extra bits as I could get just to alleviate the boredom. I shouldn't complain so, I know. It was hard work watching Monroe be a genius and my boss while he was breaking Dolores's heart.

On the set, Monroe treated her like a queen, complimenting her work, holding up her acting as an example, and similar kindnesses he showed no one else. When shooting was done for the day, he pushed her away. He told her he wasn't coming home, to his house, because he was too busy. More than once during filming I saw him with other women on his arm. I began to hate him, genius or not, for treating Dolores as he did. If he was tired of her, then he should let her go, not string her along.

Dolores held up wonderfully, except for some minor changes in appearance. She smiled as if she were in great spirits. She laughed as often as she could. Though to my ears, it often times sounded forced. I offered my support to her. I wanted her to confide in me, but she always found a way to turn the subject to something else. I hardly blamed her. I would likely have behaved in the same way.

One Sunday in March, I was getting ready for an early dinner with Elliot. Dolores had been home the whole weekend, something she had never willingly done before. I found her reading a magazine in the living room. It had been a quiet day, peaceful really, so I said, "Dee, why don't you come out to dinner with Elliot and me."

"No, I don't want to intrude," she replied not looking up from her magazine.

"Of course you wouldn't be intruding. It's just that you don't know Elliot very well, and it might give you a chance to know him better."

She looked up then. "It must be serious, primita, if I am to know him better."

I blushed, I'm sure of it. "I do like him, as I'm sure you've noticed. But that is not why I think you should come to dinner with us."

"Then it is a pity invitation." Dolores's face became so sad it was all I could do not to run to her and hold her in my arms.

"Indeed no. Can't I just enjoy the company of two of my most loved friends?" I tried to phrase my reply cooly, but the heat in my voice betrayed me.

"If you want to talk about me and," she hesitated, "me and Monroe, just talk already."

"The invitation stands. If you would talk to me about him, I would be much obliged. I have been awfully worried about you."

Dolores let out a long breath. She laid her head down on the couch. "He's grown tired of me. I knew he would, he's that kind of man." The room was dead quiet. Then she sighed again, "Every extra day he didn't turn me away I felt more confident that I could keep him. Every day I loved him more."

"At first, I just wanted the prestige of having a man like him for a lover. It wasn't long before I knew that he was the smartest, most gifted of men and the one I wanted for my whole life." She paused for a long while. "I wanted to support him in his work, be his muse. But I can see now that I was just trying to live in a fairytale."

Turning her face to the couch, she was silent. I went and sat next to her. I put my hand on her back. I wanted her to know how much I understood, how much I could commiserate, but had no idea how to tell her.

We sat that way for a long while. When her breathing evened out and I felt she had stopped crying, I said "Elliot will be here in a half an hour. You are coming to dinner with us. I won't take no for an answer."

I got up and Dolores followed. Unexpectedly, she followed my orders. When Elliot presented himself at 5 o'clock on the dot, we were both ready for him.

Our dinner was a thoroughly enjoyable one. Dolores entertained us with hilarious stories and we all had a fine night together. One of the last, I must say. But for that night, nothing else mattered.

Finally, the last week of filming was drawing to a close. We were several weeks behind schedule due to some foul weather in March. My parts had already been shot, so Mr. Hawthorne had assigned me to a comedy. Most of the other pictures being filmed at the time had been delayed. So many extras were needed to shoot the crowd scenes for *Solomon and Sheba* that whole pictures were shut down for several weeks.

Dolores made an excellent Sheba. Her exotic features were wonderfully accented for the role and her acting was beautiful. As the shooting was drawing to a close she had started to become quite thin, especially in her face. It was painful to me to watch her. I'm sure most people couldn't even tell. If they watched her closely and looked behind her smiles they would have seen what I saw. But I was already well-trained and had watched Dolores fade like this once before. Her appearance was taking on a look similar to what she had looked like before we escaped from Esther's boarding house. This time, there was no way for me to rescue her.

After my first day's work on the comedy, I found Dolores at home when I arrived. She was in the kitchen cooking. Whatever she was cooking smelled terrific and looked like enough to feed a large family, certainly not just the two of us. I went in to the kitchen and sat at the table.

"How did it go today Dee?" I asked, setting my chin on my folded hands.

She was quiet as she concentrated on her mixing bowl. After a moment she said, "Today was my last day. All that is left is some interiors with Jack going mad."

"At last," I said, "We are done with it. That was the longest seven weeks of my life." I was exaggerating, I know, but I wanted to get a reaction out of Dolores. I got more of a reaction that I expected.

She pushed the bowl away from her sharply and set both of her hands on the counter top. Without turning to me she said forcefully, "But it's going to be the best picture ever made."

How could I respond to that? There was nothing I could say without contradicting her, so I left it at that. She went back to her cooking, stirring something in a large soup pot.

After a few minutes Dolores began, "He asked me to move out for awhile. He said he needs his space while he edits the film together." I went over to her and put my arm around her. For the first time, I had a good look at her face. It was puffy and tear stained as if she'd been crying for hours. I took the spoon from her hand and set it down.

"Come now, crying while you're cooking will make the food bitter." She only nodded and let me hold her. She cried some more with her cheek on my shoulder. Her sobs diminishing, I asked her, "Now what is it we're having for dinner tonight."

"Albondigas." She didn't lift her lead.

"Have you made the meatballs yet?" She looked up and pointed to the bowl on the other side of the counter. "Well, I'll help you finish."

Dolores wiped her face and we finished cooking dinner together. She said nothing more about Monroe or about moving out. Wanting to help her, wanting nothing more than to make her laugh, I was stuck doing nothing at all. I couldn't make this kind of pain go away. I knew that better than anyone. I could have told her that everything would turn out all right, but I wasn't sure that it would.

Things went on that way for a few weeks. Dolores stayed at our home. We both made several short features. I saw a lot of Elliot. In public Dolores was as enthusiastic as ever. At home she rarely came out of her room.

Elliot began to speak to me about reconstruction in Europe now that the war was over. He had spent so many years there, spoke of the places there so warmly, that I knew he was longing to go back. I was beginning to wonder what I would do when the time came for him to leave. In all honesty, I loved him deeply. Yet, I wasn't honest with myself. I wondered if I could let him go quietly, or if I would beg him to stay. I tried to seem supportive, for deep down I really wanted him to go where it made him happy. My inner conflicts about whether or not I wanted him to be happy without me, may have made me seem less than supportive.

I wanted to be unselfish, but when I thought about the quiet happiness we had together, when I thought about his self-deprecatory humor and gentle manner, when I thought about his generosity and reasonableness, I just didn't want to see him go. Even when we argued he was a gentleman, listening before he spoke, never getting nasty or saying mean things. It just seemed so peaceful that we were together. I hate to even mention it, but he was so different than Del. Del was all energy and passion – but everything about him was on the surface. Elliot was his polar opposite, quiet and reserved, he had levels of personality and knowledge that would take a long time to really know.

We were dining one evening at Sexton's when he blurted out, "I received a communication from my brother today. I am to settle my business affairs on the West Coast. In two months time I am to leave for London."

I looked down at the table. Elliot reached across the table and took my hand. I couldn't help but to look up with more concern than I would like to have betrayed. "That's excellent news for you."

"I know it doesn't give us much time."

I squeezed his hand, "We'll make the most of it."

The rest of the evening, and in fact many more, was spent by Elliot exclaiming to me the great sights and marvels to be seen in London and Europe. He had been educated in England and so knew its ways intimately. He had lived in Paris, using it as his home base for many years, and had much affection for the city. He told me of the wonderful places he would take me in London – the Savoy, the British Museum – with weekends at a small hotel in Brighton that he adored. In Paris, he wanted to visit the Closerie des Lilas, the cafe of poets in Montparnasse, and see if the waiter Jean still had his large mustache. He described to me sitting along the Seine on the stone embankments and watching the light change as the sun went down.

I listened with great interest and not without a little longing. I have to say that his descriptions were moving to me. I did long to travel.

Elliot never openly asked me to go with him to Europe, but it was evident that he wanted me with him. With every word of praise for his favorite sights and haunts in the old country, I could tell he longed to show them to me. He respected me too much, respected my independence too much to ask me directly to go with him. It would only have led to a disagreement and we had too little time together for that. I knew what he wanted, and I really considered the option, however, I just didn't think I could go with him at that time.

I knew that when Elliot left it meant the end of our relationship and my heart was heavy. I knew that if I visited him in Europe later on things between us would be terribly different. I didn't let on how I was feeling. I wanted Elliot to enjoy our last weeks together as much as I intended to.

We spent as much time together as we could. Elliot often came to the studio lot to watch me act. I was always terribly embarrassed when he did. It was one thing to watch me after the fact on a screen, but quite another to watch me in person.

Dolores was spending a lot of time at home. She had heard nothing from Monroe, who was said to be holed up in his home office editing *Solomon and Sheba*. He had requested to Mr. Hawthorne that she not be given any starring roles for awhile so that he could call on her as needed to reshoot any scenes that might require it. I think this disheartened her a great deal, for Monroe had used an intermediary to tell her this.

At the very end of April, I had finished up with a three reel drama and had a week off. Elliot was preoccupied with tying up his business affairs. Dolores was still under Monroe's moratorium, but had yet to hear anything from him. Since we were both free of commitments for a time, I suggested to Dolores that we get away for a long weekend. It seemed to me that two independent women such as ourselves should be able to take a holiday when it felt right. When I mentioned it to Dolores, I caught her involuntarily glancing at the telephone.

Ah, so that was it, I told myself. She doesn't want to miss his call. Well, then, I would have to think of a way to get her away. She hadn't yet been to San Francisco, and I know it had been a dream of hers to visit there since she was a child, so I suggested a weekend of shopping and fine dining.

I could see her longing for Monroe's attention start to melt away as I brought up one excellent idea after another of wonderful things to do there. Although I had attended ladies college in San Francisco, I had never seen much of the city until I went with Elliot. I had been twice before with Elliot and had loved the city. I believe it may have been all the tempting shopping that finally swayed Dolores to my plan. We planned to leave on the early train on Wednesday and take the overnighter back on Monday.

As the day drew near, I could see Dolores brightening with the prospect of our holiday, despite her awkward glances at the telephone from time to time. I myself was looking forward to getting away from everything few days.

SOLOMON & SHEBA

Directed and Written by H. Phillips Monroe
Produced by H. Phillips Monroe

CHRONICLE FILM COMPANY

List of Players
Solomon – Jack Dean
Sheba – Dottie Sparks
Ramon – Tom Forman
Gwen, Solomon's first wife – Sylvia Aston
General Hectuh – Manfred Wilson
Elijah, the old minister – Henry Belting
Minister to Solomon – Charles Inslee
. . . and a cast of thousands

SCENARIO

THEN I CONSIDERED ALL THEY MY HANDS HAD DONE AND THE TOIL I HAD SPENT IN DOING IT, AND BEHOLD ALL WAS VANITY AND A STRIVING AFTER WIND, AND THERE WAS NOTHIING TO BE GAINED UNDER THE SUN.

THEN I SAW THAT WISDOM EXCELS FOLLY AS LIGHT EXCELS DARKNESS. THE WISE MAN HAS HIS EYES IN HIS HEAD, BUT THE FOOL WALKS IN DARKNESS.

FOR ALL IS VANITY AND A STRIVING AFTER WIND.

ECCLESIASTES 2, 11 - 17

(fades to title)

IN JERUSALEM OF OLD THERE LIVED A GREAT MONARCH WHO UNITED HIS PEOPLE WITH WISDOM AND STRENGTH. HIS LANDS AND HIS REACH WERE VAST. ALL OVER THE WORLD PEOPLE KNEW OF THE WISE KING SOLOMON AND CAME TO HIM FOR GOOD COUNSEL.

(fades to title)

YET ALL MEN BORN TO WOMEN ARE SUSCEPTIBLE TO THE WILES OF THE LESSER SEX. SOLOMON, BEING NOT MUCH DIFFERENT THAN HIS FELLOW MEN, FELL FOR THE GREATEST BEAUTY OF THE AGE. TRYING TO MAKE HER HAPPY WAS HIS ULTIMATE UNDOING.

The sun rises over Jerusalem. Workers are beginning their daily toils. Men come from their houses to harness donkeys to carts. Wives begin their chores. Windows open and bedclothes are shaken out. Women lean over outdoor cooking fires. Zooming over the city, upon a terrace high above the city there stands an older man dressed in layers of fine robes. He surveys the city beneath him. Spreading his arm as if giving a blessing, the long sleeve of his robe sweeping over the banister. His hands close together and the man bends over his clasped hands, eyes closed.

KING SOLOMON LOOKS OVER HIS CITY WITH WONDER AND GRATITUDE. HE THANKS GOD FOR ALL THAT HE HAS.

King Solomon turns, his robes swishing dramatically around him, and goes into his palace. He walks down flights of richly gilded stairs and is greeted by dozens of servants. He walks through the hallways with his rich clothing draping along behind him. The servants, following him, are careful not to step on the trailing cloth. Solomon walks on slowly in a ponderous manner. He looks to be deep in thought.

He enters a room that is filled with beautiful women – at least a hundred of them. All are sitting at low tables laughing and talking over breakfast. They rise when their King enters the room, each of them dressed in fine, silky clothing, they bow their heads. The King bows to them, raises a hand in benediction and wishes them well.

> MY DEAREST WIVES, GOOD MORNING, I HOPE
> YOU ALL RESTED WELL.

All of the women nod in agreement and give their husband their individual greetings.

> VERY WELL, GOOD WOMEN. I AM OFF TO ATTEND
> TO THE BUSINESS OF THE DAY.

The old king waves to the women and leaves the room. The women, smiling and in good cheer, turn to each other and start talking animatedly.

Solomon proceeds at his leisurely pace to his throne in a large ornate hall. Already there are hundreds of people lined up to see him. He seats himself comfortably on a tall, shiny throne and waves at his ministers to let the people come to him one at a time.

> KING SOLOMON'S WISDOM IS AS KNOWN AS FAR
> AS HIS MERCHANT SHIPS HAVE SAILED. KIND AND
> JUST, HE SPENDS HIS DAYS DISPATCHING HIS WISE
> WORDS TO HELP HIS PEOPLE.

A poor farmer comes first to see Solomon, he pleads his case and asks for a decision. Solomon looks kindly down at the poor farmer but shakes his finger at him and tells him that he is wrong. With a wave of his hand, Solomon sends him on his way.

Next to appear before him are two raggedy women, each clutching at a child. The women both speak at once and tug at the infant. With an indication of his hand, a minister comes to the women and removes the child from them. One of them holds on and will not let go. The other woman lets go but pleads for her baby.

Solomon asks the pleading one for her story. While the other woman scowls, the pleading woman tells her tale of woe.

THIS WOMAN'S CHILD DIED A FEW NIGHTS AGO, YET SHE CLAIMS MY CHILD AS HER OWN.

The second woman flatly refuses, saying that it is the other way around. She points to the pleading woman and then to herself, making a grief-stricken face to show her sadness.

Solomon ponders for a short while, scrutinizing each woman closely. He then straightens up and signals to his ministers to come forward. One carries the infant, the other carries a bright sword.

CUT THE LIVING CHILD IN TWO AND GIVE HALF TO ONE AND HALF TO THE OTHER!

Solomon commands his ministers who immediately begin to do as their master bids. The women shriek in horror at such a gruesome solution for the child. The woman who before was pleading for her child, now kneels before King Solomon, her face in anguish but resolute.

LET THE OTHER HAVE THE CHILD, FOR I CANNOT BEAR TO SEE IT KILLED

Wise Solomon nods at the woman's decision. Putting his hand flat out away from his side, he stays the sword of the executioner. He motions for the woman to stand up and his minister brings the child forward.

Solomon speaks gravely to the two women.

THE ONE WHO SHOWS COMPASSION MUST BE THE ONE WHO MOST TRULY WANTS TO SEE THE CHILD LIVE. THE CHILD'S TRUE MOTHER.

The minister holding the baby hands it to the woman who saved its life. The second woman is horrified to have been caught out. Without another look from her King, she is dragged out by sentries. Solomon takes the baby in his lap and tickles it until it smiles. With a warm smile, he hands the baby to its mother and the pair leave the hall happily.

For the rest of the day, Solomon attends to one problem after another. Late in the day a royal messenger appears. The messenger takes precedence over the lines of common people and their problems.

Bowing deeply before the King, the strangely garbed messenger obsequiously hands Solomon a roll of parchment.

Solomon takes the scroll and unwinds it. He reads the scroll.

TO THE HONORABLE KING SOLOMON,

HER MAJESTY QUEEN OF SHEBA RESPECTFULLY REQUESTS AN AUDIENCE WITH YOU. SHE WILL ARRIVE WITH HER ROYAL ESCORT IN THREE DAYS TIME.

Solomon nods approvingly at the message. He bids the messenger to leave with his approval. Solomon then claps his hands and his ministers rush forth. He gives them instructions for receiving of the Queen.

MAKE READY THE WEST WING FOR THE QUEEN OF SHEBA.

WE SHALL HAVE A GRAND FEAST THAT NIGHT.

The ministers bow over and over as Solomon speaks. When he is finished they rush off and Solomon resumes his task of dispatching judgements.

The day of Sheba's expected arrival, we find King Solomon once again on his parapet overlooking the city. It is afternoon and he watches for the first sign of Sheba's arrival. At last he sees a large envoy coming through the city gates.

The first to enter are the herald bearers on foot, walking ten abreast and four deep They are followed by the cavalry – one hundred fully armed soldiers aloft mighty white horses. Following are attendants followed by the Queen's ministers, nearly two hundred all together. Next come the Queen's personal attendants and servants. The ladies in waiting follow, being carried upon small palanquins. Finally, pulled by a team of ten horses comes the Queen's carriage.

Solomon leaves his post to go down and greet the Queen, long before her envoy has finished filing into the city.

Wearing a fine headdress and elaborate robes, Solomon awaits upon his throne for the Queen's entrance.

When the doors to his hall are thrown open, two lines of ten girls in flowing Arabian clothing enter the hall and walk side-by-side up to the King's throne. They split in front of the throne, one line going to each side. Revealed behind the girls are two rows of four heralds standing abreast. They too split into lines on each side of the throne. Following them are four elaborately dressed ministers in a single line – their hands folded as if in prayer.

When the ministers reach Solomon's throne, they split and face inward, creating an aisle. Revealed behind them is palanquin being held aloft by four strong men, naked to the waist. Atop the soft cushions is a woman of extraordinary beauty. She wears a simple crown of wrought gold, a sheer veil flowing from the top of her head covers the lower half of her face. The material is so fine, you can see all of her features clearly.

Solomon is clearly struck by her beauty. The Queen of Sheba is helped to the floor by the aid of attendants who have come from behind. Standing straight, she wears clothing that amplifies her striking figure. Alone she walks the few paces to stand before the King's throne. With a graceful, bowing sweep, she curtsies deeply. Looking directly into Solomon's eyes she speaks to him.

YOUR MAJESTY, I AM HONORED BY YOUR RECEPTION

Solomon bows his head in return still staring at the woman with eyes that are full of love.

YOU HAVE COME A LONG WAY FOR THIS VISIT. REST NOW AND FEAST. TOMORROW WE WILL ATTEND TO YOUR BUSINESS HERE

Solomon claps his hands several times and his stewards come forward to assist the new arrivals. There is much bustle. Solomon descends from his throne and offers his arm to the Queen of Sheba. Together, their different costumes contrasting, they walk together from the hall.

In the dining hall, Solomon sits at the head of the room filled with long tables. His wives take up many of the places. Sheba sits near to Solomon, sharing a table with his first wife, Gwen. A handsome middle aged woman who smiles a lot, but does not take part in the conversation.

Solomon makes small talk with Sheba and she gives him many shy smiles as they converse. He asks her about her homeland.

YOUR MAJESTY, PLEASE TELL ME OF YOUR HOMELAND. I KNOW SO LITTLE ABOUT IT.

Sheba vividly describes the wonder and beauty of her land. Her shy smiles are replaced by shining eyes and enthusiastic gestures.

SHEBA IS A LAND OF GREAT AND DIVERSE BEAUTY. MOUNTAINS THAT TUMBLE INTO THE SEA, PLAINS THAT CAN FEED THE WHOLE COUNTRY. OUR SHINING GLORY IS OUR SEA PORTS FILLED WITH EVERYTHING THE WORLD HAS TO OFFER.

Solomon is taken with Sheba's enthusiastic love for her land. He looks at her with misty eyes. His first wife looks on with a smug look. She knows what it means when his eyes mist over while looking at a woman.

Soon the feast is over and Sheba retires with her retinue.

Gwen stops Solomon before he can leave the hall. She indicates that she would like to speak with him in a side room where they will not be overheard. Once inside the room, she turns to her husband with a look of kindness, like one would give a sweet child. She speaks to him in admonishment.

> DEAREST SOLOMON, I CAN SEE HOW MUCH YOU LIKE THIS QUEEN OF SHEBA. I MUST GIVE YOU WARNING. I CAN SEE THAT SHE WILL BE YOUR DOWNFALL IF YOU SUCCUMB TO HER CHARMS.

Gwen looks truly upset when she finishes telling Solomon her warning. Solomon takes her hand in both of his and pats it warmly.

> THERE, THERE, MY DEAR GWEN. SHE IS TRULY THE MOST BEAUTIFUL WOMAN BUT SHE HAS A COUNTRY OF HER OWN.

Gwen doesn't quite believe her husband, but she lets him go.

The next day the great hall is empty except for Solomon on his throne and Sheba sitting on an ornamental couch nearby. They converse convivially. Then Solomon asks:

> MY DEAR QUEEN OF SHEBA, WHY IS IT THAT YOU HAVE COME TO SEE ME?

Sheba's face become's quite sad. She looks away before she answers.

> I HAVE COME TO BEG YOU TO SHARE YOUR TRADE ROUTES WITH MY OWN COUNTRY.

Sheba is clearly stricken as she announces her true purpose. She grasps her hands, pleading.

> YOUR MERCHANTS HAVE SURPASSED MY OWN IN TRADING THROUGH AFRICA. NOW MY CITIZENS NO LONGER PROSPER. SOMETHING MUST BE DONE.

Sheba goes down on her knees before Solomon, begging him. Solomon tries to console her and he pulls her up from the floor and has her again sit on the couch. He speaks to her soothingly and says that he will think the matter over.

GIVE ME A FEW DAYS, MY DEAR, AND I WILL COME UP WITH A SOLUTION

Sheba nods in agreement.

Solomon spends the next few days entertaining Sheba and her ministers. He shows them the many wonders of his city and gives them entertainments in the form of dancing girls and plays. As the days go by, Solomon finds himself more and more attracted to the young queen. Her vibrancy and beauty fascinate him. Often Solomon watches Sheba rather than the entertainment he has provided.

On the third day, Solomon and Sheba are again alone in the great hall. They laugh at a joke and seem to enjoy each other's company. Then Solomon's face grows somber. Sheba's becomes alarmed at his seriousness.

MY DEAR QUEEN, I HAVE DEVISED A SOLUTION TO YOUR PROBLEM

Sheba is joyous at the news and eagerly awaits Solomon's answer.

OH WISE SOLOMON, YOUR REPUTATION PROCEEDS YOU FOR GIVING JUST ANSWERS

Solomon nods his head in agreement at her praise. He then explains his solution.

I WILL DIRECT MY SHIPS AND MERCHANTS TO ONLY GO SO FAR AS TO TRADE WITH YOUR CAPITAL CITY. YOUR MERCHANTS WILL COMMAND THE SOUTHERN TRADE FROM THERE, BUT ...

Sheba shows her happiness effulgently. She thanks him for such a happy response to her problem. Solomon takes her hand and brings it to his heart.

BUT ONLY IF YOU AGREE TO MARRY ME

Sheba is shocked by this condition and shrinks away from the once-wise king. Solomon describes his love for her.

YOU WILL BE THE JEWEL OF MY HAREM. WE WILL RULE IN PEACE AND HARMONY FOR YEARS TO COME

Sheba is not convinced, but Solomon continues to profess his love. Finally Sheba retracts her hand. She tells him of her misgivings.

DEAR KING SOLOMON, I AM THE RULER OF MY OWN COUNTRY. HOW CAN I RULE PROPERLY FROM SO FAR AWAY?

Solomon explains that he will help her. His influence is vast, so they can easily join together their disparate kingdoms. It will all work out perfectly, Solomon tells her.

BUT YOUR HIGHNESS, I LOVE MY COUNTRY AND DON'T WANT TO BE SEPARATED FROM IT.

Again Solomon tells her it will work out perfectly.

YOU MUST STAY WITH ME FOR A YEAR OR TWO THEN I WILL GO WITH YOU TO SHEBA FOR A LONG VISIT.

Sheba is forlorn as she looks down the length of the great hall, away from Solomon. She really doesn't want to marry the old king but sees no other choice if she is to save the industry of her nation. After wiping away tears of duty and responsibility for a few minutes while agonizing over the choice before her, she turns back to Solomon and accepts his proposal.

Solomon is overjoyed and calls to his minister to begin preparations for the wedding. Sheba excuses herself.

Sheba goes to her rooms to tell her ministers. She encounters first her head minister, a handsome man nearly as young as she. She cries out to him and throws herself into his arms.

RAMON, FOR THE SAKE OF OUR PEOPLE, I HAVE TO MARRY SOLOMON.

Ramon embraces the Queen and shakes his head in denial. The two, who are obviously lovers, console each other for a few minutes. Then Sheba extracts herself from Ramon's burly arms.

WE MUST CONSULT WITH MY OTHER MINISTERS TO DETERMINE WHO SHALL RULE IN MY STEAD WHILE I REMAIN HERE IN JERUSALEM.

Ramon holds her hand trying to hold her back, but Sheba is determined – her face fixed as she stares straight ahead.

A MAGNIFICENT WEDDING

Solomon's great hall is decorated to the hilt with banners and flowers, all manner of adornment. The hall is filled with people all dressed up for the marriage of Solomon to Sheba. Solomon stands at the head of the room next to his throne. He is dressed in the finest of embroidered robes. Sheba stands at the far end of the hall, accompanied by her ministers, dressed in a simple dress of satin. She wears a jewelled crown on her head and looks truly regal. Her face is poised, but firm. She slowly walks up the aisle. A solitary tear streams down to her chin.

Solomon meets her at the bottom of the stairway to his throne platform. Taking her arm in his, they both walk up the stairs. The priest gives his sermon and marries the two monarchs by wrapping a ribbon about their two hands, binding them in matrimony.

Solomon hosts a large festival for the whole city to celebrate his latest nuptials. There is feasting and parties in every neighborhood of the city. The largest of the parties is in Solomon's own hall where have gathered the nobility of his realm. Everyone is thoroughly enjoying themselves except for the Queen of Sheba's party. In that corner, nary a one of them bestirs to smile or taste the food in front of them. Sheba, at the King's side, smiles only when convention makes it necessary, but she is quite as depressed as her fellow countrymen.

The entertainments include hundreds of dancing women, fire-eaters and conjurers, a large band playing unusual instruments, and a choir of children. The festivities are as grand as could be imagined, but Sheba remains unmoved. As the evening draws to a crescendo, Solomon leads Sheba from the hall. With a meaningful, lingering look at Ramon, Sheba follows Solomon from the party.

WEEKS GO BY ...

Sheba is laying across a couch surrounded by her own servants. Only one of her ministers remains with her, an old gentleman, who is crouched over a writing desk. Sheba stares blankly as she is fanned by her maid.

Solomon enters her apartment and exclaims at her beauty and how happy he is that she has joined his harem. Sheba smiles weakly at his exclamations. Then Solomon sits close to her on the lounge chair, holding her hand to his heart.

BUT YOU DO NOT LOOK WELL MY DARLING. ARE YOU SO UNHAPPY WITH ME HERE?

Solomon looks genuinely concerned at her distress. Sheba turns away from her unwanted husband to hide the tears in her eyes.

NO, NO, MY HUSBAND, IT IS ONLY THAT I MISS MY OWN PEOPLE.

Solomon tenderly holds Sheba's hand to his cheek and seems genuinely hurt by Sheba's sufferings. Sheba turns to him and tries to put on a happier face.

I WOULD NEVER WANT YOU TO BE SAD ON MY ACCOUNT. IS THERE NOTHING I CAN DO FOR YOU?

Sheba looks hopefully at her husband. She takes both of her hands into his and excitedly asks him for what she wants.

PLEASE, SIR, LET ME VISIT MY HOME. I WILL ONLY
BE GONE TWO MONTHS.

Solomon looks away from Sheba and lets his hand drop from hers. He shakes his head in disagreement. Sheba pleads with him, hands together in front of her in desperation. Solomon replies sadly:

OUR AGREEMENT WAS FOR YOU TO STAY TWO
YEARS. SURELY YOUR PEOPLE WON'T MISS YOU
IN SUCH A SHORT AMOUNT OF TIME.

Solomon looks hopefully at Sheba and runs a hand over her hair. Sheba nods in agreement, holding back her tears. Solomon leans forward and kisses her forehead. Then he tells her something that makes her smile, whether it is a real smile or a smile just to appease Solomon, only she knows.

MONTHS GO BY AND SHEBA IS A CAPTIVE IN THE
PALACE. SHE LONGS FOR HER OWN PEOPLE AND
COUNTRY. SHE WANDERS THE PALACE GROUNDS
AIMLESSLY AND TIRELESSLY LOOKING FOR A SIGN
OF HOPE.

Sheba dressed in the flowing robes of her fellow wives wanders in beautiful gardens walled in on all sides by the castle.

SHE TRIES TO FIND JOY IN THE SMALL THINGS.

Sheba leans over a flower to smell it, she whistles along with a song bird, she sits in a gazebo stroking the fur of a small dog. In each scene she often looks longingly towards the clear sky in the distance.

MEANWHILE. . .

SOLOMON HAS LOST TOUCH WITH HIS WISDOM.

In the great hall, Solomon is upon his throne. As usual there is a line of people formed in the long hall waiting to see the king. Two men are before him and presenting, each in turn, their sides of the problem. When they are finished speaking, they look to their king for guidance. Solomon looks at each man blankly. Then he shakes his head and swishes his hand to indicate the men should leave.

I DON'T KNOW HOW TO ANSWER YOUR DILEMMA. YOU SHOULD SOLVE IT AMONGST YOURSELVES.

Finishing his speech, Solomon rests his head on his hand, eyes closed in consternation. The ministers surrounding him look at each other and their king with eyes wide with shock. The two commoners before the king do not move to go away. They too are stunned by Solomon's dismissal.

Amongst the crowd of people lining the hall, a murmur picks up as they all talk of this turn of events.

Solomon gets up from his throne, waving away help from his ministers and leaves the hall. The ministers begin to shoo out the waiting people.

Sheba lies prostrate in her rooms. She is very depressed. Solomon enters and sits down beside her without saying a word. He takes her hand and holds it warmly. He strokes her hair. In a few minutes he gets up and leaves. Sheba watches him go impassively.

She gets up and paces her rooms, looking for all the world like a caged tiger. She grips her hands and shakes her head. Sometimes she stops and laughs mirthlessly, her eyes shining.

WHAT HAVE I DONE MARRYING THAT MAN? SEPARATING MYSELF FROM MY PEOPLE? WHAT IS TO BECOME OF ME?

Sheba wails at the walls, shaking her fists. She continues pacing the room.

Solomon stands on his terrace overlooking the city. His face is drawn and sad. He watches the industrious people below him toil at their daily labors.

WHAT IS HAPPENING TO ME? I CANNOT THINK ON THE GOOD OF MY PEOPLE FOR SHEBA'S SADNESS SADDENS ME AS WELL.

Solomon says to himself still looking over his kingdom.

He raises his hands towards the sky, his robe's sleeves falling down.

GOD, WHY CAN I NOT PLEASE THE QUEEN OF SHEBA? WHEN THE WIVES OF MY HAREM ARE SO JOYOUS, SHE ALONE CANNOT BE MADE HAPPY. WHAT SHALL I DO?

Solomon stares solemnly at the sky as if waiting for a reply. After a minute he lowers his arms and hangs his head.

All of a sudden he looks up across the city.

THE TRUMPET OF A HERALD!

At the city gates approaches the banner of Sheba. Her ministers have returned. Solomon smiles broadly.

THESE NEW ARRIVALS ARE SURE TO CHEER HER UP!

Solomon hurries away down the long staircase to greet the convoy in his hall.

A shortwhile later, Solomon enters Sheba's rooms followed by Ramon. Sheba's eyes grow wide with astonishment when she sees her minister and lover. Solomon finds happiness in her response. Seeing her greatly cheered makes him happier.

MY DARLING, LOOK WHO I HAVE BROUGHT FOR YOU, JUST ARRIVED. I KNOW THAT YOU WILL HAVE TO TAKE CONSUL WITH YOUR MINISTERS SO I WILL LEAVE YOU TO DO YOUR WORK.

Sheba smiles and thanks Solomon. With a bounce to his step, Solomon leaves the room. Within seconds Sheba and Ramon are entwined in each others arms. They murmur to each other endearments. They have been apart for a long time and hold each other while trying to make up for lost time.

Finally Ramon pulls away and looks Sheba straight in the face.

YOUR MAJESTY, YOUR PEOPLE MISS YOU DEARLY.
I MISS YOU DEARLY.

Oh Ramon, Sheba says as she kisses him fiercely. Ramon kisses her back with equal passion. Then he leads her to the couch and sits with her holding her hands.

YOUR MAJESTY HAS MADE THIS UNFORTUNATE MARRIAGE TO SAVE HER PEOPLE, YET HER PEOPLE WOULD FAR PREFER HER MAJESTY'S PRESENCE. PLEASE SAY YOU WILL COME HOME, DESPITE YOUR HUSBAND.

Ramon says the last part with a sneer and then bows his head low over Sheba's hands. She puts her hand on his head, clearly moved by his words. She puts her hand under his chin and lifts his face up.

I HAVE MISSED MY PEOPLE, AND YOU.

Again the couple embrace, time and circumstances so cruelly working against them. Sheba straightens herself up and lifts her chin in confidence.

BARGAIN OR NO, I WILL RETURN HOME. IN THREE DAYS TIME LEAVE THE CITY, BUT DO NOT TRAVEL FAR BEYOND THE CITY GATES. I WILL MEET YOU AFTER SUNDOWN AND WE WILL ESCAPE.

Ramon looks at Sheba first in shock and then with fascinated hope. He asks her how she will get away. Sheba has a steely, far away look and says:

LEAVE THAT TO ME. WE WILL GO HOME TOGETHER!

The lovers embrace once more, this time with hope in their eyes.

Solomon, so delighted that his wife is showing some happiness at last, organizes a feast and entertainments for Sheba's travelers. The few days go by very fast with Sheba meeting with her ministers about her homeland's affairs. She and Ramon keep it a secret of their plans for escape.

To make the ruse more believable, Sheba seeks out Solomon. Going up the long stairway, she finds him on his terrace. She joins him at the banister and looks out at the city that she could never call her own.

DEAR HUSBAND, I WOULD LIKE YOUR ADVICE IN THE MANAGEMENT OF MY COUNTRY. WOULD YOU MIND MEETING WITH MY MINISTERS THIS AFTERNOON?

Solomon is overcome with joy that his wife is accepting him at last. He readily agrees. In the afternoon, he enters his wife's chambers and finds them filled with her countrymen going about their business. Sheba greets him and takes him to a table with maps where they proceed to discuss and plan.

In Solomon's Hall, he sits on his throne. Sheba is beside him on the ornate couch. He wishes a fond farewell to his wife's countrymen and they bow deeply before Solomon and their Queen. As Ramon straightens, he and Sheba share a significant look. Both look away before it can be noticed.

As her countrymen leave, Sheba turns to Solomon and speaks to him. She is all smiles. Solomon smiles kindly at her in return, happy that she is happy.

As night falls on the city, Sheba and her few remaining servants skirt the city. It is important that she leave the city before the gates are shut for the night. As they approach the gates, her one remaining minister, the only one of the group on horseback, goes ahead to distract the guards. Once dismounted he leads all six guards to the guardhouse to show them his paperwork. He animatedly talks to the guards, joking with them and such, as the servants and Sheba hurry through the gates.

Once free of the gates, the women wait for the minister to ride through. The gates to the city are shut behind him. With haste they all hurry over the nearest hill. On the other side, they find Ramon and six soldiers waiting for them with spare horses. They all mount and ride away.

They reach their one remaining ship at daybreak. Ramon has sent all the others on ahead. The Queen and her people embark on the ship and sail immediately. Ramon and the Queen embrace as they lose sight of the shore.

But storm clouds brew above their heads and within a few hours, a deluge is threatening to sink the ship. The crew struggles to keep the boat afloat. Sheba stands at the helm, brave, facing the danger. Ramon is by her side. It looks like the crew will succeed as the storm seems to be abating when a large thunderbolt rains down on the ship, cracking it in two and sending it to the ocean floor.

Solomon stands atop his parapet, pacing with his hands behind his back. It is morning and the sun is rising above his beautiful city, but he takes no notice.

Solomon's minister approaches him from the doorway to the stairway. He bows deeply before Solomon.

> YOUR MAJESTY, IT APPEARS THAT THEY LEFT THROUGH THE GATES AS THEY WERE BEING CLOSED. WE FOLLOWED THEIR TRAIL TO THE SEA WHERE THEY MUST HAVE EMBARKED UPON A SHIP.

Solomon throws his head back and yells shrilly, making several people on the streets below look up in terror.

Solomon shakes his head violently and throws his arms about before tearing at his hair.

> HOW COULD SHE HAVE LEFT ME? ESCAPED FROM ME AS IF I WERE A COMMON PRISON WARDEN. WHY DID SHE LEAVE ME?

The minister continues to bow to his liege, unable to give satisfactory answers, he remains silent. Solomon continues to rant and rave. Then he turns to his minister and calls out.

BRING ME MY GENERALS. WE WILL BRING HER
BACK WITH FORCE!

Solomon's eyes shine with cruelty and the minister hurries away.

In a small room, Solomon looks over a table of a map with his three generals. He points out strategic points and discusses his plans.

TAKE THREE SIDES OF THE CITY AT ONCE AND IT
IS SURE TO FALL. DO NOT HARM THE QUEEN OR
HER MINISTERS, BUT BRING THEM BACK TO ME.

Solomon gestures fiercely as he commands his soldiers to take the Queen of Sheba's city. His features have turned ugly in his anger and hatred. The soldiers all stand stoically receiving their orders.

After much admonishment, Solomon releases his generals to prepare for the invasion of Sheba. Outside the meeting room, two of the generals stop to discuss Solomon's intentions of war. General Hectuh speaks to his younger counterpart.

OUR MONARCH HAS ALWAYS BEEN SO NOBLE AND
WISE. INSTIGATING WAR IS NOT HIS USUAL WAY. I
WONDER AT WHAT HAS BECOME OF HIM.

The younger man shakes his head in dismay at the way things have turned out and tells Hectuh:

MARK MY WORDS, NOTHING GOOD WILL COME OF IT.

The two soldiers walk away glumly, knowing they must follow their orders to the letter.

IN THE LAND OF SHEBA

On the wharf of the harbor, the Queen's minister, Elijah stands. He shades his eyes with a hand as he scans the horizon. A servant comes to the minister and hands him a scroll. He speaks to the Elijah.

SIR, ANY SIGN OF RAMON'S SHIP?

Sadly, the old minister shakes his head, indicating that he has not. He briefly looks at the scroll and then follows his servant away from the dock.

Just over the hill from the wharf, Solomon's soldiers are amassing. They have come a great distance by land in an effort to take the city by surprise. The General Hectuh is quietly giving orders to his men who are forming lines. When the men are all lined up, the general raises his sword in the air and yells attack.

ATTACK!

The trumpeters blare and the drummers begin to beat their drums. The soldiers run over the hill ready to do battle.

Carnage ensues as the soldiers quickly and efficiently take over the city. Women and children huddle in the streets. Men take up weapons against the soldiers but are no match against their swords and shields. The battle is long and deadly. The soldiers make their way, cutting through the city, towards the castle at the top of the hill.

General Hectuh takes the castle with his personal guard. They surround Sheba's ministers who are led by Elijah. The ministers stand with their backs to one another with raised hands.

Hectuh points his sword at Elijah's chest and demands information.

WHERE IS THE QUEEN OF SHEBA? TELL US NOW
OR WE SHALL HAVE YOUR HEADS!

The ministers cower in fear, shaking their heads 'no.' Only Elijah is calm. Hectuh rattles his sword at the wise old minister once again. Elijah finally speaks.

WE BELIEVE THAT OUR QUEEN WAS LOST AT SEA
WHILE MAKING HER WAY BACK FROM JERUSALEM.

Elijah hangs his head in sorrow. Hectuh looks quite shocked at this development. He soon recovers himself and indicates to his men to usher the captives away. Hectuh motions to one of his soldiers.

NEWS OF THIS MUST GET TO KING SOLOMON RIGHT AWAY. TAKE THE FASTEST SHIP TO ISRAEL.

The soldier commissioned with the errand takes off from the room at a run. Hectuh looks to the heavens, his eyes pleading, then hangs his head in sorrow.

Solomon is standing on his terrace over looking Jerusalem. He no longer looks so regal and refined. His robes are torn, his hair lays in tangles. Yet he looks over his city at dawn as is his usual habit. After staring off blankly, he begins pacing the terrace, sometimes silently, sometimes talking and gesturing to himself.

Gwen comes up the stairway with hesitation. She looks on her husband with a mixture of compassion and fear. His back is to her and she reaches out as if she is going to touch him, but at the last second pulls her hand back. To get his attention, she shuts the door to the stairway. He turns and sees her, but does not react. Gwen starts to speak.

MY DEAREST HUSBAND YOU MUST BRING YOURSELF AROUND. IT IS DISTURBING TO SEE YOU SO FORLORN AND HOPELESS.

Solomon doesn't pay any attention to her, but keeps his pacing up.

SOLOMON PLEASE LISTEN TO ME

Gwen wails at her husband who barely looks up from his nervous pacing. Crying, tears streaming down her face Gwen watches her husband as he declines ever more into madness.

I TOLD YOU NO GOOD WOULD COME OF YOUR FASCINATION WITH THAT HARLOT!

Gwen screams at Solomon, her hands balled into fists. Rage pouring out. After her outburst she turns and runs through the door to the stairs. Solomon pays no heed.

Still pacing, he looks up from time to time towards the city gates. One time when he looks he sees a horse running towards the city with great speed. This peaks his interest.

In a few minutes more, a messenger bursts through the doorway and kneels before his king. Solomon stops pacing and faces the boy. Seeing that the monarch is waiting, the boy hands to him a scroll. Solomon hastily unrolls it and reads its message. The scroll delivered, the messenger hastens away. Solomon reads.

> THE CAPITAL OF SHEBA HAS BEEN TAKEN. ACCORDING TO HER ADVISORS, SHE HAS NEVER RETURNED TO THE CITY SINCE SHE FIRST LEFT. WE CAN FIND NO EVIDENCE OF HER. HER ADVISORS BELIEVE HER SHIP TO HAVE FOUNDERED AT SEA. THEY KNOW OF NO SURVIVORS.

Solomon is stuck by the horrible news. He twists the paper to bits, his face becoming contorted and disfigured. He cries out in rage and begins ranting, pulling at his hair.

He throws his hands up to the sky and cries out.

> WHY? WHY? WHY? SHE OF SUCH BEAUTY AND SWEETNESS? WHY HAVE MY DREAMS BECOME FORSAKEN?

Solomon shakes his fists at the heavens, his face still disfigured with his madness. Then he puts his hands down and opens his mouth in a long howl. On the streets below, his people look up at the sound in fright. No longer are they happy, industrious people. Instead they cower and hide, even as they go about their chores. The wives of Solomon, inside the castle, cast themselves down in unhappiness. Solomon's ministers loll about the great hall with expressions of depression.

Solomon, standing on his terrace overlooking his grand city, gives in to his madness.

I OPENED TO MY BELOVED, BUT MY BELOVED HAD TURNED AND GONE. MY SOUL FAILED ME.

SONG OF SOLOMON 5, 6

THE END.

Chapter 20

San Francisco that May was beautiful. It was sunny and warm. The city had been washed clean by a rainstorm the day before as if it knew we were coming. Dolores and I ate at fabulous restaurants, bought beautiful clothes and hats. We rode the street car all around the city. We laughed a lot. We giggled when we saw a handsome man and indecorously rode on the sides of the street cars. In short, we acted like little girls and it was grand.

We also made the rounds at the more famous clubs, drinking champagne until the early morning hours. Dolores was the center of attention among our new male friends, and she loved every second of it. I think she may have forgotten, in the year she had devoted herself to Monroe, that she could have any man she wanted. It did my heart good to see her flirt so ravenously with new suitors. She looked as beautiful as ever.

We planned on Monday to have a quiet day. We slept in and had an amazing lunch at the hotel. In the afternoon we went to a salon and treated ourselves to beauty treatments and new hairstyles.

We had a light dinner before getting on the train for the overnight trip south. It had been such a relaxing day, such a pleasant trip, that I found myself not wanting to go back just yet, but I was due at the studio the next afternoon.

I had not made my decision regarding Elliot. Spending such an entertaining weekend in the company of Dolores made it that much harder for me. I didn't want to leave her but it would be the end of my relationship with Elliot if I let him go.

We were in the lobby at the train station waiting to board our train. I was watching Dolores rearrange her new hats in their boxes.

The porter standing attentively nearby. How could I leave her? How could I stay? Involuntarily did I think the second thought. However, I could not stop myself from the thoughts that followed. Working as an actress, for me, was just a way to make a living and pass the time. I had never been really committed to it. It was fun, but I never felt driven to do it. I certainly could do without the celebrity. It was Dolores who loved it. Her passion surrounded her when she acted a role. It was what she wanted to do, what she was meant to do.

I was just a pretty face with some gracefulness that looked good on film. I found right then in that train station that I truly wanted to go overseas. I wanted to see the world. Even as I found that I did want to go, I was still hesitant about going with Elliot. Perhaps I should work a few more years and save up my money. Then I could travel independently, go where I liked.

I told myself this was what I wanted, but deep down it didn't feel right. I got up from the lobby bench.

"Dee, I'm just going to walk around for a few minutes." Dolores mumbled something in response, still worrying over her luggage.

My head cleared a little as I moved. The decision still weighed heavily on me, even though I had come to some conclusions. I decided to pick up a magazine or newspaper to keep my mind occupied for the evening. At the newstand, I found that I had already read the magazines that had any interest for me, so I bought a copy of the San Francisco Chronicle. Tucking the paper under my arm I went back to the waiting lobby.

The train was pulling up and everyone was leaving for the platform. I caught up with Dolores and our porter just as they found the car we were on. We each took our overnight bags and watched as the porter stored our luggage. Boarding the train, we settled ourselves comfortably enough in our cabin.

As the train pulled from the station, I settled back to read my newspapers. It would be several hours yet before the porters came to let down the beds. Dolores sat across from me and appeared to be already dozing, her elbow on the window sill propping up her head.

After scanning the front page of the Chronicle, I involuntarily yelped out in shock and surprise. Near the bottom in a bold headline it read:

DOWNTOWN MADAME SAYS SHE WILL "TELL ALL"

This title was accompanied by a very ugly picture of Esther being held by policemen.

My shout had woken Dolores. I showed her the paper as I took the seat next to her. We both avidly read the article.

DOWNTOWN MADAME SAYS SHE WILL "TELL ALL"

Esther Barton, the notorious Downtown Madame who was arrested late Saturday night when police stormed her secret brothel and gambling rooms, declared to prosecutors today that she would reveal everything. Prosecutors are hoping that her information will help them bring charges against those in the city who have acted as her protectors for many years.

Barton, aged 56, has been a resident of Los Angeles for 11 years after relocating from San Francisco. Operating a boarding house for ladies as a disguise for her illegal dealings. . .

The rest of the article made no more mention of her arrest only that she was being held under numerous charges including pandering and illegal gambling.

Dolores and I barely exchanged a word as we scanned the article.

"It is the Monday late edition. Maybe we can find a copy of Sunday's paper somewhere on the train." I left Dolores rereading the article and went to find a porter. I found one sleeping on his stool in the back of the train car. Shaking him hard to wake him, I promised him five dollars if he could find me a copy of yesterday's newspapers. Then went back to our cabin.

Dolores had found a longer article in the back section of the Chronicle describing Esther's infamous days in San Francisco as a prostitute and then as a famous madame before being forced out of the city after the earthquake.

As I finished reading the article, Dolores stated bluntly, "This is not good."

I only nodded in response. I had mixed feelings about this turn of events. I was happy to see Esther get what she deserved. Yet I was also fearful for the fact that she had information that could be potentially ruinous to a lot of people. I could see that Dolores was not at all happy and extremely nervous. She had far more to lose than I did.

In a few more minutes there was a knock on the door and I opened it to find the porter with several newspapers. Apparently I hadn't been specific enough about which papers I wanted. I paid the man what must have been a half a week's wages at least and unpolitely slammed the door in his face.

There was a copy each of the Los Angeles Times and the Herald. Dolores took one and I took the other. The police raid and arrests had made the top front page. There were pictures of both Esther and Miss Prentiss fighting with police officers as they were handcuffed. I couldn't help but laugh out loud, they both looked frightfully disheveled and ugly. Dolores pursed her lips at my outburst and went on reading her paper.

The raid had taken place about midnight on Saturday. The journalist reported that the city attorney's office had been planning the raid with the police department for quite some time. Apparently, Esther had been both bribing and using blackmail to keep her business open and undisturbed. The city attorney's office had been investigating corruption in city hall. They saw the arrest of Esther as a first step to getting hard evidence against some top people in the city government.

Apparently their ploy had worked for the newspaper article did announce that she was going to give testimony to that effect. I just hoped she kept her evidence to government officials. I looked to Dolores. She was concentrating hard on the article. I squeezed her hand.

We passed a slow, sleepless night as the train traveled south. We were able to pick up morning editions of the Los Angeles papers at the station in Ventura. There was not much more in them than in the late edition from the day before. The only key piece of information we found was that prosecutors were to be interviewing both Esther and Miss Prentiss that day and were hoping to start releasing names later in the week.

The train arrived just before 8 o'clock at the Los Angeles terminal. Both of us exhausted, we rushed home. I was due at the lot for filming, Dolores wanted to go there as well to see if she was needed. To see Monroe.

We had decided that if she weren't needed on the lot she was to find out what she could about Esther's situation.

Work that afternoon was agonizing. Tired and worried, I found it hard to concentrate. On top of that, I had three hours of waiting while carpenters repaired one of the sets.

Finally, after 7 o'clock, I made it home. Dolores had told me she would bring home the evening papers. I rushed in the front door expecting to find Dolores glowering over the news, but instead found her singing a decidedly happy song while she cooked dinner.

"I take it there is good news then?" I asked her.

"Not really, no. They are going to release lists of names on Thursday or Friday. When I talked to Stephanie, she was under the impression that it would only be the names of the people in government. It makes sense. What could she get by telling giving up the names of normal patrons or, well, us?"

"We can hope. But that doesn't explain to me why you are in such a good mood."

"I saw Monroe today," she beamed at me.

"I take it you have good news then?"

"Yes! He was so sweet to me and he wants me to come back for a few days. He said he's nearly finished with the editing and could use some fun." Her eyes were twinkling, she was so excited.

"That's great Dee." I couldn't help but mirror her happiness. Underneath my smile, I was even more worried that Monroe was going to play her again – string her along and then crush her heart. As I couldn't do anything to stop it, I played happy right along with her.

On Thursday she went back to Monroe's house. There was no new information regarding Esther's arrest and we both were beginning to feel as if maybe we would be all right.

Chapter 21

I met Stephanie for luncheon on Friday. She was nervous still about what would develop from the scandal, but was feeling better about it since no new information had been released. Over lunch she told me her fears. It wasn't so much for herself that she was worried. She had become a law secretary and could support herself anywhere. It was for Harry that she worried. While not an influential attorney, he still was partner in an honorable practice and it would be the ruin of him if he were named as a customer.

"I don't know what we would do then," she told me. "For it would likely come out that I used to work there. We would have to move away, but that sort of scandal would follow Harry wherever he goes."

Stephanie's eyes welled up with tears. I patted her hand on the table to try and give her some comfort. Other than hoping that nothing further would develop from the scandal, I didn't have much comfort to offer her.

Later that afternoon, Elliot and I decided to weekend in Santa Barbara. On the drive up, the hills were bright with orange poppies. It felt good to leave the city behind and watch the rolling grassy hills pass by. More and more, I was thinking that maybe it was time for me to leave. If Dolores was on solid terms with Monroe, there could be no reason for me to stay.

I knew Elliot was hoping for an answer soon. I had been making him wait for so long. I knew it wasn't fair of me, but I also didn't want to make a decision I would regret.

Saturday was lovely. We spent the afternoon at the shore and dined at a romantic little restaurant. It was such a perfect day that I was sad when it ended, but ended it did as all days do. The next day, I found myself wishing even more that the day before had never ended, for covering the Sunday paper were lists of names. Esther's evidence.

Elliot and I were sitting outside on the private patio of our hotel room, breakfasting on sweet rolls and coffee. Elliot was reading the newspaper. I hadn't even looked at it that morning, I had awoken in such a peaceful mood. Had I taken the time to see the headlines, I wouldn't have been nearly so relaxed.

Elliot interrupted my sunny reverie by saying, "I think you haven't yet looked over the newspaper this morning?"

Realizing that I hadn't and that the implications could be enormous, I looked at him, turning my head sharply, "No. Why? Is there something I should read?"

More calmly than I could have imagined, Elliot folded the paper to the section he wanted me to read and handed it over. All I saw were a list of names. The heading above the list stated simply "Former Employees." I scanned the list and first found my professional name, followed by Dolores's.

Maggie Savoy

Dottie Sparks

I quickly refolded the paper to see what the article was. I was flustered and couldn't get the paper to fold right. Elliot leaned over, took it from me and folded it properly, handing it back. The headline, in a huge type face, read:

ESTHER BARTON SPILLS ALL

Barton delivers on names of Protectors, Collaborators, Customers and Prostitutes

Then the article began. I had no interest in the article. This was a blow. It had never occurred to me – to any of us – that she would name me as one of her prostitutes. Of course she would do that, hateful, greedy, bitter woman that she was. I recalled the verbal fight we had when I left. Clearly I remember Miss Prentiss's last words to me, "this won't be the end of it."

Still holding the paper in my lap, I stared open-eyed at the ground. What would happen now? I knew Elliot was waiting for a response from me, and an explanation most likely. I would have to tell him everything.

I hadn't meant to keep my time at Esther's a secret from him. It just didn't seem worthwhile to tell him. After all, the secret I would be revealing was not my own. Since I hadn't lived there for long, it seemed more appropriate to forget that either myself or Dolores had lived there at all, that Dolores had worked there.

Finally, taking a deep breath I looked up. Elliot watched me patiently. There were no accusations in his look, no demands. He simply looked at me, the creases around his eyes the only thing betraying an ounce of tension.

"I lived there." I began, wondering at his calm patience. "When I first left home, I stayed there with Dolores." I trailed off, not quite yet wanting to give up Dolores.

Elliot came around the table and looked in my face, his hand on my shoulder. "If you worked for her, you can tell me. Everyone makes mistakes." He kneeled down so that he could look at me directly, eye to eye.

To offer me sympathy and acceptance when the evidence before him indicated that I was not worthy of it made me realize how special he really was. Elliot was the most understanding man I had ever known and I would not let him go anywhere without me. In an instant, I made the decision to stay by Elliot's side.

"It was a mistake to live there, to be certain, but I never worked for her. I was just a boarder. But ..." Even though it was written clearly in the paper, I couldn't say what had to be said.

Elliot squeezed my hands, "What?"

"Dolores worked for that woman, she was living there when I came to Los Angeles."

"And you only just boarded with her?" Elliot inquired. "Then why would she name you as one of her employees?"

"She is a horrible woman, as you can imagine. She never would have let Dolores leave on her own, so I sneaked out our things before she could stop me. We had a loud row before I left. She threatened to ruin me." I laughed a bitter little laugh. "I think she's got her revenge."

Elliot hugged me to his chest. With my head firmly planted on his chest, I said, "Elliot, I know this is probably not the time, but when you leave I am going with you."

"My darling, you don't know how happy you've made me." I thought to myself, I did know.

We were peaceful together for some minutes before I realized that I had other, less fortunate things to attend to.

We both read the whole article and all the names. There were some very important people on the lists and some not so important. Stephanie's Harry was there. I grew so angry reading that I wanted to murder the horrible journalists that decided to ruin everyone's weekends by printing their big story.

I called Dolores at Monroe's home, something I was strictly forbidden to do. Dolores answered saying, "H. Phillips Monroe's residence," as if she were a servant.

"Dolores, it's Magda. Have you seen today's newspapers?" I asked her quickly.

"No, Monroe doesn't get the paper at home and he's been holed up in his editing room with Tucker since yesterday afternoon." She didn't know.

"Do you think he'll come out anytime soon?"

"Huh? No, not unless he comes out to sleep. I deliver his meals to the room. Why?"

I explained to her what was in the papers. There was only silence on the other end. "Dolores, I'm going to take the 11 o'clock train back to the city. Can you pick me up?"

She mumbled something that sounded like 'okay' and we said goodbye. Elliot was staying in Santa Barbara to finish up some business dealings the following day. I packed my things and he took me to the train. I got there with a lot of time to spare, but I had an urgent telegram that had to go before I left.

Elliot was so sweet to me and so understanding. He helped me in every way he could. When we arrived at the station, he took out my bags. I turned to him to give him a kiss on the cheek as a farewell, but instead he held me in his arms and kissed me fiercely. I was slightly embarrassed by such a display.

After purchasing my ticket, I went to the telegram office.

FATHER, PLEASE DO NOT BELIEVE EVERYTHING YOU READ IN NEWS-PAPERS. TELL FRANCES TOO. TELL MORE LATER. LOVE MAGDA.

My biggest worry, after Dolores, was that my father would read the Los Angeles papers and see my name. Or even worse, my mother. I knew it would upset my father greatly to think that I had been reduced to a common prostitute upon leaving his protection and had to do something to allay any fears he might have on my behalf.

The train ride gave me some time to think things through a little more thoroughly. Maybe I was panicking? With all of the important names listed by Esther, who was going to care about two minor actresses?

I had purchased copies of both the Times and Herald before leaving Santa Barbara. I carefully read through all the names. There were slight variations in each list. Such as the editor of the Herald wasn't listed in the Herald and the publisher of the Times wasn't listed in the Times. Apparently the Times had no scruples about publishing the name of its rival and vice versa. Silly really. They were all in it together.

As the train drew into the station in Los Angeles, I could see a crowd of cameramen and journalists on the platform. It seemed that they were blocking the entrance to the platform. As I was getting off the train, I saw two or three well-dressed older men break through the reporters trying to cover their faces while making for the train. I realized then that those must be others affected by the list in the newspapers. Trying to escape town it looked like. I did my best to inch around the reporters without being seen, but as soon as their first prey were out of sight, they were on the hunt for more.

Someone shouted out "There's that actress," and a huge shuffle of men came bulking towards me.

"Miss Savoy"

"Miss Savoy"

"Miss Savoy, your name is on Barton's list of notoriety. Are you trying to escape town as well."

I had been about to push through the throng and escape to the lobby. I stopped, being unable to resist answering.

"As you can see gentlemen, if you were paying attention, I have just arrived back in town." I tried to break through, but now that I had answered one question, more and more were hurled at me.

"Miss Savoy, Miss Savoy, is there any truth to Barton's accusations that you once worked for her."

I laughed, clearly and brightly. "Of course not. That is absurd. The awful woman is finally getting what she likely deserves and is doing her best to ruin many honest people."

Finally, I needled my way through the rough coats of the reporters. Bulbs flashing the whole while. Finally reaching the street, I saw Dolores's roadster a half a block away parked on the street. As I drew near I saw that she was wearing a large hat and shaded glasses. I hoped that the reporters hadn't been bothering her as well.

I got in the car and gave her an awkward hug. "How are you doing?" She shrugged and began to pull away from the curb. "I haven't even looked at the newspapers yet. I'm too scared of what I will see."

I squeezed her arm, trying to be reassuring.

We drove home. She wasn't going back to Monroe's that day. He would probably be asleep for the rest of the day, since he'd spent the last several days working on the final edit of the film.

It was probably for the best as we both needed time to think and talk.

Surprisingly, neither of us were too upset. I had thought that when the scandal started to involve us that we would become hysterical. We were both surprisingly calm. I knew that my sense of calm stemmed from my talk with Elliot. I don't know where Dolores had found hers.

I realized later, it was only the calm before the storm.

After settling in at home, after Dolores had read the lists all the way through, she said, "That horrible woman. To involve you as well, even though you had nothing to do with her business. You paid her good money then she says such horrible things about you." Dolores folded her head into her hands. "It just isn't fair."

Sitting next to her, I leaned my head against her shoulder. "It isn't fair, but it's already done."

I felt Dolores involuntarily sob. I sat up and rubbed her back. "Its all right. Really."

I told her how it had been Elliot who had discovered my name in the paper and that we had talked it through. "If he believes in me, that is all that matters. No need to worry."

"But it's my fault," she burst out. "It's my fault that you lived there. It was such a horrible mistake for me to have been there, but to have had you live with me." She cried some more, but I could tell she wasn't finished. "It was selfish of me and now you are paying for my mistakes. I was just so miserable, I needed you there."

"Dee! It's not your fault! You and I both know what a nasty woman Esther is. You can't be blamed for her lies." I made her face me, her face streaked . "I ran away with no place to go but to you. If anyone is to blame it's myself. I could be miserably married to Mr. Johnson right now, but I chose to take the risk."

"It'll be okay Dee. I know it will. This will blow over soon enough. And with all the important people on that list, who is going to care for a couple of silly actresses? Right?"

She put her arms around me and leaned her head on my shoulder. We sat quietly for a few minutes. "Primita, what about the studio? How will we face everyone?"

I hadn't thought about that yet. "I don't know Dee. Maybe we should go in there with our chins up and act like nothing happened. I don't know."

We spent the evening coming up with different plans about how to show up for work. How we could get all dressed up like princesses and walk in as if everyone there were beneath us. Or we could dress like vamps and go in with cigarettes dangling from our lips and be cool as ice.

Dolores never brought up Monroe – what she would say to him, how he would react. He was bound to find out. This we both knew. Dolores never said anything to me though, as she hadn't since she started seeing him. For all I knew, perhaps she had already told him everything. Her tense manner indicated to me that she was anxious beyond just showing up at the studio.

The night passed quietly. I thought it interesting that none of our large group of friends or acquaintances telephoned. That was scandal for you. Points out who your real friends are.

We had decided to go to the studio as usual. We thought it better just to face up to the scandal than to try and hide. I was up about 7:30 and having a cup of tea when I heard the doorbell ring. I went to see who it was, but Dolores had got there before me. From the side, I couldn't see who it was, but she was smiling.

She opened the door, her hand on the knob. A newspaper hit her square in the face. She stumbled back. I stood there, shocked.

Monroe burst through the door and caught Dolores by the arm. He picked up the paper and shoved it in her face, shaking her.

"You stupid whore. Fucking bitch. You've ruined my movie. Ruined it I tell you." Monroe continued to shake her. Dolores offered no resistance. She stared at him wide-eyed, taking his violence.

"I don't ever want see your stupid face. Never come near me. Whore, whore." These last words he screamed in her face before dropping her and storming out. Dolores pulled herself to her knees and picked up the newspaper.

I am so ashamed of myself. I was terrified into stone. I couldn't move. I didn't know how I could ever comfort her after seeing what he did to her, hearing those vile words.

Watching Dolores desperately reading the news, I forced myself to go to her. As I was reaching down for her, she held up the paper for me. She was so quiet, so sad. Her misery was so acute, crying was too happy a reaction.

I took the paper and she left the room. On the front page of the Times were profiles of many of the people from the lists given as testimony by Esther. The former mayor headed the expose. Pictures and profiles of several other men filled out the page. At the bottom right corner was the only female. It was Dolores. The photograph that accompanied the profile was a picture of her being arrested as a prostitute all those years ago. And only Dolores, with her high spirits, would have the audacity to smile right into the camera as police offi-cers ushered her into a police van.

There it was printed on the front page of the city newspaper for all to see. At least they didn't have her real name to use. She had given a false name when she was arrested.

There was no going back for Dolores now. There was nothing to cover up or hide from. With the loss of Monroe's support she would be ruined.

I went to her room, the door was closed and locked. I knocked softly. She didn't answer, so I knocked again. "Not now," was the only reply I got. I leaned against the door frame and slid to the floor. I desperately tried to think of what to say to her, something that would make her feel one tiny shred of hope.

Thinking about Papa always helped me. He had been through so much during his long life, had seen so many places and had known so many people, yet he was always cheerful. Always forward thinking. Hoping it would help, I started to speak, loudly so Dolores could hear me through the door, about our Papa.

"Dee, did you ever hear Papa say why he was such a cheerful person?" I didn't hear a response from within, so I continued. "He told me that after fought on the side of the Americans in the Mexican War, within a few months he became very depressed. He had hoped that things would change for the poor, for the people he knew. As the gringos moved in and the large ranches were broken up, he saw that nothing would change for the people who worked hard all day just to feed their families even the basics of food. He told me, if anything it got worse. For the gringo Americans treated the natives as poorly as they treated the Indians. After a year, he was fed up and that's when he signed on to a merchant ship.

"Of all the things he saw while he was a sailor, he said there were some places that were extraordinarily beautiful, both natural and man-made. He met wonderful people who could bear their burdens with ease. He also met tyrants who wanted everything to go their own way. He saw more suffering than he did beauty, yet people pulled themselves through it. Lived their lives, some happier than others.

"Papa told me, more than once, that despite the hardships you see around you, despite the hardships you have yourself, that if you begin everyday with a smile and a hopeful heart it all becomes easier to bear."

I smiled to myself as I remembered his words. Part of me wondered where they were the year before when I was so heartbroken over Del. They were there, I'm sure, within my memories, but they would have been meaningless to me at the time, I was so wrapped up in self-pity. I hoped they would have meaning for Dolores now.

"Despite making mistakes, even some very grave ones, you gotta put them behind you and do your best to enjoy the days you've got ahead. I miss Papa," the last sentence was whispered to myself. I heard no sound from Dolores.

"Dee, when you're ready, come out. We can figure out something if we do it together. Okay?" Still I received no response.

Chapter 22

That day happened so long ago, yet the pain and fear is still so fresh that it hurts me all over again. My future was set. I would leave with Elliot, so I didn't give a damn about my reputation among those two-faced Hollywood people, but my heart broke for Dolores all the same. She wanted so much to belong to that crowd, to be the cream of the crop, to be a star, to be loved. There was nothing I could do for her then.

I spent the rest of the morning listless on the couch, staring at nothing in particular, waiting for Dolores to emerge from her room. Plans and scenarios ran through my head, but there was really nothing I could do to fix the problem at hand. There was no way to make Monroe take back his words, even if he could be persuaded to change his mind.

When the telephone rang, I answered it hoping it would be Elliot. It wasn't, but I was equally pleased to find Stephanie on the other end.

"Magda? I am so sorry. I can't believe how everything has been blown out of proportion."

"I'm so glad you rang. How are you and Harry holding up?" I had wanted to telephone her earlier, but didn't want to intrude. She was dealing with her own part in the scandal.

"We're fine." She actually did sound fine. "We've talked about it and decided to move back to Harry's hometown in Northern California. He can open a practice there. I will be his secretary."

"That's marvelous," I was truly ecstatic. Something delightful was coming from all this sludge.

"And the best part is that we are going to be married before we leave. We are planning to see the Justice of the Peace on Thursday. I would really appreciate it if you and Dolores could come and act as my witnesses."

"Of course," I was truly excited now. A proper wedding to be coming from the mess. A much happier ending was in store for Stephanie. My heart panged with sorrow at the thought. Poor Dolores.

"We'll be there at 3 o'clock. Bring Elliot if you'd like. We'll have a dinner afterwards. All right?"

"Certainly. I'll tell him as soon as he gets back into town."

"Thank you so much." Her voice was warm and happy. It was encouraging to hear a glad voice. Her note changed to one of worry when she next spoke, "How are you and Dolores holding up? I can't believe that woman naming you. I hope she rots in prison forever."

I sighed, it couldn't be avoided. "I'll survive. After today's newspaper, I don't know what will become of Dolores."

"Today's paper? You mean there is more? Harry and I have given up on newspapers and the awful men who write for them and who very probably went to Esther's as often as anybody. We vowed yesterday not to read another newspaper from this city again."

"It's probably for the best," I answered, "I would have liked not to have read it either. The Times has profiles and photos of many of the people on the list – especially the important ones. They also feature Dolores and used a photo of her being arrested all those years ago."

"They didn't," came Stephanie's voice in shock. "How could they do that? It's just so mean."

We were both silent.

"What ... How is Dolores?" Stephanie stuttered out.

"I don't know. In shock maybe? She hasn't left her room since she saw it." My voice sounded flat and defeated even in my own ears.

"Oh my lord. That poor girl. I know there probably isn't anything I could do, but please let me know if I can help, okay?"

"I wish I could help her too."

"I won't keep you any longer. Please tell her we would really love to see her on Thursday. All right?"

"I will Stephanie. By the way, congratulations. I'm really happy that something decent has come of this."

"Thank you, it means a lot to me. Goodbye."

Tired from the wide range of emotions I had felt that day, I went to look in on Dolores. I found her bedroom door open, but she wasn't inside. Nor was she in the kitchen, my room, or any other room in the house. I went out to check the driveway, my mind starting to grow frantic with fear. I hadn't heard her leave, I hadn't heard her at all. I did hear an engine start while on the phone with Stephanie but hadn't taken much notice. As I reached the driveway, my fears were confirmed. Dolores had left in her car.

I was a wreck with worry all afternoon. I received a telephone call from Floyd late in the afternoon. He was extremely sweet to me, as always, and offered his sympathy. He told me a story, as he was fond of doing, of being laughed at by the press early on his career. I half listened, not really believing his troubles could be anywhere near as bad as ours.

Virginia came over around 5 o'clock. She was very sympathetic and sat with me for a long time. I felt downright guilty for my ungenerous thoughts the day before about who my friends were. We didn't talk much, as I was too upset about Dolores, but Virginia was very understanding and stayed with me until Elliot arrived. He stayed with me all night, trying to ease my worry.

Elliot read the papers that morning. I wouldn't look at them. He reported that the front page was still focusing on the scandal – more than a week after it broke – and that there was no more mention of

Dolores, me, or Harry. As far as I was concerned, as long as those three of us weren't mentioned, everyone else could go and rot.

The next morning I felt I needed to go look for her. She had taken her handbag, but nothing else. I didn't know if she had money or not. I didn't think she was in a frame of mind that would allow her to properly take care of herself. I was worried that she might do something drastic. I was just so worried.

Even though it was more than a long-shot that she had been there, I decided to start at the studio. I was hoping that someone we both knew had at least seen her.

I underestimated, by far, my fellow actors' pity in the face of scandal. After arriving, I saw that I was steadily being avoided. Although it didn't take long before the offhanded comments began reaching my ears as I desperately searched the different sets and lots for Dolores. A group of stage hands, lounging on the porch of a set, were laughing uproariously at me. Many of them I had worked with and joked with in the past. I marched up to the group and said, "If you think it's so funny, why don't you say it to me?" They all, of course, balked at my forwardness and dispersed. I was in no mood for anyone to take lightly my anxiety.

Not finding her on the likely sets, and finding no one who wanted to even approach me, I went in search of Mr. Hawthorne. He would know if she had been to the studio.

I found him walking across to the bungalow he used as his office.

"Mr. Hawthorne," I called and hurried up to him. He stopped, saw me, and looked distinctly nervous.

"Mr. Hawthorne, have you seen my cousin? Have you seen Dottie?"

He looked around nervously, as if talking to me would get him into trouble. "Please, Mr. Hawthorne, if you know anything, please tell me. She's missing. I'm terribly worried for her," I pleaded miserably.

"Um, no Miss Savoy, I, um, haven't seen your cousin. Um, I don't think she would come here, um, Miss Savoy, as, um, Monroe has banned her from the studio." He coughed nervously after his stuttering speech. This wasn't a surprise.

"What is she doing here?" Roared a voice behind me. Now I understood why Mr. Hawthorne had been so nervous. He had been expecting Monroe.

I turned to face the man. The now hideous, hateful man. "What am I doing here? I work here." I said defiantly. Monroe was at least a head taller than me and twice my weight, but I could have torn him to pieces right then.

"You don't work here any more, you don't! Not you or your whore of a cousin. Get off this property."

"I believe you are forgetting that I am under contract with this company making no less than 250 dollars per week." I held my head up with my shoulders straight. He was not going to intimidate me.

My response enraged him further. If I did shrink at his shouting it was only because he was so loud. "Get out, I say. Your whore cousin ruined me, ruined me. My movie can never be shown. Damn the day that the whore seduced me into her rotten bed."

Bellicose or not, he had gone too far. "I remember a time when you raved about your love for my cousin. Don't rewrite history now because it does not suit you." I refused to back down. He could hit me like he hit my cousin and this time the crowd who had gathered to hear our argument would bear witness.

Monroe's anger must have hit its bursting point, for he seethed for a minuted without answering and then called for his assistant directors to take me out of the lot. As they came for me, I turned to Mr. Hawthorne, who was cowering at the side of the crowd. "Mr. Hawthorne, I believe you will be sending me a compensation check for the contract you are now breaking. I expect the full amount for the four months left on my contract." This last part was said as I was being manhandled by two normally quite nice men. I did not go easily and shrugged at their grips as they tried to force me to leave. I saw Mr. Hawthorne run up to Monroe and overheard the words "money" and "ruin."

I felt better for confronting that monster Monroe. My heart was still heavy with worry for Dolores, but at least I had gotten to Monroe in some small way.

I checked as many hotels as I could, but came up with nothing. I checked in with Mr. Stuckey and with Consuela, but neither had heard from her. Poor Consuela was having a tough time of it now that Esther's had been shut down. Wrapped up in all of our own misery, I had forgotten about her. I told her I would look out for a good place for her, but deep down knew I could do nothing for her.

Tuesday passed with no word. Wednesday I waited by the telephone the whole day just hoping against hope she would call me. Thursday, as much as I had been looking forward to Stephanie's wedding, it was hard for me to tear myself away.

I hadn't told Stephanie that Dolores was missing and had vowed to keep it from her on her special day. Elliot and I arrived in good time to see the quick ceremony. Harry had invited a good friend of his whom I remembered seeing outside Esther's. A good friend indeed. Harry and Stephanie were properly married and looked very happy for it. Elliot and I sat close together during the brief exchanging of vows, holding hands tightly. I knew that he, as I myself, was thinking of a similar such ceremony performed for the two of us.

The five of us went out to dinner to celebrate and later moved on to a nightclub for dancing and champagne. I was out much later than I had wanted to be, but Stephanie deserved a fun night. I deserved a fun night. We all had a lovely time and, for just a little while, the knot of worry that had come to habitually turn my stomach, was gone.

The party broke up about one in the morning. I was bone tired and ready for bed. As much fun as the night had been, it had been a long week and I was worn out. Although as we turned the corner onto my street, I knew that the night was nowhere near finished. There were two police cars outside my house.

Elliot pulled up to the curb and I jumped out before the car had completely stopped.

"What's the matter? What's wrong?" I called out breathlessly. The officers turned towards me. There were four of them. Two in uniform, two in suits.

"You are Maggie Savoy?" Inquired the older of the two plain-clothes police officers.

"Yes, I live here. What's happened?" Elliot was by my side by this time. The lead officer looked to him.

"And you are?" he inquired matter-of-factly.

"Elliot Clayton."

"My fiancé," I interjected.

"I see," said the police officer. "My name is Detective Becker. I need to ask you a few questions. I believe you would be more comfortable if we were inside."

I nodded, too worried to care about informalities. Elliot, on the other hand, looked to interject, but I hushed him with a wave of my hand. He nodded as well and followed me to the front door. I went inside, turning on lights as I went and then settled myself on the couch. Elliot took his place next to me. He held my hand.

All four officers followed us inside. "Do you mind if the other officers take a look around?" The other officers were already starting to spread to the doorways to the interior rooms.

"Of course I do," I answered sharply. "This is my home and you have no business nosing around."

The officer took on a stern look to his face and was about to be forceful when Elliot interceded diplomatically. "I can show the officers all the rooms in the house, if you don't mind." He looked at me supportively, "Would you mind?"

"No, not if you go with them, but please don't let them touch anything." I could hear my mother's haughty tones echoing in my voice. There was something terribly wrong here, I knew that, yet I'd be damned if I let this nothing of a police officer get the better of me. He may be more than twice my age, but he would not carry our conversation.

Elliot escorted the other plainclothes policeman and one of the uniformed officers from the living room. The lead officer turned and faced me, looking directly in my face, "Miss, I need to ask you a few questions."

Putting on my haughtiest expression, "Miss Savoy to you. I demand to know what is going on."

"Miss Savoy," Becker began in a much more persuasive direction, "I would like to know where you were between the hours of 5 o'clock and 8 o'clock tonight?"

"I was with Mr. Clayton of course."

"Is there anyone who can verify your whereabouts?"

"Of course, I was attending a wedding party. It was a small celebration, but you can verify my location with Harry Stewart, Esquire and his bride Mrs. Stephanie Stewart, as well as his friend Dr. Lou Halter. We dined first at Levy's and then proceeded to the Tropicana Nightclub." I paused for a snobby effect. "Is there anything else?"

Becker hurriedly wrote down the names and places I had stated. "I'm sorry Miss Savoy, there is," he began awkwardly. "Do you know the whereabouts of your cousin and, I'm told, roommate Dottie Sparks, also known by the alias Dottie Sanchez?"

I gulped unevenly and took a deep breath. "I have not seen my cousin since Monday morning, sometime before noon." I knew the next question and answered it just as Becker began to speak. "Nor have I had any contact from her since that time. I've been worried sick and have searched for her in what capacity I have, but she left in her car so I have no way of locating her."

"I see. She hasn't been home? Perhaps even in your absence?" Becker was being almost obsequious. I could see through his methods. He did everything to appease me as I was putting on airs.

"I don't know!" I whined and wilted into tears. "If she has, I can't tell." I sucked in my breathe with a stutter. "Can't you please tell me what's going on? Please tell me."

As circumstance had it, Elliot came into the room at that moment, followed by the other two officers. I didn't know where the fourth was located, but it hardly mattered.

Elliot was angry that the officer had made me cry and ran to my side. "What have you done to her?" he demanded in a wonderfully cultured British accent. It sounded so much more intimidating than an ordinary American accent.

"Elliot, no. I think something's happened to Dottie. Maybe something terrible, but Detective Becker won't say."

I don't think Elliot was acting, not as I was acting, but his performance was effective. He held his arm around me glaring at Becker. Becker looked distinctly uncomfortable, clearly out of his own playing field.

He coughed a fake cough and cleared his throat, "Ah, no, nothing that we know of has happened to, um, Dottie. Um, well." He coughed again. "Detective Richards, can you explain to Miss Savoy the circumstances of our inquiry?" Coughing, he made his way outside.

Detective Richards, an energetic officer in his late 20s, flipped open his notepad and began the story, "At approximately 9:15 p.m. this evening, we received a call from one Charles Hanson," that was Charlie, "that there had been a violent murder at 718 Adams St." I gasped. That was Monroe's house. My outburst did not phase the young detective. "Upon arriving at the scene, officers found the bodies of a Mr. H. Phillips Monroe and Miss Harriet Atler – these identities have yet to be confirmed. On initial inspection, the deaths were caused by short range shots from a handgun that perhaps belonged to Mr. H. Phillips Monroe. It seemed the murdered were partaking in an intimate act at time of death.”

Elliot's arm squeezed me tightly. I labored to breathe. “Upon questioning, one Charles Hanson indicated that he had arrived to pick up film canisters from the deceased and had found the pair. His thoughts were that the longtime girlfriend and recently exposed prostitute, one Dottie Sparks, was the primary suspect.”

Detective Becker interrupted as he walked back into the room, “That'll be enough Richards.” He again sat down across from me. “Please, tell us anything you may know.”

I was speechless with grief. I knew she had done it. I knew Dolores so well, that there couldn't be any doubt. “I can't tell you anything.” I said evenly. No longer playing any role or trying to prove anything. “I haven't seen or heard from her since Monday. Any place she would have gone, I've checked.”

“Can you give me those names?” I gave him Mr. Stuckey's address and the names of the hotels she liked. “What about family? Is there anyone she would have gone to?”

“Never, we both are completely cut off from our family.” I must have said this more sharply than I intended, for every man in the room began looking uncomfortable.

“There is one last thing I need to tell you.” Becker obviously did not want to tell me this. “We found Dottie Sparks's car about an hour ago. It was smashed against a light pole down on Temple and Beaudry. She wasn't in the car when we found it, but it was a pretty bad crash.”

I said nothing. “Miss Savoy, if you have any information, hear anything from her, please contact me.” He laid his card on the table before me. “Goodnight.”

I didn't respond. He and the other officers left. After a minute of sitting quietly together, Elliot said, "You know it's possible that she didn't do it."

"I know Dolores like my own heart, there is no doubt in my mind that it was she." Elliot put his arm around me and I laid my head on his chest.

We must have fallen asleep like that on the couch, for I awoke with a start sometime later still sitting on the couch with Elliot's arms around me. I had been dreaming of playing hide-and-seek with my Papa when I was little. I must have been very young in my dream. The sounds of my own wild laughter when my Papa caught me still filled my ears when I awoke.

I knew where Dolores was. I didn't think it was going to be a happy reunion.

Elliot, the dear, slept soundly as I got up. I quietly went into the kitchen. Along one long wall in that room there were French doors to the back yard that I kept covered with curtains much of the time. Along the same wall were the doors to the garage and the basement. The curtain also covered the doors. As I didn't have a car and didn't need to use the storage, I seldom, if ever, went into either room. I didn't even think Elliot knew the doors were there.

I drew back the curtains to the doors. I opened the basement door first and was rewarded with a bright light coming from the fixture downstairs. I went down the stairs, with no urgency yet, no hesitation. I found, as I reached the floor, my best friend in the world hanging from the ceiling, strangled.

"No Dee, no." I murmured. Then I sat on the steps too shaken to do anything but drop my head in my hands.

Chapter 23

The next few weeks felt like they were happening to someone else, as if I were watching myself in a color-tinted picture. Before daybreak, Elliot and I decided that we would keep her death from the public. I decided really. Elliot was just kind enough to go along with what I wanted.

Dolores was dead. I couldn't bear to see or hear her vilified for Monroe's murder. There was no doubt in my mind that she had committed the murders. I knew the police linked Dolores to the murders, but I made sure they learnt nothing.

The newspapers, surprisingly, wove a tale of debauchery, murder, and kidnaping. The various theories that came out in the papers during the following weeks had to do with a narcotics deal gone bad and the murders as retribution.

After reading some of those sensationalist articles, I began to think people watched too many films. Monroe's reputation as a leading man of cinema became tarnished. I can't say that it didn't please me, knowing him as I had.

The week following Monroe's murder was horrible for other reasons than you might think. I was hounded by police, by newspaper reporters, even by Mr. Hawthorne.

Mr. Hawthorne called me frantically two days after the murder. I hung up on him. I had nothing to say to him, although it became evident he had something to discuss with me.

The following Tuesday, after repeated hang-ups, Mr. Hawthorne showed up at my front door. Elliot was not with me at the time and it made me very nervous to meet Mr. Hawthorne alone. I didn't know for certain, but had assumed, that Chronicle Film Company would be in trouble without Monroe.

Answering the door, I ushered Mr. Hawthorne into the living room. I didn't try one bit to be a pleasant hostess.

"Miss Savoy," Mr. Hawthorne began ceremoniously, "I must know where Miss Sparks has gone. I can reward you handsomely if you would tell me where she is hiding."

I eyed Mr. Hawthorne with disdain. "However much I would not like to accommodate your wishes, Mr. Hawthorne, I do not even get the joy of withholding information from you. I don't know where Miss Sparks has gone."

Mr. Hawthorne grew angry with my sarcastic speech. "You don't understand you stupid girl. I have got to know where she is. She took his film with her. We've got to get it back." He spat out the words.

"You mean *Solomon and Sheba?*" I asked, catching on to why he was so angry. "It was finished?"

"Of course," Mr. Hawthorne, generally such a quiet fussy man, was coming apart at the seams. It looked as if he wanted to curse at me or throttle me. "That's why young Charlie found them. Monroe had finished the editing that day. You know he was a month behind on delivering the film. We have got to get it or we're through." His voiced had reached a squeaky high pitch. Even though he did not raise his voice, it still hurt my ears.

"Mr. Hawthorne, if I knew where to find it, I would certainly give it back. However, I don't know where six or eight reels of film could be hidden. And, although I am loath to repeat myself, I haven't seen my cousin in more than a week." At least alive, I thought to myself. "You are searching for it in the wrong place."

Mr. Hawthorne stared at me, his eyes beady. I did my best to imitate my mother's haughty demeanor – something I had become very practiced at that week. He would not intimidate me. He opened his mouth as if to say something, thought better of it and rose to leave.

"Don't think you'll get a cent from your contract. I have no intention of paying you, broken contract or not."

"I'm sorry to hear that Mr. Hawthorne. I will file the lawsuit papers then, immediately rather than at the end of the month."

Mr. Hawthorne's eyes nearly bugged out of his head when I mentioned a lawsuit. I was determined to receive my proper due from the company. They weren't going to get off easily with me. Without another word, he left.

Harry drew up the suit papers for me. Mr. Hawthorne tried to delay settlement, for I'm certain he knew that the company would go bankrupt soon. However, sooner rather than later, he did settle his account with me.

Chronicle Film Company was in dire straits. Monroe had borrowed heavily to make *Solomon and Sheba*, relying mostly on his reputation. The company released a slapped together version of the film from extra footage they found in Monroe's house, but it was nothing like the vision that Monroe had pursued. The film was a flop, despite the sinister publicity Monroe's death provided. Before the end of the summer, one of the greatest picture making studios closed its gates in bankruptcy.

Elliot, using his money, with the aid of Harry's law expertise and local connections, kept Dolores's name out of the papers. There was hardly a businessman in the city untouched by Esther's revelations. Business transactions had routinely been arranged in Esther's rooms. After all those names were printed in the papers like a list of criminals, there were no obstacles finding men more than willing to keep another scandal under wraps and away from the journalists. The undertaker kindly came to my house in the guise of a moving van. The city clerk obliged us by predating Dolores's death certificate by a week and filing it under her real name, Dolores Santoya Esparza.

Waiting for the publicity to die down, I started to pack up the house. Our departure date had been fixed and we were to leave by the middle of June. Little had I known when I agreed to go with Elliot how very much I would be needing to get away.

When the publicity of the scandal began to die down with weeks of no new information, I quietly made arrangements for a funeral. I wanted Dee to be remembered fondly by those who truly liked her, loved her. Stephanie and Harry knew about her death already of course, since Harry's aid had been key to keeping her suicide a secret.

It was unimaginably hard to tell Mr. Stuckey, but he adored Dolores and his kindness towards her would not be changed by the succession of scandals in the past few weeks. I found him in the front room of his theater the morning before the funeral. I hadn't been to his place in many months, but it looked much the same as ever. There was now a proper window ticket booth in front, and the floors had been replaced, but it was still small and homey.

Mr. Stuckey was truly glad to see me as evidenced by the huge smile on his face. He grasped my shoulders and kissed my cheek. "It does an old man's eyes good to see you, m'dear."

"It's good to see you too, Mr. Stuckey. It's been so long since I've been here. Is business going well then?" I asked sociably.

"Pretty well, I'd say. The trick is to have a pretty girl selling tickets. I learned that when Dolores was here. No one wants to see a fussy old man in the window." He chuckled.

"It's about Dolores that I'm here," I stated, delaying the inevitable no longer.

Mr. Stuckey's face drooped in concern. "Oh?"

I gave him a rough outline of Dolores's suicide, without hinting at its correlation to Monroe's murder. When I was done telling him the sad news, Mr. Stuckey, to his credit, pulled out his handkerchief and wiped his eyes. I was steeling myself so that I would not join him. I was done with crying.

"I knew she would take it hard when her name came out in the paper. She was such a good girl." Mr. Stuckey sat on the lobby bench. "That horrible old Esther Barton ruined many a wonderful girl."

Mr. Stuckey's last sentence caught my attention. It had always been my understanding that Mr. Stuckey didn't know that we lived at Esther's. "Mr. Stuckey, you knew about Dolores?"

Sniffling a little, Mr. Stuckey nodded yes. "You weren't the only girls from the brothel that came here. I've known many such a girl, but I never saw one get out and make a name for herself like Dolores."

"So you knew, when you offered a job to Dolores, you knew already?" I was quite stunned. I really had no idea that he knew anything about it.

"Oh yes," he continued. "Since you were so keen to help Dolores out of there, I thought I could help too." He lifted his chin and smiled. "The best thing I've done, I think. It helped all of us."

I reached down and squeezed Mr. Stuckey's hand. "Thank you for your help. It did mean the world, to both of us." I told him of the funeral arrangements.

My next stop was Consuela's house. She lived on the outskirts of Boyle Heights in a well-kept, but shabby adobe house. As I approached the front gate, a teenaged girl stood up from the porch steps and went inside. Before I made it to the porch, Consuela came out. She wordlessly directed me to the porch swing. We both sat down.

"What happened to her?" Consuela asked point blank before I was able to arrange my words.

"She killed herself." Consuela nodded, eyes fixed on a distant point. We sat silently, swinging slightly on the suspended seat.

"When Esther was arrested and revealed all those names, I knew something like this would happen. She was always so ashamed of herself." I had no answer. After another long silence, Consuela continued. "Every time she came here, I could see that she still had not forgiven herself. Poor girl."

"She came here often?" I inquired, finally having something to say.

Consuela looked at me from the corner of her eyes, barely turning her face. "She did. Often enough. She didn't tell you."

I shook my head negatively. It wasn't until that moment did I realize how far apart Dolores and I had grown since embarking upon our acting careers. When we saw each other we laughed and talked, but we never really talked about what was important. A sharp pain in my chest made it difficult for me to keep my tears at bay. I would not cry.

"I'm glad you were there for her."

"No, no. I don't think anybody could have helped her," Consuela answered. "Her wounds were so deep that she could keep them hidden well. She shut people out that way. If they couldn't see her in pain, they couldn't help her."

I didn't stay much longer, just long enough to give Consuela the details for the funeral.

The next day Dolores's friends met at the Rosedale Cemetery, south of the city proper on Washington Street. It was a small party: Elliot and me, Stephanie and Harry, Mr. Stuckey, Consuela and a half dozen members of her family, and even Mrs. Haelstrom with her two youngest children in tow.

The minister gave a short sermon about the blessings of heaven. He knew only Dolores's name and age. Having a minister officiate was more a matter of tradition than Christian beliefs. When he was done speaking, I was allowed a few words.

"Thank you for coming today. I wanted Dee to be surrounded by people who loved her for herself. I'm certain that had we made her death public, the ceremony would have been flooded by her fans, but they couldn't have known Dolores but for the beauty she displayed on the movie screens."

"Dolores was my best friend. She was beautiful and vivacious, exciting and kind. She was as good a person as you will ever meet. I think that perhaps Dolores had just too much life in her, so much life that she had to share it with everyone. She ran out of it that much sooner.

"She wouldn't want us to be sad, you know. She would want us to smile and think of how she's Wowing them in heaven. I believe that is how I will think of her from now on. Flirting with all the angels and then teaching them the Bunny Hug or the Shimmy."

On those thoughts, which had just come to me, I smiled a bittersweet smile. I looked around at Dolores's friends and saw several of them smiling as well. Our small gathering broke up then. Getting and giving condolences from everyone, and for me, saying goodbye for the last time, we left as softly as we had come.

My heart was heavy once I was home. The time was drawing close for my departure with Elliot, yet I had some hard goodbyes to say before we left.

I had invited my father to lunch two days after the funeral. I needed some closure with my family and, by that time, I knew that he was the only family I had left. I also wanted, as discreetly as possible, to put to rest any apprehensions he may have about Esther's scandal.

I had made the telephone call a few days before the funeral. I waited until half past 6 o'clock, my parents' traditional dinner time, before calling. I didn't want to speak with my mother, however I wanted to know for certain my father was home.

With Elliot sitting at the kitchen table at my elbow, I picked up the ear piece and spoke into the mouthpiece to the operator. "Redlands, California, please. Santoya residence."

The various clickings began that would put through my long distance phone call. I grew nervous and handed the ear piece to Elliot, forcing him to get up to speak into the mouthpiece which I still held. "Ask for Edward," I mouthed.

Elliot got a startled look on his face then spoke, "Ah, yes, hello. May I please speak with Edward Santoya?" There was short pause. "Ah yes, of course."

Elliot handed the ear piece to me and I stepped back up to the box just as my father picked up the telephone on his end. "Hello. This is Edward Santoya."

"Um, father, its Magda." It was quiet for a few seconds and, barely audible, I could hear my mother protesting that father should take a call during dinner.

Then came my father's voice, hushed to a whisper, but joyful, "Magda! How are you? Thank you for calling me."

"Father, I won't keep you long," I said in a rush, "Are you available on Thursday to come to luncheon?"

"Thursday?" he said thoughtfully, "I have a few meetings, but they can be easily rescheduled."

"I would like for you to come to my home for lunch," I said tremulously.

"Magda, that would be delightful," he said still whispering. "I will leave by the 10 o'clock train.

Relieved that he was coming, I gave him my address.

I may not have been mentally prepared for my father's visit, but everything else was in tip top shape. My house was clean, although rather sparse in furniture. I had made a special lunch and was wearing my prettiest dress. When I heard his knock on the door at 11:45, I nearly jumped out of my skin.

I ran from the kitchen, through the living room, to the doorway. Elliot had been sitting in the living room reading a newspaper. He had barely started to fold the thing as I hurried through. I threw open the door.

"Father," I exclaimed.

"Magda!" He grasped my outstretched hands and leaned in to kiss my cheeks. I knew Elliot would politely wait in the living room until I chose to introduce him.

"Magda, is this house yours? You must be doing very well as an actress." Father looked all around him in amazement.

"Yes father, I've been living here more than a year. It's amazing what the film companies pay for such silly work." I hadn't meant that the work was silly. I had meant that the work was mostly very easy, but it had come out wrong. Before I could correct it, the subject changed.

"And are you living here with your cousin?" Father asked hopefully.

Awkward for a moment, I answered hesitantly, "Dolores used to live with me – but more about her later. There is someone I would like for you to meet." Father gave me a startled look as he assumed what kind of person he was likely to be introduced to so formally.

I led him into the living room where Elliot stood in his somber suit, looking eminently respectable and somehow wise.

"Father, I would like for you to meet Elliot Clayton, my husband."

Father's mouth dropped in complete shock even as he held out his hand to be shaken. He mouthed like a fish for a few seconds as he got his bearings and shook Elliot's hand.

"Your husband?" he exclaimed.

I stepped close to Elliot and took his arm. Elliot had agreed to go along with my farce. As I intended to sail for Europe with Elliot as his wife, official marriage or not, it only made sense, at least to me, to set my father's mind at ease that I was married. We planned on being married soon, but with all that had happened neither of us had had any time to turn to it. I was hoping that once we reached Europe we could have a romantic ceremony. Until then, we were just going to pretend for the world that we were already married.

"Elliot's business calls him to Europe. He is the representative of his family's investment firm. I've given up my acting career to go with him. We leave for the East next Tuesday." I blundered out in one breath.

I looked at my father shyly, very unsure of what his response would be. Until that point, his reactions always surprised me. I didn't know what to expect. Father looked at me searchingly, then turned his gaze towards Elliot who stood erect and proper, well-mannered yet friendly. A half-smile lighting up his face.

"Magda, I don't know what to say."

"Father, I wanted you to know before I left," I began but father interrupted me.

"Mr. Clayton, I have long since learned that I have no business in my daughter's affairs. She is far more capable of choosing her own happiness than I could ever dream to be," he spoke with deep feeling, "I think, from the look of you that she probably chose wisely."

Father held out his hand again and the two men shook. With that we settled in for luncheon. Father and Elliot had much to discuss regarding business. More than once did Father look at me with a look of pride mingled with questioning. As if he were saying by his look, "Who is this daughter of mine who has done so undeniably well for herself." It was gratifying to me to see him so pleased with Elliot.

During coffee Elliot excused himself, he had business to attend to and couldn't stay longer. After he left Father asked me about the scandal. It was a question I knew I would have to attend to at some point.

"Magda, I know it will be a hard thing to discuss with your father, but could you tell me what that Esther Barton scandal had to do with you?"

I took a deep breath, then began the tale I wanted him to know. "Dolores and I did live at the woman's boarding house when I had first arrived in Los Angeles," a grim shadow passed over Father's face, "Dolores worked as a maid for her. We left within a few months of my moving to town, both of us having got better jobs, but we left on very bad terms with Esther, Esther Barton."

I was trying to look at Father so that he wouldn't think I was lying. I really just wanted to look away, study my fingernails, anything rather than deliver this well-rehearsed speech. "I think she named us to the city attorney to get back at us for becoming rather successful."

Father looked as if he were going to say something, but I continued before he could. "That picture that the newspapers used to profile Dolores was taken before I came to the place. The house had been raided and Dolores had been arrested just for living there."

"Yet she went back?"

"Esther was giving Dolores credit, she owed her a lot of money at the time." I explained.

"Oh dear. Your Aunt Frances is going to be both saddened and relieved by this information. What about that man who was murdered? Did Dolores have anything to do with it?"

"Her involvement was completely made up by the newspapers," I lied. "Two days after our names appeared in the newspaper, Dolores ran off with her Spanish count. Have you seen in the papers the name Fausto de los Santos?" Father indicated that he hadn't. "I'm sure you've heard how Los Angeles has been over run with European nobility since the war started. Mr. de los Santos has been hobnobbing with us movie folk since last summer and had fallen in love with Dolores almost as soon as he saw her.

"She finally agreed to marry him and they left for Spain right after the scandal broke. She was probably in Chicago by the time that man was killed."

"A Spanish Count?" Father declared.

"Crazy isn't it?" I tried to pass off a laugh.

Father laughed too. "Have you met this Count? What is he like? I would love to give your Aunt as much information as possible."

"I don't know him very well, but he always seemed gentlemanly. I don't know what his title is, even what part of Spain he is from. He is about 30 and quite handsome, although he has a large scar before his right ear from an accident several years ago. His manners are perfect, as you would expect a Spanish nobleman's to be. And I know for a fact that he is very, very rich. Elliot had business with him and has been privy to some private accounts." I paused to gauge his reactions, hoping I hadn't over sold it. The truth was, I hadn't seen or heard of that count since that horrible party at the Darrows'. I hoped he was long gone from this part of the world.

"He absolutely adores Dolores. They were married in New York last week and were sailing for the Continent immediately afterwards. I just had it in a letter."

"That is tremendous news my dear," Father leaned over and kissed my cheek. "Frances will be delighted to hear it. Although it will be a sad thing not to see her in pictures any longer." His face fell a bit, "Or you, my darling. I will miss going to see your pictures."

I reached out and held his arm. "It's for the best really. Being an actress was a lot of fun, but I was never much interested in it. It was a girlish dream really. While Dolores and I made a good go of it, I never saw it as a way to spend my life."

We studied each other, and he understood me, I think. "I've always longed to travel and now I have a grand opportunity of doing so with a wonderful husband beside me."

It was too much for Father, I think, for he started to cry. Having never seen my father cry before, I joined him with tears of my own. Father didn't stay much longer. We had a tearful, yet hearty farewell. I was glad I could give my family some comfort before leaving.

The next few days were a blur for me. Over the weekend, I went out to Floyd's place for a long ride and a short goodbye. I stopped in to say goodbye to a few acquaintance who had always been friendly to me, even after the scandal. I lunched with Virginia. I bought a half a dozen hats from the Miss Tanners by way of both a thank you and a goodbye. Stephanie and I helped each other pack, for she and Harry were to leave the following week as well.

Then finally it was Monday night, the night before we were to leave. Elliot had made arrangements for my house to be looked after through his company. I couldn't bear to sell it and knew, in my heart, that one day I would come back to Los Angeles to settle.

I had been debating for weeks what to do with Dolores's things. I had them packed for a long time and meant to donate them or throw them out, but her things were the last bit of her that I had. After much deliberation I decided to store them. I knew that when I at last came back, I would want to look through them.

Deciding to store them in the basement, I took the first box down. I hadn't been in there since the night I had found her there. Even when the morticians had come, it was Elliot who had gone down with them. I had to take lots of slow, deep breaths as I went down the stairs. Not from the exertion of carrying the box, but from a creeping fear of the memory of what I'd found there before.

At the bottom of the stairs, I pulled the light cord and saw what I had expected to find – an empty room. I set the box down near to a wall and was turning to go back upstairs when I saw a small, bright beaded purse. One of Dolores'. It was lying on top of a furniture crate that we had stored here when I had moved in. My heart pounded at the sight of it lying so casually on top as if she had just tossed it there herself.

I walked over to it, very much taken aback by this unexpected find. In picking it up, I saw that behind the packing crate there was a large black suitcase. Leaning over to see it more clearly, I at once knew what it was. A film reel case. Pushing the crate aside, I examined the case more slowly. I opened it and found that 5 of the 6 slots were filled with reels of film. Picking up the first one, I read the label on the top:

Soloman and Sheba

H. Phillips Monroe

Chronicle Film Company

Reel #1

I slumped to the floor. Dolores had taken the film.

Not quite thinking things through, I got up and went up the stairs for a hammer. With a purpose that I'd rarely known, I opened the empty packing crate, neatly labeled F. Suie One Company, and pulled out the packing straw. Lugging the reel case, I placed it in the crate and stuffed the straw around. Then I sealed the crate.

If Dolores had wanted the movie released, she wouldn't have taken the reel case. Monroe had said to her that she had ruined his picture. I think maybe she believed him. If the film were released now, all the horrible things of the last month would be dredged up again. I was ready to leave it all behind, leave it buried. Perhaps I was trying to honor Dolores's last wishes or perhaps I was trying to bury the past.

I moved the rest of Dolores's things down to the cellar. Piling boxes of clothing over the furniture crate. After surveying my handi-work, I turned off the light and went back up the stairs locking the door behind me.

Elliot came for me that evening at 7 o'clock in his stately touring car. We had decided to stay at a hotel near to the train station to make sure we were in time for the early morning train. As I left my little house for what would be a long time, the sun was setting. Elliot drove to the hotel and I watched how the soft California light shone on buildings and trees, how it turned the San Gabriel mountains purple and deep blue. I looked out the window like a delighted child and took in the city for one last time. How much had happened in the few short years I had lived there – all the friends I had made, the loves I had found and lost, the amazingly charmed life I had lived.

Papa once told me how he had felt upon returning to his native land after years and years of wandering the world, his self-imposed exile.

"I had left this place with so much bitterness in my heart. I had felt and witnessed so much pain and suffering I couldn't bear to stay here – even though my sisters were here and the people I had known all my life. I had watched my parents worked to death as servants on a ranch. I'd been a soldier and had watched people die. I had tried to earn my living here even as I was treated like a dog by the invading Americanos. I had had enough and thought to find a better life to live on some foreign shore.

The only thing I discovered during my travels was that there was suffering the world over and there was nothing I could do to change it. So, I came back to my birthplace with no direction and no idea of what I would do.

When I came back, I was completely struck by the beauty of this place. As my ship came in to San Pedro harbor, my heart was in my throat. I had missed my home so much and I'd hardly even known it. In the first few weeks after I came back, I wondered how I ever could have left. Then I found that it was not the place that had changed, but myself. People still suffered at the hands of brutes. People still were wretched in the face of so much beauty. But I saw it differently. I saw it as the place where I had been born and the place that shaped me and I appreciated it in a way that I never would have if I had not left.

This place, with its yellow rolling hills and blue mountains hazy in the distance was the place of me and no matter what had happened that would never change. It was my heart and it was where I belonged.

My heart lay heavy on my chest. I could only hope that is how I would feel too. For above everything that happened, this was my home and a part of me.

Pulling up to the hotel, I saw the sun sinking into a bright red sky.

Epilogue

It was 27 years before I returned to Los Angeles and my little house there. During the interval Elliot and I married and had three children. We lived for a time each in Paris, Rome, Madrid, and London during the 1920's and early 1930's. It was a grand time to live in Europe. There were as many Americans traveling Europe at the time as there were in Los Angeles and many of our old acquaintances from the picture industry were to be met up with in Paris any given spring.

Once war became imminent, we returned to the United States and spent the war years in Elliot's family home in Cambridge, Massachusetts. In 1946, the year our son entered MIT, Elliot retired, and we returned to my little house in Los Angeles. We found a city greatly altered since we had last seen it. Many of my old friends and family were gone, yet a few still remained.

In my little house at the top of the hill, Elliot and I spent many happy years raising our youngest daughter and then our grandchildren. Elliot passed away in 1959 and ever since I have been a tolerably happy widow.

My children have all settled near to me. My oldest daughter having grown-up children herself. When I was contacted by Mr. Patterson several years ago I had been spending my days caring for my two youngest grandchildren and happily surrounded by my family.

By then, my few years as an actress seemed so far behind me. My children knew I had once acted in silent films, but as that was long before they were born they didn't much care. In the early 1930's there was a movie house in Paris that still showed silent films. Nearly every other theater had given them over for talkies. One afternoon, while passing by that theater with my eldest daughter, I found the movie house playing The Siren's Song. I couldn't resist the nostalgic urge to see once again my cinema debut. My daughter was at first bored that she must endure a film with no sound. Once she recognized my younger face (to me I looked quite the child) she was absorbed in the film. All the while, looking from my profile to the screen and back again, mouth open in shock.

That was the last time I had really thought about my acting career. Then in 1968 I received Mr. Patterson's letter. I wasn't quite sure that I wanted to revisit that time after all the years that had passed, but curiosity got the better of me and I went to visit Mr. Patterson at his school.

Steven Patterson, at the time of which I'm speaking, was a graduate student in the newly ordained discipline of Film Studies at the University of Southern California. He was researching his thesis about the teen years in Hollywood that led up to the Golden Era of pictures in the 1920's. He had been contacting many actors and filmmakers who had worked during that time. As he later told me, unfortunately many of the people famous at the time had disappeared and were untraceable.

Mr. Patterson had found me through the Los Angeles County housing records. My house had remained in my professional name since I originally purchased it in 1918. When I arrived at USC to meet with Mr. Patterson, he took me to a small soundproof studio to film an official interview with me. I was quite nervous, having shied away from cameras for nearly 50 years. However, Mr. Patterson made me very comfortable. He had done his research well and asked many well-informed and interesting questions. It was both entertaining and bittersweet remembering all those places and people from so long ago, so many which were not around any more. I had to wipe tears from my eyes as I laughed and cried over a long-forgotten anecdote.

Of course, there came a time during the interview when Mr. Patterson asked me about my cousin, Dottie Sparks. He even produced a facsimile of the picture that appeared in the newspaper following the grand opening of the Million Dollar Theater. I peered closely at the caption under the picture: Cinema Stars and cousins, Maggie Savoy and Dottie Sparks shine as they enter the new, state-of-the-art theater.

We both were smiling so prettily. Dolores was just how I remembered her, bold and saucy. My heart seized with longing for her as I stared down at the grainy picture in my hand. I had not missed her so much in many years.

"I'm sorry Miss Savoy if I caused you pain by showing you that picture." Young Mr. Patterson's apology snapped me out of my reverie.

"It's all right, Mr. Patterson. I'm glad to see the picture. Only, it brought up strong memories that I didn't even know I remembered. I'm OK now, please continue."

"Dottie Sparks was your cousin?" he continued.

"Yes and my closest friend."

"I don't mean to cause you any grief by my next few questions, but could you shed some light on the Esther Barton scandal in Los Angeles in 1919?"

I did my best to sum up that horrible time and how the scandal ruined many people, not just the corrupt politicians. When I was finished, Mr. Patterson asked, "I wonder if you would care to tell me something about Dottie Sparks relationship with H. Monroe Phillips and his subsequent murder?"

I took a deep breath and launched into the tale I had spun to protect Dolores so many years ago. A tale that I had been so committed to that, in many ways, I believed it myself. In telling Mr. Patterson, the last telling, I added that Dolores had died childless in the early 1950s, exiled from Spain with her husband and living in Argentina.

As I told my tale, I watched Mr. Patterson's face light up with satisfaction. It was a mostly happy story of romantic love and an exciting life. Far better than the truth, I thought.

Altogether, Mr. Patterson and I talked for several hours. A few days following our talk, I received a phone call from him. He had arranged for several of the pictures I appeared in to be shown for a small gathering. I took my whole family, grandchildren and all.

The night was a wonderful success. Mr. Patterson showed *The Country Cousin* in it's entirety. He only had pieces of several Kingston Sam shorts and westerns starring Floyd, but it was enough. It was great fun to watch the girl I used to be up on the silver screen again. It was satisfying to watch the astonishment on each of my children's faces and the faces of their spouses as they realized I had lived a quite exciting life when I was young.

After the pictures were shown, I met some of the other people in attendance. There were a few professors from the University, as well as some patrons of the arts. A small group of students also made up the party, Mr. Patterson's fellow students, I believe. The older viewers were a bit shy to talk to me, but the youths bombarded me with questions about early filmmaking.

Later that night, once I was home and the excitement had worn off, a longing grew in my mind. A longing for those few years, those few frightening, exciting, wonderful and sad years that I spent in Los Angeles. Most of all I missed Dee. I still had the boxes of her things in the cellar, never having had the heart to give them away. I still had the film reels she had hidden. That night I longed to see the picture that had never been shown. I longed to see the wild and beautiful Sheba as she was meant to be seen.

I had taken care of the film reels as best I knew how – keeping them cool and dry – and turning them every year or two so that the weight of them didn't compress the film. I thought that perhaps Mr. Patterson would be able to screen the film for me. However, trying to explain how I had come to have Monroe's last epic in my possession for the last 50 years would be a hard thing to explain.

I worried over it for a while before I realized that more than just seeing the film, I wanted to remember Dolores. I wanted everyone to remember Dolores. To see her at her finest. I decided then that I would tell Dolores's true tale. The time had come.

I asked Mr. Patterson to meet me at the Rosedale Cemetary the following Thursday. He appeared in good time and I asked him to walk with me. We were both silent as we walked. I'm sure he was curious to know what we were there for.

Upon reaching Dolores's grave, Mr. Patterson bent low to better read the inscription:

Dolores Santoya Esparza 1897-1919

I had purposely left the inscription plain. There were no words succinct enough for a grave stone that would convey all that Dolores was. After reading the inscription, Mr. Patterson looked up at me questioningly.

"That is Dottie Sparks' grave." I began. Mr. Patterson leaned back down to view it closer. "That was her real name."

I paused not knowing how to explain. Mr. Patterson spoke instead, "So she didn't run off with a Spanish Count? She died in 1919."

I took a deep breath trying to calm my shaking hands. "She died the night Monroe did. Dolores shot him and then hanged herself."

Had Mr. Patterson expressed astonishment or started asking questions, I think my resolve would have melted right there and no more details would be told. Mr. Patterson, instead, kneeled quietly beside Dee's grave and patiently listened to the truth.

"I don't know that I want to world to yet know Dolores's part in Monroe's death. However, there is something I would like to do that I think you can arrange."

I led Mr. Patterson back to the parking lot. I had one of my grandsons load up the film reels in my trunk that morning and right there in the parking lot, I turned them over to Mr. Patterson. The shock he expressed when he realized what I had was incalculable. He readily agreed to take responsibility for the reels. He had them cleaned and processed by a film archivist, so that the film could be projected properly. When the film was ready, he held a private screening of the film just for me.

I was mesmerized by the film. *Solomon and Sheba* was indeed Monroe's greatest film and would be able to compete even with the most modern filmmaking techniques. My heart glowed as I watched Dolores, so strikingly beautiful, in her most dramatic, and her last, role.

Watching *Solomon and Sheba* brought back a feeling I had felt so many years ago. When I was very young and still so innocent and just arrived in Los Angeles, it was the feeling that the world deserved to see Dolores, with all her vibrancy and life. It was the same feeling as when we had decided to become actresses and had started down the path that led me to where I was more than 50 years later.

It was also a sharp reminder to me how much things had changed in the long, intervening years. And yet, the feelings I had then, when I was a girl of eighteen in 1916, how those feelings were still with me, undiminished. The excitement and fear, the dread and the hope that I had experienced as I had set out on my own.

As is well-known now, Mr. Patterson found a distributor who was willing to release the film to theaters. He coordinated everything for the film's official release – finding a student to score the picture and having the University orchestra to play it; generating the transfer to more advanced film; overseeing the duplication procedures.

The world premiere of the director's cut of *Solomon and Sheba* took place at Grauman's Chinese Theater – which hadn't even been built when the picture was filmed – brought out Hollywood's royalty, past and current. In terms of Hollywood galas, it was a fairly small affair. It didn't draw the media as many epic movies do.

Yet, that night I met so many fans who came to see Monroe's finest epic and many others who came to see Dottie Sparks shine on the screen. I was amazed to find how many people still loved our early films all these years later. I felt that had the movie been released at the height of the scandals that killed Dolores, its entertainment value would have been tarnished by the shame surrounding its making. However, it seemed to me, *Solomon and Sheba* could now take its place as one of the finest pictures ever made, free of the history that weighed it down. The scandals of yesteryear were forgotten as the audience was mesmerized by the story unfolding in front of them.

ABOUT THE AUTHOR:

K.L.A. Hyatt has been writing bits and pieces and poems since she was a teenager, but only recently pursued writing novels. She attended the University of California, Santa Barbara and has worked in nearly every facet of the book industry – from development and publishing to marketing to bookselling. Currently, her "real job" is as managing editor for an insurance publisher. Moving Pictures is her first full-length novel.

For additional material about Moving Pictures, please visit the website: www.movingpicturesbook.net.